Hot Latin Docs

Sultry, sexy bachelor brothers on the loose!

Santiago, Alejandro, Rafael and Dante Valentino are Miami's most eligible doctors. Yet the brothers' dazzling lives hide a darker truth—one that made these determined bachelors close their hearts to love years ago…

But now four feisty women are about to turn the heat up for these sexy Latin docs and tempt them each to do something they never imagined— get down on one knee!

Find out what happens in:

Santiago's Convenient Fiancée by Annie O'Neil
January 2017

Alejandro's Sexy Secret by Amy Ruttan
January 2017

Rafael's One Night Bombshell by Tina Beckett
February 2017

Dante's Shock Proposal by Amalie Berlin
February 2017

Dear Reader,

Thank you for picking up a copy of *Alejandro's Sexy Secret*.

This quartet was concocted by Amalie Berlin. So I completely blame her! No, I love Amalie, and she has been one of my bestie writing buddies since pretty much day one. During one of our online chat sessions she came up with this idea about four sexy Latino doctors in the hot city of Miami, Florida.

I had so much fun planning this story with my coauthors. Surprisingly, they let me have the youngest brother—Dr. Alejandro Valentino. Alejandro has a very dark past, but that doesn't stop him from trying to live life to the fullest. And during the day he spends his time saving the lives of children in need of transplants. There's so much to love about Alejandro—it's just too bad he doesn't want to take a chance on love himself.

Enter Dr. Kiri Bhardwaj. She also carries a wound from the past that she shares with Alejandro. And working with him at Buena Vista Hospital as his boss just makes that raw hurt fresh once again.

It took a lot of work and tears to get these two together. I hope you enjoy Alejandro and Kiri's story. And please do check out Alejandro's brothers' stories: Santiago, Rafe and Dante.

I love hearing from readers, so please drop by my website, amyruttan.com, or give me a shout on Twitter, @ruttanamy.

With warmest wishes,

Amy Ruttan

ALEJANDRO'S SEXY SECRET

———

AMY RUTTAN

HARLEQUIN® MEDICAL ROMANCE™

Recycling programs
for this product may
not exist in your area.

ISBN-13: 978-0-373-21505-8

Alejandro's Sexy Secret

First North American Publication 2016

Copyright © 2016 by Amy Ruttan

This edition published by arrangement with Harlequin Books S.A.

For questions and comments about the quality of this book, please contact us at CustomerService@Harlequin.com.

Printed in U.S.A.

I couldn't have written Alejandro's story without
Amalie, Tina and Annie. You ladies are the best
to build a world with.

Annie—Mad Ron's wouldn't exist without you!

Also, I want to thank Amalie and my editor,
Laura, for taking on the monumental task of
whipping this quartet into shape.

**Praise for
Amy Ruttan**

"I recommend *Perfect Rivals*… as a place to
start for those who haven't thought of trying
the Medical line before, because this will be an
absolute treat… I give it five stars because of the
characters, the plot, and the fact I couldn't put it
down… Please read this book—*stat!*"

—*Goodreads*

PROLOGUE

Las Vegas, Nevada

KIRI WALKED OUT onto the patio of the private villa her friends had rented at one of Vegas's most luxurious five-star resorts. It was getting too crazy inside. There was a lot of alcohol and antics, including a very dirty cake that would make her *naanii* blush.

Heck, it made her blush just thinking about the racy genital-shaped cake.

There were some shrieks from her friends as the bride-to-be opened up another questionable gift. Kiri chuckled and then shouted through the open window.

"You're surgeons, you've seen those parts before!"

Her friends began to giggle again and Kiri just shook her head and sat down on one of the lounge chairs that overlooked the private pool and walled garden. Sandy, the bridezilla-to-be, was accusing her of being a party pooper on this bachelorette weekend and maybe she was, but she was thinking about her final residency exam that was coming up. Also, she was envious. Sandy had it all. She was getting married, she had a career and she knew Sandy and Tony wanted to start a family right away. It was everything that Kiri had always wanted.

The problem was she couldn't find the right guy.

Once she'd thought she'd found the right guy, the only problem being she hadn't been the right woman for him.

To get over her heartache she focused on her work. Never really cutting loose. If she couldn't have a husband and family right now, she'd have her career.

"You're my maid of honor, Kiri. You're coming to Vegas, whether you like it or not!"

"Professor Vaughan is tough, Sandy. He only picks the cream of the pediatric surgery hopefuls to work with him. I have to study. Go have fun without me."

"No, you're coming to have fun. The last three men you went on dates with you blew off because of studying. You need to have fun every once in a while too."

Kiri had come to Vegas, but had brought her books with her. She'd smuggled them like contraband in her luggage. She reached down and pulled out a notebook from where she'd stashed it. She flipped to where she'd left off, brought up the flashlight app on her smartphone and tried to cram like she'd never crammed before.

Except it was kind of difficult with that music blaring in the background.

Lord.

She rammed her fingers in her ears and held the book open with her elbows pressed against her lap and read until her glasses began to slide down her nose.

Blast.

She couldn't study this way.

Her friends had already completed their exams, knew where they were going to be practicing their surgical skills. The pediatric surgical residency exams weren't until next week. She should be back in New York and studying, not here. Of course as a maid of honor she had a bit of a duty to Sandy. And she was failing miserably. At least Sandy's sister had picked up some slack. Like arranging this weekend.

Blast that Sandy for getting engaged to Tony and having a wedding so close to exams. Who does that?

Tony was already a surgeon and was apparently somewhere in Florida, enjoying a golf weekend. Florida was probably warmer than here. She closed her notebook and shivered in the evening chill.

"I thought Vegas was supposed to be hot," she muttered to herself, and took a sip of her Bellini, which was a poor choice to have when she was already chilled.

"It's the desert. At night it gets cold. So *very* cold."

Kiri spun around to see who was speaking in the thick, Latin drawl that sent a shiver of something down her spine. Her mouth dropped open at the sight of the tall, muscular, Latino god who was leaning casually against the French doors. He had a dimple in his cheek as he grinned at her, perfect white teeth and those dark eyes sparkled in the light that shone out through the doors, promising something sinfully delicious.

"P-pardon?" Kiri said, pushing up her dark-framed glasses, which had slid down her nose again and were beginning to fog up. She cursed herself inwardly for forgetting her contact lenses in New York.

"The desert. It's very hot during the day, but at night it's *muy frio*. It's cold."

"Who are you?" she asked.

A lazy grin spread across his face. "Your friends sent me out here to lighten your mood. They said you've been a bit of a party pooper this weekend and you need to loosen up."

Oh. My. God.

She glanced over his shoulder and could see another group of bronzed muscular gods dancing to music while her friends cheered them on. This was the "entertainment" Sandy had been talking about. Male exotic dancers.

Apparently the best that Vegas had to offer.

Heat flushed in her cheeks as he took a step closer to her. He took her hand and led her into the room, sitting her down on the couch.

"Why don't you sit back, *mi tesoro*?" he whispered in that honeyed drawl against her ear that made her forget that she was always just a bit awkward around men. "Let me take care of you."

"Um…" A million thoughts were racing through her mind, but then all those thoughts melted into a pile of goo as he pushed her back against the cushions.

A familiar song that she'd heard so many times when she'd been young came across the stereo system. The kind her and her high-school friends had giggled at but which the school would never play at a dance.

Sandy and her friends began to shriek as the group of exotic dancers began to move together in a choreographed, erotic dance.

And as that Latino god began to move, his hips rolling, she suddenly understood why they didn't play that song at high-school dances. Why her parents hated that song. As she sat there on the couch, her friends screaming around her and that gorgeous specimen of a man's dark eyes locked on her, only her, he grinned at her, as if knowing she was completely aroused by him. He rolled his hips and peeled his shirt off, revealing a tattoo on a muscle-hardened chest, and she realized what she'd been missing. Why she'd been uptight. When was the last time she'd been with someone?

It had been a long time.

Kiri's leg began to tap in a nervous twitch she'd had since she was a kid, when she'd been the chubby geek that no one had paid attention to.

He moved toward her and laid a strong hand against her leg, settling the incessant tapping. His touch burned and set her blood on fire, her body reacting to the pure magnetism and sex he was exuding.

And for some reason he was focused on her.

He's being paid to do this. This is what Sandy wanted.

And that's what she was telling herself as he moved closer to her, pushing her back against the pillows, dancing just for her. He placed her hands on his narrow hips as he moved above her.

"Um…" slipped past her lips and she was mesmerized. Even though she knew it was all an act, this man held her in complete rapture. His deep, dark eyes were locked on hers and there was something about him that completely sucked her in.

Then he turned his back to her as the song ended and Kiri still sat there stunned. The Bellini she had been holding was no longer slushy but melted as she'd been gripping the glass so tightly before he'd taken it from her, deposited it on a table and placed her cool hands on his warm-skinned hips. Her heart was racing and it felt like she was on fire.

She couldn't remember the last time she'd been so turned on, so enthralled by a man. She couldn't even remember the last time she'd had sex. It had been during her residency and with Chad, the man who had broken her heart, but for the life of her all those moments with Chad were obliterated. All she saw was this gorgeous man in front of her. All she could think about was having him. That much she knew.

The last several years she'd been so focused on becoming a pediatric surgeon she'd thrown every last piece of herself into becoming the best darned surgeon in the program. So much so she'd forgotten how much she missed connecting with another person.

Just wanting a simple touch.

A kiss.

And more.

I have to get out of here.

The exotic dancers were now focused on Sandy, which was good. She left her glass of sludgy, melted Bellini on the side table and slipped out of the villa, putting some distance between her and the bachelorette party as fast as her little legs could carry her before she did something she'd completely regret.

"That was a good show tonight. Don't you think, Alejandro?"

"What?" Alejandro asked. He hadn't been really listening to Fernando, one of the dancers in his troupe, as they sat in the lounge of the hotel after entertaining that group of women at the bachelorette party. His thoughts were strictly on the beautiful woman he'd given the private dance to at the beginning. The one who had slipped out of the party when his back had been turned.

The one who was now sitting alone at the bar, nursing a glass of wine. Alejandro couldn't take his eyes off her. She had curves in all the right places and though she was short, her legs looked long and were crossed in a ladylike way and she was swirling her one foot around.

Maybe it was the tight black dress or the stilettos that accentuated her beauty; either way, he couldn't tear his eyes from her gorgeous legs.

"Yo, Alejandro? Snap out of it." Fernando waved a hand in front of his face.

"What?" Alejandro said again.

"I asked you if you thought it went well tonight. I was a bit surprised when Ricky decided to fly us in from Miami to Las Vegas, but now, with this cut from that bachelorette party and being put up at this swanky hotel until tomorrow night, I'm never going to question a thing he says again."

"Yeah, yeah, for sure." Alejandro got up from the table where he'd been sitting with his fellow dancers. "I think I'm going to stick around here tonight, rather than go out."

"You sure, bro?" another of them asked.

Alejandro nodded. "Yeah. I'm tired."

And he really didn't want to spend the large cut he'd just received on gambling and drinking tonight. Not when this was the last bit of the money he needed to pay off his student loans. This was finally his freedom from exotic dancing.

His freedom from Ricky.

He'd made it all through medical school without his older brothers finding out about what he did. They'd offered to help him pay for medical school, but they had sacrificed enough for him so he'd told them he worked down at the docks, gutting fish, and had been adamant he'd pay his own way through medical school. They didn't need to know he'd started as a dance host in a seedy samba bar before being discovered by Ricky and moving into this. Next week he was starting a residency in transplant surgery in Miami in the pediatric department of Buena Vista Hospital and he wouldn't have to dance again.

This had been his last dance and he'd never had a client walk out on him before. It was bothering him a bit.

As his friends left the bar to seek other pleasures for the rest of the night, Alejandro drummed up enough courage to go over and talk to her. He hoped he wouldn't offend her. That was the last thing he wanted to do.

He'd been a little unnerved when he'd been sent out to retrieve her from the villa courtyard. When he'd seen her, he'd been stunned by her beauty. She was curvy, but he liked a woman who was curvy. Her long black hair had shimmered in the moonlight and those large, dark eyes made him melt just a bit.

There were a lot of beautiful women he'd been drawn to over his years of dancing, but nothing like this. It was like a bolt of pure, electric attraction. He wanted to run his hands over her body, taste her lips, touch her silky hair. He was asking for trouble just approaching her, because clients were against his rules, but he had to know why she'd been so disgusted with him.

Walk away, Alejandro.

"I'll have a mineral water and a twist of lemon," he said to the bartender as he took the empty seat beside her, his heart hammering against his rib cage. He'd never felt so nervous around a woman before.

What was it about her?

"Sure thing." The bartender moved away and the woman glanced over at him, her dark eyes widening in shock. A blush tinged her caramel cheeks and Alejandro knew that she recognized him but didn't want to admit it.

"You slipped out," he said, not looking at her, keeping his gaze fixed on the rows of bottles behind the bar.

"Pardon?" she said, her voice quivering a bit.

He turned to her. "You slipped out of the show at your friend's villa."

"I don't know what you're talking about." She fidgeted with the stem of her wine glass. He leaned over and caught the scent of coconut in her dark hair and he drank it in.

"Ah, but you do, *mi tesoro*," he whispered in her ear.

The bartender brought him the mineral water and Alejandro paid him. He picked up the highball glass and took a sip, watching her as she fidgeted, obviously uncomfortable in his presence.

"Well, perhaps I was mistaken. Have a good night." He turned to walk away.

"Why would it matter?" she asked.

He turned. "Why would what matter?"

"You noticing me leaving."

"Yes, I did."

"I'm sure women leave you..." She cleared her throat. "I'm sure they leave your shows all the time."

Alejandro sat back down. "Not *my* shows."

She snorted and he was enchanted. "You're awfully arrogant."

"I have every right to be. I'm good at what I do." He winked at her and she smiled. He was getting through the walls she'd built up. Not that he knew why she'd built such impenetrable walls, but he knew when he'd been dancing for her that she'd been keeping a part of herself locked away and that was very intriguing to him.

Why would she hide herself away?

"So you're telling me that in a nightclub you notice if people come and go?"

"No, I'm not saying that."

"You just did!" Then she imitated him. "'Not *my* shows.'"

He chuckled. It was sexy the way she tried to get her high voice to deepen. Her brow furrowed and her lips pursed a bit when she did it. "That's a very good impression."

She blushed again. "So are you denying you said that?"

"No, I'm not, just that I don't dance in night-clubs, which is a polite way of saying strip clubs."

She pushed back an errant strand of her inky-black hair. "Strip clubs, then."

"I don't dance in strip clubs. I used to dance in samba bars, but the clothes stayed on. Now my services are primarily hired for private sessions like tonight. I'm *that* good. Women are willing to pay my agent whatever I desire."

She rolled her eyes. "You're laying it on thick. No one is that good."

"I am. I take pride in my work. Don't you take pride in your work?"

"I do. In fact, I'm one of the best there is."

He cocked an eyebrow, even more intrigued, and he couldn't help but wonder what else she was good at. "Really?"

"Yes. Which is why I left the party early. Work is *that* important to me. I had things to look over."

"Then how do you unwind?"

"Unwind? What is this mythical thing you're talking about?" she teased.

Alejandro couldn't help but laugh. His older

brothers often teased him about working too hard, never relaxing. Only he didn't really feel like he had the right to unwind. He had to work hard. He had too much to live up to.

"Perhaps you're right. For those of us dedicated to what we do, there is no down time. Also, there is no perfection until all parties are satisfied, and I don't think you were satisfied with my performance."

And the blush tinged her cheeks again. "I'm sorry for walking out."

"Then allow me to show you what you missed."

What're you doing?

"What?" she said, her voice hitching. "I don't have that... I don't even know your name. I can't go off with a stranger."

Alejandro reached into his jacket pocket and pulled out his business card.

"My name is Alejandro. There is all my business information. I'm fully bonded. I take my work seriously and wouldn't jeopardize that. I dance. That's all. I'm not a gigolo and nothing untoward would happen. It's hands-off."

She took the card. "Why do you want me to go with you?"

"Like I said, I don't like leaving a customer unsatisfied." He held out his hand. "Your friend paid me to put on a good show for her bridal party. Please let me finish it."

Never had he ever approached a customer, but it bothered him that she'd walked out of his performance. Or maybe it was the fact he thought she was the most beautiful woman in the world. He couldn't remember the last time he'd seen someone so beautiful.

Either way, he waited with bated breath for her answer, expecting her to say no.

She drank down the rest of her wine. "I'm probably crazy, but this is Vegas and what happens in Vegas stays in Vegas, right?"

His pulse thundered between his ears as he held her soft, delicate hand in his. "Absolutely."

CHAPTER ONE

Five years later. Miami, spring

"YOU KNOW YOU MARRIED the ugly brother, right?" Alejandro was teasing his new sister-in-law Saoirse Murphy on her marriage to his brother. His ugly brother.

Saoirse, a fiery Irish beauty, had recently married Santiago, who was rolling his eyes as Alejandro and the twins, Rafe and Dante, joined in the good-natured ribbing. They were all the "ugly brothers," but right now Santi was taking the heat because he'd been the first of the Valentino brothers to take the plunge and marry.

"It's your fault," Santi shouted, pointing at Dante and Rafe. "You two are the elders. You should be married already, then I wouldn't be getting this teasing from the baby."

Alejandro chuckled and moved out of the line of fire. He knew Dante and Rafe didn't like to be referred to as the elders, but Santi and he had always done that behind their backs.

The elders were surrogate fathers to him. As Santi had been, before he'd run off and joined the Marines. All because of a robbery in the family bodega. A robbery that had almost cost Alejandro his life, as well. He'd been caught in the cross fire, taking a bullet in the chest at the age of ten.

He'd be dead if it hadn't been for his father's heart saving his life, and because of his father's death he carried a piece of his father with him. It was a huge responsibility he carried proudly. Which was why he was now one of the best pediatric transplant surgeons at Buena Vista Hospital.

Speaking of which...

"I'm sorry, I have to get to the hospital. The new head of pediatric surgery starts today. Apparently she's a bit of a *culo duro*."

"Culo duro?" Saoirse asked Santi.

"Hard ass," Santi said to his new bride, and then he turned to Alejandro. "Don't judge the new head just yet, baby brother. She might not be as bad as the rumors make her out to be."

Alejandro ground his teeth at Santi calling him "baby brother." He hated that, just as much as Rafe and Dante hated being called the elders, but, then, it was all in good fun and he deserved it a bit for calling Santi the ugly one.

Instead of sniping back, Alejandro took Saoirse's hand in his and kissed her knuckles. "Sorry for not sticking around too long, so let me say *felicitaciones les deseamos a ambos toda la felicidad del mundo.*"

Saoirse's brow furrowed. "Congratulations… wishing both of you…"

"All the happiness in the world." Alejandro kissed her hand again.

"Suficiente idiota!" Santi said, slapping Alejandro upside the head.

"Ow, I'm not an idiot." Alejandro winked at Saoirse, who was laughing, obviously enjoying the show of them tormenting Santi.

Dante snorted and Rafe rolled his eyes while Alejandro grinned at Santi, who was busy shooting daggers at him.

"Well, I guess we should be happy he kept speaking Spanish after Mami and Pappi died," Dante groaned. "But does he have to upstage us?"

Alejandro winked at Dante. "Always, old man. Always."

He left the bodega before his older brothers started a brawl. He waved to Carmelita, who'd run the business since he was eleven. She waved back, but was focused on her work.

Outside the bodega the heat was oppressive, which was strange for a spring day. It was always hot in Miami, but this was like summer. Moist, sweltering heat. Palm trees lining the street of the old neighborhood were swaying, but the wind didn't suppress the cloying heat. A storm was brewing to the south.

Fitting.

He'd heard people refer to Dr. Bhardwaj as the Wicked Witch of the East, so it was only fitting her arrival be marked by a storm.

As he walked to his motorcycle a group of boys playing soccer in the street kicked a ball toward him and he kicked it back, waving at them. He knew most of the kids because their parents were people he'd gone to school with. People who had never left the old neighborhood, which comprised a tight-knit community of people from Heliconia, a small island nation in the Caribbean. He'd never been there as his parents had fled the country because of the horrible conditions long before he'd been born.

Only that didn't matter. Everyone here in this neighborhood was family. Everyone stayed together.

Only he had left.

His apartment was in South Beach. He was disconnected from this place because it reminded him of his parents dying, his brothers sacrificing so much of their youth for him.

It was also the place he'd first met Ricky at a scuzzy samba bar where he'd danced with lonely women. Ricky had started in the more lucrative exotic dancing, just so he could make his own way in the world.

Don't think about it. That's all behind you. Focus on now.

He had to keep his head in the game. He'd worked hard to become an attending in pediatric transplant surgery at Buena Vista Hospital. There was no way he was going to let some new head of pediatric surgery force him out.

He usually wouldn't be so worried, but apparently Dr. Bhardwaj wanted to make changes.

And changes meant cuts. He had no doubt the arrival of Dr. Bhardwaj was down to Mr. Snyder, current president of the board of directors. Ever since Snyder had taken over he'd been looking for a way to cut every single department's pro bono fund.

It was a fairly easy ride from Little Heliconia to Buena Vista. The only change was the darkening clouds rolling in.

Yes. Definitely a storm.

"Where have you been?" Dr. Micha asked the moment Alejandro walked into the attendings' locker room.

"My brother Santi just got married," Alejandro replied casually. He didn't really want to engage in conversation with Dr. Micha today.

"Mazel tov," Dr. Micha said sarcastically. "The witch is on her broom, by the way."

Alejandro cocked his eyebrow. "Oh, yes?"

Usually he ignored Dr. Raul Micha's gossip. The man was a paranoid worrywart and thankfully worked far from Alejandro, in Pediatric Dermatology, but for some reason Raul thought he and Alejandro were best friends forever.

"She's made cuts to my program already." Dr. Micha shook his head. "Cuts, can you believe it? Snyder is behind it, I'm sure. Snyder was friends with Dr. Bhardwaj's mentor up in New York, Dr. Vaughan."

Alejandro was impressed as Dr. Vaughan was a world-renowned pediatric surgeon. So at least Dr. Bhardwaj should know what she was doing, but then he recalled the word that sent a chill down his spine.

"Cuts?" Alejandro's stomach churned. This was exactly what he'd been afraid of.

"Yes. She's slashed all I've worked for."

"Buena Vista is a wealthy hospital. It's not like Seaside. Why is the board making cuts?"

"Buena Vista was wealthy," Raul said in a snarky voice. Then he peered out the door. "Oh, man, here she comes. You're on your own."

Alejandro rolled his eyes as Raul slipped out of the locker room. He pulled off his street clothes and pulled out his scrubs. Before he'd slipped his scrub top on the door to the attendings' locker room opened. Alejandro glanced over his shoulder and then did a double take as he stared into the dark eyes of the one who'd got away.

Kiri.

His one and only one-night stand from his days as an exotic dancer was standing right in front of him. He'd finished the private show five years ago and she'd kissed him. Alejandro knew he should've pushed her away, only he'd been unable to.

"Please, don't think badly of me, I've never done this," she whispered. *"Never slept with a man I just met."*

"I don't do this either." He ran his hands through her hair. *"You're the most beautiful woman I've seen in a long time."*

Her mouth was open, her eyes wide behind those dark-framed glasses she still wore. She recognized him. This was bad.

"What...? I..." She was at a loss for words.

"Sorry," he apologized, slipping on his scrub top. He held out his hand. "Dr. Bhardwaj, I presume?"

He was going to pretend he didn't know her.

Which was a lie.

He knew every inch of her. It was still fresh in his mind five years later. The taste of her skin, her scent and the way she'd sighed when he'd nibbled her neck just below her ear.

This was bad.

"Uh. Yes." She was still staring at him like he was a ghost, an unwanted ghost at that. She took his hand and shook it quickly before snatching it back. "Yes, I'm Dr. Bhardwaj."

He nodded. "I'm Dr. Valentino. Senior Attending on the pediatric transplant team."

Dr. Valentino? His name is Valentino?

Kiri had never known her Latin god's last name. Of course, she hadn't stuck around after her one indiscretion in Las Vegas.

A stolen night of passion that had led to a pregnancy, even though they'd used protection. And then that had led to a late miscarriage at twenty-three weeks, which still hurt all these years later. Staring up at the father of her lost baby boy reminded her in an instant of all the things that could've been.

Even though the pregnancy had been an inconvenience, she'd wanted her baby. She'd wanted to be a mother so badly. It hadn't been how she'd planned to start a family, but she'd been thrilled at the prospect of motherhood. And she'd tried to track down Alejandro, but when she'd called his number she'd learned he'd quit and the agent, Ricky, had refused to give her any information about Alejandro's whereabouts.

Alejandro reminded her of pain.

Yeah, lots of pain. And the wound of losing their child was fresh and raw again.

And he clearly didn't remember her, which was like a slap across the face.

What did you expect, sleeping with a male stripper?

"Yes, sorry, Dr. Valentino. It's a pleasure to meet you."

Come on, Kiri. Get it together.

She was still in shock.

Alejandro smiled, that charming, sexy smile that had melted down her walls and inhibitions five years ago.

"A pleasure to meet you too. Well, excuse me, Dr. Bhardwaj. I have a consult."

He wants to finish changing in privacy.

"Of course. Perhaps after your consult we can arrange a meeting to discuss the expectations of your department."

"Yes. It would be my pleasure."

"I want you," she whispered. *"And I've never wanted a man like this before. Please take me."*

"My pleasure." And he ran his lips over her

body, kissing her in places no one had ever kissed her before.

Kiri turned on her heel and got out of that locker room as fast as she could.

Ugh. You're the head of the department.

Kiri was angry at herself for turning tail and running. When she'd miscarried she'd promised herself she'd never run from the father if she ever saw him again.

She'd tell him everything she was thinking. Those dark thoughts she'd had as she'd recovered from her loss. Everything that had crossed her mind when she'd learned that her baby was gone.

Turn around.

Alejandro was leaving the locker room. He looked so different in scrubs and a white lab coat. Given that she'd had her one-night stand with him five years ago and he was an attending in pediatric transplants, no less, in a world-class hospital, it meant that he must've been a doctor when he'd been dancing.

Which made her angry.

Why had he been doing that? Disgracing himself?

"Dr. Valentino, a moment, if you please."

He turned.

Ha. You can't get rid of me that easily.

"Yes, Dr. Bhardwaj?"

"I'd like to join you on your consult."

He frowned. "Why?"

Good. She had him on edge. She had the power back.

"Why not? I have no patient load yet and I'd like to see how you run your practice. The chief told me you are quite the star when it comes to pediatric transplants."

Which was true. Though she had a hard time believing it until she saw it for herself. Perhaps because she'd learned long before she'd met Dr. Alejandro Valentino that you really couldn't depend on anyone but yourself.

And she wanted to throw him off his game.

One thing she had learned while going through her department's finances when she'd first arrived in Miami had been that Alejandro's department had a lot of pro bono cases. It was admirable, but the board had made it clear to her in no uncertain terms that the pro bono cases had to stop. The board wanted Buena Vista Hospital to be for the elite of Miami.

All those who couldn't afford to be a patient at Buena Vista had to be moved to Seaside or County. The aim of the board was to cater to the rich and famous. The "beautiful people," as one board member had put it.

It was a shame, but she understood that Buena Vista wanted to be at the cutting edge of health and it was a dream Kiri wanted to share.

Perhaps once they had that distinction she could convince them to open up their pockets to pro bono cases once again. Although Mr. Snyder had made it clear that pro bono cases were finished. And she almost wondered why she'd taken the job, because since her arrival it had been a headache dealing with the board of directors. In particular Snyder.

Then again, she'd have felt a bit guilty if she hadn't taken the job her mentor had put her up for.

"Kiri, this is an opportunity of a lifetime. At your age, you won't get a position like this in Manhattan. Buena Vista is a world-class hospital. Take the job I trained you for. Snyder is a friend of mine and I know he runs a good hospital and you'll be treated right."

She snorted at the memory, because it had been too good to be true.

"Of course. If you want to follow me, you can meet with my patient," Alejandro said.

She nodded and followed him down the hall. It was awkward walking beside him, both of them pretending that they didn't know each other. Of course, they really didn't know each other, other than intimately.

Kiri could remember clearly what he looked like naked. How he tasted and how he felt buried deep inside her. Yet he acted like they were strangers.

He should have some recollection of her.

He's forgotten you.

She had after all probably just been a forget-table experience for him.

Kiri knew that she wasn't particularly mem-orable to many men. Which was probably why she didn't really believe in love in the traditional sense. Even though her parents loved each other, but that was rare.

All Kiri believe in was science and medicine. Her work.

Although science and medicine had failed her that night five years ago when she'd lost her baby. That pregnancy was the closest she'd ever gotten to love and it had been snatched from her in a cruel twist of fate.

Don't think about that.

Alejandro grabbed the patient's chart from the nurses' station, smiling at the women behind the counter. She could see the effect he had on them—there were a few dreamy expressions—but as he walked past a male nurse he received a fist bump from the man.

He was charming and had everyone fooled. Just like she'd been.

"The patient we're seeing is one of the pro bono cases sent over from Little Heliconia. The patient is an eight-year-old boy with cystic fibrosis. The family only speaks Spanish. Do you speak Spanish?"

"No, well, only a bit, not enough to keep up."

Alejandro frowned. "Well, before we go in I'll fill you in on his condition and what I'll be explaining to the parents. That way I don't have to keep stopping to interpret for you." The way he said it made it sound like her presence was an inconvenience but she didn't care. He wasn't scaring her away and she knew that was his current tactic.

Kiri nodded. "Okay."

"José Agadore has end-stage liver failure. Intrahepatic bile obstruction led to the deterioration of the liver tissue. By the time County sent him to Buena Vista there was nothing to be done to help the liver and I placed him on UNOS. Today I'm going to be updating the family on his condition."

"There's no liver match yet, then?" Kiri asked, making notes. Snyder wanted notes on all current pro bono cases in her department. Each head of each department of the hospital was doing the same.

Alejandro shook his head. "And the boy is not doing well. His last panel of blood showed ascites and a bilirubin count of three point one."

Kiri flipped open the chart to see the labs and

sighed. It didn't look very promising. The more a body took a pounding while waiting for a liver, the less chance the patient had to pull through the surgery. "Has he passed cardiovascular and respiratory tests?"

Alejandro nodded. "He's just waiting. Like so many are."

Kiri nodded and followed Alejandro into the patient's room. The little boy was jaundiced and was sleeping, a nasal cannula helping the poor mite to breathe. Kiri's heart went out to the family. A mother and father huddled on the room's couch, dark circles under their eyes. They immediately stood when Alejandro stepped up to the bedside, hope in their eyes, but they didn't even glance in her direction.

"Buenos días, Señor y Señora Agadore, cómo está haciendo José esta mañana?" Alejandro asked.

"Tan bueno como se puede esperar," Mr. Agadore said, then his glance fell on Kiri. She gave them a friendly smile, but it was clear they didn't trust her. Not that she blamed them. They were scared, tired and there was a language barrier separating them.

"As good as could be expected," the father had said. Kiri had understood that. She'd heard that same phrase in several languages from countless parents whose children had been fighting for their lives, the same haunted expression in their eyes.

Alejandro turned and nodded at her. *"Permitame presente Dr. Bhardwaj. Ella es el jefe de cirugía pediátrica."*

The Agadores smiled politely and nodded. *"Hola."*

Kiri half listened, catching a few words here and there as Alejandro spoke to the frightened parents about what was happening with their son and how they had to continue to wait until a match for their son was found.

When Alejandro reached across and shook the Agadores' hands, they turned to her and she shook their hands as well. Alejandro opened the door and they walked out into the hall. She followed him as he returned José's chart to the nurses' station.

The charming, easygoing smile was gone, replaced by a man who was subdued because, like her, he knew that José didn't have much longer to live.

"How much time does he have left?" Kiri asked.

"Days," Alejandro said. "I keep my phone on, just waiting for the call from UNOS."

"Well, I hope the call comes soon. Thank you for letting me in on your consult. We'll speak again soon." She tried to leave but Alejandro stopped her.

"You can't cut my program."

"Pardon?" She asked stunned.

"I know that you've made cuts. I've heard the rumors," Alejandro whispered. "You can't cut the transplant program, any part of the transplant program."

She crossed her arms. "This is not the time or place to speak about this, Dr. Valentino."

He grabbed her by the arm and led her outside, into an alleyway. Thunder rolled in the distance and she glanced up at the sky to see dark clouds, but the heat was still oppressive. It was a bit eerie.

"What is the meaning of this?" she demanded.

"You can't make cuts," he repeated.

"I'm the head of the department. If cuts need to be made, I'll decide," she snapped.

"If you make cuts there will be hell to pay," he said through clenched teeth. His eyes were as dark and wild as the storm rolling in.

"Are you threatening me?" she asked.

"No, I'm just telling you that you can't make cuts to this program."

"I have no intention of making cuts to the program, Dr. Valentino." Then she sighed. "I'm making cuts to the pro bono program. That young boy, he's the last pro bono case that you can take."

"What?" Alejandro was stunned. "You can't."

"The board is cutting pro bono funding. They still want a world-class hospital, they'll fund research programs and equipment. They'll even fund staff, but pro bono cases must be referred to County."

"Cases like José's can't be referred to County. County doesn't have the equipment to handle children like him. Sending them to County is a death sentence. County sends cases like José's to us for a reason. We're the best."

"My hands are tied. Only those who can afford to pay for the services at Buena Vista will be treated." Then added, before she could stop herself, "You know all about what it's like to cater to the wealthy, don't you?"

His eyes were like thunder as they narrowed dangerously. "You do remember me, then."

"And you remember me. Given your age and your standing here, you must've been, what, a resident when we met?"

Alejandro cursed under his breath. "Yes."

"And does the board know what their precious Dr. Valentino did before becoming an attending at a prestigious hospital?"

"Are you threatening me?" Alejandro asked, angry.

"No." Even though five years ago when she'd miscarried and had had no one to help her, no one to hold her hand, she would've gladly threatened Alejandro then. She'd wanted him to hurt, to know the pain she'd been feeling.

"I danced to pay off student loans. That's all. Once I'd earned enough money, I quit."

"I don't care," Kiri said. "What I care about is protecting the reputation of the hospital. What if word gets out that a surgeon was an exotic dancer?"

"I haven't danced in five years. My last show was in Vegas."

Kiri's cheeks heated and he took her right back to that night so long ago. "Why did you pretend not to know me?"

"Why did you?" he countered.

"I was surprised to see a stripper as a surgeon." And she regretted the hateful words the moment they'd slipped past her lips.

"I'm not a stripper. I'm a surgeon. That's all I am. Of course, it's hard to practice as a surgeon when your program is being slashed."

"Your program is not being slashed. Only the pro bono fund. You can practice on patients who can pay."

Alejandro opened his mouth, but then a thin, long wail sounded from behind a Dumpster. It was weak, frightened.

"Was that a baby?" Kiri asked.

"Yes." Alejandro turned and they listened, trying to drown out the sounds of traffic and thunder. Then they heard the small wail again.

Weaker this time.

Alejandro dashed over to the Dumpster and behind it saw a grease-stained box filled with newspapers. Kiri knelt down beside him and gasped as Alejandro peeled back the papers to uncover a small, blue-gray baby. Very small and obviously newly born, because the cord was still fresh and hastily cut off.

"Oh, my God," Kiri whispered. "It's a baby."

A tiny infant that had been abandoned in an alleyway of a hospital. Alone and afraid.

"Fools," Alejandro cursed. "Who would do such a thing?"

And Kiri couldn't help but agree. Someone hadn't wanted this poor mite, but to abandon the baby in the heat next to a Dumpster? That was dreadful.

It was times like this that the loss hurt even more. It reminded Kiri again that life was cruel and dirty.

Life was unfair.

Alejandro whipped off his jacket and gently lifted the infant, wrapping the boy up. "Let's get him inside. It's sweltering out here and, with the storm coming, that's the last thing he needs."

Kiri nodded as Alejandro gingerly picked up the baby. She opened the door and they ran inside. All she could do was keep up with Alejandro's long strides as he called out for nurses, residents and equipment. They laid the baby down on a bed; he looked so small on the large gurney.

Alejandro moved quickly, giving him oxygen, holding the mask over his nose while they waited for an incubator.

"Who would do such a thing?" Kiri wondered out loud as she stared down at the small baby, new in this world and all alone.

Alejandro shook his head. "I don't know, but it's a good thing we found him. He wouldn't have lasted long out there. Look, his stats are very low—I'm surprised he's lasted this long."

The incubator was brought in and a resident took over respirating the baby while they ran an umbilical line to get fluids into him. Kiri reached down and stroked his tiny hand between her finger and thumb. The hand was so small it made her heart skip a beat. It made her yearn for what she'd lost.

And what she'd probably never have since her obstetrician had said she'd probably never again conceive or carry a pregnancy to term. Motherhood was not meant to be for her.

"How old do you think he is?" Alejandro asked, invading her thoughts.

"I think probably about thirty weeks. Maybe. More like twenty-eight," she whispered as they intubated the baby and transferred him over to the incubator to take him up to the nursery. She'd lost her son at twenty-three weeks. He had only been slightly smaller than this boy.

Alejandro nodded. "We probably just missed the mother. I'll let the ER doctors know to be on the lookout for her."

Kiri nodded as the resident team wheeled the incubator and the baby up to the nursery. "Good call. I'll take the little one up to the nursery and arrange for his transfer to County."

"County?" Alejandro asked, stunned.

"Yes," Kiri said. "I told you, the hospital has cut the pro bono cases."

Alejandro frowned and crossed his arms. "He won't survive the trip to County and County doesn't have the facilities of a level-one NICU."

"Then Seaside," she offered. "He can't stay here."

He shook his head. "We have the foremost neonatal intensive care unit here at Buena Vista. He needs to stay here."

Kiri didn't want to send the baby to County either, but her hands were tied.

"And who will pay for his medical expenses?

He doesn't have a family. He's an abandoned baby."

A strange expression crossed Alejandro's face. "I will pay for his medical expenses. I'll take responsibility for him. I'll act as his family."

CHAPTER TWO

"PARDON?" KIRI SAID, because she wasn't quite sure she'd heard Alejandro correctly. "What did you say?"

"I said I would pay for the child's medical expenses," Alejandro snapped. "You're not sending him to County."

Before she could say anything else to him he stormed out of the room. Kiri stood there stunned for a moment, taking in the ramifications of what he'd said.

He was going to pay for him?

She wasn't sure what she was feeling at the moment because she thought about the moment she'd planned to tell Alejandro about their baby five years ago. She'd expected him to be horrified and angry, what she'd thought would be a typical reaction in a man who was finding out he was going to be a father after a one-night stand.

Maybe her assumption of him had been

wrong, because he was offering to take this sick infant as his own.

She ran after him. "You're planning to adopt this boy?"

Alejandro froze in his tracks and spun around. "What're you talking about?"

"You just said you're going to be the boy's guardian."

"No, I said I was going to pay his medical bills. I didn't say anything about adopting him."

"Well, usually when someone offers to become financially responsible for a child like this they intend to invest in their health care and adopt."

Alejandro frowned. "I have no interest in adopting him, but I'll give him his best shot at a family. People who actually want children."

It was like a splash of cold water.

People who actually want children.

So it was clear he didn't want children. Just like she'd first thought when she'd found out she was pregnant. It still hurt, though. She'd been hoping for better from him.

His rejection of having a family, of children, was a rejection of their baby as far as she was concerned.

"You'd better get a lawyer involved," Kiri snarled.

"Why?" he asked.

"Because you'd better make sure you can be financially responsible for this child. If you try to take action and the board gets wind of it and doesn't approve, I won't back you."

She tried to leave, but he grabbed her arm, spinning her round to face him. His dark eyes were flashing with that dangerous light she'd seen before.

"Are you threatening me again?"

"No, I'm not. I'm telling you the reality of the situation." She shook her arm free. "You're one of my surgeons, Dr. Valentino. I am only looking out for your best interest."

"Best interest? It would be better if you didn't let the board cut the pro bono fund. That would be in everyone's best interests."

Kiri glanced around and could see staff were watching them now. What she did next was crucial as the new head of the department. She couldn't let Alejandro upstage her here. If she did then she'd lose any kind of footing she had.

"Dr. Valentino, if you value your career here at Buena Vista I suggest you speak to me privately about any issues you have with the board's decisions in this matter. If you continue to bring up confidential information like this in a public manner I will have no choice but to reprimand you. Do I make myself clear?"

Inside she was shaking. She'd never stood up

to someone like this before and she wasn't 100 percent sure he wouldn't just quit. Which would put her ass on the line as Dr. Valentino was a valued pediatric surgeon and brought in a lot of money.

"Crystal," he said. Then he turned on his heel and stormed away.

Kiri crossed her arms and stared down everyone who was still staring at her. They quickly looked away. Once she was sure she had sufficiently stood her ground she walked away as quickly as she could before the tears brought on by adrenaline began to fall.

"Are you out of your mind?"

Alejandro groaned as his best friend and legal counsel, Emilio Guardia, lambasted him on the other end of the phone.

"Probably," Alejandro groused. "But can it be done?"

There was a sigh on the other end. "Usually the state of Florida doesn't allow health professionals to become guardians of wards of the state. Unless we can prove that there is no conflict of interest."

"There is no conflict of interest. I'm not gaining anything financial from helping this baby."

Which was the truth. He wasn't. In fact, according to Kiri, he was risking it all by helping him. She'd made that perfectly clear to him, but he really had no choice. If the baby was sent to County he'd die.

"Can you send me over the medical records you do have on the boy and I'll apply for an emergency injunction? I don't see why a court wouldn't approve of you having guardianship over the boy, especially if they can't locate the family in the next forty-eight hours. For now, I can at least keep him at Buena Vista."

"Thank you, Emilio." Alejandro was relieved. "I'll get those medical records over to your office as soon as possible."

"I'll watch for them."

Alejandro hung up the phone and ran his hands through his hair. He hadn't believed it when he'd heard that little cry from behind the Dumpster.

He'd been so angry that the board was cutting the pro bono cases that when he'd heard the cry it had shocked him. And then to find that little guy, premature, barely clinging to life in the hot Miami sun...

It had infuriated him.

There was no one to fight for this baby. Just him. Dr. Bhardwaj had made it clear that the onus was on him. Last night he'd tossed and turned, thinking about how Kiri had appeared to be angry about the fact he was willing to pay for the baby but not adopt him. Having a family was something he'd never planned on. Not with his uncertain future. His heart, his father's heart, which beat inside him, could fail. In fact, the median survival rate for a pediatric transplant patient, such as he had been, was twenty-two years. He was nearing that. Once he started to have problems, he'd be put back on to UNOS to wait for a new heart that might never come. And Alejandro wouldn't leave any child without a parent.

He knew the pain all too well. His future was far too unpredictable.

Yeah, he loved kids, but he knew the pain of losing your parents. He wouldn't wish it on anyone. The best thing would've been to let the baby go to County instead of getting involved, but he couldn't just let this baby get lost in the system.

The baby would die if they moved him now. Of that Alejandro was certain so there was really no choice, he had to fight for the boy.

Just like Dante, Rafe and Santi had done for him.

He, at least, had had someone to fight for him when he'd been lying in a coma, his parents dead. His brothers had made the decision to take their brain-dead father off life support and direct their father's heart to him because it was a good match and without it Alejandro would also have died that night because of the robbery.

Alejandro had been a priority on the list back then. And at least he hadn't been an infant. Children as young as six could receive a heart from an adult. It was harder to find an infant or a child's heart.

Alejandro and his father had been a perfect match.

His brothers had given him a second chance to live. They'd sacrificed so much to give him a life. This little boy had no one and Alejandro seriously doubted that they would find the baby's family.

The baby was alone, fighting for life, and Alejandro was going to make sure he had a chance.

What about after you save his life?

The thought caught him off guard.

You're lonely.

He was lonely, but he was used to this life. This was what he'd resigned himself to when he'd finally been old enough to understand the ramifications of his lifesaving surgery. Any chance at happiness like Santiago had found had died that day. And when his transplanted heart stopped beating, no child would mourn him like he mourned his parents.

There was a knock at his office door and he looked up. "Come in."

Mr. Snyder walked in. "Dr. Valentino, a word."

Great. Apparently word got around fast.

Alejandro gritted his teeth. "Of course. Please have a seat."

Mr. Snyder took a seat. He smoothed down the lapels of his expensive designer suit and cleared his throat. "I wanted to speak to you last night, but you'd left."

"My shift was over," Alejandro said, "so I left for the evening."

"You're certain it wasn't because of your dressing-down?" There was a glint of pleasure in Snyder's eyes.

Alejandro fought the urge to toss him out of his office. "I'm quite busy today. How can I help you, Mr. Snyder?"

"It's come to our attention that you're trying to keep that abandoned baby here."

"Yes. What of it?"

"I'm surprised you're trying to do this. Hasn't Dr. Bhardwaj told you that all new pro bono cases have been suspended pending a restructuring of the board?"

"Yes," Alejandro snapped.

Mr. Snyder sneered. "Dr. Valentino, are you purposely disobeying the board of directors' decision?"

"No, I'm not. That baby is not a pro bono case."

Mr. Snyder blinked. "I don't see parents and the last I heard the infant is now a ward of the state of Florida."

"Not for much longer, Mr. Snyder." It took every ounce of strength not to belt Mr. Snyder across the head. He knew these kinds of men. They got a bit of power and they thought they ruled the world, and he knew Mr. Snyder was taking great pleasure in it.

Mr. Snyder was a pretentious snob.

"What do you mean?"

"I mean I have contacted my lawyer and very soon I will be guardian of that baby, meaning that I will be financially responsible. I will be paying all the medical bills."

"Why would you do that?" Mr. Snyder asked.

"It's my money. I'll do what I like with it."

Mr. Snyder shook his head and stood. "No good can come from this. That child should be sent to County, like all the other wards of the state."

"Well, he's not. And if we're done talking, I do have to get back to my work. Paying patients, as per your request." Alejandro smiled at him a little too brightly. It was enough to tick off Snyder, who left his office in a huff.

Alejandro raked his hands through his hair. *Oh, Dios mío.*

This was not how he wanted to start his week at Buena Vista, with the president of the board of directors breathing down his neck and the new head of pediatric surgery being his one and only one-night stand who knew about his sordid past.

There was another knock at the door and Alejandro cursed under his breath, wondering if Snyder had come back to spew more vitriol and threats at him.

"Come in."

Kiri opened the door and his pulse quickened at the sight of her, but he also didn't really want to see her either, since she was the one who had delivered the devastating news about the pro bono program.

It's not her fault.

"Are you okay?" she asked.

"Of course. Why wouldn't I be?" he asked, trying not to look at her.

"You know I had to dress you down yesterday."

"I know," he sighed. "My apologies, Dr. Bhardwaj. I was angry yesterday."

"I get that," she said. "Dr. Valentino, you can't take responsibility for that infant."

"I have to," Alejandro said. "He doesn't stand a chance if he's shipped off to another hospital. Especially not County."

"You know that I don't want to do that either, but the board—"

Alejandro held up his hand. "You don't have to explain board politics to me. I'm very familiar with that. Snyder was just here."

"Oh, great," she said sadly, then she looked concerned. "I told him I'd handle it."

"Your job is safe, I'm sure. It's me he doesn't like and he never has. Probably because I don't kiss his ass," he snapped.

"I don't either," Kiri said defensively.

"And what about Dr. Vaughan?"

"What about Dr. Vaughan?" she asked, confused.

"Oh, come on, I'm sure there was some smooching involved."

"I ought to slug you," she hissed. "I worked hard and Dr. Vaughan recommended me for the job."

Alejandro felt bad about his gibe. He was just on edge. "I'm sorry. Snyder has got me all riled up."

"I can see that. Can I sit down?" she asked. "I hate hovering by the door."

He may be angry at board politics, but that was no reason for him to behave like an animal. Especially in the presence of a lady. Carmelita had smacked him upside the head numerous

times in his youth when he'd stepped out of line
when it came to the fairer sex.

*"Eres todo un caballero. Comportarse como
tal."*

You're a gentleman. Behave like one.

"Of course." Alejandro stood and pulled out
a chair for her. "Sit, please."

She sat down and then he took his seat again.
"So what do I tell the board about the baby?"

"My lawyer is getting an emergency injunction to stop the transfer. I'm hoping as the head
of pediatric surgery you can delay things on your
end for a couple of hours."

She nodded. "I can, but if that injunction
doesn't come by the day's end then I have to
send him to County."

"Not Seaside?" At least at Seaside he had family who could watch out for the boy.

"No," she said sadly. "Wards of the state are
to be sent to County."

Damn.

"Well, I appreciate you doing all you can do
to delay it. I'm dead serious about taking financial responsibility for the boy."

A strange expression passed across her face,
like pain, but whatever it was it was quickly
gone. "Why are you doing this?"

Alejandro shrugged. "Wouldn't you if you
could?"

"Your job is worth this?" she asked.

"Are you going to fire me?"

"No."

"Then, yes, it's worth it. The boy needs medical attention, the best medical attention that this city can give him, and that's here at Buena Vista. He needs a chance at life. I can give him a shot, even if it's only financially."

That strange expression passed across her face again. "How very gallant of you."

"What's with the sarcastic tone?"

"There's no sarcastic tone."

He frowned. "Why does this make you so mad?"

"Look, I want what's best for that baby too, but doing this is just throwing it in my face. In the board's face. You're basically saying that you don't care about the new policies being handed down to you by your boss or the board, you're just going to do what you want."

"That's not it at all," Alejandro snapped. "This is about saving that child's life."

Her eyes narrowed. "I understand that."

She couldn't believe that she was trying to talk him out of it. It was so unlike her. When had she changed so much? When she'd decided to become a pediatric surgeon she'd wanted to save them all too. She was just as idealistic as Alejandro. And then reality had hit her hard. She'd lost patients and had learned how cruel life was. She'd become jaded, but never had she shared those dark thoughts with another surgeon until now.

Strange emotions were raging inside her. Watching him fight so hard to save this little baby melted her heart, but also reminded her that he hadn't been there to save theirs.

Not that there had been anything that could be done about that. She knew that, but he hadn't been there and he'd made it clear he never would be.

It just hit so close to home.

When she'd seen that little baby in the dirty box, covered with newspaper and thrown away, it had cut her to the very core.

And it had ticked her off.

Alejandro had stepped up to take responsibility for the boy.

Would she have done the same as him? Kiri would like to think so, but she wasn't sure if she could as head of the department.

So she envied him a bit, envied his bravery in doing such a thing.

"Look—" Her words were cut off as Alejandro's cell phone rang.

"Hello? Yes, this is Dr. Valentino." He listened

to the voice on the other end. "Where is it? I see. I'll be there as soon as I can."

"Is everything okay?" she asked as he hung up the phone.

"Yes, but I have to go." Alejandro stood up.

"Who was that?" Kiri asked.

"A liver for José. It's in New Orleans and I'm going to retrieve it."

She was shocked. "Do you always do your own retrievals? Why don't you send a resident?"

Alejandro shook his head. "I want to make sure that our piece of this liver is done right. I want to make sure everything goes smoothly for José's new liver. This is his last shot."

Kiri nodded. "I'll make a call to the airport and charter a plane."

"Thank you."

Kiri stood. "Can I go with you?"

He was surprised. "You want to go with me? Why?"

"I want to see you in action," she said. "I was planning on observing this surgery once a match was found. And right now I'm still getting my footing."

"I'd rather you stayed here," Alejandro said. "To make sure they don't ship that baby off to County."

Kiri smiled at him. "I've already put a stop to that. The baby is having tests. I have to be the one to release the baby to County. No one else. The baby is safe."

She waited while he mulled that over. He dragged a hand through his dark curls, making them wild and unruly. Sexy as hell too.

"I can't go," he shouted in frustration.

"Why not?"

"No other doctor speaks fluent Spanish and I have to prep José. I'm going to have to leave the recovery to a transplant team in New Orleans and a resident." He cursed again. "I don't want to do it, but I don't really have a choice."

"I'll go and retrieve José's liver. You stay and prep José," she offered.

"Are you sure?" Alejandro asked. "Have you done a retrieval before?"

She shot him a look and he chuckled. "What am I talking about? Of course you can. You sure you don't mind?"

"I wouldn't have offered if I minded. Prep José and I'll call you when the liver is retrieved. Also, call the charter. I want to leave as soon as possible," she said.

Alejandro nodded. "I'll see you at the ambulance bay in fifteen minutes."

"Okay." Kiri stood and then let herself out of his office. She'd be missing a board meeting, but she didn't care. She was a surgeon and this was her job. To help little José out. It would be better for the parents and for the boy if Alejandro prepped them for what was going to happen.

Kiri changed out of her business attire and into scrubs. She grabbed her new identification and a Buena Vista jacket, which would let the Parish Hospital in New Orleans know where she was from, since they were expecting Alejandro.

Fifteen minutes later she was in the ambulance bay. An ambulance was waiting to whisk her to the airport. Alejandro was standing there, waiting for her, holding a cooler that would transport José's liver.

"Thank you for doing this."

"It's no problem. Look, I know I've been a bit of a hard ass and dropped quite a bomb on you yesterday and then we had our public disagreement, but part of my vision for the pediatric team of Buena Vista is working together as a team."

He nodded. "I like that vision. You'd better go. Call me when you have the liver."

"I will."

Kiri glanced back once more to see Alejandro still standing there, watching her climb into the ambulance, an unreadable expression on his face. She knew that look. He wanted to do the retrieval himself and he'd be pacing until she called him with the news that it was okay.

She understood that. She respected it.

"You ready to go, Dr. Bhardwaj?" the paramedic, Mike, asked.

"You betcha. Let's go."

As much as she hated flying, at least the flight to New Orleans would be short and a life depended on her.

She may not have been able to save her baby or everyone, but she could save this family's son.

And that gave her an inkling of hope that she hadn't felt in a long, long time.

CHAPTER THREE

THIS WAS THE PART she didn't like and Kiri hoped that no one knew that she was shaking in her boots as she was called to the operating table to retrieve the liver. It was the ending of a life.

And she hated that.

The worst part of a job. Which was why she specialized in general pediatric surgery over transplant surgery. She gave props to Alejandro for dealing with this every day. Life and death involving children.

Parish Hospital had a surgical resident helping her as she watched another surgical team remove a kidney. It was decided she would remove the entire liver out of the donor and then an attending from Parish, who was a bit of a specialist in dividing livers, would do just that. One piece for José and the rest of the liver would go to another person, because the liver was an amazing organ that had the ability to regenerate itself.

It was just that in José's case neither of his

parents were a good match for him and were unable to do a living donation. Which was why the boy had gone on the UNOS list and why she was here.

She'd done several retrievals, but in New York she had just overseen them as she'd become an attending. The retrieval had been done by the student she'd been teaching, but only when the transplant attending hadn't done it themselves, that was.

There was a lot of pressure riding on this retrieval. She was very aware of that. Alejandro had made it clear that this was José's last shot.

You should've stayed in Miami. You should've hired an interpreter.

No, it was better that Alejandro was there. If she had been that boy's mother and couldn't speak the language, she'd want the surgeon she was familiar with to stay and look after her child. If she were a mother, she'd feel the same.

Only you're not a mother and you probably never will be.

Kiri stared down at the liver and decided where to start the resection. The other part of the liver would go to the next doctor waiting in the wings. A resident stood across from her, while a scrub nurse waited for instructions.

"Scalpel." Kiri held out her hand and the nurse set the number ten blade into her palm, handle first. She was the more experienced surgeon, so she removed the liver from the donor patient and placed it in the ice-cold preservation liquid where the Parish Hospital surgeon waited to split it.

José was a child and only needed half of the liver. The left lateral segment was destined for him.

Thankfully, the liver was healthy. There was no damage, no bleeding, spots or cysts and no signs that the liver was deteriorating, things they looked for during a transplant surgery. They would go over it once again before they placed it in José.

Kiri placed it into a stainless-steel bowl of preservation solution. Another resident whisked it to the general surgeon who would divide it. Kiri removed her gloves and got the cooler that would transport the liver part back to Miami.

Once the splitting was complete and she was in the ambulance she would call Alejandro and let him know they were on their way, which would give him time to get José anesthetized and into the operating room, so it would just be a matter of transplanting the organ into José.

It was a delicate dance and Kiri was impressed that a man like Alejandro would take up such a specialized and difficult field, especially given his background. Wasn't he worried about people finding out?

And she could only imagine the public relations nightmare that it would cause if the general public did find out what the respected surgeon had done in his past.

As she mulled over trying to explain that to the board of directors if they ever found out, a memory of Alejandro crept into her mind.

The tattoo of the large eagle covering his chest.

She remembered running her fingers over the tattoo, tracing the delicate pattern and swirls of ink.

"It's an interesting choice for a tattoo," she whispered as he ran his hands down her back and she tracked the gentle ink designs with her fingertip.

"It covers a scar," he said as he kissed her neck.

"A scar? It must be a large scar."

He nodded. "Yeah, ever since I was a kid. When I became an adult I covered it with something meaningful to me."

"An eagle?"

"Sí."

"Why?"

"No more questions."

He grinned and kissed her, causing her to

*forget all the questions she still had about him
and just feel the way his kisses fired her blood.*

"Dr. Bhardwaj?"

Kiri shook thoughts about Alejandro out
of her head and stepped forward, opening the
cooler filled with preservation solution. The surgeon from Parish Hospital gently placed the liver
segment inside.

Once they were sure the liver was safe and
that the left branches of the artery and bile duct
hadn't been damaged, Kiri closed the lid and
moved out of the operating room. Once she had
got out of her gown and scrub cap she followed a
nurse out to the ambulance bay, where an ambulance was waiting to rush her back to the airport.

She pulled out her cell phone and hit the number she'd programmed in to direct her straight
to Alejandro.

"Dr. Valentino," he said quickly.

"It's Kiri. The liver is viable and I'm on my
way. Should be there in a couple of hours."

"I'll prep him." Alejandro hung up on her and
she slipped the phone back into her pocket as she
climbed into the back of the ambulance with her
precious cargo.

The paramedic who rode in the back with
her secured her in her seat. She wasn't going to
take her eyes off the liver and it was protocol at
Buena Vista. She was responsible for the organ.

With her nod, the siren started up and the ambulance raced out of the bay at Parish Hospital.

Even though the sirens were blaring, they were trying to make their way through the crowded French Quarter at dusk. Already there were partygoers out, horse-drawn carriages and tourists everywhere.

The paramedic driving was cursing under his breath.

Come on.

She glanced out the back window and behind her the crowd of people filled in any space that they had just cleared. Finally the ambulance got a break in the crowds and headed out on Canal Street and onto the expressway that would whisk them on an elevated highway west to Louis Armstrong Airport.

She closed her eyes as the ambulance rocked slightly, whipping down the highway to the private charter plane that was waiting to take her back to Miami.

"Parish Hospital isn't placed in the best location in New Orleans," the paramedic across from her said. "The French Quarter this time of night is bad."

"I can only imagine, but it's not as bad as rush hour in New York," Kiri said, sharing a smile with the paramedic. They didn't say anything else. Kiri didn't have much to say because, like the paramedics, they all knew that a life had ended.

Even though the donor had been an adult they had still been someone's child. Someone who had been loved. Lives would be saved tonight because of the generous donation, but also tonight there would be people mourning.

Loved ones grieving.

Once she was on the plane she'd feel better, but she wouldn't be at ease until the liver was in José and the boy was pulling through.

Only then would she relax.

Alejandro stared down at José lying on the table, intubated and waiting for the liver. The boy was on veno-venous bypass and Alejandro had almost finished removing José's damaged liver from his body. He wanted to make sure that he left good lengths of vessel so that when he reanastomosed the donor liver it would take.

This was José's one shot.

Just like it had been yours.

Any transplant surgery was hard for him, even after all this time, because at one time he'd been on the table, hooked up to bypass as a young boy, his father being taken off life support in the operating room next to him so that Alejandro could be given a fighting chance at life.

His brothers having to make the monumental decision to end their father's life and become orphans themselves so that Alejandro could go on living. Every surgery stirred those memories in him, but he still wouldn't change it for the world. When he'd visited his father's grave months later, because he'd been in the ICU when his parents had been buried, he'd promised his father he would save others.

He'd dedicate his second chance at life to transplant surgery.

He would help other children. Other families.

The operating-room door opened and Kiri entered, masked, carrying the cooler.

"It's about time," he said under his breath, barely glancing up as he worked over José.

"Like I can control the speed of a plane," Kiri said. She handed the cooler off to Alejandro's resident, Dr. Page, who had fresh preservation solution ready and waiting.

"Are you going to scrub in and assist?" Alejandro asked. He wasn't sure why he asked, but he figured he might as well make the offer, because she was probably going to stay anyway.

"You read my mind."

He grinned to himself and watched her as she headed back into the scrub room to get properly attired.

Once she was scrubbed and gowned she joined

him on the opposite side of the table, and the nurse handed her the retractor.

"You've done a nice job of dividing the bile duct," she said. "Have you removed his gallbladder too?"

"Yes, to avoid future complications, and thank you for the compliment, Dr. Bhardwaj."

"My pleasure," she said.

"And I didn't thank you properly for flying to New Orleans and back to retrieve the liver. It was a lot easier on my patient and his family for me to be here."

She nodded. "I thought as much. I'm sure they were thrilled."

"Yes, and scared beyond belief."

"I don't blame them. If it were my child…" She trailed off and cleared her throat. "It's good you were there and I'd never been to New Orleans before. Not that I saw much of the city."

"That's too bad. It's a great city," Alejandro remarked. "The Café du Monde is one of my favorite places for café au lait and beignets."

"Beignets?"

"Fried pastries covered in icing sugar. Beautiful, but evil." And he winked at her.

She shook her head. "I'm not much into baked goods."

"Oh?"

"I'm more of a savory person. French fries."

"I don't think that's a specific New Orleans food."

"I didn't say it was," Kiri said. "Before my parents moved to New York they lived with relatives in London, England. So when we visited my family there before visiting the rest of the family in Mumbai, we had traditional fish and chips on the banks of the Thames. It was the best."

"Were you born in Mumbai?" he asked.

"Nope, New York City. Manhattan, to be precise. Where were you born? You speak fluent Spanish."

"How is the liver looking, Dr. Page?" Alejandro asked, ignoring her question. He had been born in Miami, but he didn't feel like talking about Heliconia at the moment, the country his parents had come from, because it would remind him of that day he'd lost his parents. It was bad enough the ghosts of that memory haunted him every time he went into the operating room, but he wouldn't talk about that day.

The day he'd been shot.

And if on cue his scar twinged in memory of it, his heart skipping a beat to remind him.

"It's looking great, Dr. Valentino. Ready when you are," Dr. Page said.

"I'm ready."

"Walking with the liver," Dr. Page announced,

and she stopped beside him. Alejandro set down his instruments and gently reached into the stainless-steel bowl to lift out the liver. The sounds of the operating room were drowned out. All he could hear was his own pulse thundering in his ears as he steadied himself and focused on gently placing the liver where he needed it to be in order to transplant it into José's body.

Giving José that second chance at life, like he'd been granted.

A life of antirejection drugs and taking care of yourself, but for the price of life it was something that Alejandro was willing to pay, just like José and his family were.

"You're awake!"

Alejandro's eyes focused and he saw Dante and Rafe hovering over him. Santi was slumping in the corner, sulking. His eyes were red.

He tried to talk, but couldn't. His throat hurt and it wasn't the only thing.

"Don't try to talk," Dante said. "You've just had surgery to replace your heart and they just removed the tube from your throat."

He glanced over at Rafe, who nodded. His eyes were red too, bloodshot.

"Do you remember what happened?" Dante asked.

Alejandro nodded and winced as tears stung

his eyes. The sound of shots still seemed to be ringing in his ears.

"The police are going to come and they want you to look at pictures. Do you remember the men who came in?"

Alejandro nodded, because he would never forget those scary men with the guns. Then he grimaced, his chest hurting.

"You were shot. Remember?" Dante said again. "Don't try to move. You're still recovering. Please take it easy."

And then he shot a look at Santi, asking silently where Mom and Dad were. Santi would know why Mami and Pappi weren't here. He needed them. He wanted his parents.

Santi's eyes were dark, hollow. "Mami and Pappi are dead. You have Pappi's heart."

He heard screaming in his head, realizing that he was crying out in his mind when he was unable to do it physically. Only the screams were the monitors and his brothers were calling for help as he had a seizure.

"It's a nice job," Alejandro said, shaking those memories from his head. He didn't want to think about his parents right now. Those nightmares of the shooting, there was no place for them. He had to stop thinking about them. He needed to focus on the surgery as he began a caval replacement. Usually he would take the approach of navel preservation cavocavostomy, but in José's case his IVC was completely fried so Alejandro used the donor IVC to replace José's.

"I didn't split it, just removed it," Kiri said.

"Still, you kept all the arteries intact. It's a beautiful liver."

Kiri nodded. "It'll give him the best shot."

"It's the best part of the job," Alejandro said, then he grinned at her.

"What is?" she asked.

"Giving them their best shot. Every child deserves a chance at life."

"Y-yes…of c-course." She stammered over her words, like she was trying to swallow down sadness.

Had Kiri lost someone? A child, perhaps, who still haunted her? When she'd come into his office he'd noticed that she didn't wear a ring on her finger, but that didn't mean anything. Not really. She could still be involved with someone.

She could have a family. The thought of her with another man made him angry. Not that he had any claim over her other than a one-night stand five years ago when he'd still been dancing. One heated one-night stand that still stuck with him.

Since Kiri he hadn't seriously dated anyone. He'd just thrown himself into his work, but there were times he recalled her hands on him, the scent of her, the taste of her, and the thought of her with another man was just too much for him to take at the moment.

"How did your family take to moving down here from New York City?"

She cocked an eyebrow above her surgical mask. "I'm an adult. My parents took it fine, I suppose. They really don't have a say over where I go."

"Not your parents. I mean your husband or significant other."

"I'm not married and there's no significant other, not that it's any of your business."

"I was just curious. You don't have to snap at me."

Her dark eyes narrowed. "How about we focus on the surgery?"

"I like to chat when I'm doing surgeries. Besides, you had no qualms when we were talking about café au lait and beignets."

"I suppose I didn't. Still, we should focus."

"I am."

"How so?"

"Chatting helps me focus."

"Really?" she asked in disbelief.

"What helps you keep your focus during surgery, then?" he asked.

"Silence." There was a twinkle in her eyes.

There were a few snickers of laughter and

Alejandro couldn't help but smile. This was why he'd been attracted to her all those years ago. She was feisty, fiery. She might act like a bit of a wallflower, but she wasn't.

She was far from it, deep down.

They didn't say anything further as Alejandro finished the surgery. Before he closed they took José off bypass. And he held his breath, waiting for the donor liver to pink up and let him know that it was being accepted by the body for now. There was always the chance that it could be rejected later on, but Alejandro wouldn't close until he saw the blood flow back into the liver.

That would let him know that he'd done his job well for now.

"Take him off bypass."

The machines whirred to a stop and Alejandro watched the liver.

Come on.

The liver pinked up and he said a silent prayer that it had taken so well. "Excellent job, everyone. Let's get this little man closed up and into the ICU."

"Fine work, Dr. Valentino," Kiri said.

He nodded in acknowledgment, but didn't look at her as he finished his job. He probably should let a resident close, but he wanted to see José's case through. He'd brought the boy this far.

And he'd promised José's mother that he would see it through. That he wouldn't leave José's side.

Once it was done and José was stabilized Alejandro finally stepped away and let residents and nurses take care of his charge. He would check on José in the ICU before he left for the night. Kiri was already in the scrub room, cleaning up, as he peeled off his mask, tossing it in the receptacle.

"There's a lawyer pacing the halls, looking for you," Kiri said. There was a hint of censure in her voice.

"It's not a malpractice suit," Alejandro snapped. "If that's what you're thinking."

"I wasn't thinking that. I assume it's your injunction about the baby, but it doesn't look good for a lawyer to be pacing the halls of the hospital, waiting for a surgeon."

"Are you afraid of the image he'll cast?" Alejandro teased as he ran his hands under the water.

"Yes." She toweled off her hands. "Especially as he's looking for one of my surgeons."

He grinned. "I am one of your surgeons?"

"Of course. I am the pediatric head. You're a pediatric surgeon, are you not?"

"Absolutely." He grinned and waggled his eyebrows at her.

She rolled her eyes, but a smile played at the corner of her mouth. "You're pathetic."

"I thought you were just praising my prowess in there?"

"You're very infuriating. Where did you learn to be so annoying?"

"I have three older brothers, all of them in the medical field."

"Oh, good Lord."

He couldn't help but laugh. "Don't you have siblings?"

"We're going to start with the personal interrogation again, are we?"

"Hey, I like to get to know my colleagues."

She cocked an eyebrow and crossed her arms. "Really? Can you tell me a bit about the scrub nurse in there, then?"

Alejandro grinned. "Of course. Her name is Elizabeth. She's a married mother of four. She's been my scrub nurse for a number of years. I like her because she anticipates exactly what I need during transplant surgeries. Her favorite color is yellow and she loves Cuban food."

Kiri's mouth dropped open. "Are you kidding me?"

"I make conversations in there when things are going well. It's how I can focus. Why do surgeons have to be so serious all the time?"

"We're serious because we're dealing with lives."

Alejandro shook his head. "And we're human too. It makes for a more relaxed atmosphere. Since you're unlikely to be in any of my other surgeries, what does it matter how I run my operating room?"

He grabbed a paper towel and dried his hands, then threw the towel in the garbage. "Now, if you'll excuse me, I have a lawyer to speak to."

He walked past Kiri, leaving her standing there stunned.

And he didn't care.

It was unlikely she'd be in the OR with him again. She was taking over a department and soon she'd have her own patient load to deal with. He would only have to deal with her if there were consults or meetings.

He was an attending, not a resident who needed to be taught a thing or two.

It was better this way. It was better to keep his distance from her, because he'd promised himself a long time ago he would never get married.

Never get involved with someone, not after what had happened with his parents and the pain their deaths had caused. Not when his father's heart could give out. He was very aware of heart transplant stats. His time was limited.

And he would never put someone he cared about through the pain of loss.

It was better this way. He could bear the pain himself.

Can you?

And he would never put someone he cared
about through the pain of loss.
Besides, this way he could bear the pain
himself.

CHAPTER FOUR

KIRI WAS WALKING the halls of a darkened Buena
Vista. She'd been working late again and as she
walked she realized that no one else was around.

What was going on?

She turned and the lights dimmed. Alejandro
was at the end of the hall dressed in a suit, his
head lowered, his hands behind his back. She
was completely confused.

"Dr. Valentino?"

*Music started and he began to dance. Just
like that night in his hotel room in Vegas. Right
down to the same suit.*

Kiri sat down in a chair that suddenly appeared. She wanted to tell him to stop dancing, that it wasn't appropriate to do his routine
in the hospital, but she lost her voice and suddenly it didn't matter that he was doing this in
the hospital.

She was transfixed as he undid the knot in his
tie, slowly pulling it off. Those dark eyes were

glittering in the dim light and were focused on her. Holding her captive.

Kiri realized then she was at his mercy. Her body thrummed with need as he pulled off his jacket and shirt. She ran her hands over his body, over his hard, rippling muscles. Then he leaned over her, his lips brushing her ear.

"Mi tesoro," he whispered. "I want you forever. Always. Only you."

She closed her eyes and waited for a kiss.

Instead a blaring noise echoed in the hall and he moved away...

Kiri woke with a start. Her alarm clock was going off. It startled her and as she groggily reached for her glasses, she fumbled to find the alarm and shut it off.

With a sigh she sank back into the pillows. Sunshine was peeking in through the venetian blinds that covered the bank of floor-to-ceiling windows in her apartment bedroom.

"Good Lord," she groaned. Alejandro was invading her dreams again and even though it had just been a dream her body was craving the kiss she'd been waiting for. The kiss that was in her imagination. She hadn't had an erotic dream about Alejandro in a long time.

Any dreams she'd usually had about him since the miscarriage had brought tears to her eyes and reminded her of what she'd lost. What she'd been denied.

So dreams about him were more like nightmares.

Except for the one she'd just had, which still made her blood burn with need.

The sun coming through her windows was a bit blinding, but it was worth it. She'd chosen South Beach because she liked to be near the ocean, she liked the art deco buildings and there was no city obscuring her view of the ocean.

Her apartment was also a decent size and there was a pool for people in the building to use. It was perfect.

Unlike her small rabbit hole of an apartment in Manhattan.

The only downside was that South Beach was loud at night, but no louder than New York City, so it really didn't bother her all that much that there were boisterous nightclubs and loud music at night. It reminded her of home.

She glanced at all the boxes still littering her apartment. She had the day off so she could do some unpacking, but instead she decided that she was going to go down to the pool and soak up the sun. Kiri had been in Miami for just over a week and she'd been in so many meetings that she hadn't had a chance to really make the most of the Florida sun. Checking her weather on her phone made her smile.

In New York City it was raining, dreary and cold.

For the first time she was glad she wasn't there.

She got out of bed and opened her blinds, squinting as the brilliant sun filled her apartment. It was warm and made her feel alive again.

How long had she been living in a fog?

After she'd lost the baby she'd retreated into herself. Work had been the only thing that could numb the pain. Her life had been on autopilot. She couldn't even remember the last time she'd had a day off. Keeping busy had occupied her mind and kept it off her loss.

A vision of Alejandro holding that little baby from the Dumpster had hit her hard. Would he have been so caring if he'd been holding their baby?

How could he? He didn't even know about his son and he'd made it clear that he didn't even want a baby.

And if their baby boy had lived, she wasn't sure she'd have the position she had now at such a young age, and she doubted very much whether, if she had a child, she would've moved so far from her parents and sister.

She would've wanted to give her child a family.

Cousins, grandparents and aunties. The kind of family she'd had when she'd been growing up. They say everything worked out for a reason, but she would gladly give up all she had to have had a chance to keep her child. A chance to be a mother.

Stop it.

Kiri shook her head. There was a no point in thinking about the past. She was going to change into her swimsuit and head down to the pool. It was her day off and she was going to enjoy it.

She put in her contacts, showered and brushed her teeth so she was ready for the day.

She found her bathing suit and grabbed a couple of magazines from the stack she had and headed down to the aqua pool in the courtyard. Maybe later she'd stroll through her neighborhood and walk along the white sandy beaches.

The whole day was hers.

It was warm outside, but not warm enough to tempt her to go swimming just yet, even if the pool was heated. So instead she found a lounge chair and made herself comfortable. As she relaxed in the chair she realized that she wasn't the only one here.

One of her neighbors was swimming laps in the pool.

She watched him, his muscular arms cutting through the turquoise water with ease. She couldn't help but admire him and then he stood and pulled off his swimming goggles, the water running down over his bronzed body, and she found herself staring at that eagle tattoo she knew all too well.

"Alejandro?"

He blinked a couple of times. "Kiri?"

"What're you doing here?" she asked.

"I live here," he said. "What're you doing here?"

"I live here."

Great. Just great.

He laughed. "Well, isn't that so like the universe, trying to make sure we're together?"

"You mean karma? Are you saying I'm being punished?" she teased.

Alejandro laughed and climbed out of the water and she tried not to let her gaze linger too long on his lean, muscular body. Her blood heated as all those naughty thoughts from her dream started creeping back into her head.

He grabbed his towel and dried his face with it before wrapping it around his waist and pattering over to where she was lounging.

"I hope you put on sunscreen. It may not be that hot out, but the sun packs a nasty punch."

"I'm a doctor. I know and, yes, I did." She began to flip through one of her magazines, trying to ignore him, but it was no good. He sat down beside her and her heart began to race as the memories of her lingering dream filled her head.

"So when did you move in?" he asked.

"About a week ago. I'm on the eighth floor."

"I am, as well. I'm Eight B."

"You're kidding me?"

"No, why? What apartment are you in?"

"A. You're my neighbor?" Just what she needed.

"Well, not technically. You're across the hall from me. I face the ocean and you have a lovely view of the pool here."

"I think I would rather face the ocean." She sighed. "I have a partial ocean view from my bedroom, by the way."

Why did you just say that?

He grinned lazily. "Well, maybe you'll have to show me your view sometime."

"Uh…" She faltered. "Perhaps."

He ignored her. "The ocean is a nice view. Definitely better from where I grew up. You couldn't see the ocean from where I lived as a child."

"So you're a native Miamian. Is that the right term?"

He chuckled. *"Sí."*

"Well, is it a nice place to grow up?"

He shrugged. "Here it is. I've always liked

South Beach, but where I grew up it was a bit different."

"Where was that?"

"Little Heliconia. It's a poorer part of the city on the mainland. My parents were from Heliconia and settled near other Heliconians."

"Ah, that explains why you're fluent in Spanish. Were you born there?"

"No, here in Miami," he said. "I've never been to the motherland, as it were."

"I didn't realize both of us were children of immigrants."

He lazed back in the chair. "I believe that all Americans are immigrants. It's just some have been here longer. So you have the day off?"

"I do. And apparently you do, as well." She tried to feign disinterest in him, but he wasn't taking the hint.

"I'm on call," he said absently. "I have one of my best residents taking care of José. I checked on him early this morning and I will probably go in tonight. However, I'm ready to race up there if I get a call."

Kiri nodded. "And the John Doe infant?"

"I was granted guardianship of the baby and he's stable. He's going through a few more tests with the pediatric cardiologist," Alejandro said. "I haven't seen him since we found him."

Kiri found that remark stung. Why didn't he

want to adopt the baby eventually? Why else would he offer to be financially responsible and go through all the trouble of being the baby's guardian if he wasn't going to adopt him?

Because he didn't want kids. He probably liked his life the way it was. She was trying to do that, as well. Enjoy what she had been dealt without thinking about what she didn't have.

Which could be rectified if she ever found the right man to settle down with and adopt. That was still a possibility.

Then she realized he'd mentioned cardiology.

"Cardiologist?" she asked, concerned.

"His heart is giving the cardiology team some concern. They think he was born at about twenty-eight weeks, but if he has a congenital heart defect he could be younger."

"Poor mite," she whispered. "You sure you still want to be financially responsible for him? I mean, the costs already racking up…"

"I'm sure," he snapped. "End of discussion. I'm responsible for him. Once he's better, then he'll have a shot of being adopted into a family who will love him."

"You still don't want to adopt him?"

He frowned. "What gave you that idea? I haven't changed my mind. I'm not interested in a family."

"Because you're currently his guardian, I thought you might change your mind."

"No, I'm not cut out to be a father. Kids were never on the plan. I don't want kids. End of discussion."

It was like a punch to the throat. *Kids were never on the plan* and *I'm not cut out to be a father.* The words made her stomach turn and gave her the answer she'd always wanted. Alejandro wouldn't have been happy if she'd come to him pregnant.

He wouldn't have been there for their child.

It just would've been her. Only she'd never got that chance.

She shut her magazine. "Well, I think I've had enough sun for the day. I think I'll go unpack some boxes."

"You just got here," he said. "Stay."

"I really have a lot of unpacking to do."

"You say that like you're about to dive into a pool of scorpions. Why don't I show you around?" he suggested.

No.

Only she did want to get to know the neighborhood and Alejandro had grown up in Miami. Like it or not, he was her only friend here. It couldn't hurt, as long as she kept reminding herself they were just colleagues. Nothing more, because it was clear Alejandro did not want the same things as her.

"Are you sure?"

"I wouldn't have offered if I wasn't sure." He stood. "Say we meet in the lobby in thirty minutes? That gives us enough time to change and I'll take you out on the town."

"I don't know whether I should be thrilled or terrified."

He grinned, flashing those brilliant white teeth at her. "Always thrilled with me. Or have you forgotten? Make sure you wear pants."

"What? Why?"

"I drive a motorcycle. Skirts and motorcycles don't mix. Well, at least I'm sure those who wear skirts think that. I don't mind looking." Then he winked.

Kiri rolled her eyes and tried not to laugh as she collected up her things and headed back to her apartment. She had never been on the back of a motorcycle before and it frankly terrified her a bit.

Live a little. That's why you came to Miami.

She'd come here not only for the job but for the change. To escape the fog she'd found herself in in New York City. Staying in the same place, she couldn't escape the pain of her loss. This was a fresh start.

Not really since you're going out with the father of your baby.

Kiri groaned as she set her things down on her dining-room table, glancing in the mirror hanging on the wall. "What have I done? What am I doing?"

Alejandro was pacing as he stared at the elevator.

What am I doing?

He was still asking himself that question as he waited for Kiri to come down to the lobby. He didn't know what had made him invite her out. That hadn't been his plan. He'd been going to catch up on some paperwork and perhaps drift over to the hospital. That's usually what he did on his days off. Not that he was really off, he was on call. There just hadn't been any calls yet.

The doors of the elevator opened and Kiri stepped out.

He sucked in a quick breath, bracing himself for the fact she soon would be behind him on his bike, so close to him. And she was just as gorgeous as she'd ever been.

Capri pants, espadrilles and a cotton blouse that made her skin glow. Her long silky black hair was tied back and braided.

"You're staring at me. Am I dressed okay? You said pants, but all my pants are woolen and more for winter wear in New York. I haven't had a chance to unpack my spring and summer long pants."

"You're fine. You look nice."

More than nice.

A blush tinged her cheeks. "Thanks. So where are you taking me?"

"Would you like some lunch first? I know a great place."

She nodded. "Sure. What's it called?"

"Mad Ron's."

She blinked. "Mad Ron's? Should I be worried?"

Alejandro shrugged. "Depends if Ron is there or not."

"There's a Ron?"

"Of course, it's called Mad Ron's."

Kiri shook her head and they headed down to the parking garage together. He handed her the extra helmet he'd been carrying and stowed her purse in the pannier. He waited until she climbed on behind him, her arms wrapped around him, before he started the engine and pulled out of the parking garage onto Collins Avenue.

Her grip tightened as they headed out over the McArthur Causeway.

"Relax," he shouted. "Enjoy the view."

Kiri's nails dug into his flesh so he doubted she was enjoying the view, but Alejandro liked taking the causeway. The islands were dotted with beautiful, expensive homes and large yachts were docked in the channel outside the homes.

He could so be a boat person. Then he could sail around the world, not a care in the world. And if his heart gave out then he could die at sea. It would be peaceful.

Only that was just a fantasy. He'd made a vow to be reliable, work hard and not waste a second of life.

He wouldn't let his *pappi* down.

His father had worked hard to get to America and open that bodega to support his family. To give them a better life than they could possibly live in Heliconia. Too many sacrifices had been made on his behalf. Alejandro took his duty very seriously.

It wasn't long until they arrived at Mad Ron's. He just hoped that his brothers weren't inside. He didn't want to have to explain Kiri, even though there was nothing to explain. His brothers would know something more had passed between them.

Even if that something more had been five years ago.

And he couldn't risk his brothers finding out what he'd done.

The dancing had been the only time he'd been free. It hadn't been his favorite job in the world, but it had let him have just a taste of freedom.

It was a secret that only he and Kiri knew about. And he was tempting fate by taking Kiri to Mad Ron's, which wasn't far from his family's bodega and Little Heliconia, but it was a weekday and he was hoping Dante and Rafe were working and that Santi was in a bit of a honeymoon phase with Saoirse and wouldn't be making an appearance.

He parked the bike out front. Loud music was blaring from the open door. The palm trees surrounding the building swayed in a gentle breeze, rustling the fronds and the bamboo wind chimes hanging outside.

Kiri handed him the helmet. "I thought we were going to explore South Beach. I wasn't expecting a ride over the water."

"You've been stuck in Miami Beach too long. You've driven the causeway in a car before."

"Yes, but there was something about not having the safety of metal surrounding me…"

Alejandro chuckled. "Well, I'll buy you a mojito. That will calm your nerves."

He breathed a sigh of relief when he scanned all the plush red leather booths and didn't see any sign of his brothers or Mad Ron, which was probably a good thing.

Gracias a Dios.

"Would you like to sit outside and enjoy the breeze?" he asked.

Kiri nodded. "That would be nice."

Alejandro waved to Ángel, who was working behind the bar. They took a seat in the farthest corner of the patio. The palms and hibiscus bushes were covered in fairy lights, but they weren't on right now.

Actually, they had the whole patio to themselves, which was nice in one way and a bit awkward in another.

Kiri sighed and leaned back in the chair. "It's wonderful out here."

"Worth the motorcycle ride?"

"Not sure about that. Ask me when we have to drive back over that causeway to get back home."

He grinned. "Well, if you pried your eyes open you could enjoy the sights of the islands with all the beautiful homes and all the big yachts."

"Do you have a yacht?"

Alejandro cocked an eyebrow. "As you're technically my boss, you know how much I get paid. No, I don't have a yacht."

"I figured you had some money stashed away from your days of dancing." Then she blushed. "I'm sorry. I didn't mean to assume or bring that up."

"No, it's okay. Nothing much is left. I paid off my school loans, if you recall. The rest went to a down payment on my condo five years ago."

"What did your parents think of your cho-

sen career path before becoming a surgeon?"
she asked.

"Not much. My parents died when I was ten."

"I'm sorry," she said, and she reached out to
touch his hand. "Did you have other family to
take care of you?"

"No, my parents were the only ones who came
to America from Heliconia, long before I was
born. The rest of my family is back on the island,
but I have never really met them. It was just me
and my brothers. They're all older. The twins
Dante and Rafe were legally adults at the time
our parents died. Santi was only thirteen and I
was ten. My brothers took care of me."

"That was nice of them. You said they were
all in the medical world. What do they do?"

"They're all doctors." He smiled as he thought
about his brothers. He was proud of them and he
was sure that his *mami* and *pappi* would have
been proud of them all too. They had all worked
hard to get where they were. "Dante is a neu-
rosurgeon, Rafe is a epidemiologist and Santi
was in the army as a doctor, but currently he's a
paramedic. He recently got married."

"Are the older two married, as well?"

"No, I think they're confirmed bachelors."
Like me.

Only he didn't say that out loud. Usually he

did when he was talking about his brothers, but for some reason he didn't want to tell Kiri that.

"Besides, they're too ugly to get married." He winked at her.

"I'm sure they love it when you call them ugly."

"Oh, yes, I'm the baby. I'm *perfecto*."

"Ha-ha, yeah, sure," she teased.

"And what about your family? I know your parents come from Mumbai. Do you have any siblings?"

"Yes, I have an older sister. She's married with a couple of kids. They're great kids. I miss them." There was a hint of sadness in her voice.

"Then why did you move so far away from them?" he asked.

"The job was too good to pass up and the kids are older now. It's not too cool to hang out with boring aunt Kiri anymore."

Alejandro chuckled. The waitress came out and handed them menus. "We'll have one of Ángel's mojitos and a virgin mojito for me, please, as I'm driving."

The waitress nodded and left.

"How strong are these mojitos?" Kiri asked with trepidation.

"Strong enough, or so I hear. I don't drink."

"I remember," she said, blushing again. She picked up her menu. "What should I try? I'm not really used to Latin cuisine. Other than Mexican."

Alejandro grimaced. "That's not the same."

"Then you pick. I'm pretty adventurous."

"Are you?"

"Okay, now you're scaring me with that evil grin."

"If I had a long mustache I would be twirling the ends and laughing maniacally."

She rolled her eyes, but chuckled under her breath. "Well, I guess I'm mostly adventurous. I don't eat beef."

"Really? Why?"

"I'm Hindu."

"Chicken is probably your safest bet, then," he said.

The waitress came back with the drinks then. She set a huge mojito down in front of Kiri, whose eyes widened at the sight of it. His alcohol-free mojito was smaller, but was still a big glass of slushy goodness.

"Would you like to order anything else?" the waitress asked.

"Yes, two orders of *pollo asado* please."

The waitress nodded. "Coming right up."

"What did you order?" Kiri asked.

"It's chicken. You'll like it." He leaned back in his chair. "It's been a while since I've been to

Mad Ron's. I've been busy working on my pro bono program at Buena Vista."

She sighed. "I'm sorry about that, but the board was very clear. Or rather Snyder was."

"I know. You're just doing your job but, still, it's not the right decision."

"My hands are tied. José got his liver and this baby will be taken care of. You can't save them all."

"We should be able to save them all," he said.

"You're right," she said soberly. "We should, but it's not like Buena Vista is closing its doors to children. We can still save children."

Alejandro sighed. "It just doesn't feel like it's enough."

"It never is," she said, and that hint of sadness was in her voice again.

"Who did you lose?" he asked, catching her off guard.

"Pardon?"

"I'm a good reader of people and there are moments where you seem so sad I can't help but wonder who you lost. I lost my parents and I'm familiar with that expression."

She shrugged but wouldn't look him in the eye. Instead she poked at her mojito. "I didn't lose anyone. I hate to see children suffer. It's the worst part of the job."

"Of course." Kiri was right, Alejandro knew

that. Not being able to save all the children was the hardest part of the job. It tore his heart out when he lost one of his little patients, but there was something more to it than that for her. Something deeper.

He knew that pain. A pain he would never bring on anyone else.

Before he could ask any more questions his phone rang. "It's the hospital."

Kiri leaned forward. "Well, answer it."

"Hello? Yes, this is Dr. Valentino. Yes. Are you sure?" His heart sank as he heard the other doctor on the other end tell him what he didn't want to hear. "Okay, I see. Thank you for letting me know. I'll be in to check on him later."

He hung up the phone and let the words sink in.

Dammit. He'd been hoping for better news. This was not the kind of news he wanted to hear, especially in light of their conversation.

"Is it José? Do you have to go?"

Alejandro shook his head. "It's not José. That was the cardiology team about the baby."

"Oh, I see." And Alejandro knew that she understood exactly what had been said on the other end of the line.

The baby needed a new heart.

The baby had been officially put on the UNOS list, because without a new heart that little miracle baby he'd found in a cardboard box behind the hospital would die.

And the odds of finding an infant heart in time were very slim indeed.

CHAPTER FIVE

THE REST OF the lunch at Mad Ron's was pretty somber after Alejandro had fielded that call about the baby. She wasn't sure if it was because of the cost involved or the fact that they probably wouldn't be able to find a heart in time.

Either way, it hurt her, as well.

She'd never wanted that infant to be sent to County. She'd wanted to keep him at Buena Vista where the top surgeons in Miami could take care of him, but her hands were tied. There was no more money in the pro bono fund for anyone.

Still, she felt responsible. Like it was her fault this child might not make it.

Like you blamed yourself when you miscarried.

She shook that thought away. It had taken her a long time to stop blaming herself for the loss of her child. And who was she kidding? There were moments she still blamed herself.

"I can't believe he survived as long as he did," Alejandro murmured.

"So he has hypo plastic left ventricle, double outlet left ventricle, tricuspid atresia, atrial septal defect, ventral septal defect and pulmonary stenosis?" Kiri asked. "You're right. It's a miracle he made it out in that heat."

Alejandro nodded. "They put him on UNOS because the only way to stabilize his heart, which is totally out of rhythm, is to give him a Fontan procedure. The problem is that the pulmonary resistance is high because he's a newborn. It takes months to drop, so they can't do the Fontan. The baby doesn't have months to wait for the procedure and because his heart disease is so complex, his little heart is swelling, so it's better to wait for a new heart."

Which would be costly. But she didn't say that. He knew. They both did. Usually transplants weren't done on babies so young. It was rare, but they could do it.

"You never know what could happen. It's true that more adults die than children, making infant and children's hearts harder to come by, but since older children can take adult hearts, he has a better shot of landing an infant or a small child's heart. If his current heart is enlarged there should be space to take a toddler's heart."

Alejandro nodded. "Yes, that's not what I'm worried about, though. As his guardian I can't do the transplant surgery. Heart transplants are one of my specialties. I'm the one the cardiology team calls when a heart transplant needs to be done on a child. A baby's vessels are so much more delicate. Especially a preemie's."

"Yes, that is a conundrum. You may not be able to perform the surgery, but you can stand over the surgery and guide a resident."

He shook his head vehemently. "A resident is not touching that baby."

"Oh, no? Who is, then?"

He then stared at her. "You are."

"Me?" She had done pediatric heart transplants, but she wasn't sure if she could operate on that child. Not when Alejandro was the guardian. It hit a little too close to home for her.

"You are the head of pediatric surgery. I want you to be the one to do it."

"I'm not a transplant specialist. You need to have one of your residents do it," she argued. She didn't want to risk hurting the baby.

She just couldn't.

He shook his head. "No, you're a good surgeon."

"How do you know? I've only ever assisted you once."

"I saw for myself how you retrieved that liver. You may not have split it, but the veins were easy to graft back into José. I also have my sources." He grinned deviously.

"Your sources?" she asked.

"I like to check out my competition. You were Dr. Vaughan's top student and Dr. Vaughan only chooses the best. I'm sure you've done these procedures before under his tutelage. I know he's done infant heart transplants and I know you have, as well."

"I'm not really your competition, I'm the head of the department and I'm not a specialist in transplant surgery."

"Everyone is competition," he said seriously. "Something I've learned the hard way."

"Really?"

He took a drink. "When you have to work and fight your way through a competitive program and specialty and you're a minority, you have a longer way to arrive at the destination. I fought the whole way. I worked hard to get where I am and I'm very protective of what I have."

Kiri smiled. She understood that all too well. Being a woman of an immigrant family, short and a bit of a wallflower when she'd been younger, she'd had to learn to speak up in a very competitive surgical program.

She'd learned to fight for everything she wanted, as well.

Even if she lost that fight. She never gave up.

You've given up on one thing.

And she tried to not think about the fact that

she was never going to have another baby. She'd decided after she lost hers that she was never going to put herself through that kind of pain again, and her obstetrician had told her she had a hostile uterus so it would be unlikely she would conceive again, let alone carry a child to term.

"You're sad again," Alejandro remarked.

"What're you talking about?"

"As I said, I can read people." He leaned forward. "You went somewhere else. Your thoughts drifted. Where were you?"

Nowhere.

"I'm not sad," she said, plastering a fake smile on her face.

Liar.

Where she was was a dark place. A place where all her dreams had been laid to rest.

Alejandro stared at her with those piercing dark eyes seeming to read her soul. "Something is bothering you."

"Well, I am far from home. I've spent my whole life in New York City, rarely traveling except once to Vegas…" Then heat flooded her cheeks as she thought of the one time she had traveled there. "And then to see family. That's all the traveling I've done."

"How was the wedding?" he asked, a twinkle in his eyes.

"What wedding?" she asked, confused.

"The bachelorette party from five years ago. You were the maid of honor, I believe? The trip to Vegas."

"Oh, right. It was good. They're still together."

"Well, that's good." He smiled. "So this is your first time in Florida, then?"

She nodded. "It is and I have to say I'm not missing the cold at all. I like this heat and the sun."

"It's not always this beautiful. In the summer it gets humid and then there's hurricane season."

"We've had hurricanes in New York."

"You're right, you have. I guess, then, that Florida—other than the fact we don't usually get snow and we have alligators—is really no different from New York."

"Alligators." She shuddered. "I'm not a fan of reptiles or bugs."

"Perhaps we'll have to take a drive down to the Everglades and I'll take you out on a fan boat into the swamp. See if we can spot some gators."

"No, thank you!" And Kiri shuddered again. "I'm fine right here, in the city, where it's some-what safe."

This time it was his turn to have a strange look pass across his face. "The city is not as safe as you think."

"Well, no city is safe," she agreed, but she could sense there was tension between them.

"But I seriously doubt that an alligator is going to take an elevator and knock on my door." She was trying to ease the tension between them.

He laughed, his eyes twinkling, his demeanor relaxing. "Not an alligator, but maybe other beasts."

"Now that I've been to Mad Ron's and surprisingly haven't been knocked on my butt by the mojito, probably because of the chicken, is my tour of Miami done for the day?"

Alejandro grinned. "Hardly. There's still so much to show you."

"Should I be afraid?"

He shrugged. "Don't you trust me?"

"I don't know you well enough to trust you," she teased.

"Don't you?"

"One night together and one surgery does not equate to knowing each other. I have secrets and I'm sure you do, as well."

And she meant what she said. She was sure that he had secrets, just like her.

Alejandro reached into his wallet and pulled out some money, weighting it with an empty plate so that it wouldn't blow away in the wind.

"What're you doing?" she asked.

He cocked an eyebrow. "Paying?"

"No way. Let me. You drove me here."

He chuckled. "No. I'm paying. You're my

guest. I insist." He stood and held out his hand. "Come on, trust me. Nothing will happen to you. You trusted me once before."

And look how that turned out.

Only this time she wouldn't end up in his bed. She was just enjoying her first real day out in Miami. Ever since she'd arrived here it had been nothing but work. Kiri also found that she liked Alejandro's company.

She wasn't so lonely when she was with him. Yeah, she had friends and a loving family, but there was a void in her heart that wasn't as noticeable around him. And he was here, her family was not.

She took his hand and he helped her to her feet. Kiri didn't know where he was leading her, but at that moment she didn't care. There were so many times she didn't live. It was exciting to see where he was going to take her.

He waved to the waitress as they left and headed back to his motorcycle. This time when she climbed on the back she wasn't as nervous as she'd been before, but her pulse still raced because she was going to be so close to him again.

Even after all this time, he still affected her.

She was still attracted to him.

The memory of his lips on her skin, bringing her to ecstasy, was forever burned into her brain. And as she sat behind him on his motorcycle, her arms around him, she could feel those rock-hard abs again.

And instinctively she ran her hands over where the tattoo was, feeling the hard ridge of his scar that the tattoo covered.

She heard him suck in a breath but he didn't say anything. All he did was rev the engine of his motorcycle, causing her to grip tight as he pulled out of the parking space at Mad Ron's and headed out onto the Miami streets.

This time as they drove through the city she was able to appreciate the architecture. The Spanish influence.

He headed toward the Bay of Biscayne and she couldn't help but wonder where he was taking her. They were traveling in the Coconut Grove area of the city on a tree-lined street, which offered nice shade. There was a Spanish gatehouse and Alejandro slowed down, turning into the drive. They drove through a parkland of what looked like an estate before he pulled into the main parking lot for visitors.

"Where are we?" Kiri asked, handing him her helmet again and then running her hands through her hair.

"Vizcaya. It's a European-inspired villa in the heart of Miami. It's one of the most beautiful places in the city and I thought you'd like to see it. I've been here many times, so I can tell you what we're looking at. You don't need to get the audio tour."

"It's a museum?"

"Do you have a problem with museums?"

"No, I like them," she said.

He grinned. "I thought you might."

"Why, because I'm such a nerd?" she teased.

Alejandro cocked his head to one side. "Hardly."

They walked side by side through the gardens. This time Kiri paid for admission into the museum since Alejandro had paid for drinks and the lunch. Vizcaya looked like something that would be found in Spain, in a place like Barcelona. It was very European and totally out of place in Miami, but she was enchanted by the grandeur as they wandered through the main house.

"So who built this place?" she asked.

"James Deering. It was a vacation home in the Jazz Age."

Kiri grinned as they moved through rooms full of art deco and luxuries of the early 1920s. She could almost picture ladies in flapper attire and liquor flowing freely despite Prohibition.

"It's an interesting name for his home. Vizcaya. I like it," she said.

"There's a lot of speculation about why he named it Vizcaya but, yeah, I have to agree with you, it does roll off the tongue. It's sexy and mysterious, which is probably what he was going for."

They walked out of the main house and she gasped at the sight of the Atlantic Ocean. The water was calm and the sun was sparkling over the gentle lapping of waves. In the distance they could see Key Biscayne. And the water was dotted with large white yachts.

"I wonder where they're heading."

Alejandro shrugged. "The Bahamas or Caribbean. Or nowhere. There are a lot of yachts that just stick around Miami."

Alejandro watched her as she leaned over the garden wall and stared happily out at the yachts in the water. He couldn't help but smile and he couldn't remember the last time he'd had this much fun.

He'd worried that the day he'd originally planned was going to be so boring.

He'd come to Vizcaya before on his own. He liked walking through the gardens and the home, but he'd been here so many times he forgot what it was like to walk through it with someone who had never been.

Alejandro had been worried that she wouldn't like it as much as he did. It was a special place to him. His parents had liked this place. They'd often come here, bringing him. His brothers didn't seem to care much for it, but Alejandro loved it here.

His mother had loved the European gardens and they would wander for hours out amongst the hardwood trees. She'd said it reminded her of home and his father would always hold his mother's hand. Alejandro loved running along between the hedges, they were so uniform, like green walls. Everything was lush and verdant.

So different from their home in Little Heliconia.

They were happy here.

Carefree here.

And on days like today, with the warm breeze and the calm waters, he could almost feel their presence again. The day of the shooting they had been going to finish up at the bodega and head to Vizcaya to walk around the gardens. His brothers hadn't been going, just Alejandro and his parents.

"Why do you want to go to Vizcaya again?" his father teased his mother.

"You know I like it and on days like this, calm, it reminds me of when Heliconia was just like this. I want to walk amongst the trees. It relaxes me."

"And how about you, Alejandro? Do you want to go to Vizcaya again?"

"Sí," *Alejandro answered. "I like it there. I like to run through the grass."*

His mother shot his father a look. "You see? He needs to feel the grass on his bare feet."

"Okay, we'll go to Vizcaya again." Then his father took his mother in his arms and kissed her. "You know that I would do anything for you, mi tesoro."

"Put your hands up!"

His mother screamed.

Alejandro shook the horrible thought out of his mind. He'd never forgotten the sound of his mother's screams. The sound of bullets and of him lying on the floor, staring at his father who was unconscious, lying in a pool of blood, his hand outstretched towards his mother.

He didn't want to think about his parents or that horrible moment. He should've died that day too.

"Come on, let's go wander around the gardens." And without thinking he took Kiri's small hand in his and led her away from the water into the gardens. She didn't try to pull her hand away.

He'd almost lost his cool when she had been running her hands lightly over his chest, tracing his tattoo through his shirt.

He knew what it was like to really have those

soft fingertips trace his skin. And just thinking about it caused his blood to heat with desire.

Even after five years he wanted her. And he'd never wanted a woman like this before.

It scared him.

What am I doing?

He couldn't lead her on. There was nothing he could offer her and she was his boss. All they could be was friends.

He let go of her hand as they wandered along the outer perimeter of Vizcaya's gardens. He had to get out of here. He had to put distance between them. It was bad enough that they were working together and that they lived across the hall from each other, but he couldn't take her out like this.

To the places which reminded him of his life when it had been happy and easy.

To the time when he'd been an innocent boy, before he'd been forced to grow up.

"Mami and Pappi are dead."

Santi's words haunted him again.

"You know what, I really think I should get to the hospital and check on the baby. I know that I can't be his doctor, but maybe you're right, maybe I should school a resident on doing the transplant. I also want to make sure the cardiology team has got him on the UNOS list."

Kiri tried to hide her disappointment. "Okay, sure."

"I'll take you back to your apartment before I head to the hospital."

"You could just take me to the hospital. I should check on a few things, I planned to anyway. There's no sense driving all the way back to South Beach and then back into Miami just to drop me off," she said.

"I don't know how long I'll be. How will you get home?"

"I can take a cab," she said.

Guilt ate at him, but it was for the best. "Okay. Let's go."

They walked in silence back to his motorcycle. This time when she held him, he could sense the distance in her.

It's for the best, he reminded himself again. He dropped her off at the hospital's main entrance before he headed to the parking lot.

Kiri climbed off and retrieved her purse, handing him back his spare helmet. "Thanks for lunch and Vizcaya. I had a good time."

"You're welcome. I'll see you later." It was a lie. He was going to try and avoid her as much as he could. He wouldn't hurt her. He liked her too much.

She nodded and headed into the hospital.

You're an idiot, Alejandro.

CHAPTER SIX

KIRI HADN'T SEEN ALEJANDRO for a couple of days. Not since he'd dropped her off at the hospital. Something had changed at Vizcaya and she wasn't sure what, but it was probably for the best. It wasn't like anything could happen between them.

He'd made it clear he didn't want kids or a family. He wasn't going to adopt that baby and Kiri didn't want to give up on her dream of becoming a mother.

A dream of a family.

Besides, she was his superior. There was no way anything could happen between them while they worked at the hospital together.

She couldn't jeopardize her career for a man who didn't want the same things she did.

She cleaned her hands with hand sanitizer before she walked into the neonatal intensive care unit to check on some patients.

"Good morning," Kiri said to the head NICU nurse, Samantha, who always seemed to be there.

"Good morning to you too, Dr. Bhardwaj," Samantha said cheerfully.

"How are my two surgical patients today?" Kiri picked up the chart of the first baby, Maya, who had been born with her organs on the outside. Kiri had done the first surgery yesterday to start correcting the problem. It would take some time to slowly return the organs back to their rightful positions, but she had no doubt Maya would make it. She'd done so well in the surgery and was thriving post-op. Hitting all her milestones for recovery.

"Maya's stats are good. Blood pressure and oxygen levels are stable. She's tolerating treatment well," Samantha said. "She's a fighter."

Kiri nodded and pulled out her stethoscope, listening and examining the incision and the bag that covered the organs.

Her next patient was a simple cleft-palate fix. She'd done the first surgery the day before Maya's.

"How's he feeding?" Kiri asked, as she disposed of the gloves she'd used to look at Maya and put on new ones.

"When I feed him, he does well. Mom hasn't been down to feed him. She's not handling the cleft palate well," Samantha said.

Kiri frowned. "Why? It's a simple fix. I mean, parents are never happy their children have to go through this. It's not pleasant, we all want healthy babies, but he's healthy other than this."

She glanced at where the John Doe baby was. The boy who was clinging to life, who had been thrown away.

It could be worse.

"I know, but she refuses to come down and I can't always feed him. I have other patients to care for so he still has an NG tube and receives feeding from there."

"Perhaps it's postpartum depression?" Kiri suggested. "Perhaps that's why she hasn't been down?"

"She's from a very wealthy family on Fisher Island. The family's money comes from a cosmetic line. The baby, the heir, was supposed to be on their reality show next month, but now he can't be. Mom doesn't want him to be seen like this, so she's disengaged."

Kiri shook her head. "Get her a psych evaluation. Money or not, it sounds like postpartum depression."

"Her OB/GYN tried to get that. Snyder put a stop to it because he's friends with the child's father who thinks it's ridiculous."

Kiri rolled her eyes and muttered, "Ridiculous."

The boy would be fine. Cleft palate was a serious issue, but could be fixed. It just took time. Some people wouldn't care about appearances. Some people just wanted a baby.

Like me.

Her gaze fell on the incubator at the far end.

John Doe. The child she and Alejandro had found.

She disposed of her gloves and wandered over. He wasn't her patient, he was on Dr. Robinson's service until a heart could be found. After she did the transplant he'd be on her service, but she couldn't help but check on him.

"How is our little John Doe doing?" Kiri asked, peering into the incubator. Her heart melted at the sight of the small soul hooked up to so many machines.

"He's a fighter too," Samantha said proudly. "It's too bad Dr. Valentino hasn't come to see him. I feel bad because this baby is all alone."

Kiri's stomach clenched. She was alone here too. Miles away from family and friends. She understood.

Life was unfair.

"I'll hold him. I mean, I found him too and I will be his doctor when a new heart is found."

Samantha smiled and nodded in approval. Kiri put new gloves on as Samantha opened the incubator. Together they maneuvered all the wires and cords and wrapped him in a blue hospital blanket.

Kiri picked him up. He was so light, so delicate.

"See that! His stats stabilized," Samantha remarked. "He's benefiting from the touch."

"I can see," Kiri whispered, smiling down at that little face. John Doe wasn't the only one benefiting from the touch. It did something to her, deep inside. She handled babies all the time in her job, but this was different.

She rarely cradled them. Rarely held them against her own heart to savor the feeling of something so tiny and fragile against her chest.

It felt so right.

So good.

It was wonderful.

Tears filled her eyes as she thought of that brief moment she'd held her tiny son. Holding the little John Doe made her yearn for what she'd lost and what she'd never have. Her child had been in her arms so briefly before he'd been taken away. He'd never taken a breath. Never cried. Never had a chance.

"Okay, I'll put him back. I have to get to a consult." Her voice quivered and she tried not to cry.

"Sure thing, Dr. Bhardwaj." Samantha took

the baby from Kiri and together they got him settled back into his incubator.

"Thank you for letting me hold him," Kiri said. "I can see all our patients are taken care of here."

"Thank you, Dr. Bhardwaj," Samantha said. "And your holding him really did help. I'm a huge believer in skin-to-skin contact. Maybe if Dr. Valentino came by he could hold him, as well. It would help him out."

Kiri nodded. "I'll let him know."

She quickly left the NICU and tried not to cry.

She was angry at letting herself feel that way again and when she rounded the corner and caught sight of Alejandro at a charging station, charting, she saw red. He was part of her pain, because he was the one who'd got her pregnant.

The condom broke. It's not his fault.

Only she was too emotional to listen to rationality. Their baby was gone.

"Valentino," she snapped. He looked up, surprised.

"Yes, Dr. Bhardwaj, how can I help you?"

"You're John Doe's guardian. Visit him. Hold him. You're a doctor, you should know that human contact is essential to healing. You should know better."

She didn't wait for his response. She kept

walking, not giving him a chance to respond because if she lingered she knew she'd cry.

When she was far away from the NICU and Alejandro, Kiri leaned against a wall and took a deep steadying breath, trying to get her emotions under control.

"Dr. Bhardwaj?"

Kiri opened her eyes to see Dr. Prescott from the emergency room standing in front of her. He looked concerned.

"Are you okay?" he asked.

"I'm fine. How can I help you, Dr. Prescott?" she asked.

"You know your John Doe in the NICU?"

"Yes," she said, but she knew. Deep down she knew what Dr. Prescott was going to say.

"We think we found the mother. We did a blood test when she came in for a postpartum infection, which we treated. The lab work came in and it's a match."

Kiri smiled. "Great work. Is she still here?"

Dr. Prescott nodded. "She is, but she doesn't speak English. Just Spanish."

Dammit.

"I'll get Dr. Valentino. We'll be down to the emergency room soon."

"Okay." Dr. Prescott left and Kiri girded her loins to deal with Alejandro again. Hopefully the mother really did want her child. Perhaps she'd had a change of heart and she wanted to see her baby. Kiri could only hope.

Perhaps John Doe would get a happy-ever-after.

Alejandro was still standing there at the charging station, charting. He saw her coming and did a double take, glaring at her.

"Kiri, what—?"

Kiri cut him off. "They found John Doe's mother."

He cocked an eyebrow. "Are you sure?"

"Dr. Prescott is positive. They ran blood tests. She came in because of a postpartum infection."

"Does she want to see the baby?" he asked.

"I don't know. She doesn't speak English. Perhaps you could speak with her?"

Alejandro nodded. "Let's go."

They walked in uneasy silence side by side down to the emergency room. Which was fine.

She had nothing really to say to him. If the mother wanted the baby back then maybe this whole situation with the John Doe and Alejandro could end. He'd no longer be the guardian and could do the surgery himself.

Dr. Prescott was waiting for them when they got to the emergency room floor.

"Dr. Valentino, thank you for coming down," Dr. Prescott said.

"No problem, Dr. Prescott. You said she doesn't speak English?" Alejandro asked.

"Not well. She could tell us sort of what was wrong. If you could translate for me that would be great."

Alejandro nodded. "Sure thing."

They all stepped into the isolation room. John Doe's mother was very young. That was the first thought Kiri had when she saw her. She saw a frightened young girl whose eyes darted back and forth between the three of them. She was ready to run.

"Hola, soy Dr. Valentino. Cuál es su nombre?"

"Luciana," she said, with a hint of relief in her voice.

Alejandro went on to explain what Dr. Prescott was saying to her about the postpartum infection and the medication. Once that was done Dr. Prescott slipped from the room. It was then time to ask her about the baby.

"Cuándo dar a luz, Luciana?"

He was asking her when she gave birth. That was when the girl became guarded. Even though Kiri couldn't understand what she was saying or what Alejandro was saying, she could see the change in personality. She was lying to him. She didn't want anyone to know about the baby.

Alejandro's words became quick, blunt, and Luciana's eyes narrowed. Then she turned her head and wouldn't say anything more. She was done talking. Kiri's heart sank. This was not the happy ending she was hoping for.

Alejandro shook his head. He stood up and they left the room, shutting the door.

"Well?" Kiri asked, though she knew.

"She doesn't want the baby. I'm going to send legal counsel and a translator down so she can officially relinquish her rights."

"Why doesn't she want the baby?"

Alejandro sighed. "She was assaulted. The father of the baby is unknown. She said looking at the baby reminded her of the assault. I'm going to have Prescott recommend a trauma counselor, as well. I told her what her baby was dealing with, but she doesn't care. She's only eighteen."

"She's just a child herself," Kiri murmured.

Alejandro nodded. "So our little John Doe is officially a ward of the state of Florida. I asked her if her parents or any other family members would want him, but, no, her mother is the one who delivered him and dropped him off at a hospital. She didn't know it was this one or she wouldn't have come here."

Alejandro didn't say anything further to her. He went to speak with Prescott. Kiri glanced back into the isolation room. Luciana was crying, but she was angry. And confused, of that Kiri was certain.

She didn't want or probably couldn't afford John Doe anyway. With the complication of his congestive heart disease, it was probably better that the boy had been dropped off. Someone would want him when he was all better.

Someone would love him.

Why not you?

He'd managed to avoid Kiri for four days after she'd called him out and after being told the baby's mother had been found. Luciana had officially signed him over to be a ward of the state and had given up all her rights.

Alejandro had a lot of mixed emotions about it all. And it appeared Kiri did too. He was angry that the young woman had been assaulted, but it was sad the little boy had to suffer and be born as the result of something so violent.

He just threw himself into his work and rarely went home. Alejandro picked up the chart in the neonatal intensive care unit to check on the child, who was intubated and hooked up to different monitors. He'd been avoiding the neonatal intensive care unit because he didn't want to get attached. Only he couldn't stay away.

Not since that day Kiri had called him out, because before that he'd gone to the NICU and seen Kiri holding the baby close to her heart. Seeing her hold John Doe, her eyes closed and an expression of bliss and agony on her face, had been unnerving.

And an image of Kiri holding his baby flooded his mind. Only he couldn't have that. A bullet had denied him. An uncertain future had also decided his fate. He lived life to the fullest, but he was destined to be alone. He shook that thought away and focused on the child he was legal guardian to. There was so much wrong with his heart.

Hang in there, amigo.

He shook his head as he read over his chart. So young, born too early, no parents and to have so many problems. It wasn't fair.

Of course, life wasn't fair.

Alejandro knew first-hand what that was like, both personally and as a doctor. He set the chart down and then put on some gloves. Even though he knew he shouldn't, he opened the incubator and touched the little boy, placing his hand over the boy's little head.

So tiny. So fragile.

And then he ran his hands over the boy's body, before that tiny fist curled in a reflex action around his finger. A strange rush of emotions flowed through him as he stared at the little baby.

Other than working with children, he didn't have much experience with babies as he was the youngest of the brothers. He still remembered the first time he'd handled a sick preemie. He'd been so afraid that he was going to break the little girl, but his teacher had given him confidence.

Now he had no problem holding even the most fragile of babies. Which was good considering that he was going to be an uncle soon and he'd have to show Santi a thing or two about holding a baby.

He chuckled to himself, thinking about Santiago becoming a family man.

Santiago was the last person in the world he'd thought would settle down. Saoirse had certainly tamed his brother.

Perhaps you can be tamed?

"Do you want to hold him?" the NICU nurse Samantha asked as she finished charting on the incubator next to infant John Doe. "You should."

He should say no, but instead he said, "Sure, I think that would be good for him."

Samantha nodded. "Yes, it would be, Dr. Valentino. Skin-to-skin contact is sometimes the best therapy for these sick little mites."

Alejandro took back his hand and then sat in the nearby rocking chair. He peeled off his white lab coat.

Samantha looked up from where she was

readying baby John Doe. "Dr. Valentino, skin to skin means you need to take your scrub shirt off."

"Do you think that's wise? I understand the importance of skin-to-skin contact, but I'm not related to the baby."

Samantha fixed him with a stern stare. "You're his guardian. He has no one else."

Alejandro understood how that felt. So he peeled off his scrub shirt.

Samantha raised her eyebrows at the sight of his large tattoo, which hid his heart-transplant scar, but she didn't say anything. As a nurse, she'd probably seen worse.

She brought the baby over to him and with a lot of finesse because of the different cords and lines attached to him she placed baby John Doe against his chest and then covered the infant with a blanket.

Alejandro gently place his hands against the baby's back, holding him there. And even though the boy had a bad heart, just holding him like that did something. The monitoring tracking the baby's heart started to stabilize a bit into a steady rhythm, which was saying a lot for an infant with a bad heart.

Samantha smiled at him. "You know, miracles do happen. It's a good thing the parents dropped this little guy off at Buena Vista and that you found him, Dr. Valentino. We all know what you're doing and we want to help any way we can. We heard that the hospital is cutting the pro bono fund."

"It's not the hospital cutting the fund, Samantha. It's the board. Snyder in particular, who is currently president of the board of directors."

"Not surprising, but still you can't bear the financial burden on your own. We all want to help. We want to do a collection. We want to do something to help this poor baby."

Alejandro smiled. "That is very kind of you."

"My son was born with congestive heart failure. They told me to let him go so many times when he was a baby, but I didn't listen to them. He had a heart transplant when he was ten years old and he's just started college."

"I'm glad to hear that, Samantha. You never know what can happen. Miracles do happen." He said it all the time, but he wasn't sure if he believed it. The statistics didn't lie.

Samantha nodded and moved away to the next incubator.

Alejandro stared down at the little boy against him, so tiny against his chest. It was like holding a delicate bird.

"You'll be fine, amigo. You'll see. We'll get you a heart and you'll be fine."

"You should name him, instead of calling him amigo."

Alejandro looked over to see Kiri standing in the door of the NICU, her hands deep in the pockets of her white lab coat. She wasn't wearing the dark-framed glasses that she usually seemed to sport when she was wearing scrubs and working on patients. Instead she was dressed in business attire, a tight pencil skirt and heels, which elevated her from five feet five to maybe five feet seven.

"How can you walk in those things around here?" Alejandro teased.

She glanced down at her feet. "With difficulty, but I find when I'm addressing the board of directors I want to appear a bit taller, or taller than Snyder, at least." She stuck out her leg and he admired her shapely calf. "That's why I bought these shoes. They were expensive."

"Designer, then?"

She nodded. "I much prefer my sneakers or sandals. And I definitely prefer wearing scrubs and not having to wear panty hose."

Alejandro chuckled. "So why are you lurking around the NICU today if you're supposed to be in meetings?"

"I was checking on a couple of my patients." She nodded in the direction of the other end of the NICU. "They're not as badly off as your little John Doe."

"I don't think any baby currently at Buena

Vista is." He glanced down at John Doe. "You're right, though, I should name him. John Doe and amigo don't suit him in the least."

"No, he needs a name and an identity if he's going to win his fight. He's got a long road ahead of him." Kiri took a step closer and reached out as if to touch the child, but then thought better of it. She put her hand back in her pocket and stepped back again, which made no sense as he'd seen her holding him a few days ago. "So do you know any good names?"

"My mother always said that names give us strength and pay homage to our culture. I would like to name him something like that."

"I can't help you with naming. Unless you'd like a completely boring name like John Doe."

"How about an Indian name? Why don't we both name him? We both found him, let's both have a hand in naming him."

A strange expression passed over her face. "No, you name him. I—I wouldn't know… You name him."

He couldn't help but wonder why she didn't want to help name him, but he didn't press the matter. "Gervaso, it means warrior. He needs a strong name."

Kiri smiled. "That's a nice name and very different. I don't think I've heard it before. How do you spell it?"

"*G-e-r-v-a-s-o*. Gervaso."

"It's nice," she whispered.

"My mother liked it. It's my middle name, actually."

"Well, it's better than baby John Doe and definitely better than amigo."

"Are you sure you don't want to give him another name?" Alejandro asked.

"Positive. I'd better go check on my patients." She turned and headed to the far side of the NICU, picking up a pair of gloves before she opened an incubator.

He didn't know what had got into her and he didn't care.

Right now his focus was Gervaso and getting him healthy again so that he could get adopted and live a long, happy life.

You can live a long time. You can be happy.

Only the moment he thought about Gervaso going off with someone other than him it caused him a pang of pain. Would it be so bad if he became the boy's father?

Yes. You can't. What if you die? What if your heart fails? What if...?

It wouldn't be fair to the baby. He needed parents. He needed a stable home.

And Alejandro couldn't give him those things. Everything was so uncertain.

"Samantha?" Alejandro called out.

"Yes, Dr. Valentino?"

"I have to finish my rounds. Can you help me put him back?"

"Of course, Dr. Valentino." Samantha put on fresh gloves and gently took little Gervaso from him and they got him settled back into the incubator.

"Also, make sure you change his chart and the application for his birth certificate. His name is Gervaso, not John Doe. *G-e-r-v-a-s-o.*"

Samantha smiled. "Will do, Dr. Valentino."

Alejandro pulled on his scrub shirt and picked up his white lab coat from the back of the rocking chair. He briefly glanced at Kiri's back and then got out of the NICU as fast as he could, because he was scared of the emotions little Gervaso and Kiri were stirring in him.

They were unwelcome.

Were they?

Kiri had been completely unnerved when she'd walked into the NICU and seen Alejandro holding that wee baby boy skin to skin. It had stirred so many emotions in her. When she'd first found out she was pregnant and had been trying to get hold of Alejandro she'd pictured him holding her child like that.

It was one of the silly fantasies she'd clung to.

She hadn't cared if he didn't want her, but she'd wanted her baby to have a father.

Of course, he didn't want kids and she'd lost her baby and she hadn't thought about that little fantasy in a long time. When she'd walked into the NICU and seen it playing out live it had made her feel weak in the knees. He was so sweet, holding that small baby against his chest. So gentle, so kind.

It had completely unnerved her.

She'd wanted to reach out and touch the baby again, but she'd stopped herself. She didn't want to get emotionally attached to a child who was going to be adopted by a loving family after he pulled through his heart transplant.

And then Alejandro had asked her to help name him. It was almost too much.

She didn't want to grow attached to a baby she was going to lose again. A baby who wasn't hers.

There were a lot of names that she'd thought of when she'd been considering names for her child, but those names were too precious and had been buried along with their son.

She knew that Alejandro had been avoiding her and, truth be told, she'd been avoiding him too. Kiri didn't know what had happened at Vizcaya, but those walls that had been coming down had been built up fast again.

And it had reminded her too that he was able to get past her defenses easily.

She'd known it was better for both of them if she kept her distance so she'd thrown herself into her work. She'd planned meetings, begun to see patients and had got very good at navigating the halls without seeing him.

Until today.

Kiri finished checking up on the babies in the NICU and then discarded her rubber gloves. She made quick notes and instructed the NICU nurses on care. As she was leaving the NICU she glanced at Gervaso's incubator.

He was so small.

She took a step closer and her heart skipped a beat as the image of Alejandro, holding the wee baby skin to skin, invaded her mind and overtook her senses.

And, though she shouldn't, she pulled on a pair of gloves and reached inside to touch the baby. Her eyes filled with tears as she ran her fingers over his little back, over his legs to the tiny feet curled under his bum. The hospital identification bracelet looked so large on his skinny little ankle. There was a hint of dark hair on his head…

This was what she'd imagined her baby to look like and it was almost all she could do not to start sobbing in the NICU.

She pulled her hand out of the incubator quickly and discarded the gloves in the receptacle. She'd thought that by leaving New York she'd been escaping the ghosts that haunted her. Walking the halls of the hospital where she'd lost her son had been too hard for her, and she'd thought that by coming to Miami she'd escape.

Kiri had never counted on the father of her baby to be in Miami.

She left the NICU and headed to her office, until she got paged to the emergency room. There was an incoming trauma. Children were hurt.

Kiri's stomach flip-flopped and she ran as fast as she could in her heels toward the emergency room. There was no time to change. It didn't matter. This was her job. Children needed her. When she got down to the emergency room, it was in chaos.

It was like a war zone almost.

"What happened?" Kiri asked, as she threw on gown and gloves.

"A school bus was in an accident. Multiple trauma," the emergency doctor in charge said. "Most of the kids have minor injuries, but one of them is unresponsive. She's in Pod Three."

Kiri nodded and headed straight for Pod Three.

The little girl was unconscious and the code team was shocking her.

"We have a sinus rhythm," the resident in charge of the team said.

Kiri rushed forward and jumped into the fray. "What do we have here?"

"She was thrown from the back of the bus when the accident happened and was hit by a car."

Kiri cursed under her breath. "I need a CT scan stat. I want her checked for head injuries and internal bleeding." She lifted the girl's shirt and could see extensive bruising on her abdomen. She palpated and she could almost guarantee that there was internal bleeding and the girl would require a splenectomy.

She listened to her chest and could hear fluid.

"I need a chest tube tray," Kiri shouted over her shoulder. It was handed to her and she inserted the chest tube, blood filling the tube as it drained from the lungs. "Let's get this girl up to the CT now."

"Right away, Dr. Bhardwaj." The resident moved fast as they got the little girl stabilized and started to push her gurney through the havoc of the emergency room to get her a stat CT scan.

Once she had the scan she would know how to approach the surgery. Who she would need in there. They got her straight into the CT scan and Kiri waited as the scans came through. As they appeared on the computer screen she was glad to see that there was no intracranial bleeding, but there was a lot of free fluid in the abdomen as well as a few broken ribs, probably puncturing her lungs. She needed a cardiothoracic surgeon to work on her lungs while Kiri removed the spleen, which was the source of the internal bleeding.

"Page Cardiothoracic and let's prep an OR," Kiri said to her resident. "Get her ready."

The resident nodded and Kiri headed straight for the locker room to change into scrubs. This little girl was going to be in surgery for some time.

And Kiri was going to make sure that the long hours that this girl was in surgery were going to be worth it. She was going to make sure this little girl lived to see another day.

CHAPTER SEVEN

"Suction, please," said Kiri as she worked on the little girl's spleen. There was no saving it and Kiri was in the process of removing it. The lungs had not been badly punctured and the ribs had been set. The lungs were patched. The cardiothoracic surgeon on duty, Dr. Robinson, was monitoring her, just to make sure that another leak didn't happen.

"Kids are quite resilient," Dr. Robinson said offhandedly. "I'm sure she'll pull through. She's a lucky little girl. Someone three times her age would have a harder recovery. If this accident had happened on the bridge she could've been thrown into the water or the ambulances might not have gotten to her in time."

Kiri nodded, but didn't respond to Dr. Robinson. She knew very well that this girl was lucky to be alive. She didn't wish to engage in any banter, she just wanted to make sure this little girl was stabilized so she could update the parents, who she knew were in the waiting room.

And as she was working on the spleen she noticed there was damage to the kidneys, as well.

Blast.

"How is her urine output?" she asked over her shoulder.

"She hasn't had any urine output," a nurse responded as she checked the bag.

Dammit.

The kidneys were probably shutting down, which meant this girl might need a transplant if both kidneys were shot. That's the last thing this poor girl needed after all she'd been through. Hopefully they could be repaired.

Though she didn't want to see Alejandro again today, she needed him in the OR. She needed him to check on the girl and assess the kidneys while she continued to work on the spleen.

"Can someone page Dr. Valentino to come to the operating room? I want him to check out this patient's kidneys."

An OR nurse went to the phone and paged Dr. Valentino. She could hear the murmur across the room, but she ignored it. She ignored that her own pulse began to race at the thought of seeing him again.

Focus.

Kiri continued to work on the spleen, but then

the left kidney began to bleed. "Hang another unit of packed cells. And suction, please. Where the heck is Dr. Valentino?"

Definitely kidney trauma and Alejandro needed to be here. She needed him.

The doors to the OR from the scrub room slid open and Alejandro, capped and scrubbed, came into the room.

"It's about time," she snapped.

"Dr. Bhardwaj, what seems to be the problem?" he asked as a nurse gloved and gowned him.

"We have a female, age ten, who has blunt-force trauma to the abdomen after she was thrown from a school bus during an accident. Her urine output has been nil and the left kidney has blood pooling behind it. I need your assistance as I'm working on the spleen."

Alejandro nodded and took his spot across from her. "And the spleen is damaged beyond repair?"

Kiri nodded. "I'm performing a splenectomy. Her ribs were broken, but Cardiothoracic has cleared her of any trauma to her diaphragm, heart or lungs. There was a small puncture to her left lung but that was patched by Dr. Robinson. It's all in her abdomen."

Alejandro whistled under his breath. "It must have thrown her far to damage the kidneys."

"She was hit by a car," Dr. Robinson said.

"Poor girl." Alejandro began his examination. "The left kidney is torn, but it can be repaired. I'll place a shunt." Then he looked at the other kidney. "Minor tear in the ureter. Let's get this girl on bypass so toxins don't build up and I'll get to work."

"I'm almost done the splenectomy then I can get out of your way," Kiri said.

And she wanted to get out of his way.

"You're not in my way, Dr. Bhardwaj. I can work around you," Alejandro said without looking at her as he got to work on the patient.

She couldn't help but admire his dedication to the task. How he was able to repair such a small organ. Those strong hands so delicate as they worked on the young girl. They moved in unison, not needing to speak as they focused on their work. It was like they had been operating together for a long time. She hadn't had this rapport with another surgeon since she'd worked with Dr. Vaughan.

"Do we know her name?" Alejandro asked, breaking the silence.

"Casey," Kiri said. "Why?"

"I like to know." He glanced up at her. "It helps me to connect to my patients and I like to talk to them, to let them know that they're going to be okay. And, Casey, you'll be okay."

Tears stung her eyes as he talked to the little girl so gently.

"You have a way with kids," she said.

"I like kids," Alejandro answered as he worked.

"Yet you don't want kids?"

His brow furrowed over his mask. "Liking kids and wanting kids are two different issues. Something I don't want to discuss."

"Hey, I'm just trying to get to know my colleague better."

"It's a very personal question," he said.

"It's no different from you grilling me about my lack of significant other the first time we operated together."

Alejandro's eyebrows popped up and he chuckled. "Touché."

"Wrong use of that word, my friend."

"How so?" he asked.

"It means to touch. We're not touching." And then her cheeks heated when she realized what she'd said. Those dark eyes of his twinkled behind the surgical mask but he didn't say anything else to her.

"Casey, you're doing great," he said. Kiri smiled.

What was with him and names?

And it reminded her that she'd never named her baby boy. Their baby. She'd planned to name a boy after her father. She shook her head. She couldn't think about that right now.

As she finished the splenectomy Alejandro was still working on the damaged kidney and shaking his head, which made her heart sink.

"There is nothing I can do," he said. "I'm going to have to do a nephrectomy."

"And the other kidney?" Kiri asked.

"The ureter isn't that damaged and the kidney is intact and not bleeding. It will be fine. We'll keep her in the hospital and I'll monitor her and give her the right medicines to help with elimination until the ureter on the right kidney heals. A shunt will help." Then he stared at her. "And if her parents can't pay to keep her here, will you ship her off to County?"

It was a pointed barb. And as she'd be the one to sign off on it, she was powerless to stop the board's will.

"You know that's beyond my control. And she has parents. She's not a ward of the state."

"Good, because I would do everything in my power to keep her here if she was going to be shipped off. She's my patient."

"You can't pay for every child."

He grunted in response. What she wanted to tell him was that she'd try her best to keep Casey here so that Alejandro could monitor her, but that was beyond her control. It was bad enough that the Buena Vista board of directors was seriously considering shutting the ER doors, because they were tired of vagrants and those who couldn't pay coming to their hospital, but that was for the head of trauma to deal with. Not her.

In this case of the school bus accident they had been the closest hospital and they were a level-one trauma center. Whether the board liked it or not, they couldn't close their doors to those who were hurt.

Especially not children.

Perhaps that was how she could persuade the board of directors to allow Casey to stay if her parents weren't able to pay the hospital bill. It would be good press for the hospital if they allowed the young girl who was hurt in a school bus accident to be treated by their world-class physicians.

Like Dr. Alejandro Valentino, who was saving this girl's life by operating on her kidneys and probably saving her from going on the already taxed and full UNOS list.

And then she thought about little Gervaso. He was priority, but she was worried that he wouldn't make it to get his heart transplant and what would that do to Alejandro? She knew the pain of losing a child.

"I'm finished with the splenectomy," she said.

"I'll go give the parents an update about her condition."

Alejandro nodded. "Thank you, and let them know that once I'm done with the nephrectomy I'll come out to speak with them."

"All right." Kiri headed to the scrub room and peeled off her gown and gloves. This was her least favorite part of the job, telling parents who were scared beyond belief the status of their child. Telling them their child was ill and undergoing a serious surgery to save their life.

At least Casey would probably pull through.

Casey would probably live.

The nephrectomy and the ureter repair took longer than Alejandro had anticipated, but the bleeding in the cavity where the damaged kidney was had stopped and the ureter had been repaired. Casey was producing urine again, thanks to a shunt and some elimination medicines that would help her as she healed. At least Casey still had a viable kidney. She didn't have to go on UNOS. She was broken, but she could be repaired and go on to live a full life.

You can too. You can have a full life. You're just scared.

He shook that thought away. There was no time to feel sorry for himself. He was here to give an update to his patient's parents.

As he walked into the waiting room he was surprised to see that Kiri was still sitting there with the parents, talking with them.

Kiri saw him first and gave him an encouraging smile then stood up, which caused Casey's parents to jump up and stare at him with terrified hope.

There was no other word for it. He knew that look too well.

"You must be Casey's parents." He held out his hand. "Dr. Valentino."

"How is our daughter?" Casey's mother asked, clearly terrified, not taking Alejandro's hand after her husband had shaken it.

"She's fine. She's in the pediatric intensive care unit. She sustained multiple injuries to her abdomen as well as several broken ribs. As Dr. Bhardwaj told you, we had to remove her spleen and one of her kidneys."

Casey's mother covered her mouth with her hands and was trying not cry. "Is she going to be okay?"

"Yes, she will be. People can live with one kidney. I'll refer her to a nephrologist, who will monitor her over time. We're going to keep her in the hospital for at least a week so I can monitor her progress and watch to make sure that the shunt I placed doesn't slip. She will be on some medications for some time to help her eliminate urine and aid in the healing process."

"Can we go see her?" Casey's dad asked.

"Of course," Alejandro said.

"I'll take them up there," Kiri said. She walked by and squeezed Alejandro's arm in thanks as she led the parents out of the waiting room. He was exhausted and he had to find a good strong coffee and take his own medication.

Just like he did every day at this time. The antirejection medication so he wouldn't lose his father's heart.

It's your heart now.

Only it wasn't. Alejandro knew it was his dad's and that was why he was living. The ultimate gift from his father. Which was why Alejandro had dedicated his life to surgery.

He wanted to give back.

For as long as he could, because who knew how much longer he had? How much time his father's heart would beat for him?

He grabbed his wallet out of his locker and then headed outside where there was a coffee cart that sold particularly strong Cuban coffee day and night. The sun was just setting. The city was full of gold and red and he wished that he was back at his apartment, watching the sun set over the ocean.

This was his favorite time of day.

When the world slowed down just a bit. When he could thank the powers that be for another day on earth. Another day of saving lives.

Of course, in South Beach the world didn't slow down all that much and the nightlife would be gearing up. The clubs would be pumping out loud music and hordes of people would be wandering the streets.

Tourists mostly, but still the streets hummed with a different pulse and it had been so long since he'd gone there to feel life, the energy flowing through the music. It had been so long since he'd danced.

"What will it be tonight, Dr. Valentino?" the barista asked.

"Tall and dark with two shots of espresso, please." Alejandro opened his wallet and pulled out the money.

"Coming right up."

Alejandro rolled his shoulders. They were stiff and sore from the surgery, but the pain was worth it. That little girl would go on to live another day. Even if she was minus a couple of organs.

She had another shot at life.

The pain on the parents' faces, though, had been too much to bear for him. Which just affirmed his choice not to have a family.

"Here you go, Dr. Valentino."

Alejandro took the coffee and paid the barista. He wandered over to the row of benches just outside the main hospital doors and sat down. He closed his eyes and listened to the city.

His city. When he'd danced, he'd been working all over the country, but Miami was his home. It always would be, even though he'd lost his parents here and had even lost a brother who'd gone off and joined the army for a time, he still loved it. He would always come back here.

His parents were gone, but at least Santiago had come back.

There was just something about this place that spoke to him. Miami had a hold on him. It was his first love.

His only love.

Is it?

And then he couldn't help but think of Kiri. After their time in Las Vegas he'd tried to find out more about her. He'd wanted to get to know her, but Ricky hadn't had that information or at least hadn't been willing to share it.

Ricky had been a bit difficult that way and he had not been happy when Alejandro had decided to leave.

"You'll come back. You'll need money and you'll come back. They always come back."

Alejandro had promised himself he would never go back to dancing like that. Which was why it was imperative that no one found out about his past.

Of course, that had never concerned him until Kiri had shown up. It was good Ricky had never shared that information. He had no right to get attached to her. To lead her on when his time was limited.

"Can I join you?"

Speak of the devil.

He opened his eyes to see Kiri standing there. She looked as tired as him. He should tell her to leave, but he couldn't. He was lonely.

"Of course." He slid over and she sat down, slumping over.

"I was not prepared for a splenectomy today," she said.

"Who is prepared for splenectomies?"

"I am, when I plan the surgery because of a preexisting condition, but an accident like that? It's something I'll never get used to." Kiri shook her head. "So much trauma."

"You're a surgeon, you have to live for the moment." He took a sip of his coffee; it was bittersweet, just the way he liked it, and it woke him up.

"I know, it's just… It's so hard watching a kid go through that. I sometimes wonder why I chose to work with kids."

"Why did you?" he asked. "If it weighs so

heavily on you, why did you choose to work with kids?"

She shrugged. "I don't know, probably because they're worth saving."

He raised his eyebrows in question.

"And adults aren't?"

Kiri laughed softly. "No, it's not that. I just... I love kids and I want to help them. Why did you decide to become a pediatric transplant surgeon?"

Alejandro sighed and set down his coffee cup. He lifted his scrub shirt. "You see the eagle?"

"I remember the eagle," she said tenderly, and a delightful blush tinged her cheeks.

"And you know there's a scar there. Touch it and tell me what you think it is."

She reached out and traced her hand over it. Not just the touch of a lover, but this time as a doctor.

"I would say heart surgery. Have you had heart surgery?"

Alejandro nodded. "A heart transplant, to be precise. When I was ten."

She gasped. "I'm sorry to hear that."

"Well, I'm okay now." He winked at her. "I decided when I was ten that I wanted to be like the surgeon who saved my life. I wanted to save other kids. I wanted to help. So I worked hard to become the surgeon I am today."

"Why did you cover it with an eagle?" she asked.

"To remind myself to always soar and because women don't particularly find it sexy if their exotic dancer has a big old ugly scar across half their body."

She chuckled. "I guess not."

"Tattoos are hot," he teased, waggling his eyebrows. "Although it did hurt like you wouldn't believe and took a few sessions to complete."

"I don't doubt it."

"Are you off tonight?" he asked.

What're you doing?

He didn't know. She was his boss, it was probably a bad idea, but he needed to be with someone. Someone he didn't have to pretend around.

Someone who knew him.

Not many did.

"Yes, I'm done now. How about you?"

"I was on my way out the door when you paged me."

"Sorry about that," she said. "I thought if she needed a transplant you would know right away. I should've paged someone else."

"Never be sorry. It's my job and I take it very seriously. I want you to know that. You know who I was before I was a surgeon. No one else does."

"I wouldn't tell anyone your secret. Our secret, remember? I was there that night and indulged too."

His blood heated as he thought of that night. Not so much in the private villa where he'd been dancing for her and her friends, but when he'd seen her at the bar. Alone and sad.

And even though he shouldn't, he couldn't help himself.

"What're you doing tonight?" he asked.

"Nothing. Why?" she asked, frowning. She looked confused.

"We're going dancing."

"Dancing?" She sounded panicky. "Do you think that's wise?"

"I know. It's probably not right, but I think I'm your only friend here in Miami and we're just going dancing. That's all. It's harmless."

"I don't dance," she said.

He slugged down the rest of his coffee. "Tonight you will. I'm taking you to a samba bar and we're going to dance. We're going to celebrate saving Casey together."

"Well, then, shouldn't we invite Dr. Robinson, as well? He helped," she teased.

Alejandro wrinkled his nose. "No, it's just going to be us two. Have you seen Dr. Robinson dance?"

"No, I haven't." Kiri chuckled. "Have you?"

"Yes. It's bad."

"No worse than me, then."

"You've seen me dance, though." He grinned as she began to blush. "I can teach you. Come on, there's a samba bar near our apartment. We don't even have to take the motorcycle. We can walk."

She bit her lip and he waited with bated breath to see if she would take him up on his offer. One part of him hoped that she wouldn't, but another part of him really hoped that she would. He felt like celebrating tonight. Tonight he wanted to dance and he wanted to dance with her.

He didn't want to be alone.

"I shouldn't," she said. "But I will. Why not?"

"*Excellente.* I will pick you up at ten o'clock. Be ready. Wear a dress." He crushed his coffee cup and tossed it in the garbage bin as he stood. "I'm looking forward to this. I promise you'll have fun, Kiri."

"Promises, promises. I'll hold you to that, you know. I'd better have fun." She was teasing.

"I guarantee you'll have a good time."

"You guarantee it?"

And before he could stop himself he took her hand and kissed her knuckles, before whispering, "Absolutely."

"No worse than me, then."

"You weren't dancing, though." He grinned as she began to blush. "I can teach you, Cohr could be a sailor for how out of practice he is when it comes to..."

CHAPTER EIGHT

KIRI WAS SECOND-GUESSING the choice of dress as she stared at herself in the full-length mirror in her bedroom. It was short, tight and a one-shouldered emerald-green number that always looked good on her. She always wore this dress when she went dancing.

It was probably dated, but this dress made her feel comfortable.

It had been a long time since she'd worn it, though.

What am I doing?

Not only had it been ages since she'd been dancing, but she shouldn't be going out with Alejandro. Not when he was one of her surgeons. It could be detrimental to their careers, but Alejandro was the only person she'd connected with here.

The only person she knew.

She almost canceled. She was going to, except he knocked on her door.

"*Hola*, I…" He trailed off as his gaze raked her from head to toe.

A blush crept up her neck and bloomed in her cheeks. Her pulse raced as those dark eyes settled on her.

"You look…stunning."

"Thank you. You said to wear a dress."

"Yes, well, that dress suits you." He cleared his throat. "Are you ready to go explore South Beach and samba bars?"

"I think so," she hedged.

"You only think so? You don't sound very certain."

"Should we really? I mean, given my position at the hospital…"

He held up his hand, cutting her off. "We're going as colleagues. Nothing more. We're celebrating, that's all. We're friends, yes?" He held out his hand. "So are you coming?"

No. Don't do it.

It had been so long since she'd had fun. Kiri took his hand and went with him. Once they were outside the cool chill of air-conditioning gave way to a sultry night. It wasn't too bad as a breeze was rolling in off the ocean.

"How far are we going?" she asked.

"Not far. Stick with me."

Kiri did exactly what Alejandro suggested as they moved through the crowds. She stuck close to his side as they moved through the crowded streets toward a samba bar on the busiest street of South Beach. She could hear the Latin music pouring out onto the street. It was loud, but not obnoxious. It seemed to fit with the mood of the crowd, the vibe in the air.

"Slow down, you have longer legs than me," she teased as she tried to keep up.

Alejandro stopped and looked at her legs, grinning. "They look fine to me. Damn fine. I happen to like your legs. If I haven't said so already, I'm so glad you wore a short, tight dress."

"Be serious," she said, but she was pleased he thought she looked good. The last time she'd felt even remotely good about herself had been in Vegas.

Don't think about that night.

"That's not the point. Slow the pace down. I can't keep up with your march."

"I'm just eager to dance with you. To dance in celebration of our success with that little girl today." And as if to hammer his point home, he spun her around in the crowds.

Kiri laughed at his enthusiasm.

Alejandro gripped her hand tight as he moved through the crowds. Or actually it was almost as if the crowds parted for him. And as they moved through the people she could see more than a few women who stopped to check him out.

And to check out her as well, the competition, as it were.

It made her feel slightly uncomfortable to be sized up by other women. It reminded her of the times when she'd been a little girl, chubby, in hand-me-downs from her older sister, a bad haircut and big, thick glasses.

You're not that girl anymore.

She was a confident, talented surgeon with a great job at a respectable hospital. Although she couldn't blame the women for checking out Alejandro. He looked so good in his tight white shirt and dark denim. He had perfect hair, he was tall and ripped and had a devastatingly charming smile, with a dimple to boot.

So sexy.

It wasn't just his looks, though. It was his personality. His charisma. He had this hold on people. Kiri was pretty sure that he was aware of this and he used it to his advantage, and given that it was Friday night and the street outside the club was packed, she was glad he knew his way around.

Alejandro spoke with the doorman. They shook hands and laughed and the velvet rope was lifted for them to enter the club, much to the protests of the crowd waiting.

"Come on," Alejandro said.

"How did you get in? There's a huge line waiting to get in here."

"I grew up with the bouncer and the club owner. Plus, I started dancing in a club like this."

She stopped in her tracks. "You mean…"

"No," Alejandro said quickly as he led her into the darkened club. "I just danced. My friend would hire dancers to dance with lonely women who were on their own. That's how I was discovered by Ricky, who got me into the exotic dancing side. Of course the club Ricky found me in was in Little Heliconia. The club owner I know has become very successful."

The club was filled with people dancing and there were dancers on a stage by the bar in brightly colored costumes covered in feathers dancing to the Latin beat. It was like being at Carnival in Rio, only more contained.

It was overwhelming. She gripped Alejandro's hand tighter as she took it all in. It was like an attack on the senses, but then she felt excited to be here. The music made her sway a bit. She'd been dreading this, but now that she was here she thought this might actually be fun. As long as she kept her cool around Alejandro and didn't let her attraction to him sway any of her decisions.

"Why did you choose dancing for Ricky over this?" she asked, shouting a bit over the noise.

"Dancing for Ricky paid way more. I would still be dancing here, trying to pay off medical school, if I hadn't taken that job." And then he spun her as they headed out onto the dance floor. "I was one of the best dancers here."

He brought her out of the spin and tight against his body as he led her into a dance. Her pulse was racing, being so close to him. His arms wrapped around her as their bodies moved together.

"I don't doubt it," she said, and then she cursed herself inwardly for sounding a bit like a schmuck. She tripped and he caught her.

"Legs wobbling still from the forced march?" he teased.

"No, I don't dance very well. I'm not very coordinated in heels. I can barely walk in them. And, besides, I told you I don't dance."

He smiled down at her. "You're doing fine."

"Ha-ha. You're too kind."

Alejandro frowned. "No, you're doing fine. Just grab the rhythm."

"Says the man to the woman who is rhythmically inept."

He chuckled and then his hands moved from hers and he put them on her hips, guiding them to the rhythm of the music. "Just feel the music. Close your eyes and forget everything else."

It was hard to forget everything else while his

hands were on her hips, guiding her in a very sensual dance. Her body was very aware that Alejandro was touching her and she was glad a layer of clothes was separating them.

"There you go," he said. "You've got it." He took her hands again and led her into the middle of the dance floor, his hands holding hers as he led her through a very simple dance. His dark eyes twinkled and that irresistible grin made her feel a bit weak in the knees. She couldn't help but admire the way his body moved.

She'd enjoyed watching him in surgery; his fingers working on the most delicate structures was like a dance in itself and this was just an extension of that. It was an assault on her senses.

He had been the only man to ever make her feel something. He'd made her feel desirable, sexy, and it was a rush to feel that way again in his arms.

Five years had not dulled the desire she still felt for him.

He spun her round again and she laughed as the colorful dancers all around her and the flashing lights blurred in a dazzling light.

He was laughing too as he pushed and pulled her through the dance and she just listened to his advice and found the rhythm of the music and moved her hips. His eyes were dark and she recognized that look, the lust in his eyes, and her heart fluttered.

She had to be careful tonight or she might be swept away.

The song began to wind down and he spun her round and then brought her close, holding her tight against him. His breath was hot on her neck as their hips moved together.

The song ended and people began to clap. She pushed herself away from his embrace and joined in applauding the live band.

Another song started up and before she had a chance to say no, because she was still trying to regain composure from the last dance, he brought her close, holding her tight. His hand held hers as he led her through a slower dance.

She glanced up to see him staring at her.

"What?" she asked.

"Nothing." He looked away. "I was just going to compliment you on your supposed lack of dancing skills."

She stepped on his foot and they laughed together. It was nice to be real with him. Kiri didn't have to pretend.

"See, I told you I'm no good at this."

"You're very good at this." He smiled at her.

Kiri's heart skipped a beat. She thought he was going to kiss her and she wasn't sure if she'd be able to stop him.

"It's hot out here on the dance floor. Do you mind if we stop?" she asked over the din of music.

"Do you want something to drink?" Alejandro shouted.

"Yes. Some water would be great. The crush of people in here, it's so hot."

He nodded. "Let's go that way, where there's a quieter bar."

Kiri took his hand and he led her off the dance floor. They found a small table tucked into the corner of a bar. She sat down and he went to get the drinks. He brought back two bottles of what looked like expensive water.

"How much did that cost you?" she asked.

"Probably more than an alcoholic drink. This water might be made of gold."

She laughed and took a drink. It was ice cold and heavenly. "Thank you for the water. This place is popular."

Alejandro nodded. "It's one of the best in South Beach and a definite tourist trap."

"I can see why. Not only are people dancing but this place is crawling with professional dancers."

"They often do a dinner show early in the evening, but you need reservations for that."

"I'm sure those are hard to come by."

He nodded. "That's really for all the tourists."

He took another swig of his water. "You did so good out there. You can dance, you're just being modest."

"I'm not being modest. I really can't dance, but you're a good teacher."

"*Gracias*. I did do a bit of that too."

"What?" she asked.

"Teaching dance, but again Ricky paid me so much more to do exotic dancing." He frowned. "I loathed it so much, but it afforded me my freedom."

"Aren't you afraid that one of our patients would've seen you? I mean, look at me."

He shrugged. "I have thought of that, but I didn't do my exotic dancing in Miami. I was quite insistent that I be sent outside the greater Miami area. I didn't want my brothers finding out. They didn't know that I was doing any sort of dancing as a way to pay for my schooling. They thought I was working at the docks in a fish-processing facility."

Kiri wrinkled her nose. "And that was better?"

"To my older brothers, yes. I didn't have the guts to join the army like my brother Santiago."

"Who taught you to dance?" she asked.

"My mother. She taught me and I just kept dancing, even after she died." He smiled wistfully. "She wanted me to be a dancer, I think, like her brother Jorge. Jorge died when she was young, before she came here. She always talked about Jorge's dancing."

"And your bothers didn't know you danced even then?"

"No, they would've teased me so it was a secret. Just me and my mother knew about it." He cleared his throat. "If someone were to recognize me I'd pretend I didn't know them. Honestly, most people don't remember a male exotic dancer's face. The only reason you remember me is because of what happened afterward."

His gaze was intense and she looked away.

"Yes," she whispered, and the reason his face was burned into her brain was because no other man had made her feel that way, because she'd stepped out of her comfort zone and allowed him in, and look where that had got her.

"Come on, let's have another dance." He stood and held out her hand and as much as she wanted to, she just couldn't.

"I'd rather not press my luck. I think I'll sit this one out."

"Are you okay?" he asked, squatting down in front of her. "Too many people?"

She nodded. "Yeah, I just need some air. It's really crowded in here."

He nodded. "Okay, let's get out of here and

take a walk on the beach. It's been an exciting day."

She was relieved that he understood her need to get out of the crowded club. She took his hand and let Alejandro lead her out of the overcrowded club. Her head was pounding because of the loud music, but it wasn't that. Being with him like this, getting to know him was going to make it harder to walk away. She liked being with him, but they didn't want the same things. There was no future for them.

It ate away at her soul.

They crossed the street, dodging the cars that were pretty much at a standstill because of people looking for parking and partygoers going from bar to bar.

Once they were on the opposite side of the street it was a short walk over some small dunes and through some long grass to the beach. It was dark and overcast. There was a strong breeze blowing in from the ocean, but it was nice. They kicked off their shoes because sand was starting to fill them.

Even though it was dark, the sand was soft and warm against her feet.

It was exactly what she needed at that moment.

"Looks like a storm is rolling in," Alejandro

remarked. "Or rather it feels like a storm is rolling in. I can't tell since it's dark."

Kiri glanced out over the water, but all she could see was darkness, though she understood what he meant. The air felt different. The wind was stronger, with a haunting whistle to it. And then there was a distant roll of thunder.

"Maybe we should head for shelter?" she asked.

"It's still far off. We can walk on the beach back to home. Would you like that?"

"Yes. It will be better than the crowded street."

They walked in silence, right down by the shoreline, letting the cold water wash over their toes. It felt so good. There was another flash of lightning, this time closer, and they stopped to watch it light up the sky in the distance. And then a bolt of thunder cracked across the sky over the ocean.

"Beautiful," Kiri murmured.

"It is. I never tire of watching it."

"Have you ever watched a hurricane come in?" she asked.

"Only when the whitecaps come rolling in. I'm smart enough to know that when a hurricane is coming you seek shelter. As one man said once, it's not that the wind is blowing, it's what the wind is throwing around that causes the most damage."

"Sound advice."

"Though I do understand the appeal of chasing a storm. The danger in it. I find them fascinating."

She stopped to look up at him. In the streetlights shining down onto the beach, and as the lightning flashed, she could see the wind rippling his white cotton shirt.

"You like to live dangerously, then?"

"No, but I like the idea of living dangerously. The only time I lived dangerously was when I came up to you in that bar five years ago." He took a step closer and tilted her chin so she was looking at him. Her heart hammered against her chest and her body ignited in a thousand flames. He still had a physical effect on her.

So much so that she lost all sense of control around him.

And she didn't like to lose control. She couldn't lose control when it came to Alejandro. She'd learned the hard way what it was like to lose control around him. He cupped her face, strands of hair tickling her cheek, and no matter how much she wanted to fight it, how much her inside voice screamed that she should push him away, she just couldn't.

She closed her eyes and let him kiss her.

His lips were gentle against hers, familiar, and so many emotions came bubbling to the surface. Anger, sadness and lust. It had been so long since she'd been kissed by a man she couldn't remember when it had been.

She'd only been on a couple of dates after she'd lost the baby, but now, with Alejandro's arms wrapped around her, she couldn't recall them.

All she could remember was him.

Everything else was forgotten as she melted in his arms. Kiri wanted to stay there. He made her feel safe, he made her feel alive again.

What're you doing?

She pushed him away. "I can't."

"I'm sorry, *mi tesoro*," he whispered. "I didn't mean for that to happen."

My treasure. Only she wasn't his treasure and she resented the term of endearment.

Kiri nodded as his words hit her with a cold dose of reality. "It's okay, but please don't call me that. I'm not your treasure. I never will be."

A strange look passed on his face. "Of course. I'm sorry."

"I'd like to go home now. I have some more meetings tomorrow that I have to prepare for. It was a long, emotional day. This was probably not wise. I should've just gone to bed."

"Of course. I'll take you home." There was no lingering by the beach this time. They walked the rest of the way in awkward silence along the beach until they got to their condo.

They rode the elevator up to their floor in silence. She tried not to look at him. If she did, she might cry or do something she'd regret.

And Alejandro walked her to her door only because his own door was across the hall from hers.

"Kiri," he said gently, those dark eyes of his making her melt, "I am sorry if I made you feel uncomfortable."

"It's okay." She was trying not to let her emotions overwhelm her.

He rubbed the back of his neck. "I got carried away, but I want you to know that I don't regret what happened between us. Not then, not now."

What he said made her pulse race.

"I don't regret what happened between us. Not then, not now."

Kiri didn't regret it either, but she knew that if Alejandro knew what had happened he might regret ever having laid eyes on her. He might regret ever sleeping with her.

The thing was, even after her loss she'd never regretted the choice she'd made. It had hurt, but she'd never regretted going with Alejandro that night. That night had been the most wonderful night in her whole adult life.

No man had ever treated her like that before. Or since.

So, no, she didn't regret it either. She wished that she could have more, but there couldn't be any more between them. She was technically his boss. She'd come here to prove herself, not to fall in love. She couldn't fall in love with a man who didn't want kids. Still, she wanted him to know. Wanted him to share it with her.

He had the right to know.

For so long that pain had been very hard to bear and she'd sworn to herself five years ago that she would never ever go through it again. Telling him would probably push him away for good.

So it was better this way. He deserved to know.

It was better to keep Alejandro at a distance. That kiss had been too dangerous.

It was too dangerous for her heart.

"Alejandro, five years ago, after our night together, I fell pregnant."

"I… What?" he asked, his eyes widening. "Pregnant?"

"I lost the baby. I tried to find you but…" Tears streamed down her face. "I can't ever go through that pain again. You deserve to know. I'm sorry. So sorry."

She didn't give him a chance to respond because she began to cry harder. She had to get away from him. Kiri pulled out her keys, her hands shaking as she unlocked her door.

"Kiri…"

She shook her head. "I'm sorry." She slipped inside her apartment and shut her door quickly so she didn't have to see the stunned expression on his face or the hurt. She didn't want to talk about it because she couldn't handle it right now.

At least he knew now.

At least now she could move on without him, without the guilt of keeping the loss of their child a secret, because she was sure he wouldn't want anything to do with her again.

CHAPTER NINE

SHE'D BEEN PREGNANT?

The words sank in and he was still numb. Still in shock.

Kiri had been pregnant?

After standing in the hallway, feeling stunned, for a few moments he unlocked his own door and went into his apartment. It was so hard to walk away from her door when all he wanted to do was ask her how she'd lost the baby. He wanted to hold her, console her, because she'd faced that loss on her own.

He hadn't known.

He'd almost been a father and that thought scared him. She'd also been the only one to ever get to him.

He'd had a couple of other casual flings, but nothing compared to Kiri.

And now the more he got to know her, the more he wanted her.

Which was a dangerous thing. He needed to

know her pain. He wanted to console her, process it, but at the core of all the rush of emotions swirling around inside him he wanted to make love to her again.

To let her know in the only way he knew how that it was okay.

He was okay.

They could separately be okay.

When they had been out on the dance floor together, his hands on her hips, all he'd been able to think about had been taking her, making her his. And he'd been very aware of the way other men had been looking at her and that had infuriated him.

She was his.

She's not, though.

And he had to keep reminding himself of that fact. When they'd been standing out on the beach, watching the storm roll in, it had reflected exactly what he'd been feeling in his very soul at that moment, watching her standing there, wisps of her silky black hair escaping and blowing across her face.

The absolute peaceful smile on her face, but then the pain. He hadn't wanted her to feel pain. He'd wanted to take it all away. It was all he'd been able to do not to carry her off.

Alejandro had wanted her. Just like he'd

wanted her back in Vegas. Nothing had changed, she was still the woman he desired above all.

So he'd kissed her.

And he'd sworn he could feel her melt into him. For one crazy moment he'd been lost and then she'd brought him screeching back to reality. She'd lost his baby. He couldn't be with her because he didn't want to hurt her. She deserved a man who could give her everything. Everything she wanted. Marriage, children. He couldn't give her those things. He may have got her pregnant once before, but he couldn't do that again.

Though he'd been shot and injured, they'd told him his father had died because of a brain hemorrhage, but Alejandro was certain that the hemorrhage had been caused by the shock of seeing his wife and son fall first. His father had truly died of a broken heart and subconsciously given up the will to live. In the foggy recesses of his brain from that moment, he recalled his mother being shot first, of crumpling into his father's arms while his father had screamed her name, and then he'd felt the sting of a bullet.

Alejandro shook his head, trying to drown out the sounds of his father screaming. He rubbed his scar, which burned.

He couldn't imagine loving someone so deeply and then losing them. And he couldn't do that to another person. It was too much to bear. Which was why he never opened his heart. Had never let another person in. Yet Kiri always seemed to find a way in. His walls weren't safe when he was around her, which was why he had kissed her on the beach.

Why he couldn't resist her. He would never be able to resist her.

She lost our baby. He had already caused her pain and hadn't been there.

And she had tasted so sweet.

Outside the storm raged, just like a storm raged in his heart. Thunder rumbled and he leaned against his window in the darkness, staring out. He could see the once calm ocean was becoming choppy as the storm rolled onto shore.

Go to her.

And though he knew that he shouldn't because of their positions at the hospital, he couldn't help himself. He needed her. He turned and left his apartment and knocked on her door, his heart jackhammering, his blood on fire.

She answered. Her hair was down and brushed out and she'd changed out of the dress into a nightgown. Her dark eyes were swollen and red from tears.

"Alejandro?" she said, surprised to see him.

He didn't answer her; instead, he reached down and kissed her again. Possessively. He wanted to let her know that he wanted her. He would always want her, and even though she was not his to have, he would never not desire her. And he wanted her to forgive him for not being there when she'd needed him most.

She was under his skin, burned into his memories.

No one could live up to her.

Though he could never have her, she was his.

Kiri melted and kissed him back, her arms around his neck and her fingers tangling in the hair at the nape of his neck. He pushed his way into her apartment, almost expecting her to stop him again, but she didn't. He closed the door with a swift backward kick.

"I'm so sorry, Kiri, for your loss. For what you went through alone. I don't know how to help you. How to make things better. I just know that I want you. More than that night in Vegas…"

"Alejandro," she whispered, laying her head against his chest. "What're we doing?"

"I don't know." He cupped her face and ran his thumbs down her cheeks. "I don't know. I want you, but if you need more from me, if you need a promise of something more, I can't give you that and I'll leave. I just swore a long time ago that I wouldn't ever…" He sighed and dragged his hand through his hair. "My heart transplant."

"You're afraid it will fail?"

He shook his head. "Yes, when I was ten I had the heart transplant because I was shot when my parents' bodega in Little Heliconia was robbed. My mother died at the scene, but my father died during surgery to save his life. My life was hanging in the balance and since my father was brain-dead my brothers directed my father's heart to me as we were a perfect match. I carry a piece of a man I admire greatly inside me. It's a huge responsibility and it reminds me every day that I have to work hard to be the best doctor I can be. I can't be selfish. I promised him that I would dedicate my life to medicine." He was going to say more about how he didn't know how much time he had left, how he'd never hurt her again, but he couldn't.

Her eyes filled with tears for the horror that he had endured at such a young age and her heart went out to him for the brave decisions he'd made since that dark time. "I'm so sorry for your loss, Alejandro. You went through a shocking and terrible ordeal—and at such a young age. I'm wowed that you've dedicated your life to saving others as you yourself were saved. Your parents would be filled with pride to see what you've achieved. It's so admirable. I understand."

"It's not a burden, it's just how I've lived. I had to tell you, I just had to know if you still wanted me even though I can't promise you anything beyond this."

She bit her lip. "I do want you and I don't need a promise. You've made it clear about how you feel, but what about our jobs?"

"No one has to know. We can just have tonight."

"I just need tonight," she whispered. "To chase away the ghosts."

"Are you sure? You deserve more than I can give."

Kiri shook her head. "All I want is you. Right here. Right now."

A flash of lightning illuminated her apartment and he heard the rain splash against the glass of her windows. The storm had come and there was no turning back now. No stopping it now. He scooped her up in his arms and carried her to the bedroom. He set her down and then cursed under his breath.

"What?" she asked.

"I don't have protection. Seducing women is not something I do very often."

"I can't get pregnant again," she said sadly. "I'm unlikely to conceive. Added to that I have a hostile uterus, which makes the odds of carrying a baby low as well…I won't get pregnant again. I refuse to, so I take birth control."

"Are you sure you want me to continue?"

She nodded and then undid the buttons to his white shirt. "I want you, Alejandro. I've always wanted you."

The moment her hands pressed against his bare chest he lost it and he knew he had to have her. There was no going back and perhaps he was putting his heart at risk, but it was just for this moment. Another stolen moment.

He kissed her again, running his hand down her back, cupping her bottom to pull her closer against him.

"I've thought only about you for the last five years," he whispered against her neck. "Only you."

"Me too." A little moan of pleasure started in her throat as he kissed that spot on her neck that he remembered so well. Alejandro nearly lost his mind with desire. This was what he'd been dreaming about for so long.

"If I'm not careful I'm liable to take you right here."

"Is that bad?" she teased, running her hands down his back.

"Yes, I plan to take my time with you."

Alejandro pressed her against the mattress, running his hands over her body but pressing his body against her so he could feel her curves pressed against him. He reveled in the softness of her skin, her hair, as he kissed her again.

"Touch me," she whispered. "Please."

"With pleasure." And he cupped her breasts, squeezing them, but that wasn't good enough for him. He wanted to kiss every inch of her skin.

Apparently it wasn't enough for Kiri either because she pushed him away and took off her nightgown, baring her beautiful naked body to him. Her skin glowed in the darkness, the flashes of lightning illuminating her.

With hurried fingers she helped him out of his clothes so that nothing was between them. She ran her hands over his skin, causing gooseflesh to break out over his body.

"I love your hands on my body," he whispered.

"I can tell," she teased. Then she teased him with the tips of her fingers. Running a finger lightly down his neck, over his chest and then tracing the tattoo. Her hand splayed against his abdomen and slipped lower, gripping him in the palm of her hand.

"*Dios,*" he groaned.

"I love it when you speak Spanish." Still holding him, she leaned forward and nibbled his neck. "You're completely at my mercy."

"*Sí.*"

Her dark eyes glittered and she grinned devilishly as she stroked him. He sucked in another breath. His whole body was alive, every nerve on fire as she touched him. He tried to hold back a moan but he couldn't.

Kiri touching him was driving him wild and he was afraid that if she kept it up he would come. Only he didn't want her to stop.

"Oh, mi Dios, no se detienen," he grunted, bucking his hips at her.

"What did you say?" she asked, dragging her lips over his chest.

"Oh, my God, don't stop."

"Then I won't." Her mouth was on him then and his hands slipped into hair and he started speaking in Spanish, not even knowing what he was saying because he was being driven wild with pleasure.

Growling, he pushed her against the mattress, pinning her there below him.

"Now who is at whose mercy?"

She bit her lip and tried to wrap her legs around him, but he let go of her wrists to push open her legs.

"I want you, Alejandro."

"I know, but now it's my turn. I've wanted to taste you for so long."

"Taste wh…? Oh, *mi Dios,*" she gasped as he did exactly just that. Torturing her the way she had tortured him.

"You've picked up Spanish quite well," he teased her.

"How do you say 'I want you inside me now'?"

"Te quiero dentro de mí ahora."

"Te quiero dentro de mí ahora."

"Sí."

"That wasn't a question. That was an order."

"Was it, now?" he teased her again, running his tongue around the most sensitive part of her, making her cry out. "Say it again. I want to make sure you're saying it right."

"Te quiero dentro de mí ahora. Please."

"Por favor."

"Sí," she said, arching her hips at him.

"Okay." He moved over her, staring down into her eyes. Kiri pulled him down for another kiss as he entered her with one quick thrust.

"Dios," he groaned. She was so tight, so hot. It took all his control not to take her too fast, but her body arched and she began to match his rhythm so that he sank deeper into her, and he couldn't hold back. He slipped a hand under her bottom, bringing her closer and angling his thrusts as he quickened his pace.

It was hard to hold back, but he managed it until Kiri came, crying out his name as she tightened around him. Only then did he allow his own sweet release.

When it was over he rolled away, trying to catch his breath, and he realized that he wanted more of her.

"That was amazing," she whispered in the darkness. He could hear her panting and he grinned.

He rolled back over and grabbed her, dragging her across him, her soft body against his. She kissed him gently on the lips.

"That was amazing," he said. "You're amazing."

She smiled at him. The wind howled outside as she settled against him and he stirred to life again. He wanted her again. And she seemed to want more as she sat astride him, sinking down on him, riding him, but this time making love to him slowly. Tenderly.

Yes. He wanted so much more of her. So much that it scared him and he realized that he was a lost man.

Kiri woke with a start. She reached out, expecting to find Alejandro there, but he wasn't. This time he'd left, instead of her. Her stomach knotted as she thought of him sneaking out, but really he was just doing exactly what she'd done.

And they hadn't made any promises.

He'd told her he couldn't offer her anything and she'd accepted that because she couldn't give him anything either. And since they worked together, what they'd done wasn't right.

All they had were these couple of stolen moments and a lost child.

That's all they had together.

Outside the sky was gray, the ocean was gray and turbulent, and the beach was littered with driftwood and seaweed. It was a miserable day outside as the remnants of the tropical storm lingered into the morning.

She got up, because she couldn't lounge around in bed all day, though that's what she wanted to do. The moment she sat up she caught sight of his white shirt lying crumpled on the floor where she'd tossed it.

Kiri picked it up and held it to her face, drinking in his scent. Tears stung her eyes and she thought of what she'd almost had with him. While he'd expressed remorse for her he hadn't seemed to feel much at all about it himself, which confirmed her belief that he didn't really want children. That saddened her because being with him had been so much more this time because she knew him. She understood him. She loved being with him. She enjoyed his company. He was a friend.

No, he was more than that.

I'm in love with him.

And the thought scared her because it was something she'd been trying to deny for a long time. She could talk herself out of it before because all Alejandro had been then was a one-night stand. She hadn't known anything about him, not even his last name.

Now it was different. Kiri knew a lot about him. She knew his last name. Knew he'd grown up in Miami and his parents had been immigrants from Heliconia. He was dedicated to his work, he rode a motorcycle, he loved to dance and he was charming.

He treated his patients and his coworkers with a level of respect she'd never seen from a brilliant surgeon before.

He was charming, sexy and passionate about medicine.

And he'd suffered a devastating tragedy as a child. With far-reaching consequences. Only he'd turned his life around, had turned the darkness of his past into something bright and wonderful.

Alejandro was the perfect man. Only she couldn't have him because he didn't want the same things she did.

She was in love with a man she could never have. She tossed the shirt away.

Get a grip on yourself.

Alejandro had made it clear to her last night that he couldn't be in a committed relationship and she had done the same. She'd promised him that it would be okay, that he didn't have to commit to her.

She was a big girl.

She was independent. Things could carry on like they had before. She would make sure of it. Only as she stared at the crumpled shirt on the floor she knew that nothing would be the same between them again.

Kiri only hoped that she hadn't totally jeopardized her career in Miami.

Even though she missed New York City like crazy, Miami had grown on her. She loved the weather and the culture. Loved working at Buena Vista.

This was her home now.

And she wasn't going to let anything stand in her way.

Even her feelings.

CHAPTER TEN

"YOU'RE LATE, DR. BHARDWAJ."

Kiri tried not to roll her eyes as she walked into the small boardroom where she was meeting with the head of the board of directors today. She really detested these meetings with Mr. Snyder, who only saw the bottom line instead of the lives.

"Thankfully, Dr. Prescott was able to meet with me in your time slot," Snyder snapped.

"The head of trauma?"

Mr. Snyder glanced up at her briefly from his paperwork. "The former head of trauma."

Her stomach sank into the soles of her feet. So they were planning to close the trauma department, and Prescott had been so helpful in finding Gervaso's birth mother.

Dr. Prescott didn't deserve this. This was not how a hospital should be run. A hospital needed a trauma department.

"Do you think closing the trauma department is wise?" she asked.

"We're not planning on closing the trauma department. Dr. Prescott quit. He took another job. He was just handing in his resignation. I'm on the lookout for a new head of the trauma department, so if you know anyone or can recommend someone out of the pool of attendings we have here I would appreciate any recommendations. Besides, your only concern is pediatrics. You're not Chief of Surgery."

It was a barb, meant to keep her in her place.

Kiri took a deep breath and counted to ten. "I'll keep my eye out. I haven't quite met all the attendings outside the pediatric department."

Mr. Snyder nodded. "You're running your department like a tight ship. I have to say, the board of directors is quite pleased with your summary."

"Thank you," Kiri said, but if Snyder was pleased with her she didn't take that as a compliment. The cuts she'd made when she'd first arrived didn't sit too well with her.

"We just have one concern, about Dr. Valentino," Snyder said.

Her stomach did a flip again. "What about him?"

"We want to keep him, he's the best specialist in pediatric organ transplant that we've ever seen. His survival rate is high, but these pro bono cases have to stop. We're trying to save money and attract a very specific clientele here."

"I couldn't very well send José Agadore elsewhere. He was too ill to move and Alejandro spoke his language. The family were at home with him. It wasn't long before UNOS called and we were able to give him the liver transplant."

Mr. Snyder cocked an eyebrow. "Yes, but the antirejection meds aren't being paid for by the family. They should be, but Dr. Valentino is paying for them."

Kiri was taken aback. "What?"

Mr. Snyder ignored her and pulled out another file. "And this John Doe in the NICU, why wasn't he shipped to County? That's where wards of the state of Florida in Miami go. They don't stay here."

"I'm aware of that, but you'll notice that Dr. Valentino was approved to be guardian of the baby. He's footing the bills. The child needs a heart transplant."

Mr. Snyder pulled off his glasses and rubbed his eyes. "We don't want to lose Dr. Valentino, he's too gifted, but this has to stop. This charity. The only way to keep away the people who require pro bono services is to stop all charitable donations."

Kiri clenched her fists under the table. She

knew exactly what Mr. Snyder was implying. He meant riffraff. Whatever riffraff was. "Dr. Valentino is not doing the baby any harm and it's his money."

"You need to talk to him." Snyder sent her a pointed stare that made her blood boil.

"I'll talk to him. That's my job," she snapped.

Snyder glared at her. "Remind him that while it may be his job to save his patients medically, it's not his job to save them financially."

"Is that all? I do have *paying* patients to see."

"Yes." Snyder waved his hand, effectively dismissing her like he was a lord and she was a lowly serf.

Kiri stood and left the meeting. She was fuming and she had an inkling this wasn't the board of directors speaking but Mr. Snyder personally. How could Dr. Vaughan, a man she admired so much and who was all for pro bono cases, be friends with someone like Mr. Snyder? She had to find a way to appeal to the rest of the board about their pro bono fund.

Babies like Gervaso and others didn't deserve to be shipped off to County because they were unwanted. They deserved to be cared for by the best team of pediatric doctors in Miami. She was worried about Alejandro forking over so much money. It was attracting the wrong attention and he had to lie low for now.

Until she could get the heads of the hospital together to convince the entire board that the pro bono fund needed to be reinstated.

She found Alejandro in José's room. He was talking to José's parents, and before she could even knock on the door she saw him reach into his pocket and bring out bottles of prescription medicine.

Dammit. What're you doing?

Kiri was angry at Alejandro for endangering his job like this. With Gervaso's case he'd gone through a lawyer and a judge had approved it. The hospital's hands were tied, but this? This was going too far.

José would be on antirejection medications for the rest of his life. Alejandro couldn't be doing this. José's family had to be on some sort of drug plan. The boy had cystic fibrosis as well. Was Alejandro supporting the medication for that too?

Now he was stepping out of line with the doctor-patient relationship.

She knocked on the door. "Dr. Valentino, can I speak with you privately?"

He glanced over his shoulder and nodded, holding up a hand to let her know that he would be one moment.

Kiri moved away from the door and headed

into a private exam room, waiting for Alejandro to come in.

It wasn't long before he was there.

"Close the door, please," she said, not looking up at him. She was fuming. He was putting his career at risk. If he was fired for conflict of interest he wouldn't be hired by another hospital if Snyder had any say over it. Then who would take care of Gervaso?

It was highly irresponsible.

"You're very serious." Alejandro closed the door behind him. "What's wrong?"

"I just got out of a meeting with Mr. Snyder."

"I can tell from your expression that your meeting with him didn't go too well."

"No, it didn't." Kiri sighed. "I don't know how to say this, but they're concerned about your behavior recently, first with baby Gervaso and second with José."

He frowned. "What do they have to be concerned about?"

"They're worried about you paying for too many things." Kiri scrubbed a hand over her face. "You're too charitable."

"I don't understand. Why is that a bad thing?"

"It's not, it's just bad here."

"Why?" he asked.

"Mr. Snyder cut the pro bono fund."

"I know, but it's not coming out of hospital

funds. It's coming out of my pocket. The bills are getting paid so why do they care?"

"Alejandro, they're worried that it might get around that there's a surgeon on staff who is willing to shell out money. It's a conflict of interest. They don't want to attract the wrong kind of attention."

He snorted. "I know exactly what he means by that."

"Look, I know too. I hate that, but you can't save everyone." And then she paused. She was starting to sound like Mr. Snyder and that bothered her.

"I'm not saving everyone, financially that is. I'm Gervaso's guardian."

"What about José? I heard that you're paying for his medication. You can't do that. It's a conflict of interest. You can't go out of pocket for them. It's attracting attention. You could lose your job and then what will happen to Gervaso?"

"You make it sound like I'm stealing the medication," Alejandro snapped. "For your information, I'm not paying for José's medication."

"You were pulling pill bottles out of your pocket."

Alejandro reached into his pocket and held up the bottles. "You mean these? These that say 'Alejandro Valentino' on them? I was showing José's family the medication that José will be on for the rest of his life. Just like the cystic fibrosis medication. They need to understand the importance of the antirejection drugs."

"Mr. Snyder had a bill showing that you paid for some of José's meds."

He shook his head. "I took José's parents' money and went down to the pharmacy to deal with the pharmacists. The pharmacists here don't speak Spanish. I do. José's parents paid me back. They're on a drug plan through their insurance and their pharmacy is in Little Heliconia, but the hospital won't allow me to discharge José until his parents pick up meds and show the attending physician that the child is taking the antirejection meds. It's hospital policy. Since José's parents don't drive and were planning to take a cab, I didn't think it was right for them to pay extra money that they don't have to get to their pharmacy in Little Heliconia and back again to get their son."

Kiri's heart melted. Alejandro was so good and she felt like a heel for thinking the worst of him, for letting Snyder sway her into believing the worst in him.

Alejandro was good and suddenly she felt like the harbinger of doom and gloom. "I'm sorry. I didn't know. I am very relieved, by the way."

He gave her a half smile. "It's okay. I get it.

You were under pressure from the board and Mr. Snyder. I can go speak to the board if you want."

She shook her head. "No, you don't have to do that. I'll explain to them, it makes sense now."

"I hate board politics," he grumbled.

"Me too."

An awkward silence fell between them.

Alejandro took a step closer to her. "Since we're alone…"

He bent down and kissed her on the lips.

"I have been thinking about you all morning."

"What're you doing?" she asked, stunned.

"Kissing you," he said.

"I know, but last night you said it was just going to be one time."

Alejandro took a step back like she'd hit him. "And kissing you to thank you is taking it too far?"

"Yes," she whispered. "Because kissing me like that makes me want you more."

"You want me?"

This time Kiri gripped his lapels and pulled him down into a kiss that she knew she would regret, because kissing him like this tore down her walls completely, shattered them, and it scared her that she wanted him this badly.

You're at work. You can't have him. He's bad for your heart.

It was that sobering thought that made her

push him away. Why was she so weak when it came to him? Why couldn't she control herself when she was around him?

"We can't do this," she said.

"We can."

And she glanced up to see those dark eyes full of lust, the same dark, burning desire that she was feeling for him.

"I want you too, Kiri. You make me crazy with wanting you."

This was wrong. She should stop him, but she couldn't. She wanted him so badly she didn't care anymore.

She'd been numb and living in a fog so long. She wanted to live again.

To feel.

And not feel the blinding, raw pain she'd buried deep inside.

She just wanted passion. Release.

In this room it was just the two of them.

Just them, and that's what she wanted, even though she knew he didn't want that. It wasn't a permanent thing so right now she'd savor every moment that she had with him.

She crossed to the door of the exam room. Turned the key in the lock, sealing them in, shutting out the real world.

Hot and wild with need, she shimmied out of her underwear and hiked up her skirt as she helped him undo his scrub pants. He was hard and ready for her. Just like she was ready for him. She'd been ready for him the moment she'd laid eyes on him.

Alejandro hefted her up and pressed her against the wall, inching up her skirt. She wrapped her legs around his waist, her hands gripping his shoulders, holding on for dear life as he thrust into her.

"Kiri," he moaned. "Why do I want you so much?"

Kiri didn't answer; all she did was bite her bottom lip so hard she tasted blood. She was trying not to cry out in pleasure.

If all she could have was this moment with him, she was going to revel in it.

"You feel so good… *Dios*…" he moaned against her neck as he thrust into her.

She wanted to tell him she loved him. There was so much she wanted to say to him but couldn't because she didn't want to get her heart broken. He'd been so clear that he couldn't give her anything.

You should've resisted him. You should've kept far away.

And she'd tried to resist him, so many times, but each time she'd failed. He was always there and she was drawn to him. She was a weak fool and she tried to stop the tears of emotion that were welling up inside. The last thing she wanted to do was cry. She didn't want Alejandro to see her tears.

Right now she just wanted to savor this moment of being with him. Of him buried inside her, their bodies pressed together as they moved as one.

She came quickly and he followed soon after.

This was all so wrong. Wanting him when he didn't want more, but when it came to Alejandro she was so weak. So very weak.

Hot tears streaked down her cheeks and he saw them.

"Are you okay?"

"No."

He wiped the tears away with his thumb. "Tell me about it."

"What is there to tell?"

"A lot more. How did it happen? How did you lose our baby?"

She sighed. "Because of my hostile uterus, my cervix dilated. They couldn't stop it. I was only twenty-three weeks along. There was nothing to be done."

His head dropped. "A boy or a girl?"

"A boy." Her words caught in her throat. "His lungs weren't ready. He never took a breath."

He nodded. "I'm sorry that happened to you. Was he buried?"

"In Manhattan."

Alejandro nodded again and she began to cry more as he held her tight. "I'm so sorry."

"I know. Me too." She gave him a wobbly smile, but still couldn't help the tears.

He smoothed the tears from her face as her sobs subsided. He kissed first one damp cheek and then the other. Carefully, tenderly. Then he caught her lips with his own in a slow, lingering kiss that ignited the fires of passion in her once again.

What're you doing? Stop this.

Only she couldn't because she was so helplessly in love with him. He was the only one for her. He was the only one she wanted. She was completely ruined for all other men. It was him or nothing.

You're a fool.

"I can't get enough of you, Kiri," he murmured as he broke the contact momentarily. "Why is that?" he asked.

"I don't know."

"Do you want me to stop?" he asked, kissing her neck now. "I'll stop if you want me to."

Yes, the rational part of her screamed, the part of her that wanted to protect her already fragile heart from being hurt again. Only she couldn't say no. She didn't want to say no.

"No, I don't want you to stop."

I never want you to stop.

"Good, because I don't think that I can," he moaned as he thrust into her.

"Then don't," she whispered, pulling him down to kiss him again.

So very weak.

He held her tight against him as their breathing returned to normal. This was not how he was going to get over her. Last night, being with her, he'd realized it wasn't just that he desired her or that he was attracted to her.

He was in love with her and it terrified him to his very core.

His plan had been to avoid her for the next few days, but he was slowly coming to realize that he needed her. Like air or water. He wanted to be with her. He wanted to forget about the pain he'd caused her. The guilt ate away at him. He hadn't been there. She'd been alone. Yet one moment with her and what had happened? They'd locked themselves in an unused exam room and he'd taken her twice. He just couldn't get enough of her when he was around her. He just had to have her again and again.

There's a solution to your problem.

He shook that thought away. He couldn't give her all she deserved.

"I'm sorry," he whispered. "I didn't mean for

that to happen." He helped her back up from the exam table, which wobbled slightly as they got up.

"It's okay, neither did I." She straightened her skirt and hair, while he pulled up his scrub pants.

"This is going to be tricky."

"What is going to be tricky?" she asked.

"Us around each other."

"Agreed," Kiri said. "Very tricky."

"So what're we going to do about it?" he asked.

"Try harder not to succumb?" she suggested.

"Unless we just say screw it and date." The words shocked him as well as her. He didn't want to date her, or that was the plan, but being around her he couldn't get enough of her. He'd been very clear when they'd first got together and now he was reneging on the deal. Alejandro could see the disappointment on her face. She didn't want to be serious with him.

Which was what he'd wanted in the first place. And all the percentages of heart-transplant survival rates swirled around in his mind. Twenty-two years was the median and he was at twenty-one. He could be on the UNOS list next year. He was being selfish in wanting her.

It terrified him.

"Alejandro..." She was going to say something more, but then her pager went off. "It's the baby!"

"What?"

"Gervaso, it's a 911 page."

"Oh, God, no." He ripped open the door.

His heart raced at a thousand beats a minute as he thought about all the things that could go wrong with Gervaso's heart. And all the variables terrified him. They ran out of the exam room toward the neonatal intensive care unit. When they got there Dr. Robinson and his team were working on Gervaso. The NICU had been cleared of all nonessential personnel and Alejandro winced as he saw them use the defibrillators on the tiny infant.

Gervaso couldn't die.

He was supposed to live. That's why the mother had dropped him at the hospital, wasn't it? That's why he and Kiri had been destined to find him. Gervaso was supposed to live. He wasn't supposed to die in a world-class facility while waiting for a heart. He wasn't supposed to die like his son had died.

The child he hadn't even known he'd had until recently.

The child he'd never wanted.

The child he'd lost.

His blood. His flesh.

Now Gervaso was dying. He could see that.

You can't let this happen. This is not how it's supposed to be.

Alejandro took a step in but Samantha stopped him. "You can't, Dr. Valentino."

"I'm his doctor. His transplant doctor," he said fiercely.

"You're not, though, Alejandro," Kiri said gently. "You're his guardian. You're not allowed in there."

"You're all the family he has," Samantha said. "And family is not allowed in there when the doctors are working. You know that."

It hit him hard. Like a punch to the gut.

Gervaso's family. That was him. He didn't want to be that baby's family. He just wanted to help the baby get a new heart. To have a second chance and then find his real family.

You can be his family. You are his family.

And as the boy's family he couldn't go in there. His hands were tied and he felt completely useless standing there.

"What am I going to do?" He cursed under his breath a few choice words and raked his hands through his hair. "He needs me. I'm the best transplant surgeon there is."

"I know you are," Kiri said. "But he doesn't have a heart yet. There's nothing you can do and legally there's really nothing that you can do because you're his guardian."

"Someone has to be there, someone who can help," he pleaded with her.

"I'll go," Kiri said. "I'll take care of him."

Alejandro nodded as Kiri slipped inside the NICU to help. And all he could do was stand by and watch helplessly as his only chance for any kind of family was on the other side of a glass partition.

And it was slipping away from him.

"We're losing him!" Dr. Robinson shouted. "I need zero point zero one of epinephrine stat! Damn, this kid's vessels are so small. I can barely get a Norwood done on him."

Kiri couldn't do much to assist Dr. Robinson, but she was there, watching little Gervaso struggling to live. His little heart was giving out and everything was moving in slow motion. So all she did was hold the retractor and try to help Robinson navigate the small, delicate vessels of a preemie's heart.

Gervaso's heart.

And she was taken back to that moment when she'd been bleeding out and learning the sad truth that her baby was gone.

Even though Gervaso wasn't her child, she didn't want him to slip away. Alejandro may deny that he was that child's family, but she saw the way he was with him. He'd named him. Alejandro was this boy's family.

Alejandro was about to lose another child and it tore her up completely and she felt like it was her fault because at this moment she was useless.

Come on.

She closed her eyes and said a little prayer.

Then she heard a heartbeat and she opened her eyes.

"We got him," Dr. Robinson shouted.

"He's going to be okay?" Kiri asked.

"For now, but this will happen again and the next time he won't survive. He needs a new heart."

Kiri nodded. "I'll check with UNOS again."

"Let them know what happened here today. It will probably bump him up on the list," Dr. Robinson said.

"I will." Kiri looked down at little Gervaso, intubated and so small. In that small face she saw her lost baby and she couldn't help but reach out and touch his little fist. Longing shot through her.

Hold on.

She had to get out of the operating room. She couldn't stand to see Gervaso like this. To know that Alejandro would be heartbroken if the baby died. It was all too much for her because she understood that pain and if she lingered then she was in danger of having that happen to her again. She couldn't let that happen again.

Kiri peeled off her gown and gloves and scrubbed out.

She headed out of the OR and saw Alejandro pacing in the hall. His expression was broken and he looked defeated. Even though he didn't want to admit it, he cared.

"Well?" he asked the moment his gaze landed on her.

"He's stabilized. I'm about to call UNOS and let them know about his progression. We're hoping this will bump him up the transplant list."

"Okay."

Kiri touched his arm. "He's a fighter."

"Can you honestly say that he'll pull through this?" Alejandro asked. "The odds are against him."

"Miracles do happen." Though she was one to talk. She wasn't even sure that she believed in miracles.

"I want you to do the surgery."

"I can't," she whispered. "Don't make me."

"Make you?" Alejandro snapped. "What're you talking about?"

"I can't operate on that baby."

"Why? You're not related to him." Alejandro froze. "You care for him?"

"I…I don't think… You can get a neonatologist to work on him."

"Kiri, he's not a neonate, he's premature, yes, but he falls under your jurisdiction. You've done heart transplants and I need you to do this. I need you to save him. For me. Please."

"Don't make me operate on him. I can't do it. I can't lose another baby." Tears slipped from her eyes, because there was no controlling them now. When Gervaso had coded and she'd watched them trying to bring him back from cardiac death, it had all become too real for her. When she'd miscarried their baby, she'd been far enough along to hold their son in her arms. To weep over him and to bury him in a tiny white coffin.

She couldn't do it again. If Alejandro wasn't going to adopt Gervaso, she was. So she didn't want to operate on him.

"What're you talking about?"

"Our baby," she said. "I lost our baby."

Alejandro frowned "I know. I know you did."

"If Gervaso dies, it will be my fault this time."

"This time?" he asked confused. "Whose fault was it last time?"

"Yours, your fault…I blamed you for so long. You weren't there to help me."

"It was my fault that our baby died?" He shook

his head in confusion. "How? I didn't know. I would've helped had I known."

"Yeah, sure, you've made it clear you don't want kids. You have no idea the depth of my pain. You're not the one who lost the baby," Kiri yelled, all the anger that she'd been keeping pent up inside her coming out. "You don't know what I went through. The pain I felt. I did it all alone. You weren't there!"

"How could I be there? I didn't know!"

"Exactly. It was my pain to bear. Not yours."

"It could be my pain to bear, but you're scared. So scared you won't even help out a child who needs you. Losing our baby wasn't your fault any more than it was my fault, but if you don't do this surgery on Gervaso you will be responsible for his death. It will be your fault!"

Kiri slapped him hard because he was right but also because she wanted to hurt him. She wanted him to feel the sting of what she'd gone through when she'd lost their baby. He would never know the pain, because he hadn't been there.

Alejandro held his cheek, his eyes like thunder.

"I'm not the only one afraid," she said. "You're so afraid of having a family because you lost your parents. You say that you carry a piece of your father inside you, you want to be like the man he was, but from what you're telling me you're nothing like him. Your father brought your family to a new country to give them a new start. It sounds like your father was a brave man and you're too afraid of loving and losing that you're losing what you could have. You're a coward, Alejandro Valentino."

She turned on her heel and ran from him because she didn't want him to see her cry. He didn't deserve to have her tears. To share in this pain. It was a little too late for that, but then again he was right to call her a coward too.

She was afraid of losing a child again.

The pain was too much. It hurt too badly and she was terrified of feeling this strongly for someone. She was terrified of acting on her feelings for Alejandro, of admitting out loud that she was in love with him. And she was terrified of loving Gervaso. Of wanting to be a mother so desperately but too afraid of losing it all.

That she wanted all Alejandro had to offer, even though he wasn't even sure about what he was offering yet.

He didn't even know if he wanted Gervaso for the rest of his life.

Could she really put her heart at risk like that? Especially with someone who didn't want kids?

Her smartphone rang. She cleared her throat. "Dr. Bhardwaj speaking."

"Yes, this is the United Network of Organ Sharing. Are you the surgeon responsible for Gervaso Valentino?"

"Yes," she said, her voice shaking.

"We have a heart at County. It will be ready in the next couple of hours. Are you able to come?"

Her hands shook because it was so close that she would go and retrieve the heart and because it was so close she knew that somewhere in this city someone was mourning a loss. Tears stung her eyes. They could bear the pain and so could she. She had to.

She was a surgeon.

She cleared her throat. "Yes. I will be there within the hour."

She hung up the phone, gripping it tightly in her fist.

She could do this.

She *had* to do this.

CHAPTER ELEVEN

ALEJANDRO STOOD THERE, STUNNED. The imprint of her palm was still stinging his cheek. He'd deserved it, though. He'd said heartless things to her. She had lost their child alone. He hadn't been there; she hadn't deserved that. He should've been there. His child had died.

Things she didn't deserve, but he was still trying to process the rush of emotions flowing through him. Emotions that he'd kept at bay for so long.

He wasn't sure what he was feeling.

And then it hit him that he'd lost a baby and he was on the verge of losing another. He stared at Gervaso in the neonatal intensive care unit, isolated and hooked up to so many machines. The nurses who were handling him were now gowned and masked.

If a heart wasn't found it would be only a matter of days before his little body gave out. And if Gervaso died, what would become of his heart?

Dios mio.

He was completely helpless and lost.

How had his brothers coped?

How had Kiri coped? And then tears rolled down his cheeks. He couldn't remember the last time he'd cried. And then it hit him. He remembered in complete Technicolor the last time he'd cried. It was a memory he'd blocked because it was too painful.

The last time he'd cried had been the night Santiago had left for the Army. They'd just gotten the note and Alejandro had realized that he was on his own. Dante and Rafe were working hard to support them all.

He'd decided that, being fifteen, he was too old to cry, even though being alone in the night had scared him. At night he'd remembered the shooting, losing his parents. Even before then the night had always scared him. He'd cried because he'd missed his mother, who had soothed his bad dreams. He'd cried for his father who'd always had a joke.

He'd cried for Dante's and Rafe's smiles and gentle good-natured ribbing and Santiago, who had always been in the next bed, snoring his head off.

He'd been alone and had missed his family.

So he'd cried one last time when at fifteen and had never shed another tear again, because he'd been on his own. He'd had to take care of himself. He hadn't had a family anymore.

Except now he did.

Kiri and Gervaso were his family. As much as he wanted to deny it, he couldn't. Now he was on the verge of losing another family and it was too much to bear.

You have to bear it.

He couldn't ever have a family. His future was so uncertain. How could he give Gervaso and Kiri any sort of life? He was living on borrowed time. And as he thought of that, his head spun. Beads of sweat broke out across his brow.

Alejandro glanced up to see Kiri coming towards him. He wiped the tears away because he didn't want Kiri to see them. As she got close he saw she was wearing a Buena Vista jacket and was carrying an organ transplant cooler.

She gave a solemn nod, keeping a professional calm about her, though from her red eyes he could see she'd been crying. Tears he'd caused. "There's a heart at County Hospital."

"Kiri," he said, "you don't have to do this. If you can't—"

"I do have to do this." She glanced through the NICU's glass windows sadly. "There's no one else to do this. Gervaso deserves a chance at life."

"I'm sorry," he whispered.

"I'm sorry too. It will be okay. He'll pull through." Kiri cleared her throat. "It will give him a chance to live. A chance for a *real* family to love him, since it's clear you don't want to adopt him."

It was a dig and he deserved it. He knew in that moment that Kiri's heart was lost to him.

"But you're going to retrieve—"

She held up her hand to silence him, her dark eyes flashing. "I know very well what I'm going to retrieve. I know what I'm walking into. Don't remind me. I'm not doing this for you."

Her voice trembled a bit and he wanted to pull her close and tell her he was sorry that he hadn't been there for her five years ago when she'd delivered their child. He wanted to tell her that it would be okay. She could do this. Only he knew she didn't want to hear it from him now. Not when he was making her do this for him.

This impossible thing that would hurt her and possibly close her heart to him forever.

"Thank you," was all he managed to say.

"You asked me once to give him a middle name," Kiri said.

"I did. Names give strength."

"I know," she whispered. "Aatmaj is my father's name. It means 'son' and I think it's fitting, don't you?"

"Was that what you were going to call our

baby?" he asked, trying not to let her see that it was eating him up inside, but it was. He'd lost a child, one he'd never known he'd had.

A child he hadn't even known he'd wanted.

Until now, because it had been with her.

The woman he loved.

The woman he'd lost.

The only woman who had been able to reach him, but he couldn't say those words out loud. If he said them out loud then there was a possibility that it wouldn't come true. That Gervaso would die and he'd be alone.

He'd lose his heart.

It's already lost.

She nodded once and then turned, walking away from him to retrieve Gervaso's heart.

He nodded solemnly and all he could do was drop his head and pray for all the things he'd never known he'd wanted.

All the things he was so close to losing.

And he couldn't leave it like this.

He started to run after her and caught her as she was heading out of the ambulance bay. He caught her by the arm, spinning her round and kissing her.

It caught her off guard and he was almost expecting her to slap him again, but instead she kissed him back, touching his face in reassurance. He needed that.

"Thank you," he said again.

Kiri's dark eyes twinkled with unshed tears, tears she was fighting to hold back. "You're welcome, but don't ever do that again. I don't need your kisses or want them."

Thanking her had not been what he'd wanted to say, but he'd found himself choking on the words. How could he say it when he wasn't sure he could give her his entire self? And she'd made it clear she didn't want him, but what did he expect?

He let her go, watching her as she climbed into the back of the ambulance. Alejandro watched until it left.

He wandered away from the ambulance bay and, feeling lost, he found himself standing in front of the church chapel. There was no priest in there, but that was okay. Alejandro didn't need absolution right now.

Don't you?

He hadn't been inside a church in so long. His brothers had never really enforced it. The only time in his youth he'd gone after his parents had died had been when the nuns at school would force him to go.

He took an uneasy step and then stepped back.

There had been so many things he'd done wrong with his life, would he even be welcome? And his whole life he hadn't even been sure he believed in God. Not after what had happened to his parents. Taking a deep breath, he walked into the chapel.

There were prayer candles burning so Alejandro picked up a fresh one and lit it. He set it down and closed his eyes, sending up a prayer for Gervaso. For Kiri and her strength and for himself. For the child they had lost.

All he wanted was another chance at a family, a chance at happiness, and he was worried that he'd blown it. The chapel began to spin and he felt light-headed.

He was standing there helplessly like a fool, staring at a wall of flickering candles, when he got a page about Casey.

Dios mio. Not another one.

Right now he had to bury all the feelings raging inside him. Right now he had to be a surgeon. He left the chapel and headed up to the pediatric critical care unit where they had been monitoring Casey since her surgery.

When he got to Casey's room his resident rushed the chart over to him and he could see from the catheter bag that Casey was bleeding again.

"She spiked a fever and complained of pain, separate from her incision pain, and then her urine output stopped."

"The shunt has probably become dislodged,

which has torn open her ureter most likely." Alejandro cursed under his breath. "Get permission from Casey's parents and prep her for surgery."

"Yes, Dr. Valentino."

Alejandro headed off to the scrub room. He had to focus on Casey right now and he had to bury all the anxiety he was feeling about Gervaso right now. Another child needed him.

Kiri had been dreading this moment. It was like she was reliving her loss over again. She closed her eyes as she waited for the surgeon to call her forward. She'd be the last to go up. The heart was always the last organ to be removed. And then a life would end.

Don't think about it.

She learned that the donor in question had been born with a chromosome disorder and was brain-dead, but it didn't make it any easier and she sent up a silent prayer for that little one, an old Hindu prayer that her grandmother had taught her. Just a simple prayer that would send blessings, for the parents who were grieving, for the little life that had never had a chance.

"Dr. Bhardwaj?"

Kiri stepped forward.

"Walking with the heart," the doctor said, carrying the bowl with the preservation fluid. They placed the heart in a bag with fluid into her container. She snapped it shut. When she was out of the operating room she called Buena Vista.

"Robinson speaking."

"Prep Gervaso Valentino for a heart transplant. I will be there in thirty."

"Will do."

Kiri disconnected the call and moved as fast as she could to the ambulance bay. She was trying to process all her feelings now, to get them out of the way so that she could operate on Gervaso. If Gervaso died Alejandro would never forgive her and she would never forgive herself.

Dr. Robinson would be there, but he'd never done a transplant on an infant this small before. Usually it was Alejandro who handled transplants this small. It was his specialty, only his hands were tied. He couldn't be in there. If he was it could jeopardize any future adoption for Alejandro if he wished to pursue it, though she seriously doubted he would. She hadn't even seen him shed a tear for their child.

At least she had done transplants on babies this small and the two of them could do this together.

They had to do it.

She had to save Gervaso, for Alejandro's sake. *And for you.*

That thought scared her, but it was true. She

didn't want to lose Gervaso and she didn't want to lose Alejandro. Even though Alejandro had made it clear he didn't want her.

She wanted them to be her family.

For so long she'd been mourning her loss and been too afraid to reach out and take what she actually wanted. She wanted a family. Wanted to be a mother, more than anything.

She wanted love and she didn't want to spend her life alone.

The ride to Buena Vista was smooth. Kiri drowned out the sounds of the siren blaring and held tight to the cooler that held the heart. When she got to the hospital she was whisked up to the operating room where Dr. Robinson and the team were prepping Gervaso.

She handed the heart to a scrub nurse and scrubbed in. The nurse would take care of the heart and place it in preservation fluid. Dr. Robinson would be placing Gervaso on bypass and removing his wee damaged heart while she inspected the donor heart and went over the plan of attack.

You can do this.

She walked into the operating room and saw the little body on the table…

"It was a boy."

Kiri held out her arms and took the tiny boy

*wrapped in a towel. His eyes hadn't even opened
and he was so small.*

*"My baby." She wept. The pain was too in-
tense, so hard to bear that she didn't know how
she was going to go on living. "My baby." Her
little boy who she'd been going to name after
his father.*

She shook the memory away because this
baby was stronger. This was her baby and he
would live.

Oh, God, please, help me.

The nurse gowned and gloved her. She went
over to the heart in the stainless-steel bowl. Such
a small heart, but it was good.

"The baby is on bypass, Dr. Bhardwaj, and the
old heart has been removed. We're ready for the
donor heart," Dr. Robinson said.

Kiri nodded and headed over to the table,
taking over the lead position. A nurse placed a
head lamp on her head and magnifiers over her
glasses so she could see all the small vessels.

"Walking with the heart," a nurse shouted.

"I'm glad you're here to help," Dr. Robinson
said. "I'm used to working on teenagers and
adults. Alejandro has the lighter touch for the
young ones."

"I'm glad you're here too, Dr. Robinson. You're
the heart specialist. We can do this together."

Dr. Robinson's eyes crinkled as he smiled behind his mask. "You bet we can."

Kiri took a calming breath as the nurse stood next to her, holding the heart. Gently Kiri reached into the bowl and lifted it out, knowing that right now she was holding everything that mattered to her in the palms of her hands.

You can do this.

Once Casey's shunt had been stabilized and she was back to producing clear urine, Alejandro got her back up to the ICU and on a new regimen of medications that would help with the flow. He talked briefly to Casey's parents and reassured them that their daughter would be okay.

I wonder how Gervaso is?

He glanced at the clock on the wall of the waiting room because he couldn't even go down to the surgical floor and be near the operating room. It wasn't allowed.

Instead, he paced, watching the clock.

How do people wait?

It was driving him mad, waiting. While he waited he tried to take his mind off Gervaso's surgery and he thought about what Kiri had told him about Mr. Snyder and how they'd wanted the baby to go to County. He thought about all the other children who were now being sent to

County because Buena Vista wasn't taking pro bono cases.

Alejandro knew that he couldn't work in a place like this anymore. He had to help every child, no matter what their situation in life.

That's what his father would do.

That's what his father had done.

He'd helped those who'd come to his bodega, those who'd been unable to afford to buy anything. His father had helped the needy.

"I came here to make a better life, Alejandro. I couldn't make a good life in Heliconia. There was no life left there to live, but here I can help. I can take care of you, your brothers and Mami. And I can take care of everyone who needs me. That is a life worth living. That is a rewarding life."

He scrubbed his hand over his face before he pulled out his phone and punched in a familiar number.

"Hello?" Santi sounded tired on the other end.

"It's Alejandro."

"Is something wrong? You never call me."

"I know I don't," Alejandro said, and then he sighed. "Why did you marry Saoirse? I thought you never wanted to get married."

"I didn't, but I fell in love. I couldn't help it. I fell so deeply in love with her that the thought of living without her outweighed my fear of possibly losing her."

Alejandro nodded. He understood what Santiago was saying.

"You still there?" Santi asked.

"I am. I'm just thinking."

Santi snorted on the other end. "Well, that's a first."

"I'm adopting a baby," Alejandro blurted out. The other end went silent.

"Now who is at a loss for words?" Alejandro teased.

"That's a huge responsibility," Santi warned. "What brought this on? You're not one for responsibility beyond your work."

"I know, but he has no one. He's undergoing a heart transplant right now."

"You're calling me during a heart transplant?" Santiago yelled into the phone.

"I'm not doing it. I can't, I'm already his guardian."

"Well, that was fast," Santi said.

"Not really. I applied a couple of weeks ago. I found him, you see. He was abandoned and sick and the hospital cut the pro bono fund."

Santi cursed under his breath. "Really? That's not good."

"I know. I'm thinking of leaving. Going somewhere I can help those in need. I thought I was living like Pappi this way, but if I can't help those who need it, then I'm not really."

"Alejandro, you have to do what's right for you. You have a piece of Pappi in you, yes, but that shouldn't define your life. Our parents wanted us to have freedom to choose our paths. Your life is your life. Live it."

"My time is limited."

"Who says?" Santi snapped.

"Medicine? Come on, Santi. You're a doctor too. You've read the reports."

"Yes, I know, but you didn't get a transplant because of heart disease and Pappi was in excellent health when he died. You know the statistics better than anyone else. You've lived this long. Live your life, *idiota*!"

"Oh, yes? Is that what you're doing now?" Alejandro teased.

"Yes." Santiago laughed. "It took me a long time to realize this and you're even a bigger dunderhead than me. You're stubborn."

Alejandro laughed. "Thanks."

"No problem. Do what's right for you, Alejandro. Step out of Pappi's shadow, stop being afraid of what you can lose and just take what life gives you. Live it."

Alejandro disconnected the call. Santiago was right. He had been too afraid to open up his heart because of the what-ifs. There would always be what-ifs and did he really want to live his life not knowing what could come of it? It might be messy. It might hurt, but it would hurt more if he didn't try.

He wanted it all.

And for the first time he wanted what his parents had had.

It was hours that he stood in that waiting room. Alejandro got a taste of what it was like on the other side and he didn't like it much.

Was this what it had been like for his brothers? Was this what he'd put them through?

It was absolute torture. He was used to being in the operating room, not outside, wondering if Gervaso was alive or not.

He raked his hands through his hair and made up his mind to go to the surgical floor, whether he was allowed to or not.

You could jeopardize your adoption of him.

The doors of the OR opened and Kiri stepped out. She was looking for him and then her gaze landed on him and she smiled, nodding.

"Oh, *gracias a Dios*."

She nodded. "He survived, but the next twenty-four hours will tell the whole tale. He could still reject the heart."

Alejandro nodded. "I don't care. I will be there for him."

"Good."

"I'm going to adopt him."

"I'm glad to hear that." She grinned. "He's supposed to be your baby."

"This is hard for me to say…"

"What? Have you changed your mind?" And she looked ready to hit him if he gave her the wrong answer.

"No, I want to adopt him, but I wonder…I can't help but wonder…" Only he didn't finish the rest of what he'd been going to say because the world began to spin and his knees crumpled beneath him.

"Alejandro!"

Kiri's screams were muffled but they sounded like his mother's. And as he laid his head against the cold tile of the floor he knew his time was up. His heart was racing, and then it froze, and as he lay there, the world disappearing from sight, he could hear his parents' voices again.

This was the end.

"Alejandro!" she screamed, and reached out to try and catch him, but he fell to the floor, just slipping out of her hands.

"No," she cried out. She checked for his pulse, but there was none.

"I need a crash cart *now*!" Kiri yelled over her shoulder.

A Code Blue was called. She straddled him and checked his airways before starting CPR.

"You're not going to die on me!" she shouted at his lifeless body as she pumped his chest. "You're not going to die. Damn you!"

The crash team came running. She could see the looks on their faces as they realized that their Code Blue was Dr. Valentino.

Then Dr. Robinson was there, fresh from the operating room.

"Kiri," he said gently. "Let me. It's plain to see you're family."

Kiri stopped her compressions and let the crash team take over. Dr. Robinson guided them as she watched the man she loved lying there, no pulse, no heartbeat, on the cold hard floor.

She couldn't lose him; she couldn't raise Gervaso without him.

She needed Alejandro. Always had.

Oh, God.

Tears streamed down her face.

"Clear!" Dr. Robinson shouted, and a shock went through Alejandro's body.

Please. Not him too.

"Charge to one hundred," Dr. Robinson said. "Come on, Valentino, work with me for once in your life!"

Kiri closed her eyes, holding her breath as they shocked him again. Then she heard it. After the thump of the shock a heartbeat, faint on the monitor but it was there. It was a rhythm.

"Good. Let's get him to the CT scanner. Let's see what caused his heart to fail."

"He had a heart transplant as a child!" Kiri shouted.

Dr. Robinson nodded. "I know. Who do you think writes his prescriptions?"

He left Kiri standing there as they carted Alejandro away. She'd never even had the chance to tell him how she felt about him. Just like she'd never got to say that to her baby.

Their baby.

On the floor was Alejandro's phone.

He had brothers and they deserved to know. She picked it up and saw Alejandro had recently been speaking to Santiago.

Alejandro needed his brothers.

She pushed redial and took a deep breath.

"You again?" a deep voice said on the other line. "Now what do you want? You seriously never call me this much."

"It's not Alejandro," Kiri said, trying to keep her voice from shaking.

"Who is this?"

"Dr. Bhardwaj at Buena Vista. Alejandro collapsed and needed to be resuscitated."

There was silence. Then a sharp cry of pain. "Is he...?"

"He's alive, but going in for testing. You need to…" She trailed off as she began to cry. "You need to come down here."

"I'll be there as soon as possible."

Kiri ended the call and then went to wait for Alejandro's family. If she didn't, she might lose her mind.

It was only a matter of minutes and a paramedic faintly resembling Alejandro came running into the trauma department. He made a beeline for her.

"Are you Dr. Bhardwaj?"

"Yes, and you're Santiago?"

"Yes. I couldn't get hold of Dante or Rafe. I figured just me is good enough for now."

"He's in the catheterization lab. There was a block that stopped his heart."

Santiago nodded grimly and they walked to the cath lab, where they watched Alejandro on the table. Dr. Robinson was threading the catheter to remove the block.

"Mio Dios," Santi murmured, crossing himself. "I can't take this. We almost lost him once. I knew a day would come when he'd need to go back on UNOS, but I thought he had more time. I prayed he had more time. I can't lose him, we can't…I just thought he had more time."

"I know," she whispered. "It's been about twenty or so years?"

Santi nodded. "Yes, about that since our parents died. Do you know how they died?"

"He told me," Kiri said gently.

Santi cocked an eyebrow. "I assume you're more than his boss, then?"

She nodded. "Yes."

"He'll pull through," Santi said, turning his gaze back to his brother. "If he doesn't, I'll kill him."

Kiri smiled at Santi, watching him watch Alejandro, worry on his face.

It was more than she could take at the moment. She slipped away and went to the NICU. She saw Gervaso in his incubator, clinging to life, a new heart giving him a chance.

She gowned up and went into the isolation room. She couldn't touch Gervaso. He needed time to heal and touch right now would put too much stress on his body. Knowing that she couldn't touch him made her begin to weep.

She needed to heal too. Needed Alejandro. Needed Gervaso.

She needed her family.

If only God would give her a chance, but even if Alejandro didn't make it Gervaso was hers. It was a done deal with her heart.

Her heart belonged to him and it belonged to Alejandro.

Fully and completely, whether he liked it or not.

CHAPTER TWELVE

Damn.

Alejandro winced in pain as he slowly opened his eyes to see Santiago at the foot of his bed, glaring at him.

"What the…?"

"Shut up," Santiago said. "Do you know how much you scared the ever-loving heck out of me?"

"What happened?"

"You had a heart block, *idiota*."

The monitors began to beep as his pulse raced.

"Don't overexcite yourself. You're fine. No rejection of Pappi's heart. You'll be fine. Scar tissue is not your friend. That was the culprit."

Alejandro relaxed. "Did they do surgery? I'm numb so I can't tell."

Santi shook his head. "No, just a catheterization. You're lucky, amigo. You were put back on UNOS, though, but you're low on the list. There are more options for you and that heart before you need a transplant."

"Good, that's good. Do the elders know what happened to me?" Alejandro asked.

"Yes, they're relieved you pulled through." Santi grinned. "They threatened you with death if you didn't make it."

Alejandro chuckled. "Kind of a moot point by then."

"I did the same. I planned on torturing you when we met up again one day. You scared me."

"I scared you?" Alejandro teased. "Nothing scares you."

"Some things do," Santi said, and he nodded over at the chair beside the bed, where Kiri was curled up, sleeping. "You were lucky. Don't blow it."

"I won't," Alejandro said. "Though I'm on the transplant list again, what kind of life—"

"Let her make that decision. She knows," Santi said. "Live life, you moron!"

Kiri stirred. "Is he awake?"

Santi nodded. "Yes, and I'm going home to my wife." With one last squeeze of Alejandro's foot and a knowing glare Santi left.

"Kiri," Alejandro said.

She sat on the edge of the bed. "You scared me."

"I'm sorry."

"Don't ever do that to me again."

"I can't guarantee that. My heart—"

"Is fine for now. You're on UNOS, but not a priority. I'm a surgeon. I understand the implications," she said, interrupting him. "Your heart is fragile, but so is mine. You can't use that as an excuse to push me away. Not anymore."

He grinned. "So I guess that answers my question from earlier."

She looked confused. "What question?"

"I was going to ask...I was hoping that we can adopt Gervaso together. I'm the father and you're the mother."

Tears filled her eyes. "Can we? I mean, you want me to adopt him with you?"

"Yes."

"I don't know what to say. How can we?"

He nodded. "We can, but we should get married first."

"Married?"

"*Sí.*" And he held his breath.

She sighed. "Alejandro, if you're just asking me to marry you to expedite the adoption application, then I can't marry you. I know you just had an attack, but I won't marry you for that."

"I'm not asking you because of Gervaso. I'm asking for me." He gripped her hand. "I want you, Kiri. I've always wanted you. I want to have a family again. I can't live without you. The thought of losing you terrifies me, but I can't not take the chance. I'll risk everything to have you. To make a family with you."

Tear began to roll down her cheeks. "How can I make a family with you? I lost our baby."

"We'll make a family with Gervaso. You and him, that's all I need."

"And if Gervaso doesn't make it?"

"I'll have you. I love you, Kiri, *mi tesoro*."

She broke down in sobs when he said those words. His hand was still clutching hers and she couldn't believe that Alejandro was saying these things.

"I love you too," she finally managed to say. "I was too afraid to love, too afraid to lose. Losing our baby almost killed me and then I almost lost you. I didn't think I could ever love again, but I love you, Alejandro. I love you."

She leaned over and he wrapped her in his strong arms and then cupped her face, kissing her in his recovery bed.

She still was terrified about what the future held, whether Gervaso would make it or not and whether Alejandro would too, but at that moment she didn't care. It was a risk she was willing to take because it was a chance to live. Fully.

"How is Gervaso?" Alejandro asked.

Kiri nodded and took his hand. "Strong."

"Really?" There was a smile on his face.

"Yes."

"I think he'll live," Alejandro said, as he leaned back.

"Babies are resilient and he's definitely a fighter." She smiled up at him. "I'm scared, though. Scared of losing you both."

"Me too, but you don't have to do it alone this time. I'm here. I'm sorry that you had to bear the pain of loss without me. If I…" He trailed off, his dark eyes moist. "I'm sorry, Kiri."

And she held him. "It's okay. We have each other now."

So they held each other close, holding on as they talked about Gervaso. How they knew he would survive, the boy they hoped would be their son. Planning for a future together.

Praying for a miracle and never letting each other go.

Kiri wanted to wait a week after Alejandro was discharged and given the all clear before they decided to go down to City Hall and make their marriage official. She wanted to stay close to Gervaso's side and make sure that he didn't reject the heart.

Gervaso was strong.

A definite fighter, and each day that went by he grew stronger. Just like his father.

"So is today the day?" Alejandro asked as he

came into the neonatal intensive care unit where she had been sitting with Gervaso. She couldn't hold him but she was watching him and checking his stats often. "We got our license four days ago."

"I think so. He's doing well and Dr. Robinson is on duty." Kiri smiled at Samantha, who was hovering. "As is Samantha. I think we can leave for a couple of hours to get married."

"Married?" Samantha shrieked. "That's wonderful! I had no idea you two were an item."

Alejandro chuckled. "We met a long time ago and have been in love since then. We just didn't know it."

"He's stubborn," Kiri teased.

Samantha snorted. "Don't I know it?"

"We're getting married so that we can put in the adoption papers tonight to formally adopt young Gervaso here." Alejandro laid a hand against the incubator. "My lawyer said that we have a better chance adopting him if we get married."

"I'm so happy," Samantha gushed. "For the both of you. It's the right thing to do clearly, and I'm so happy for Gervaso. Such a sad story ending so right."

Kiri shot Alejandro a knowing look. She stood and took Alejandro's hand as they walked out of the neonatal intensive care unit.

"Did you manage to find some witnesses?" Kiri asked. "The only people I know in Miami are you and the people I work with."

"I wrangled up a couple of unwilling participants, but they don't know why."

Kiri cocked an eyebrow, intrigued. "Who did you get?"

"My brothers Dante and Rafe."

"I'm finally meeting the infamous elders?" She grinned. "I can't wait to see what they look like. So if you didn't tell them we're getting married, what did you tell them to get them to go down to City Hall?"

"I told them I was being tried for public indecency. I broke the news of my exotic dancing days to them and they were not happy. So they think I'm being charged with that. They're mad. First the heart block and now this. Getting arrested is on the elders' no-no list for me."

She laughed. "You're terrible."

He grinned. "I know, but I like to have fun with the elders."

They took Kiri's car to City Hall and parked it. When they walked into the building they saw the tall, dark-haired, olive-skinned twins scowling and searching the crowds of people, probably looking to string Alejandro up by his short hairs.

They were devilishly handsome, as well.

Kiri had met Santiago when Alejandro had

had his heart issue and had then met Saoirse just after Gervaso's surgery. She'd been taken aback by the brother that Alejandro had called ugly. When she'd first met Santiago she hadn't understood why the brothers all insisted on calling each other ugly when it was far from the truth.

One of the brothers' gazes landed on Alejandro and his fist clenched as he moved through the crowd toward them.

"I think you're in trouble," Kiri whispered.

"I think you're right."

"Alejandro Gervaso Valentino, you have some explaining to do!"

"Dante, that's Dr. Alejandro Gervaso Valentino, if you don't mind."

Kiri squeezed his hand in warning not to provoke his brothers, who looked ready to murder him.

"You're lucky I don't kill you right here, baby brother. I would if it weren't for Pappi's heart," Rafe snarled. "Exotic dancing? Public indecency? You're a doctor, for God's sake, and you're recovering! What are you thinking about?"

"That was all a ruse, old man."

Dante frowned. "For what?"

"The heart block?" Rafe asked.

"No, that was real. The arrest."

"What the...?" Dante looked like he wa

going to murder someone and that someone was Alejandro.

"I needed two witnesses. I'm getting married today."

Dante and Rafe exchanged looks.

"You're what?" Dante asked.

"This is my fiancée, Dr. Kiri Bhardwaj."

Kiri felt uneasy as the brothers' gazes fell on her, but they instantly softened and they smiled at her warmly. Just like Alejandro.

"A pleasure," Rafe said, taking her hand and kissing it. "I've heard so much about you from Santiago, but given the fact you're engaged to Alejandro I thought Santiago was just pulling a fast one on me."

Kiri chuckled. "I assure you I'm quite real."

"Why are you marrying this ugly one?" Dante teased. "You're picking the wrong brother."

Kiri laughed while Alejandro scowled.

"I love him," Kiri said, shrugging.

"She's delirious," Dante said in an aside to his twin.

Rafe nodded and then turned to Alejandro. "No, seriously, what is going on?"

"I'm in love with her and we're adopting a baby."

"A baby?" Dante and Rafe said in unison.

"*Sí*, a baby." Then Alejandro proceeded to tell the whole story, right from the first time he'd met Kiri to Gervaso's heart transplant a couple of weeks ago.

"So, you see, I needed two witnesses and I knew you two elders wouldn't come down to City Hall because you would think that I was pulling your legs, so I told a little white lie."

"We're happy for you," Dante said.

"It's about time you grew a pair," Rafe said. "Seriously, Alejandro, Mami and Pappi would be proud."

Kiri smiled as Alejandro hugged both his brothers tight.

"We're going to be late," she piped up. "Our appointment is in ten minutes."

"Right, let's go." Alejandro took her hand and the elders followed them into the judge's chambers.

Alejandro handed the paperwork to the judge and stood in front of Kiri, holding her hand. He grinned down at her.

"I love you, *mi tesoro*."

"And I you."

The ceremony was simple, then Kiri signed the certificate and so did Alejandro.

They were married.

"You may kiss the bride," the judge said.

Alejandro tipped her chin and pressed a kiss against her lips. "Thank you for bringing me back my family."

"Thank you for being my family," she said. "Thank you for helping me find my way to the world of the living again. I was so lost."

"Me too," Alejandro whispered, pulling her close. "Now let's get these papers off to the adoption lawyer so we can make Gervaso a part of our family."

"*Sí,*" Kiri teased.

Dante and Rafe welcomed her to the family and the four of them went to the next building to file their marriage certificate with their adoption papers. After that was done Kiri and Alejandro took Dante and Rafe to the neonatal intensive care unit at Buena Vista to meet the soon-to-be newest member of the Valentino family.

"So should I call you Dr. Bhardwaj or Dr. Valentino?"

"I think there're enough Dr. Valentinos to last a life time," Kiri teased.

"Fair enough, but you know there are never enough Valentinos. Miracles do happen," Alejandro said encouragingly.

"I hope you're right."

And she hoped that miracle would come true, but for now she had all she could ever want.

EPILOGUE

One year later

KIRI WALKED ALONG the beach, watching as Alejandro jogged ahead, chasing after Gervaso, who was toddling at full speed through the sand and the surf. Against all the odds and his preemie start, their little fighter had mastered first walking then running around the time of his first birthday.

He was thriving a year after his heart transplant, though Kiri knew he might have to go back on UNOS again one day. Just like Alejandro.

Alejandro was good about going to his appointments and taking care of himself. He was on the list, but so far with close monitoring there had been no further heart failure.

So Kiri just lived every day to the fullest, enjoying the time she had with her family.

She couldn't believe that she'd been married to Alejandro for a year already. Shortly after they'd married Kiri's parents had descended from New York City to meet their new son-in-law. Her parents were thrilled that she'd gotten married but not that she'd gotten married at City Hall.

So while they'd been in Miami Kiri had married Alejandro again for a second time in a traditional Hindu ceremony, which her parents had always wanted for her.

And Alejandro had teased that there was no escaping him now.

The newlyweds and Gervaso had taken the painful trip to New York City to visit the grave of the child they'd lost, which had allowed Alejandro to mourn and to mourn with her.

And on the anniversary of his parents' deaths she'd gone with him to the graveside to pay her respects to the people who'd raised four strong, proud men.

She still missed her family and friends back in New York City, but after becoming a Valentino and adopting Gervaso she became part of an even larger family.

It was what she'd always wanted.

"Come back here," Alejandro shouted, interrupting her thoughts as he playfully ran past her after Gervaso, who loved splashing through the little waves that broke on the shore. Kiri grinned as little footprints appeared on the sand before the waves washed them away.

The little boy was laughing and screeched when Alejandro closed in on him then hefted him up and swung him around. Gervaso sported a crop of dark curls and had the bluest eyes that Kiri had ever seen. The scar from the heart transplant was barely visible over the top of his T-shirt, but that didn't stop the precocious boy from running amok. It didn't slow him down one bit.

One of Gervaso's first words had been spoken when he'd pointed to his scar and Alejandro's scar and said, "Same."

"Mami!" Gervaso cried out through fits of giggles.

"I'm coming," Kiri called out, but they'd gotten so far ahead of her she had a hard time catching up.

Unfortunately she was moving a bit slower than those two were.

She looked down at her belly. She was seven months along and she was apparently carrying an elephant. Once she'd found out she was pregnant she'd had her cervix sewn up and had been put on a light workload up until last month, when she'd been told she should no longer work.

Which was fine. It was harder to stand for long periods of time now. Not with what seemed like a gigantic child growing inside her.

Her sister-in-law, Saoirse, had warned her that Valentino babies were large.

"Big heads!" she'd teased.

Kiri had laughed then, but now she believed it. "I have to sit down," she shouted over the laughter. She grabbed one of the many beach chairs along South Beach and sank down into it. It was heavenly, though she didn't know if she'd ever be able to get out of it again. Still, it was nice not to be walking around so much.

They'd spent the day house hunting in South Beach, because Alejandro wanted to live near the ocean and they were outgrowing the one-bedroom condo that Kiri owned. They'd sold Alejandro's condo to pay for Gervaso's heart-transplant surgery, but not long after they'd paid the hospital bill Mr. Snyder had been booted off the board for giving a bad reputation to Buena Vista and the pro bono fund had been reinstated.

It seemed the press had got wind that a surgeon had applied to adopt an abandoned baby to save the baby's life when the hospital had threatened to turn him away.

And since Alejandro was a renowned pediatric transplant surgeon the press had eaten it up. It had been a small victory, but worth it.

Buena Vista was now the kind of hospital they could both be proud to work in.

Kiri leaned back in the chair and put her feet

up. The sun was setting over the ocean and the nightlife on South Beach was starting to kick up a notch.

Alejandro came back with Gervaso on his shoulders. "You know, on second thought I think we should expand our search area."

Kiri cocked an eyebrow. "I thought you loved the ocean. And Gervaso clearly loves the ocean, he's absolutely soaked."

"I know. Sorry about that, but he loves the waves. For what it's worth, there's a huge wet spot on my back."

Kiri chuckled. "I have no sympathy for you. So why do you want to widen the house hunting? I though you loved South Beach."

"I do, but we can go outside Miami. We could go to an island even."

"No way, not an island. I'm not driving over a large bridge every day."

He shrugged. "You do it now."

"Yes, but at least South Beach and Miami Beach are hard pieces of land and not islands that could flood." She shook her head. "No islands."

"How about a yacht?"

"No yachts. Besides, all your stripper money is gone, yes?" she teased.

He glared at her. "I could always go back to it."

"I don't think so. You're mine."

Alejandro bent over and kissed her. "So where were *you* thinking?"

"There're a lot of nice houses down by Vizcaya," she suggested. "On the mainland."

Alejandro grinned. "A good school district too."

"Exactly." She rubbed her belly again. "I'm really dreading having to trade in for a minivan soon."

He laughed. "You'll look good driving a minivan."

"You're driving it, buster."

"I don't think so," he teased. Then he set Gervaso down beside her. He curled up against her belly, rubbing his baby.

"Baby," Gervaso said. "Mine."

Alejandro placed a hand against her belly and the response was a strong kick. "Not long now. We'd better speed up our search. I want to be in the house before the baby comes."

"I agree." Kiri laid her hand over Alejandro's and the baby kicked up at them, as if knowing that they were talking about him or her. Kiri hadn't found out the gender as she wanted to be surprised.

It was a miracle she was pregnant, but she'd heard tell of women who spontaneously conceived after adopting and that's exactly what had happened. Seven months ago when all the final paperwork had come through, announcing they were finally Gervaso's parents, they'd celebrated in style that night.

And now they were on the fast track to a family. If they could only find a house that would suit them both.

"Did you ever think that you'd be here?" Kiri asked. "You were so adamant about not having kids."

He shook his head. "No, I never did, because I didn't think I'd live to see this."

"You're a transplant surgeon—people beat the odds all the time."

He grinned at her. "I knew I shouldn't have walked up to you in that bar in Vegas."

"Well, you told me that what happens in Vegas stays in Vegas. And look where we are," she teased. "It certainly didn't stay in Vegas."

"I'm glad of it, *mi tesoro*."

"Are you?"

He gave that charming smile as he leaned over and kissed her gently on the lips. "Absolutely."

* * * * *

Contents

This book employs a simple
rating system to help choose
which places to visit:

   'top ten'

 ◆◆◆ do not miss
◆◆ see if you can
◆ worth seeing if you
have time

Maps and Plans

INTRODUCTION

Toronto's skyline, dominated by the CN Tower, on the shores of Lake Ontario. The lakefront setting makes it a metropolis with something of a seaside atmosphere

INTRODUCTION

'Toronto...a kind of New York operated by the Swiss'. *Globe and Mail*, 1 August 1987

Metropolitan Toronto is that rarity among major North American cities – a community of many small-town virtues and few big-city vices, with trees to balance the skyscrapers and racoons in its ravines. It has all the advantages of a city of two and a half million, an art world, theatre, television production, 5,000 restaurants, major-league baseball, hockey and football and that ultimate symbol of sporting prominence, a domed stadium, yet its crime rate is negligible and its downtown full of life.

In Toronto people live in the heart of the city as well as the suburbs and stroll its leafy streets day or night not only with impunity but with pleasure, a state of affairs which may not be all that remarkable in Europe but is almost unknown in major western hemisphere communities.

It is a likeable city, despite being a jumble of office towers, apartment buildings and family homes interspersed with churches, statues, the odd fountain and solemn public buildings, all sprawled out along the north shore of Lake Ontario in the province of Ontario and all dominated by the high-reaching, 1,815-foot (553-m) spire of the Canadian National Railways television tower, which adds a futuristic cast to the lakefront skyline.

For one thing, the city is clean and free of graffiti, not depressingly so but more like Scandinavia than London, Paris or New York. And things run on time and people queue up politely. And though they are not folksy in the manner of, say, Moscow residents, who have a village chattiness and peasant humour that yields nothing to the competition of big-city life, Torontonians do not have the hard veneer of New York or Chicago residents. What many do have is Presbyterian reticence, inherited from the Scots pioneers of the new land, that can be broken down with one friendly question or a passing smile. Then, like all small-town people they are quick with advice and help.

To European visitors it is all very American, with gun-toting police, big cars, bars instead of pubs and a careless disregard of distance – workers in the same office may live 60 miles (95km) apart and routinely drive a 120-mile (190-km) round-trip to visit each other of an evening. To Americans it is very British, with its

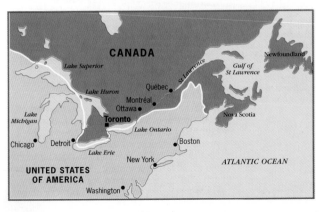

INTRODUCTION

It may not have the grandeur of some cities, but it is a pleasant blend of older buildings (above, Old City Hall) and modern tower blocks

King Street, York Street, Queen's Park (the site of the provincial legislature), neat and liveable downtown, profusion of teapots (the US cup of tea is full of lukewarm water with a bag at the side) and British pronunciations (herbs, not 'erbs and a definite Scottish 'oot' and 'aboot' sound when going out and about).

It is, in fact, a fine blend of the two, the best of both worlds, in a way, with a largely British heritage, but moulded and amended by the American experience. And that is true in language, schools, government, right through the whole fabric of society. There are lots of fish and chip shops in Toronto, for instance, but you get ketchup with your vinegar and your chips

are called French fries. And at the other end of
the scale, if you go to court you will find crown
attorneys and Queen's Counsels – but all of them
will be North American-style lawyers combining
the functions of barristers and solicitors.
With all its attributes, though, Toronto is not a
city of grandeur, no London, Paris, Lisbon or
Buenos Aires. It grew up on the pioneer ruts of
Muddy York's narrow streets and has few
sweeping prospects or grand boulevards. Most
downtown thoroughfares are dully commercial
and Yonge Street, the city's heart, is common-
place where it is not tawdry, lined with raucous
bars and record stores and fast food outlets.
Only the 12-block length of University Avenue
leading north from Front Street to the solemn
bulk of the legislative buildings at Queen's Park
has any sense of style and occasion. And
unfortunately, despite its breadth, central boulevard and sweeping prospect, the street is dull.

Origins and Dimensions
The area known to the world as Toronto is, of
course, actually five cities and a borough, four
of the six with names transported from Britain
(York, North York, East York and Scarborough)
and two with names of North American origin
(the original Toronto and Etobicoke), the whole
spread over a 25-mile (40-km) stretch of Lake
Ontario shoreline 90 miles (145km) from
Niagara Falls and the US border.

There are areas of the city that have that sense
of style but they are mostly residential
neighbourhoods which came into being as the
city grew, areas such as Rosedale and Forest
Hill where huge old mansions slumber beside
shady streets. For anyone with an interest in
architecture these are communities to visit.
Though each community has its own government
for local matters, all work together collectively
as Metropolitan Toronto. (It should be noted that
some, though by no means all, Torontonians
pronounce the name 'Traana' but you will be
understood if you say a proper 'Toronto'.)
It sprawls over fairly flat land, with no
spectacular hills except at Scarborough Bluffs in
the east, where 330-foot (100-m) cliffs offer

a lookout which takes in many waves but no hint of the far shore (not surprisingly, since the lake is from 30 to 53 miles (48 to 85km) wide). But three major rivers, the Humber, the Credit and the Don, as well as numerous creeks and ravines, twist and turn through the urban areas, bringing a breath of the country with wildlife which includes racoons, rabbits, foxes, squirrels and birds of all descriptions. Add that effect to Toronto's green canopy of trees and its public gardens and you have again a big city that retains small-town touches. In the heat of summer (which can reach over 30°C/90°F) it is the waterfront that casts a spell: promenades by the lakeside; harbour tours of every ilk (moonlight cruises, day runs, dinner sailings); ferry rides to Toronto Islands, which

The waterfront is an ever-present attraction to visitors, whether for strolling along the lake, joining in the fun at Harbourfront or taking a trip on a ferry to the Islands

Downtown Entertainment
Attractions for visitors are spread right across the 244 square miles (632sq km) of the metropolitan city, but for most the major lures lie in the downtown area of the original Toronto, at the heart of the community, with its harbour, islands, theatres and concert halls, museums and galleries, hotels, restaurants and shopping.

rim and protect the harbour, to picnic by the water and drift in canoes down shady lagoons; concerts and hot dogs at Harbourfront and a stop for a beer and an enveloping Cinesphere movie at Ontario Place, a wonderland of domes and towers built over the water not far from the site of the first tiny European settlement, a French fur trading post established in 1720. There may be a thousand other things to do in summer, but put the waterfront high on your list. And do not overlook it in spring, when a stroll along Harbourfront's breakwater offers the lift of fresh lake breezes or in autumn, when the colour change from the north comes blazing down the ravines. The change is best seen north of Toronto (there are bus tours and route maps for rental car drivers), but more than a hint of its scarlet and yellow glory can be enjoyed right in the heart of the city.

The city in winter is another matter. The lake warms the air enough to save Toronto from the worst of nature's outrages but the bitter winds and slushy streets and temperatures that can drop below -17°C (0°F) tend to send residents and visitors alike indoors and underground, where happily they find buried between Yonge Street and York Street, one of the world's largest subterranean cities, six blocks long by two wide, 3 miles (5km) of tunnels with 1,000 shops, entertainments, bars and restaurants, complete with waterfalls, growing plants and even trees.

The north end of the tunnel leads to The Eaton Centre, a four-block, three-storey complex of shops, stores, snack bars, restaurants, high-fashion boutiques, greengrocers and a branch of the department store whose name it bears. It was built on the lines of Milan's Galleria purely for shopping, but the results were so pleasing it has become a major tourist attraction.

Back in the 1950s the city was known as Toronto the Good, usually said with some disgust, and though it is a lot more relaxed now it still could not be described as wild and woolly. Bars open at the respectable hour of noon and close at 01.00hrs, you buy liquor at government stores, Sunday is still a day of rest for most people and there is no gambling other than on race horses and lotteries.

The skyscrapers of 20th-century downtown Toronto

That said, it is not dull. West End and Broadway shows play the theatres, restaurants serve the foods of the world, it is a major sports city (in 1992, the Toronto Blue Jays became the first baseball team outside of the United States to win the World Series), your choice in bars is almost unlimited and there are attractions unique to the city, as we shall explore in later chapters. And if cities cramp, then visitors can always try jogging the length of Yonge Street (pronounced 'young'), the central thoroughfare, though it might take some time. The longest street in the world, it starts at the water's edge and runs north and west as Highway 11 to Rainy River, Ont, on the Minnesota border, a distance of 1,168 miles (1,880km).

BACKGROUND

For a city with such a proper image there is an awful lot of rum in Metropolitan Toronto's history; and not a little accident. It sits where it does, for instance, not by choice but by chance. It grew up around a British fort that evolved from a British fur trading post that superseded a French trading post that was located at the site of a small Indian village. And the village existed only because the level piece of ground between the Humber and Don Rivers was the spot where tribes canoeing south from Lake Huron reached Lake Ontario after portaging the lower reaches of the Humber. Down that trail over the centuries had come Hurons and Iroquois, Ottawas and Menominees, Shawanoes and Sacs, Foxes and Mississaugas, war parties and scouts, hunters and nomads, all moving freely in an endless land. And down that trail in early September 1615, came the young French explorer Etienne Brulé, who lived among the Hurons as a scout for Samuel de Champlain and who spelled the beginning of the end for the natives' free-roving way of life.

He was the first European to see the future site of Toronto, though he was not the man staid city fathers of later years would have chosen for the role – someone combining the courtliness of Sir Walter Raleigh with the holiness of St Francis of Assisi. Brulé was not close on either count.

Pioneer's log cabin

BACKGROUND

Described as vulgar and barely literate, he brawled, drank, and womanised until a drunken quarrel over a native maid went too far and he was beaten and eaten by his Huron friends. Brulé made no notes and he drew no maps on his visit to the lakeside site the Hurons called Toronto ('meeting place' or 'plenty' in their tongue – we will never know which because the Iroquois wiped them out a few decades later), but he reported back to Champlain and the portage north became a favourite route of such adventurers as La Salle when heading west through the Great Lakes to explore the Mississippi. (It took them to the Holland River, Lake Simcoe, the Severn River, Georgian Bay and Lake Huron, a shortcut that avoided the back-breaking portage at Niagara and the long haul through Lake Erie and upstream against the Detroit River current.)

But while the route was recognised as valuable, the site was not, at least for another century, though somewhat earlier than that some visitors from La Salle's fort at Cataraqui (now Kingston) set the tone for future conventions if not an example for Toronto the Good.

The Iroquois Confederacy had moved north into former Huron territory along the shores of Lake Ontario by the late 1670s and some had settled near the mouth of the Humber at a village of typical long houses called Teiaiagon. And among its first European visitors were the men from Cataraqui.

What happened then is recorded in a work of the time titled *Histoire de l'eau de vie en Canada:* '…Six traders from Katarakuy named Duplessis, Ptolemee, Dautru, Lamouche, Colin and Cascaret, made the whole village of Taheyagon drunk, all the inhabitants were dead drunk for three days; the old men, the women and the children got drunk; after which the six traders engaged in the debauch which the savages called Ganuary, running about naked with a keg of brandy under the arm.'

It is hard to understand what lusts that debauch called Ganuary was designed to gratify, but the report certainly proves that life on the frontier was not all candle-making and churchgoing.

By 1720, the French had recognised the necessity for a fur trading post at the portage

The Gooderham Building

point, if only to intercept Indians on their way to the English traders south of the lake. By 1750 the battle for furs was so intense they replaced the trading post with a proper fort on the east side of the Humber and called it Fort Toronto, the first use of the name for a settlement. However, it was soon eclipsed by a larger bastion, called Fort Rouillé after the colonial minister in Paris, which briefly flourished as a centre of the fur trade before being torched by its garrison during a British attack in 1759. A single plaque on a stone pillar on the waterfront grounds on the Canadian National Exhibition near Ontario Place marks its site. Little else remains to recall its existence or its passage. The British, who resumed trading amid the ruins and earned a bitter reputation among administrators and settlers for debauching the natives with liquor, agreed to buy 500 acres (200 hectares) from the Mississauga tribe in 1787 for 1,700 pounds sterling's worth of trade goods and food, including 24 brass kettles, 200 pounds of tobacco, 47 carrots, 10 dozen looking glasses, 24 laced hats, 2,000 gun flints, one bale of flowered flannel and, naturally, this being the future site of Toronto, 96 gallons of rum.

The town of York, built and named by John Graves Simcoe, the lieutenant-governor, was soon designated the capital of Upper Canada and almost as soon won a reputation for hard drinking. There were six taverns for a population of just over 400 and they were not held to modern hours, it seems, since landlords are on record as complaining they had to get up most nights to serve rum.

So widespread was York's reputation for tippling, in fact, that a writer at the *Constellation*, a newspaper in Niagara, commented that the words 'We, the inhabitants of the Capital' should always be translated to read: 'We the inhabitants of York, assembled at McDougall's over a glass of grog…'.

Fort York and the town were captured in April 1813 by US forces during the War of 1812, though the victory cost the invaders the life of explorer and brigade commander, General Zebulon Pike and several of his soldiers when the powder magazine was blown up by the retreating British.

(During the US occupation the new parliament buildings were burned down with an unexpected effect. British troops attacking Washington, DC set fire to the president's residence in retaliation for the York blaze and to hide the scorch marks the building was painted with whitewash: hence the name White House.) However, the occupation lasted only a few days, then the US troops went home and the Town of York went on about its business. And it went right on growing. By 6 March 1834, when it became the City of Toronto, it had a grand total of 9,254 residents and a fiery mayor, William Lyon Mackenzie, who felt so strongly about the need for responsible government that three years later he led an ill-planned and short-lived rebellion. Defeated, he fled to the US but returned just 12 years later after a general amnesty, to run for the legislature – and win. More, Mackenzie, who was the grandfather of William Lyon Mackenzie King, a Liberal prime minister of Canada earlier this century, was such a hero that in 1858, when he retired, public subscription bought him a home which is still standing, as a museum, at 82 Bond Street. Responsible government came without rebellion as, in 1867, did independence, and the city kept growing, drawing immigrants mainly from Britain but with a trickle from the rest of Europe and, in the early years, a stream from the US, lured to Ontario by the abundance of land. Nor had the French altogether disappeared from the scene with the loss of Fort Rouillé. There had always been French Canadian Torontonians since the days of St Jean Rousseau from Montréal, who had set up a trading post near the mouth of the Humber as early as 1780. It was he, in fact, who piloted the British schooner *Mississauga* bearing the new lieutenant-governor into the harbour where Simcoe was to build his capital. And the skipper of that Royal Navy ship was one Jean Baptiste Bouchette. The Scots came in great numbers, fleeing the Highland Clearances, and the Irish, fleeing famine. By the early 20th century, the Toronto police force was mostly Irish – but in contrast to US cities these were Ulster Irish, Protestants all. The make-up of the force has changed, of course, and so has the whole pattern of

So popular was the rebel William Lyon Mackenzie that the people gave him a retirement home, now a museum

immigration and city settlement. Up until World War II Toronto was an Anglo-Saxon bastion but the post-war years brought a wave of Europeans, Dutch and Italian, Greek and German, Portuguese and Poles. And now new waves have rolled in, from the Caribbean and Latin America, from India and Pakistan, from Vietnam and Hong Kong, all forming part of the new fabric of the city. On the positive side, for visitors, this has meant that the somewhat staid ways of the old Toronto are disappearing, that there are restaurants and entertainments of every kind representing cultures from around the world, and that the population is far more varied and colourful than it was once upon a time.

But there are negatives, too, of which the visitor should be aware – trends to indicate Toronto is growing less law-abiding as it grows more diverse, with more reports of street gangs, drugs and violence. It is a long way from New York city yet. It is still a safe place, as it has been since Etienne Brulé hefted his canoe down the Humber, and you can still ride the subway in safety and walk the night-time streets. But now the little straggle of huts at the end of the portage is coming into the modern age.

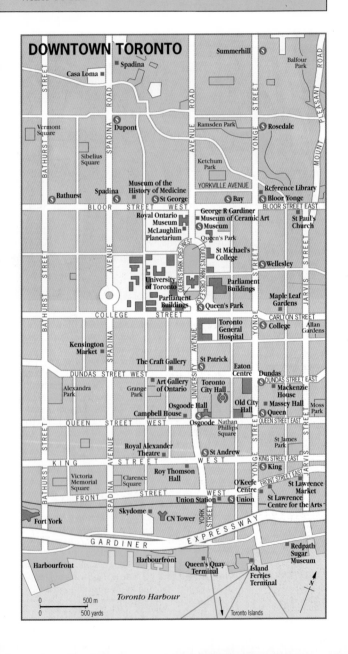

DOWNTOWN TORONTO

Summerhill

Balfour Park

Casa Loma ■   Spadina

Vermont Square

Dupont

Ramsden Park   Rosedale

Sibelius Square

Ketchum Park

YORKVILLE AVENUE

Bathurst   Spadina   Museum of the History of Medicine   St George   Bay   Reference Library   Bloor Yonge

BLOOR   STREET   WEST   BLOOR STREET EAST

George R Gardiner Museum of Ceramic Art   St Paul's Church

Royal Ontario Museum   Museum

McLaughlin Planetarium   Queen's Park

St Michael's College

Wellesley

University of Toronto   Parliament Buildings   Maple Leaf Gardens

Parliament Buildings   Queen's Park

COLLEGE   STREET   CARLTON STREET

Toronto General Hospital   College   Allan Gardens

Kensington Market ■

The Craft Gallery   St Patrick   Eaton Centre   Dundas

DUNDAS   STREET WEST   DUNDAS STREET EAST

Alexandra Park   Art Gallery of Ontario   Toronto City Hall   Mackenzie House

Grange Park   Old City Hall   Massey Hall

Osgoode Hall   Moss Park

Campbell House   Queen   QUEEN STREET EAST

QUEEN   STREET   WEST   Osgoode   Nathan Phillips Square   St James Park

Royal Alexander Theatre   St Andrew

KING   STREET   WEST   KING STREET EAST   King

Victoria Memorial Square   Roy Thomson Hall   O'Keefe Centre   St Lawrence Market

Clarence Square   St Lawrence Centre for the Arts

STREET   FRONT   WEST   Union   FRONT STREET EAST

Union Station ■

Skydome ■   CN Tower   Fort York

Redpath Sugar Museum

GARDINER   EXPRESSWAY

Harbourfront   Harbourfront   Queen's Quay Terminal   Island Ferries Terminal

0   500 m

0   500 yards

Toronto Harbour

Toronto Islands

N

WHAT TO SEE

A Divided City

Following John Graves Simcoe's original plan, downtown Toronto is laid out in a grid pattern. This centres on Yonge Street, which runs straight north from Lake Ontario and forms the dividing line for East and West street designations. King Street East runs in that direction from Yonge, King Street West the opposite way. In both cases the numbers start at Yonge and climb as you move away. North and South streets are numbered from the lakeshore.

Attractions in and around the city can be reached by taxi, limousine or rental car, of course, but all can be visited by public transport too, and specific instructions on how to reach them by bus, streetcar or subway can be obtained from the Toronto Transit Commission or TTC (tel: 393 4636), open daily, 07.00–22.00hrs. (For more information, maps and brochures call the Metro Toronto Convention and Visitors Association on tel: 203 2500 or visit its main kiosk in front of the Eaton Centre at Yonge Street and Dundas Avenue, where it shares space with Five Star Tickets. Other booths are scattered about the Metro. Some of these may be closer to where you are staying, so telephone the association for exact locations.)

The subway is fast, efficient, graffiti-free and basically simple. It runs in a giant narrow U down Yonge Street from Finch Avenue, through Union Station,

Looking out over downtown Toronto from the CN Tower

WHAT TO SEE – ART GALLERY OF ONTARIO

The Henry Moore Sculpture Centre in the Art Gallery of Ontario

the hub of the system, and north again under University Avenue and Spadina Avenue to Wilson Avenue. The long cross-town Bloor Street Line runs from Kipling Avenue, in the west, under Bloor Street and Danforth Avenue to Kennedy Road in the east, with a surface spur running north and east to Scarborough Town Centre.

These lines all intersect with surface streetcar and bus routes and just one ticket, with transfers, will take you through the whole Metro-wide system for a small cost.

Exact change is required on streetcars and buses so it is wise to buy several tokens or tickets if you plan to make much use of the system.

On the following pages are descriptions of some of the many and varied places the system can take you.

◆◆◆
ART GALLERY OF ONTARIO ✓

317 Dundas Street West
British sculptor Henry Moore dominates this gallery even with its array of 12,000 works by artists ranging from Rembrandt to Picasso. His is the first work you see as you approach the gallery and a huge Henry Moore Sculpture Centre houses 131 bronzes and original plasters, 73 drawings and 689 prints, many donated by the artist after Toronto bought his bronze, *The Archer*, to grace its new city hall. The Canadian Wing displays changing examples from the museum's huge collection of works by such artists as Emily Carr, David Milne, Homer

Watson, Cornelius Krieghoff and the Group of Seven (see page 42). There are 50 new and renovated galleries.

The Grange, behind the gallery and accessible from it, is an historic Georgian mansion, the oldest brick house in Toronto and the gallery's original home. It has been restored as an elegant Canadian gentleman's residence of the 1830s and is staffed by costumed and knowledgeable interpreters of pioneer life. Admission is free with gallery admission. For information tel: 979 6648.
Open: Wednesday and Friday 10.00–22.00hrs; Thursday, Saturday and Sunday 10.00–17.00hrs.
Closed: Monday and Tuesday.

◆◆
BLACK CREEK PIONEER VILLAGE

1000 Murray Ross Parkway/Jane Street and Steeles Avenue
A whole mid-19th-century Ontario village, complete with human and animal inhabitants. Watch the blacksmith, weaver and printer at their crafts, explore the grist mill and walk the boardwalks. See, hear and smell what it was like to live in the rural Canada of Victorian times. More than 30 buildings, including a general store, town hall, schoolhouse and hostelry are spread out around a pioneer farm and mill stream. Costumed villagers and farm folk add authenticity as they explain the troubles and joys of pioneer life. Visitors can take sleigh rides or go skating or cross-country skiing in winter when the buildings are closed.

Open: May to December, daily 10.00–17.00hrs (18.00hrs on holidays and in July and August).
Closed: 31 December to early March (tel: 736 1733 or a 24-hour tape tel: 661 6610).

Visitor's to Black Creek Pioneer Village enjoy a taste of what life was like in Victorian days

◆◆◆
CANADA'S WONDERLAND ✓

9580 Jane Street, Maple, Ont
A lively 370-acre (150-hectare) theme park some 20 miles (30km) north of Toronto city hall featuring the Smurfs and Flintstones cartoon characters in Hanna Barbera Land, strolling musicians, water and thrill rides (and tame ones, too, for the small fry) and, at the Kingswood Music Theatre (tel: 1-832 8131), big-name musicians and singers for adults.

A major draw is the Salt Water Circus, featuring sealions and dolphins. There is plenty of noise and activity designed to keep you moving and spending;

Casa Loma has everything a dream castle should have

food is not cheap (and you are not allowed to bring a picnic) and the only places to sit in the shade are often the show pavilions, which can cost you again. But children love it. There are Wonderland Express GO buses from York Mills and Yorkdale subway stations (tel: 665 0022 for times and fares). *Open*: weekends in May and early autumn, daily in June, July and August, from 10.00hrs; closing times vary. Admission package prices also vary widely in cost and coverage. For details on hours and prices and for general information tel: 1-832 7000.

◆◆◆
CASA LOMA ✓

1 Austin Terrace
On a slight rise in the city's heart stands a 98-room castle built early in this century by millionaire royalist Sir Henry Pellatt, who spent a fortune on it, then found the taxes too high

and turned it over to the community. Though it was three years in the building and many more in the dreaming, he lived there for less than 10 years and never realised a major objective, to play host to members of the British royal family. Described by one critic as 'a mixture of 17th-century Scotch baronial and 20th-Century Fox', Pellatt's castle, restored to its original grandeur, has everything a romantic would want: secret passageways, an 800-foot (244-m) underground tunnel, wine cellars, towers, stables, 30 bathrooms, 25 fireplaces, a palm room, a marble swimming pool, a kitchen range large enough to cook a whole ox, a shooting gallery and a bowling alley. You can explore it on your own and as you wander you can easily imagine Sir Henry and Lady Pellatt entertaining 3,000 guests at some grand ball, the

tinkle of laughter in the great galleries, the swish of silk, the shuddering resonance of the mighty $75,000 pipe organ. There are frequent Murder Mystery games played at the castle, which offers a perfect background.
Open: daily, 10.00–16.00hrs (09.30–16.00hrs July and August).
Closed: Christmas, New Year's Day and weekdays in January and February (tel: 923 1171).

◆◆◆
CN TOWER ✓

301 Front Street West
The world's highest public observation deck and a possible sight of the spray from Niagara Falls 30 miles (48km) away across Lake Ontario are just two of the attractions of this 1,815-foot (553-m) tower, the world's tallest free standing structure. The **360 Revolving Restaurant** at 1,150 feet (350m), reached by an outside, glass fronted elevator (not for the faint of heart) gives you a 360-degree rotating view of the city, the lake and miles of countryside every 72 minutes. Or you can study the displays of the Ecodek high in the sky or shoot up another 447 feet (136m) on an inside elevator to the Space Deck at 1,465 feet (447m) where glass windows bank inward so that you can look not only out but down. Note that all this requires not only a brave head for heights, but good visibility to make the trip worthwhile.
If high places are not for you, consider going down instead of

Always on the skyline, the CN Tower

up. Visit Tour of the Universe in the basement beneath the tower where the ride is only simulated (see page 36).
Open: daily, all year. Summer: 10.00–midnight; winter: 10.00–22.00hrs. To find it, just look up. It can be seen from anywhere along the lakeshore and from many other parts of Toronto.
For information tel: 360 8500.

◆
COLBORNE LODGE
South Entrance, High Park
Built in 1837 by artist/architect/ engineer John George Howard and his wife, Jemima, and superbly sited on a high rise in High Park overlooking Lake Ontario, this is one of the oldest surviving picturesque Regency villas in North America. Howard bequeathed the house and 165 acres (67 hectares) of grounds to the city to form the nucleus of Toronto's largest park – now 400 acres (162 hectares) thanks to other donations – so that it sits surrounded by nature, tall trees and lush lawns, ponds and pools and gardens. The house is exceptional in the elegance of its design but Howard was an engineer, too, and it had its practical side with a wine cellar, summer and winter kitchens and Toronto's first indoor bathroom. Most of the original furnishings are on display along with Howard's watercolours of early Toronto and there are costumed guides to talk about the lodge, the Howards and John Howard's role in the development of the city. Take a picnic lunch to the park, use its biking paths or playgrounds or just its shady

lawns and offer yourself the lodge as a bonus.
Open: guided tours in summer, Monday to Saturday 09.30–17.00hrs; Sunday and public holidays noon–17.00hrs; in winter: September to December, Monday to Friday 09.30–17.00hrs; Saturday, Sunday and public holidays, noon–17.00hrs; January to March weekends and public holidays only noon–17.00hrs.
For information tel: 392 6916.

◆◆
FORT YORK
Garrison Road off Fleet Street
Built in 1793, blown up by the retreating British during the American invasion of April 1813,

Military history is peacefully re-enacted at Fort York, the scene of the bloody battle in 1813

rebuilt in 1816 and restored in this century, the fort offers a look at a national military past that was a little more turbulent than most visitors imagine.

Within the powder magazines, blockhouses and barracks are restored period rooms and exhibits to tell that story and there are uniformed guides to enact and explain the day-to-day military and social life of the men and women who lived there in colonial times. As well, there are marches and 19th-century military drills to the shrill of fifes and the beat of drums. The fort was the birthplace of Toronto and perhaps deserves better than being surrounded by traffic arteries, as it is, but within its fortified walls it is possible in the traffic's lull to imagine briefly those early days. And if you wonder why it is not by the water's edge as it once was, it is not the fort that has been moved, but the lake. Landfill has shifted the shoreline south, leaving the fort high and dry north of Lakeshore Boulevard.

Open: summer: Tuesday to Sunday 09.30–17.00hrs; winter: Tuesday to Friday 09.30–16.00hrs; weekends 10.00–17.00hrs, but visitors should call to confirm current times.

For information tel: 392 6907.

◆◆◆
GEORGE R GARDINER MUSEUM OF CERAMIC ART

111 Queen's Park, opposite the Royal Ontario Museum
The only museum of its kind in North America, this division of the Royal Ontario Museum is full of pottery treasures, 2,000 objects from high-heeled ceramic slippers to exquisite chocolate cups, mystical dragons, exotic perfume bottles and fragile flowered teapots. The Renaissance of Raphael and Michelangelo shines in the bold, bright colours of Italian majolica, English delftware recalls the reign of the Stuarts and Cromwell's Puritans and there are American pots dating back as far as 2000 BC. As well,

exhibits include more than 100 18th-century Meissen porcelain figures inspired by the Italian *commedia dell 'arte*.
Open: Tuesday to Saturday 10.00–17.00hrs; Sunday 11.00–17.00hrs.
Closed: Mondays and national holidays. Admission to the ROM entitles you to tour the Gardiner. For information tel: 586 5551.

◆◆◆
HARBOURFRONT ✓

Queen's Quay, York Street to Bathurst Street
The federal government acted as fairy godmother to turn this rundown waterside industrial

Harbourfront, a fun place for all

strip on Queen's Quay into a year-round people place for waterfront strolls and dances, concerts, lectures, sailing, entertainments, shopping and outdoor and indoor cafés. There's a walk that follows the water's edge and tables and benches for picnics, an antique market, craft works (pottery-making and such) and, if the budget allows, upmarket shops in a magnificently renovated warehouse, Queen's Quay Terminal, which also houses the Premiere Dance Theatre. Stop at Queen's Quay Centre for a programme of events, which can range from ballet to ice canoe races. Some of Harbourfront's original appeal has been lost since it introduced apartment blocks to its lands but it is still a wonderful place to visit on a sunny afternoon and interesting any time. Do dress warmly in winter, though, when winds can be bitter.

Open: daily, 10.00hrs–midnight.
Closed: Christmas and New Year's Day.

For general information, tel: 973 3000; for box office information tel: 973 4000 .

◆
HOCKEY HALL OF FAME
BCE Place, 30 Yonge Street
This shrine of the unofficial national sport of Canada offers photographs, trophies, movies, artefacts, sticks, skates, goalie masks and histories of the game, the teams and the stars. But you have to be a fan or someone with real curiosity about the sport to get the most out of the exhibits. Canada's Sports Hall of Fame is in the same building

and offers a look at a broader range of activities.

Open: spring/summer: Monday to Wednesday 09.00–18.00hrs; Thursday to Friday 09.00–21.30hrs; Saturday 09.00–18.00hrs; Sunday 10.00–18.00hrs; autumn/winter: Monday to Saturday 09.00–18.00hrs; Sunday 10.00–18.00hrs.

For information tel: 360 7765.

◆◆◆
MACKENZIE HOUSE
82 Bond Street
This is the home that his friends gave the fiery little rebel, William Lyon Mackenzie, in 1858 on his retirement from the provincial legislature. A printer, newspaper publisher and politician who fought with words then with bullets for responsible government, he had led the disorganised anti-government forces in the Upper Canada Rebellion of 1837, then fled to the US when the revolt was quickly suppressed. But so popular were he and his cause that when he returned 10 years later he was re-elected to the provincial legislature where he served for another 10 years. (His daughter, born during the years of exile, was the mother of William Lyon Mackenzie King, Canada's prime minister during World War II.) Attached to the gas-lit Victorian townhouse is an exhibition gallery where his tempestuous story is told, and a reconstructed 19th-century printing shop, complete with his hand-operated Washington flat-bed press and its original type. In the house itself costumed guides explain the family's lifestyle and

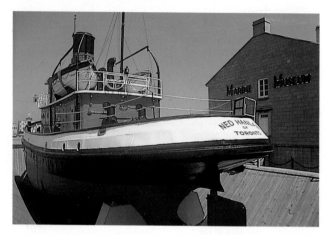

demonstrate domestic chores in the restored Victorian kitchen. Afternoon tea is served.
Open: summer: Tuesday to Saturday 09.30–17.00hrs; Sunday and public holidays noon–17.00hrs; winter: Tuesday to Friday 09.30–16.00hrs, Saturday, Sunday and public holidays noon–17.00hrs.
For information tel: 392 6915.

Summer visitors can go aboard this restored harbour tug, an exhibit at the Marine Museum

◆◆
McLAUGHLIN PLANETARIUM
100 Queen's Park
You sink back in slothful comfort and the universe is yours, along with a laser-beam rock concert, if that is your desire, at this division of the Royal Ontario Museum. Under the 92-foot (28-m) dome 80 projectors and a superb sound system surround you with the starry gleam of the night skies and images of the distant planets, exploding stars, black holes and other phenomena. There's a three-dimensional model of the solar system and a 2,000-year-old sundial as well as computer games to illuminate the mysteries of the heavens. Shows change frequently. Children 6 to 15 must be accompanied by an adult, children under that age not admitted.
Open: daily, all year.
Closed: Monday in winter, Christmas Day, New Year's Day.
For information and show times tel: 586 5736 .

◆
MARINE MUSEUM OF UPPER CANADA
Exhibition Place
The stories of the fur trade and of Great Lakes warships and ferries are told here, along with the history of Toronto's harbour and a look at how the colonies used water transportation for fun and profit. There are superb ship models, too, and in summer, from May to October, visitors

can swarm over a restored 1932 harbour tug named after the 1880 world sculling champion, Toronto's Ned Hanlan. There is a nice little restaurant (The Ship Inn) in the basement that is open for lunch only, and the building itself is interesting. It served as the officers' quarters of Stanley Barracks, circa 1841, and was used as a quarantine station during World War I.

Open: Monday to Saturday, 09.30–17.00hrs; Sundays and holidays, noon–17.00hrs.

Closed: Christmas Day, Boxing Day (26 December), New Year's Day and Good Friday. For information tel: 392 1765.

Tiger at the zoo, where animals roam freely (well, almost) in re-creations of their natural habitats

◆◆◆

METRO TORONTO ZOO ✓

Meadowvale Road, Scarborough Highway 401
Some 710 acres (287 hectares) of woods, pastures and orchards have been transformed into African savannah, Malaysian rainforests, Western prairies and other habitats in this most modern and humane of zoos. The animals came first when the zoo was designed and they roam relatively freely over accurate re-creations of their home turf in outdoor reserves that mimic the terrains and even some artefacts (a Mayan temple, for example) of Africa, Australia, Eurasia, Indo-Malaya and the Americas. Meanwhile, in huge pavilions, climate control offers weather that is ideal for such diverse creatures as orangutans, kooka-burras, beavers and alligators. There's a silent electric monorail train with air conditioning to take you where the deer and the

antelope play, a Zoomobile for a longer overview, four walking trails for the energetic (though some spots in the zoo are reachable only by train) and what was until recently the biggest McDonald's in the world to sustain you (though a picnic lunch would also fill the gap). Cross-country ski tours amid the animals are a winter extra.

Open: daily (except Christmas) 09.30–16.30hrs in winter, 09.00–19.30hrs in summer. Easiest to reach by rental or private car but accessible on public transit with a long bus ride. For information tel: 392 5900.

◆
MONTGOMERY'S INN

4709 Dundas Street West at Islington Avenue
A handsome example of United Empire Loyalist or Late Georgian architecture, this

14-room inn has been restored to its appearance during its heyday in the late 1840s when it was a centre of social life for the country around. Built in 1830 by Irish immigrant and militia captain Thomas Montgomery, it is not to be confused with the Yonge Street tavern of John Montgomery, which also flourished in the 1830s and was a meeting place for William Lyon Mackenzie's rebels of 1837. Costumed staff demonstrate the crafts and the cooking methods of the time.
Open: Tuesday to Friday 09.30–16.30hrs; weekends 13.00–17.00hrs.
Closed: Monday, Christmas Eve and Christmas Day, New Year's Day and Good Friday.
For information tel: 394 8113.

◆◆◆
MUSEUM OF THE HISTORY OF MEDICINE
288 Bloor Street West
Everything from an Egyptian mummy to a Victorian baby's bottle can be found in the four small rooms of artefacts and exhibits that constitute Canada's major medical history museum. The mummy was autopsied in Toronto 14 years ago (no single cause of death was found) and is part of a display on that procedure. The bottle is part of the Drake paediatric collection of feeding objects, which dates from ancient times to 19th-century Europe. Scores of other exhibits illustrate 3,000 years of health care. Fascinating.
Open: Monday to Friday, 09.30–16.00hrs. No admission charge for individuals.
For information tel: 922 0564.

◆◆◆
ONTARIO PLACE
955 Lakeshore Boulevard West at Exhibition Place
Built on and over the waters of Lake Ontario, this 96-acre (39-hectare) amusement park of steel and glass 'pods' looks like a set for a futuristic movie but offers very down-to-earth entertainment, everything from beer gardens and children's water games (take bathing suits) to a six-storey, wrap-around IMAX Cinesphere theatre, an open-air amphitheatre with big name entertainment (free with general admission) and a World War II destroyer, HMCS *Haida*. Can't be beaten on a warm summer afternoon or evening.
Open: mid-May to early September, Monday to Sunday 10.30hrs–midnight.
For information tel: 314 9811 or 314 9900 (recorded message).

◆◆◆
ONTARIO SCIENCE CENTRE

770 Don Mills Road at Eglinton Avenue East
A wonderland of hands-on science as entertaining as it is instructive. Touch, feel, manipulate, experiment, play… and learn. Among hundreds of other intriguing things, chat with a computer, guide a module to a landing on the moon, handle enough electricity to stand your hair on end (50,000 volts), hear a whisper, though not necessarily a romantic one, across a crowded room, run a television camera or appear on screen. Children are fascinated but so are adults. Plan for a visit of at least four

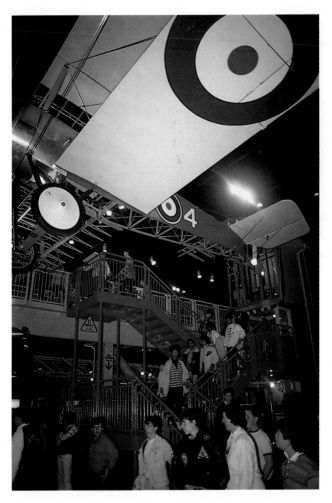

With all its 'hands-on' exhibits, the Ontario Science Centre is one of Toronto's most fascinating and instructive attractions

hours and use the map you are given on admission to make the best use of your time.

Open: Saturday to Thursday 10.00–18.00hrs; Friday 10.00–21.00hrs.
Closed: Christmas Day only. For information and extended summer hours tel: 429 4100 (switchboard), or 696 3127 (recorded info).

◆◆◆
PROVINCIAL PARLIAMENT BUILDINGS

Queen's Park Crescent
Built to look governmental and imposing in the late 1800s, these pink sandstone and marble buildings sit magisterially at the top of University Avenue in grassy, tree-shaded Queen's Park, a name often applied to the buildings themselves. The corridors and rooms are large and airy and the Legislative Assembly chamber on the second floor is suitably formal. There are tours during business hours and visitors may attend sittings of the House (free tickets are necessary) when the 125-member assembly is in session (roughly October to December, February to June). The best time is usually the Question Period, from 14.00 to 15.00hrs, when the opposition parties get a chance to attack the government on matters of current import.
For information tel: 325 7500.

Provincial Parliament Buildings, home of the Legislative Assembly, Romanesque and suitably imposing

◆◆◆
ROYAL ONTARIO MUSEUM ✓

100 Queen's Park, Avenue Road and Bloor Street
One of the world's few major museums to combine art, science and archaeology, it is famous for its Ming tomb (the only one in the Western world), its general Chinese collection (the finest outside China) and its dinosaur skeletons, West Coast and Plains Indians displays and Egyptian relics, among many things. Visit the mastodon, stegosaurus and other giants in their prehistoric jungles, plumb the dark recesses of the Bat Cave, where special effects bring thousands of the little creatures to life, cringe from the real and very lively tarantulas, scorpions and giant hissing cockroaches in the Life Sciences

gallery, or ponder the meaning of life in the new Gallery of Evolution – amid the mummies of those who sought eternity so long ago on the banks of the Nile. One could spend a day or a week or a month among the fascinating items in the main building without even glancing toward the three other nearby divisions of the museum (listed separately), the McLaughlin Planetarium, the Sigmund Samuel Building (Canadiana) and the George R Gardiner Museum of Ceramic Art.
Open: summer: Monday, Wednesday, Friday and Saturday 10.00–18.00hrs; Tuesday and Thursday 10.00–20.00hrs; Sunday 11.00–18.00hrs; winter: Tuesday 10.00–20.00hrs; Wednesday to Saturday 10.00–18.00hrs; Sunday 11.00–18.00hrs.
Closed: Monday in winter.
For information tel: 586 5549.

◆◆
SIGMUND SAMUEL BUILDING
14 Queen's Park West
The scope and skill of Canada's pioneer craftsmen is on display at this division of the Royal Ontario Museum, a haven for antique buffs and lovers of beauty. Period room settings, showcasing the finest in early Canadian silver, glass and woodenware, are a major attraction, but so are the antique toys, weathervanes, farming implements, household tools and cooking utensils. On show, too, are paintings, pottery and

Dinosaur skeletons in their prehistoric jungle setting at the Royal Ontario Museum

sculpture by such artists as Cornelius Krieghoff, William Eby, Thomas Nesbitt and Louis Jobin and a magnificent set of miniature models of pioneer artefacts made early this century by a craftsman born before Confederation (1867).
Open: Monday to Saturday, 10.00–17.00hrs; Sunday 13.00–17.00hrs.
Closed: Christmas and New Year's Day.
For information tel: 586 5540.

◆◆◆
SKYDOME ✓

1 Blue Jays Way
Among the newest attractions in the city, this 8-acre (3.25-hectare), multi-million-dollar sports dome in the heart of downtown Toronto was opened in 1989. A retractable roof 282 feet (86m) above the playing field, high enough to put a 31-storey building underneath, rolls back on sunny days to let baseball and football fans and concert-goers enjoy the outdoors, rolls shut in stormy weather. The figures are staggering: it holds 52,000 for baseball, 54,000 for football, 65,000 for concerts, has 24 fast food outlets, including four McDonald's (one of the largest in North America), and contains a 364-room hotel (with 70 rooms overlooking the field), a health club, a theatre, games booths and a $13 million television studio. As well, the giant central video display board for replays and messages, called, fittingly, a Jumbotron, measures 115 feet (35m) by 33 feet (10m). The Dome is the home of Toronto's

major league baseball team, the Blue Jays, and the Toronto Argonauts of the Canadian Football League, but can be used for a variety of sports, concerts and exhibitions. Prices for games and concerts vary with the event (check local newspapers for details) but there are tours at fixed prices.
For information tel: 341 3663 or 341 2770 for tourist information (tours daily in summer 10.00–18.00hrs).

◆
SPADINA

285 Spadina Road beside Casa Loma
Complete with gaslight and original furnishings, this 1866 mansion sits in six acres (2.5 hectares) of parkland and garden and reflects the elegant world of Toronto high society at

Spadina House, whose furnishings reflect the life of four generations of the Austin family

the turn of the century. Four generations of the Austin family lived in the home and the furniture, art and decorations reflect the changing times, with Victorian, Edwardian and art nouveau influences.

Guides introduce visitors to the upstairs/downstairs life of the Austins, their children and the domestic staff. The garden, one of Toronto's finest, offers more then 300 varieties of plants in an original setting. The house, incidentally, is pronounced 'Spa-DEE-na' though the street is pronounced 'Spa-DIE-na'.

Open: summer: Monday to Saturday 09.30–17.00hrs; Sunday and holidays noon–17.00hrs; winter: Tuesday to Friday 09.30–16.00hrs; Saturday to Sunday and public holidays noon–17.00hrs.

Closed: Christmas Day, Boxing Day (26 December), New Year's Day and Good Friday. For information tel: 392 6910.

◆◆
TOMMY THOMPSON PARK
Leslie Street

A place for birdwatchers and nature lovers. This vast, and growing, landfill project once known as the Leslie Street Spit has become a paradise for birds and for people who want to escape the high-rise city except as a view across the bay. Ironically, it is that very city that keeps the 3-mile (5-km) spit growing now that harbour traffic has diminished and a breakwater is not as necessary. Rock and earth from the sites of the new skyscrapers still has to be put somewhere and the spit is the place. But it serves a good purpose since the park has become home to the largest gull population on the Great Lakes as well as a sanctuary for egrets, geese, ducks, herons, terns and hundreds of smaller birds. Closed weekdays, the park can be reached at weekends by taking the Queen Street

The striking architecture of the City Hall environs is reflected in the pool of Nathan Phillips Square

streetcar to Leslie Street and walking south or, on Sundays, by taking a bus from there that travels the length of the spit every 20 minutes. Other than that vehicle (and the trucks full of fill) admission is restricted to pedestrians and cyclists.

◆◆
TORONTO CITY HALL
100 Queen Street West at Bay Street
A marvel of modern architecture when completed after years of acrimony in 1965, the building, with twin towers cupping an oyster-shaped council chamber, is still eye-catching, though its efficiency as a workplace is somewhat less admired. Nathan Phillips Square, which fronts it, hosts sunbathers, demonstrators, rock concerts, brass bands, picnickers and people-watchers in summer, and skaters on the frozen waters of the reflecting pool in winter. British sculptor Henry Moore's monumental work *The Archer* presides, weathering down the years. There are free tours weekdays, none on holidays.
For information tel: 392 7341.

◆◆◆
TORONTO ISLANDS
across the harbour
Another waterfront attraction that may just be the best because so much of it was contributed by nature, not man. The six islands, which stretch in an arc across the waterfront to form the harbour, are reached on Metro Parks Department ferries which leave from a dock south of the Westin Harbour Castle Hotel at the end of Yonge Street (but note that the dock is reached via walkways at the west side of the hotel, near the end of Bay Street). Avoid the trip on summer weekends when the islands are thick with people; but on weekdays they offer cool breezes and a bucolic retreat for lazing, sunning and picnicking.

The Toronto Islands make a cool retreat across the harbour, with plenty of activities on offer

There are beaches and swimming but the lake water is cool to the uninitiated and sometimes polluted (signs will warn visitors if it is). Shady lagoons and canals wind hither and yon and at Centre Island you can rent paddleboats and canoes to explore their lengths. Or you can rent a bicycle for a leisurely tour of the parkland. Food is available and there is a small, 14-acre (5.5-hectare) amusement area called Centreville, which is modelled on a turn-of-the-century village. There is an admission fee and it has 15 rides, games, arcades, miniature golf and a small petting farm for children. In winter the ferry service is less frequent but available for cross-country skiers or well-bundled walkers. Fares are minimal but changeable. Contact the Parks Department tel: 392 8193 for times and fares or tel: 203 0405 for Centreville information.

◆◆
TOUR OF THE UNIVERSE
Base of the CN Tower
A trip to the year 2019 and a spaceship flight to Jupiter played absolutely straight, with a 3-D boarding pass, check-points, customs, immigration and health controls, inoculations (by painless – and harmless – light beams), seat belts and a 70mm-wide-screen simulation of flight that can have you gripping the armrest. Rated among the top 10 rides in North America (though it is not technically a ride), it is all superbly done with the finishing touch being the deadly serious way in which it is all handled. You may think it is a game but they play it for real, which adds greatly to the effect. Journeys last approximately one hour.
Open: all year, with summer hours 10.00–22.00hrs and winter hours varying. Earthlings 12 years of age or under must be over 3 feet (1m) tall to make the voyage.
For information tel: 868 6937.

Excursions from Toronto

There are multitudes of day trips and weekend jaunts one can make out of Toronto, to Old Fort Henry at Kingston or the beaches or ski slopes of Georgian Bay, to a hundred villages or beauty spots for such things as fall fairs, maple sugar or autumn colour. The city sits just south of a vast cottage country and just north of the US border, so there are attractions in every direction. But four top the list by a considerable margin, one for its sheer magnificence and power, one for its period charm and the other two for their artistry.

◆◆◆
NIAGARA FALLS ✓

Just 90 miles (145km) away around Lake Ontario, one of the natural wonders of the world thunders away the years carrying 34½ million gallons (157 million litres) of water a minute over Canada's Horseshoe Falls in an awesome display of raw power. It is the major falls at the site, 177 feet (54m) high and carrying 90 per cent of the water (the others are Rainbow Falls on the US side of the border and Bridal Veil Falls), and it is magnificent, no matter the viewpoint or the season. You can look down at it from towers, go behind its downfall, approach it from below in what seems a very tiny boat or simply stand by the brink mesmerised by the sight and the sound. If the weather is pleasant get some idea of the scale first by taking a walk of just under a mile (1.5km) along

The American Rainbow Falls thunder into the Niagara River

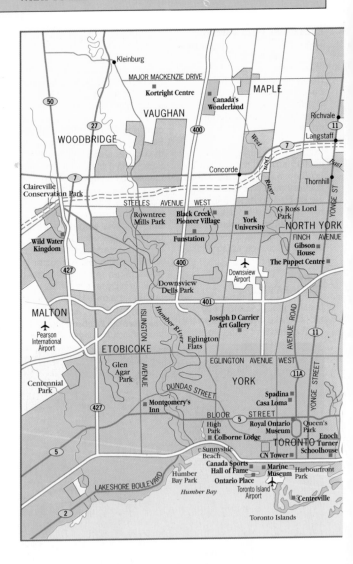

Kleinburg

MAJOR MACKENZIE DRIVE

Kortright Centre

Canada's Wonderland

MAPLE

Richvale

VAUGHAN

WOODBRIDGE

Langstaff

West Don River

Concorde

Claireville Conservation Park

Thornhill

Yonge St

East Don River

STEELES AVENUE WEST

Rowntree Mills Park

Black Creek Pioneer Village

York University

G Ross Lord Park

NORTH YORK

Wild Water Kingdom

Funstation

FINCH AVENUE

Gibson House

The Puppet Centre

Downsview Airport

Downsview Dells Park

MALTON

Pearson International Airport

Joseph D Carrier Art Gallery

Humber River

Eglington Flats

AVENUE ROAD

ETOBICOKE

EGLINGTON AVENUE WEST

Glen Agar Park

ISLINGTON

AVENUE

YORK

11A

YONGE STREET

Centennial Park

DUNDAS STREET

Spadina

Casa Loma

Montgomery's Inn

BLOOR

STREET

High Park

Royal Ontario Museum

Queen's Park

Sunnyside Beach

Colborne Lodge

TORONTO

Enoch Turner Schoolhouse

Canada Sports Hall of Fame

CN Tower

Marine Museum

Harbourfront Park

Humber Bay Park

Ontario Place

Toronto Island Airport

Centreville

LAKESHORE BOULEVARD

Humber Bay

Toronto Islands

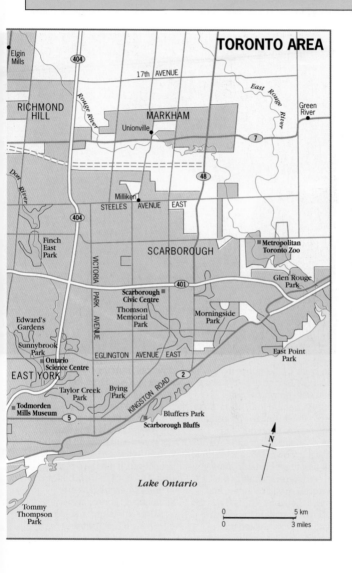

TORONTO AREA

Elgin Mills

17th AVENUE

East Rouge River

Green River

RICHMOND HILL

Rouge River

MARKHAM

Unionville

Don River

48

Milliken

STEELES AVENUE EAST

Finch East Park

VICTORIA PARK AVENUE

SCARBOROUGH

Metropolitan Toronto Zoo

Glen Rouge Park

401

Scarborough Civic Centre

Thomson Memorial Park

Morningside Park

Edward's Gardens

Sunnybrook Park

Ontario Science Centre

EGLINGTON AVENUE EAST

East Point Park

EAST YORK

Taylor Creek Park

Bying Park

KINGSTON ROAD

2

Todmorden Mills Museum

5

Bluffers Park

Scarborough Bluffs

N

Lake Ontario

Tommy Thompson Park

0   5 km
0   3 miles

the brink of the gorge from Rainbow Bridge to Table Rock, then gain entrance to the tunnels behind the falls through Table Rock House. For a small fee you are fitted out with raincoat and boots and take an elevator down 125 feet (38m) to the first tunnel, which offers you three different views of the incredible wall of water. And wall is the word. Curtain has too frail a connotation to describe that battering, deafening downpour. Get another close-up view of the falls aboard the *Maid of the Mist*, which you will find at the end of a well-signed trail down the gorge. Again you pay a small fee and don rain gear, but this time you see the downfall from the front, bobbing about like a cork on the surging waters (it operates from mid-May to late October).

Views from the look-out towers are scenic enough but they do not give you the vision of brute power you get, deafened and drenched, at the base of the falls. The towers are a better bet at night when the falls are illuminated (approximately 21.00hrs–midnight in summer, 19.00–22.00hrs in winter). In addition, in winter, when ice formations and frozen spray can create a fairyland effect, citizens join the Niagara Parks Commission, hotels and businesses in creating a Christmas-time effect with

Horseshoe falls illuminated: the best time to view Niagara Falls from a tower is at night

◆◆◆
NIAGARA-ON-THE-LAKE

Best known these days as the home of the world's only annual Shaw Festival, this little town of some 13,000 on the shores of Lake Ontario was once the capital of Upper Canada (1791–6). It lost that title – and the legislature – to the upstart Fort York, because the authorities said it was too close to the US border. And, for once the authorities were right. In 1813 the Americans came in and burned the place to the ground. However, the gracious 19th-century homes that arose from the ashes of Newark, as it was then called, are with us yet and lend the town its special appeal. It is small enough to explore on foot and one of the joys of a visit is a stroll through the old section and along Queen Street. There one finds gift and antique shops, tea rooms and ice cream parlours, all with a carefully studied old-fashioned air, which comes to its fullest flower in the Niagara Apothecary museum with its graceful 1866 bottles and beautifully labelled 19th-century jars. An ideal plan is to arrive early for the theatre and spend some time strolling through the town, then enjoy a picnic by the water or a dinner at one of the local hostelries. Accommodation tends to have an old-fashioned air, as well, with bed & breakfast establishments and several inns doing a roaring business in the summer theatrical season. The festival,

thousands of coloured bulbs in a three-month (mid-November to mid-February) Festival of Lights. The town of Niagara Falls itself is very commercial but the falls, on Niagara Parks Commission land, make up for any gaudiness. The Parks Commission, incidentally, owns land right along the 35-mile (56-km) length of border and its gardens are famous. They are well worth a drive, say while on the way from Niagara Falls to Niagara-on-the-Lake. The falls can be reached from Toronto by car on the Queen Elizabeth Way, by bus, by special coach tours (Gray Coach Lines tel: 393 7911) and by train (VIA Rail tel: 366 8411).

which began as a low-key tribute to Shaw in 1962, now presents a full May-to-October season devoted to the witty iconoclast and his contemporaries, with no less than three theatres on the go. For tourist information tel: 1-468 4263 (there's a charge from Toronto) and for festival information tel: 361 1544 (toll free) from Toronto. Niagara-on-the-Lake is 80 miles (130km) from Toronto and can be reached by car using the Queen Elizabeth Way or by Gray Coach.

◆◆◆
McMICHAEL CANADIAN COLLECTION
Kleinburg
The Group of Seven, formed by that number of artists back in 1920, captured Canada on canvas with a realism that caught the eyes of the world. This is one of the great collections of the group's work, but alongside it there is also an important collection of works by other Canadians such as Emily Carr and Clarence Cagnon and Indian and Inuit art and sculpture. The whole is magnificent and the setting, over-looking the beautiful Humber River valley, is unbeatable.
Open: 1 May to 31 October, daily 10.00–17.00hrs; 1 November to 30 April, Tuesday to Sunday, 10.00–16.00hrs. About an hour north of Toronto by car using Highway 400. For information tel: 1-893 1121.

◆◆◆
STRATFORD
Stratford as the home of William Shakespeare is a familiar concept, and in this little community 98 miles (157km) west of Toronto that tie is perpetuated, even though the original Stratford-upon-Avon lies several thousand miles to the east. More than 150 years ago citizens of what was then a tiny hamlet renamed the Little Thames River the Avon and set about cultivating a relationship with the Bard based on nothing more than a name. But in 1953, when the Stratford Festival was born with Alec Guinness playing Richard III upon a makeshift stage under a tent, the link was completed. Today Stratford offers one of the Ontario's great cultural experiences, presenting not just Shakespeare and other works in the Festival Theatre but every form of theatre and music, ranging from folk songs to opera in the Avon Theatre and Third Stage and in privately owned theatres. It attracts stars from around the globe and patrons from just as far away.
There are 172 acres (70 hectares) of parkland along the Avon and 19th-century public buildings and homes to admire and, best of all, there is a sense of peace, a calm, unhurried pace that fits in well with Shakespeare. The season is May through October. Tourist information can be obtained from the Stratford Visitors bureau tel: 519/271 5140 (long distance from Toronto) and festival information by calling a Toronto number, tel: 373 4471. Stratford can be reached by car from Toronto using Highway 401 west or by train (VIA Rail) or bus (Gray Coach Lines).

PEACE AND QUIET

Wildlife and Countryside in and around Toronto
by Paul Sterry

Toronto lies on the shores of Lake Ontario and within easy reach of extensive areas of forest in southern Ontario. This makes it an ideal centre for visitors who appreciate scenery and natural history, the lake itself attracting wildfowl, waders and gulls in large numbers and woodlands harbouring varied mammals, birds and plants. The further away from Toronto you travel, the more natural is the landscape with many of the forests further north relatively unspoilt. The wildlife around the city itself is representative of the region as a whole. A wide variety of insects abound in the forests, as do woodland birds such as woodpeckers, warblers, hawks and flycatchers. Large mammals are often seen: deer, moose and bear are common and in Algonquin Provincial Park are especially confiding.

Gentle giant. Although formidable to look at, the moose is actually a shy vegetarian

PEACE AND QUIET

From a botanical point of view, the forest floors are a delight, being rich in mosses, ferns and orchids. For a few days in the autumn, the burnished leaves are a memorable sight and when they fall they create a patchwork of shades which vie, in terms of colour, with fungi of all shapes and sizes.

Toronto and Lake Ontario

Stretching south from the waterfront of Toronto, Lake Ontario disappears into the distance like a huge, inland sea and, to add to the maritime effect, many of the birds that it harbours would be equally at home on the eastern seaboard of North America. Terns and gulls breed on some of the remote headlands and islands while in winter, vast numbers of waterbirds dot the surface of its waters.

Harbours and beaches play host to mixed flocks of herring gulls and ring-billed gulls, the former being the more numerous of the two. Although superficially similar, ring-billed gulls can be identified by their slightly smaller size, the pale eye with a dark 'eyebrow' and the 'ringed' bill. From autumn to spring, a variety of more unusual species sometimes joins these flocks and careful scrutiny could reveal glaucous, Iceland, Franklin's or Bonaparte's gulls in among the larger birds. Autumn and winter are the seasons for the wildfowl which congregate around the shores of the lake and tens of thousands of birds are often recorded in a season. From the Toronto Islands and lake-shores to the east of the city, vast rafts of birds

can be seen. Numbers are often under-estimated since bobbing and diving birds are difficult to count and it is often only when flocks take to the wing that a true idea of the numbers involved can be obtained.

Canada geese mingle with scaup, bufflehead and long-tailed ducks, and many other species are also seen during spring and autumn migration. By late winter, most of the male ducks have acquired their breeding plumage and often display to each other in separate-species flocks. In among the ducks, double-crested cormorants sometimes swim and dive for fish and lucky observers may see great northern divers (common loons) resplendent in their black and white summer plumage.

In most years, the level of Lake Ontario drops slightly by late

*Named for their native homeland –
Canada geese and goslings*

summer and even a slight drop
exposes beaches along its
shoreline. These are much
favoured by migrant waders
which pass through in vast
numbers from late July to
October. Semipalmated
sandpipers, dunlin, lesser
yellowlegs and least sandpipers
are all abundant in suitable
habitats and identifying them can
prove a stimulating challenge.

Marshes and Pools
Wetland habitats abound in
southern Ontario and provide an
endless source of fascination for
anyone with an interest in natural
history. Birds and mammals
patrol the pool margins and open
water, many species feeding on
fish and amphibians. These in
turn prey upon aquatic larvae of

the biting insects that can make
the visitor's life a misery during
the summer months.
Open marshes with sedges and
rushes are found beside river
courses and much of the forest
is also decidedly wet underfoot.
Alder woodland, in particular, is
often swampy and pools of open
water are not uncommon, thus
providing ideal habitats for
American toads and gray
treefrogs, which spend much of
their lives on land but have to
return to the water to spawn.
Whether in water or land, the
marshes' smaller inhabitants
have to be constantly vigilant
since green herons, great blue
herons and American bitterns
are ever alert for a meal. The
latter species, with its mottled
and streaked brown plumage,
shows remarkable camouflage
as it creeps stealthily through
the vegetation. The instant that it

PEACE AND QUIET

spots a meal, however, this apparent lethargy disappears and a lightning strike secures the victim.

American woodcock and sora rails skulk around the margins of ponds and lakes, which are often fringed with reed-mace (cat-tail), searching the muddy margins for insects, snails and other invertebrates. Blue-winged teal and the most elegant of wildfowl, the wood duck, keep close to cover while, in the open water, pied-billed grebes swim and dive and belted kingfishers and ospreys plunge from overhead perches.

Muskrats
There are mammals to be seen in Toronto's marshy habitats and conical heaps of vegetation built in the shallows are a sure sign of the presence of muskrats, endearing rodents which build their homes out of reach of land predators. They are often seen swimming across the water to reach them and can be identified by their long, naked tails which are laterally flattened. The muskrat's diet is largely plant material but by contrast mink are strictly carnivorous. Rather shy animals, they are competent swimmers and somewhat similar to, although smaller than, the river otters with which they coexist.

Algonquin Provincial Park
Lying less than 220 miles (350km) north of Toronto, Algonquin Provincial Park is a vast area of Canadian wilderness. Its 3,000 square miles (7,700sq km) comprise lakes, rivers, marshes, rocky outcrops and extensive forests containing both deciduous and coniferous tree species. The wide variety of Algonquin's trees is due to its position at the geographical divide between the coniferous forests, which dominate northern Canada, and the mixed woodlands of the Great Lakes region. This diversity has encouraged a wonderful range of other plants and animals to the park, many of which are more characteristic of sub-arctic environments.

Despite its great size, Algonquin is still accessible to both the casual visitor and the intrepid explorer. Between Huntsville and Whitney, Highway 60

traverses the southern tip of the park and from here and the forest tracks and side roads, there is plenty to be seen. Well-informed rangers at the Park Museum will advise you on the best spots on a day-to-day basis and should also be consulted if you wish to venture further into the wilderness. Facilitating this, a network of hiking trails and over 620 miles (1,000km) of canoe routes allow further exploration and designated campgrounds and lodges afford overnight stays.

Some of Canada's finest wilderness areas are to be found within Algonquin Provincial Park

Around the margins of lakes on which great northern divers (common loons) and ospreys fish, grow woodlands of maple, birch, cherry, balsam and spruce. Warblers and red-eyed vireos forage among the foliage for insects, while in moss-covered glades and clearings, orchids, and plants of Labrador tea and leather-leaf grow in profusion. Algonquin is perhaps most famous for the variety and the often confiding nature of its mammals. Beaver, white-tailed deer, moose, black bear and red fox are common and frequently seen, but it is the park's timber wolves which are most renowned. During the late

summer and autumn, their howls are a familiar sound as family parties gather together before the onset of winter. Visitors have little to fear from these impressive predators because, despite their reputation, much of their diet is fruit, carrion and small mammals and birds. It is only in the dead of winter that large packs form to hunt down quarry as large as deer or moose.

The Wildlife of Algonquin Provincial Park

Although the short-term visitor to Algonquin cannot fail to be impressed by its scenery and wildlife, a longer stay will yield a far greater variety of plants and animals. By exploring the forest trails at length, the visitor will come across more retiring creatures and have time to observe some of their more intriguing activities.

Larger lakes are often grazed by moose. These huge beasts, males of which have immense

Beavers

The signs and handiwork of beavers are conspicuous throughout the park. These industrious rodents, which may weigh as much as 55lbs (25kg), build dams which flood considerable areas of woodland and, surrounded by water, the beavers construct their 'lodge'. Built of twigs and mud, their home is only accessible from beneath the water's surface, making it invulnerable to attack from many predators. Bark and twigs of aspen, birch and maple are their favourite food and they sometimes fell whole trees to serve as a winter larder.

Beavers will sometimes fell a whole tree for winter food

sets of antlers for most of the year, are especially fond of plants growing under the water's surface. Moose have long legs and can swim extremely well, so that during the height of summer, when biting insects are at their most troublesome, they spend much of the day almost completely submerged. Sometimes the only sign of their presence is a nose, ears and antlers. Many of Algonquin's other inhabitants are more inconspicuous but, fortunately, most of the birds can be located by their calls or songs, which to the trained ear are readily distinguishable. Some of the forest dwellers, however, do not give any clues as to their whereabouts and must be located by persistent observation or luck.

The spruce grouse is just such a creature: neither shy nor afraid of man, this remarkable bird knows exactly where to sit in the undergrowth to get the best effect from its mottled plumage. In dappled light it is almost invisible among the tangle of fallen leaves and twigs and to enhance its camouflage, it also shows great reluctance to move. Once it has been found the bird allows a close approach and to be able to sit quietly and watch a spruce grouse close-to is a memorable experience.

The Forests of Ontario

Canada is renowned for its forests and despite the activities of large-scale commercial foresters, much of the country is still cloaked by trees. Even within the boundaries of Toronto, Morningside Park and James Gardens hold interesting, semi-natural woodland and within a short distance of the city, fascinating tracts of forest can still be found harbouring a wealth of plant and animal life. The forests of Ontario are strikingly different according to their position within the state. Those immediately around Toronto are largely a mixture of deciduous trees (those whose leaves fall in the autumn) with a smaller proportion of conifers, which generally retain their leaves throughout the year. However, as you travel north in the state, the proportions change and conifers predominate with black spruce, white spruce, larch and jack pine being among the commonest species.

The reason for this change in forest type is the latitude and climate of the land past and present. At the time of the last Ice Age, much of Canada lay under a blanket of ice which excluded vegetation almost completely, but as the ice retreated northwards, hardy plants began to colonise this new landscape of pools and marshes. The first to do so were the larches, spruces and birches which now comprise the boreal forests, but as the climate warmed up further south these species were replaced by the less hardy trees such as maple, red oak and oak which reach the northern limit of their ranges.

The air is often filled with the scent of pines, and as a testament to its clarity, lichens, which are especially sensitive to pollution, festoon the trees. Red squirrels chatter noisily and scamper among the branches, pausing to nibble the seeds from fir cones, their dexterous hands assisting them greatly in this process. Black bears forage on the ground for berries, fruits and small mammals, while in the foliage above, warblers and flycatchers hunt for insects among the lichens and leaves. Woodpeckers, such as the northern flicker, bore holes in the trunks and branches in search of wood-boring insect larvae, especially where the tree is dead. On the other hand, the delightfully named yellow-bellied sapsucker, often drills into living wood, causing the sap to run.

Forest Life

The forests bordering the Great Lakes contain a rich variety of trees and the leaves of the deciduous species which predominate produce stunning colours for a few autumn days prior to their being shed. During the spring and summer, the woods are full of new life, but the falling leaves forecast the onset of winter when food is most difficult to come by and survival is the name of the game.

The wildlife of the woodland has adapted to these seasonal changes in a variety of ways.

A chipmunk searching for insect food in tree bark

For example, although some birds can endure the harsh winters, many migrate south to more temperate regions. Most reptiles, amphibians and insects survive in a state of dormancy and mammals, too, have had to adapt in order to survive the hardships of the biting Canadian winters.

White-tailed deer have little option but to persevere until the ice and snow relinquish their grip on the land, their thicker winter coats giving them added insulation. Beavers, on the other hand, retreat to their snug lodges around which they have already built up a large supply of winter rations. Other mammals, such as the charming eastern chipmunk, build up their own fat reserves and hibernate through the worst of the weather. Come the spring, with its promise of bountiful food supplies, the chipmunks soon wake up and make up for lost time and energy reserves.

April and May sees the arrival of returning migrant birds whose songs add to those of the resident species. Each songster is advertising his presence within a territory and trying to lure a mate. If successful, a nest is built with different species occupying sites from the forest floor to the tree canopy.

By May and June, plant life burgeons in the woods and this encourages a wide range of herbivorous insects such as caterpillars. The fate of many of these is to feed the hungry mouths of young birds, but there are sufficient survivors to give rise to colourful butterflies such as spice-bush

swallowtails, mourning cloaks, fritillaries and skippers.

Moths are also abundant but hide by day among fallen leaves or on tree bark. After dark, they are often attracted to car headlights or outside lamps, and many species, such as hawk moths, are surprisingly large. These too are preyed upon and form the diet of a variety of nocturnal animals such as bats and the common nighthawk.

Toronto's Warblers

During the harsh Canadian winters, the forests of southern Ontario, although stately in their mantle of snow and ice, are comparatively silent: those creatures that have not hibernated or moved south for the winter are quietly and busily engaged in the search for food. In the springtime, however, the woods come alive with bird song and this joyful sound helps rejuvenate the life of the forest. Many of the songsters are warblers, of which at least ten species regularly breed within a short distance of Toronto. A further 10 species breed more locally in Ontario and several more, such as Cape May warbler, palm warbler and Nashville warbler, pass through on passage. In fact, on a good day during spring migration, it is quite possible to see more than half the number of species which breed in the whole of North America, and on top of this there will be vireos and flycatchers to look at.

Some warblers, such as the yellow warbler, black-and-white warbler and chestnut-sided warbler, prefer the deciduous

PEACE AND QUIET

This yellow warbler is one of at least 20 species of warbler that might be seen around Toronto

woodlands which border the Great Lakes, while other species, like the Canada warbler and Blackburnian warbler, haunt the coniferous woodlands so typical of northern Canada. Since Algonquin Provincial Park harbours a good mixture of both forest types, it is a particularly rewarding spot to search. Some of the species found here have somewhat misleading names: despite their titles, ovenbirds, which resemble miniature thrushes, and American redstarts both belong to the family of North American wood warblers. Spring is a particularly rewarding time of year to look for warblers because the males of most species will be singing and even migrant birds on passage join in the chorus. Although by July and August, most birds will have finished breeding and, therefore, singing too, the numbers of birds make

up for this because both adult and juvenile birds will be present.

By late summer, identifying them can prove a real challenge because of the variation in plumages. In many species, males have a different plumage from females, summer plumage is different from winter and juveniles are different from adults. The end result is that, at this time of year, no two birds ever seem to look exactly alike!

Farmland and Open Country

Toronto and the surrounding countryside of Ontario has been occupied by human beings for centuries and during this time they have had a profound influence upon the environment. The most noticeable effect has been the clearance, in many areas, of the trees which once cloaked the region. Much of this land has been, and still is, used for agriculture, but where the fields have been allowed to revert to the wild, an interesting selection of wildlife can be found and the open terrain makes observation all the more easy. In drier areas, milkweed plants with their umbels of pink flowers are quick to colonise, the leaves becoming food in the summer months for the brightly coloured and poisonous caterpillars of monarch butterflies. Skipper and swallowtail butterflies also visit flowers to feed on the nectar, and grasshoppers and

Spice-bush swallowtail

bush crickets hop among the low vegetation, many falling victim to vigilant eastern kingbirds or ground-hunting eastern garter snakes. After dark, moths take to the wing, many being consumed by common nighthawks, birds with large eyes and gaping mouths which catch insects on the wing. They nest in a simple scrape on the ground where their cryptic

plumage renders them almost invisible as they sit motionless throughout the day. Also nesting on the ground are killdeer, elegant plovers whose name derives from their loud alarm call. Their two black breast bands and conspicuous chestnut rump in flight make them easy to identify.

Overhead, American kestrels and red-tailed hawks patrol the skies scanning the ground for small mammals and birds which scurry into the cover of long grass and low shrubs in which horned larks build their nests. Strikingly marked bobolinks and eastern meadowlarks use low bushes as convenient perches. The latter species also uses these lookouts as song perches, while bobolinks sing in flight over their territory.

By the late summer and autumn, flowers and bushes have started to produce their seeds and fruits, and red berries attract the attentions of ravenous cedar waxwings, unmistakable with their subtle pink plumage and conspicuous crests. Prior to migration, large flocks of red-winged blackbirds and brown-headed cowbirds wheel through the skies, descending like a cloud to the ground to feed.

Buffalo and Niagara

The Niagara Falls are among the most spectacular and widely visited natural wonders of the world and few people can fail to be impressed by their splendour. However, while visiting this world-famous beauty spot, the keen observer can also see a wide variety of

54

waterbirds on the Niagara River, many of which may even be seen from the *Maid in the Mist* boat which travels to the foot of the falls.

The attraction of the Niagara River to the birds that frequent its waters lies partly in its position between Lakes Ontario and Erie and partly in the fact that it seldom freezes over. In addition, migrant landbirds pass through the Niagara peninsula in spring and autumn and add further variety to an already exciting species list.

From the road which runs parallel with the river, huge flocks of gulls can be seen. At all seasons, herring and ring-billed gulls predominate, but at any time of year, apart from the height of summer, small numbers of up to 10 other species may be seen. Glaucous and Iceland gulls are relatively large, white-winged birds and therefore easy to pick out in flight, whereas kittiwakes, Franklin's, Bonaparte's and black-headed gulls stand out because of their smaller size.

On the waters of the river, small numbers of divers and grebes mix with often sizeable flocks of ducks. As on Lake Ontario itself, bufflehead, goldeneye and canvasback are common with many other species occurring in smaller numbers. Long-tailed ducks, often known as 'oldsquaws' on account of their cackling calls, can also be numerous. The drakes have long tail-plumes from which they gain their name and these show up especially well in flight. Like the shores of Lake Ontario to the east of Toronto, those of

Lake Erie to the west of Buffalo are excellent for migrant waders, generally referred to as shorebirds in American books.

During April and May, and from July to October, more than a dozen species can be seen in a single day. Short-billed dowitchers, dunlin, pectoral sandpipers, turnstone and semi-palmated sandpipers abound, the numbers of adult birds being supplemented in autumn by juvenile birds in smart, fresh plumage.

Migration

Toronto's climate is one of extremes: the summers are hot, but in winter the grip of ice and snow can be unremitting. Some animals can tolerate these extremes while others avoid the winter by hibernating or migrating south before the weather changes for the worse. Many of Toronto's passerine birds feed on insects and consequently have to move south in winter in order to feed. Some species move relatively short distances in response to prevailing weather conditions, but others make predictable and annual long-distance migrations covering thousands of miles.

Broad-winged hawks and barn swallows are among those which undertake journeys which may take them as far south as Central and South America. While migrating, these birds often become concentrated in certain areas, and although nowhere around Toronto can compare with Point Pelee in western Ontario, the shores of

The drake's tail feathers make the long-tailed duck unmistakable at all times of the year

Lake Ontario and Long Point, 125 miles (200km) southwest on the shores of Lake Erie, still yield impressive numbers of birds in spring and autumn. In the winter, these same areas can also be good for visitors from the arctic because, surprising as it may seem, to them Toronto's winters are comparatively mild. Glaucous and Iceland gulls are regular migrant visitors and there is a good chance of seeing snowy owls and rough-legged buzzards as well.

Migration in the animal kingdom is not entirely the province of birds. The autumn migration of caribou from arctic Canada south to better feeding grounds is well known, as is the movement of salmon up rivers to their spawning grounds.

Monarch Butterfly
There are few examples of animal travel more remarkable than the journeys of the monarch butterfly which take the species from as far north as the Great Lakes south to Mexico for the winter.
Unlike bird migration, the whole journey of the monarch butterfly is not performed by the same individual.
At the onset of spring, millions of butterflies leave their wintering valley in the Mexican Sierras and fly north, stopping *en route* to mate and lay eggs on milkweed plants. The subsequent generation then continues to journey north and after the process has been repeated several times, monarchs finally reach Toronto. After one brief generation, they embark on the return journey: truly a remarkable feat for such a delicate insect.

Maples

As Canada's national emblem, the maple leaf signifies the importance of the tree both to the country's environment and to its economy. Depending upon the species, the wood may be used for timber, the sap can be used to make maple syrup and maple sugar, and the trees themselves are an integral part of Canada's landscape.

In the woods and forest bordering Lake Ontario up to six species of maple may be found growing. By far the most important of these is the sugar maple. As its name implies, it is this species which is most important as a source of sap, the technique for its extraction

The beginning of the fall – the changing colours of maple leaves in early autumn

having first been perfomed by indigenous Indians. The timber of sugar maple is also important; since it is both hard and strong, it can be used for anything from furniture to veneer.

In the autumn, one of the glories of the deciduous woodlands of southern Canada is the changing colours of the leaves. The colours vary from red to golden yellow depending on the species, and as they cascade on to the woodland floor they create a beautiful mosaic of shape and hue underfoot.

FOOD AND DRINK

Visitors to Toronto will find the same styles in food as they will in any other major city of North America – the basic Anglo-Saxon roast beef, steaks, chops and apple pie, the heritage brought by early settlers overlaid with all the influences of Europe and the rest of the world.

Cuisine which can be identified as definitely Canadian may be less easy to find in Toronto than in other provinces. You can taste the pea soup and *tourtière* of Québec, which found their way west to Ontario long ago, but there are dishes such as the Acadian delicacies of New Brunswick which can only be found in that province. Because Ontario's growing season for fruits and vegetables is relatively short, it depends upon places such as Mexico, Chile and California for its fresh produce in the winter and there is never a shortage of tomatoes and avocados, passion fruit and cauliflower at any time of the year.

But oh, in summer, the glory of the first sweet and tender corn, the huge vine-ripened tomatoes and the slim asparagus stalks when they finally come out of the fields!

And then comes autumn, the true harvest, time of sweet squash and pumpkin pies, turnips and the sharp crunch of crisp apples. Or those same apples in dumplings of pie dough seeped through with maple syrup and cream. There are overweight Canadians and such dumplings are one reason why, though most feel the game is worth the candle.

One of the oldest and best

Fresh fruit – but mostly imported

traditions in Ontario rural communities is the church supper, with ham and scalloped potatoes that are brown and crisp from the oven and platters piled high with corn on the cob, dripping with butter. Apple pie and sharp, well-aged Ontario Cheddar follow … and one could die happy.

You might enjoy such a meal if you have friends in Toronto who invite you to their home, or if you travel extensively through the Ontario countryside, but it is not something easily found in city restaurants.

Barbecued meals, on the other hand, are easily available and in that respect Toronto restaurants mirror the tastes of the average citizen, for Torontonians spend a lot of time at their backyard barbecues in summer. Having waited so long for warm weather they are determined to squeeze every last drop of enjoyment out of it. And in this – and many other respects – they do not differ significantly from their US neighbours.

Tea in Toronto
To a large degree, the Canadian food experience mirrors that of much of the northern United States, although you will be assured of getting a decent cup of tea (poured from a teapot) instead of a cup of lukewarm water and a tea bag on the side. However, it must be admitted that, with the exception of a few of Toronto's elegant hotels, there is no such thing as afternoon tea, unless you drive into the surrounding countryside and hunt down a tearoom.

While most Torontonians would agree that food is expensive, the city is in the midst of a love affair with convenience foods – not simply fast food (although there are all the usual chain operations) but fantastic gourmet ready-to-heat foods sold for equally fantastic prices. Toronto's restaurant menus cover the world, with the cuisine of France and Italy being by far the strongest and the most recent trend coming from California. There is no shortage of domestic beer (which is like German and Dutch beer in strength and taste) nor of imported beer, and there is never a problem in choosing a good bottle of wine to go with your meal. The problem may arise when you go to pay the bill, for mark-ups on wine, first by the government, then by the restaurants, can be horrendous. Unfortunately, you cannot beat the system, for it is illegal to 'brown-bag' it (arrive with your favourite bottle of plonk under your arm) as you can in, say, Sydney or sections of New York city, and, given Ontario's greed for sin taxes, the practice will never be condoned. Happily, an increasing number of places will now let you order by the glass and you can always fall back on a carafe of the house wine.

Eating Out
Interest in food seems to be at an all-time high in Toronto with trendy new restaurants opening every few weeks. That is partly due to the fact that it is a big, still-growing city, with tastes influenced by immigrants, and partly to the fact that like many

North American cities it has a populace that is growing more adventurous in its eating habits. It is no problem to find a restaurant in Toronto. After all, there are more than 5,000 of them. But recommending them can be a problem. New stars can rise quickly, find favour for a little while and wane just as quickly. And in the case of many of the city's new breed of young chefs, by the time you arrive to check out the rave reviews, he or she has decamped to follow a new path. For that reason some new spots have been omitted from the following listings, which concentrate on places that are

Every opportunity is taken to enjoy refreshment al fresco

not only superb in themselves but stand an excellent chance of being still in business when a reader wants a dinner.

(Ideally, one should complement this list with the latest reviews in *Toronto Life* magazine and in two of the major newspapers, *The Toronto Star* and the *Globe & Mail*, whose listings can change by the week as the chefs come and go.)

Most restaurants accept credit cards, but it is wise to make sure they will honour your particular brand (especially in some of the smaller eateries).

The service charge is not included in Toronto and tipping in the region of 15 per cent (before the 8 per cent Ontario sales tax) is appropriate.

FOOD AND DRINK

North American

Bloor Street Diner, 55 Bloor Street West (tel: 928 3105). Well situated for uptown shopping binges, this is high-tech dining with a vengeance. Choice recorded jazz in the background and burgers to match, along with speedy service. Open all week, 11.00–03.00hrs. Moderate prices.

Fred's Not Here, 321 King Street West (tel: 971 9155). Popular with theatregoers, puts an emphasis on smoked or grilled entrées – game, Brome Lake duck and swordfish are a few – prepared and served with aplomb. Imaginative décor and pleasant service but, since it is one of the city's popular eateries, be sure to leave enough time if you are intent on making the opening curtain. Moderate prices.

Hart's, 225 Church Street (tel: 368 5350). Relaxed and casual with good daily specials chalked around the walls at handy intervals. A no-nonsense menu includes pastas, hearty soups, burgers and a first-rate Caesar salad. Friendly staff and always a clutch of regulars at the bar.

Closed on Sundays. Inexpensive.

Metropolis, 838 Yonge Street (tel: 924 4100). One of the few places for the Canadian touch, they're doing inventive things with Oka and St Benoit cheese atop onion and cider soup, wild rice puddings and Huron Country rabbit. And for a taste of Canada, Ontario-style, try the Upper Canada Ale and Creemore Springs Lager. Highly recommended. Closed on Sundays. Inexpensive.

Pickle Barrel, 595 Bay Street at Dundas (tel: 977 6677). This combined restaurant and delicatessen offers all-day breakfasts, tremendous desserts and vast portions of pastas, salads, BBQ and fish specials at keen prices. Chicken dishes and the deli meat plates are especially good value. There is another outlet with similar fare at 151 Front Street West. Inexpensive.

*An Atlantic Canadian dish,
breaded rabbit with rice*

Cafés

Future Bakery & Café, 1535
Yonge Street (tel: 944 1253). A
simple bakery specialising in
European staples has
mushroomed into a small chain
of excellent little cafés supplied
from a central dairy and bakery.
The food is fresh, filling and
innovative, with everything from
coffee and cakes to full-scale
meals with a European flavour.
A hit with everyone from
students to business people,
they make a wonderful place to
while away an hour or so
watching the world go by. Other
branches are located at 95 Front
Street East, St Lawrence Market,
2199 Bloor Street West and 739
Queen Street West. No
reservations. Inexpensive.
Studio Café, Four Seasons
Hotel, 21 Avenue Road (tel: 964

0411). An up-market hotel café
and restaurant, this place offers
a broad range of innovative and
healthy eating options from
across the culinary globe.
Reservations recommended.
Moderate prices.

Continental/International

Bemelmans, 83 Bloor Street
West (tel: 960 0306). With its
polished wood, brass, marble
and glass it is somewhere
between a chophouse and a
private club and although there
is a large and varied menu, it is
the bar scene that is the big
draw. An outdoor patio for the
summer months and civilised
hours for nighthawks. Monday
to Friday: 11.30–03.00hrs,
Saturday: 11.00–03.00hrs.
Sunday: 11.00–midnight.
Inexpensive.
Bistro 990, 990 Bay Street (tel:
921 9990). Across from the
Sutton Place Hotel and close to
the movers and shakers of
Queen's Park, it is basically a
sophisticated bistro, all arches
and terracotta and cathedral
ceiling. Appealing *à la carte*,
with an emphasis on fresh,
simply prepared dishes,
delicate iced soups in summer
and a wealth of good desserts.
There is also a *prix fixe* menu
which will keep you happy
through four courses.
Expensive.
Café Victoria, (King Edward
Hotel) 37 King Street East (tel:
863 9700). Sunday brunch may
never taste this good again. The
board groans with beef
Wellington, lamb, roast pork
and cold turkey. Pâtés and egg
dishes and a profusion of breads
and rolls almost complete the

picture. (Leave room for fresh fruits and cheesecake). The stylish elegance of this grand hotel adds to the enjoyment. Inexpensive.

The Daily Planet, 40 Eglinton Avenue East (tel: 440 0030). Big and casual with a menu to match, it is handily placed for shopping on north Yonge Street and popular for late night snacks after the movies. The Sunday brunch crowd staked it out as a bargain long ago, so get there early to avoid queues. Open until 01.00hrs Monday to Saturday and 11.30–23.00hrs Sunday. Inexpensive.

Duke of York, 39 Prince Arthur Avenue (tel: 964 2441). Well situated for Yorkville's galleries and boutiques, it is a nicely converted house with a chef who likes to surprise the palate. Perhaps a soy and rice vinegar accompaniment to grilled salmon, or a mix of sage and walnuts. Closed on Sundays. Expensive.

Ed's Warehouse Restaurant, 270 King Street West adjacent to the Royal Alexandra Theatre (tel: 593 6676 or 593 6672). When Ed Mirvish does anything he does it with style and verve. Thanks to him the Royal Alex was saved some years ago, and, more recently, he has given new life to London's Old Vic. The Warehouse is pure show biz with 400 Tiffany lamps, 1,300 seats and signed photos of all the greats who have appeared at the Royal Alex over the years and it is chock-a-block with antiques. Prime roast beef and steaks are served and the enjoyment and value cannot be topped. Inexpensive.

Right next door are **Ed's**

Ed's Warehouse – or maybe Ed's Chinese, Ed's Italian, Ed's Seafood or Old Ed's?

Chinese, **Ed's Italian**, **Ed's Seafood** and **Old Ed's** – again, excellent value and good fun. Dress codes have been abandoned (there was a time when no tie meant positively no admittance). No reservations taken unless you happen to be a party of 20 or more. Monday to Saturday: noon–14.00, 17.00–22.00hrs; Sunday: 17.00–21.00hrs. Inexpensive.

Hard Rock Café, 283 Yonge Street (tel: 369 9458). It may not be an original choice of somewhere to eat, but the tried and tested 'Hard Rock' formula is a winning one if you are after burgers, fries and all the trimmings. This was the first 'Hard Rock Café' to open in North America, but has been joined in Toronto by the 'Hard Rock Café–SkyDome, which also offers the standard classic diner menu and a stand-up guitar bar, but has the added

bonus of a tremendous view across the playing field at the Skydome. It is located at Suite 3300, 1, Blue Jays Way (tel: 341-2388). Moderate prices.

Jennie's, 360 Queen Street East (tel: 861 1461). Art deco prints, a cosy atmosphere and a young chef with an inventive mind which dwells sometimes on the Orient. Curried Bombay shrimp and beef teriaki can share the table with delicious garlic cheese bread. Sunday brunch and patio dining in the summer. Moderate prices.

Panama Joe's, 124 Danforth Avenue (tel: 463 0085). Go for lunch if you are in a tropical mood. A live palm, lots of bamboo and Mexican artwork along with some of the best corned beef sandwiches in town, as well as upmarket pastas and calamari. At night the dance crowd hits the scene. Open until 01.00hrs Monday to Saturday. Moderate prices.

Rotterdam, 600 King Street West (tel: 504 6882). Crowded watering hole, noisy, but alive, with a menu featuring beef and chicken along with seafoods and salads. Pick your way through a huge list of beers and consult with friendly servers. Moderate prices.

Scaramouche, 1 Benvenuto Place (tel: 961 8011). It has been the stamping ground of many of Toronto's new breed of young, innovative chefs and its lustre is undimmed. Creative cooking with a French slant and superb desserts, all enjoyed over a spectacular view of the city. Good pasta bar (less expensive) in the adjacent lounge. Closed on Sundays. Very expensive.

FOOD AND DRINK

Senator, 249 Victoria Street (tel: 364 7517). The Senator has been in business since 1948, serving up regular North American-style breakfasts, lunches and dinners in an easy-going setting. For something more formal try the adjoining 'Dining Room', which specialises in steaks and seafood, or drop into the Senator Jazz Club for live jazz six times a week. Moderate prices.

Chinese

Champion House, 478 Dundas Street West (tel: 977 8282). For lovers of the fiery Szechuan style, plus spectacular Peking duck. Large menu and the waiters really hustle. Closed on Tuesdays. Moderate prices.

Lichee Garden, 595 Bay Street (tel: 977 3481). This welcoming Toronto institution has been in business since 1948, and has won a brace of awards for its food and service. These days it is hardly the cheapest Chinese restaurant in town, but is still a reliable favourite among locals and visitors alike. Open daily. Moderate prices.

Pink Pearl, 120 Avenue Road (tel: 966 3631). Uptown chic in the Cantonese manner. Nicely served as befits the

Toronto's Chinatown, the third largest in North America, has more than 100 Chinese restaurants

surroundings. Pick your way through the many *dim sum* offerings after you have broken your bank at the Hazelton Lanes boutiques. Moderate prices.

Sai Woo, 130 Dundas Street West (tel: 977 4988). An institution of Chinatown with a never-ending menu. It was one of the first Chinese restaurants in Toronto and is also one of the most famous. Traditional Cantonese style cooking. Excellent pickerel. Open daily, 11.30–02.30hrs. Inexpensive.

Danish

Danish Food Centre, 101 Bloor Street West (tel: 920 5505). Small, cafeteria-style restaurant with wonderful open-faced sandwiches, salads and pastries. They also do a brisk take-away trade. Inexpensive.

French

Arlequin, 134 Avenue Road (tel: 928 9521). This is an elegant but relaxed restaurant in which to enjoy food with an accent on the south of France. It is also a first-rate stop if you are buying food for a picnic as its succulent pâtés, quiches and unusual salads are available to take away. Attentive service. Closed on Mondays. Moderate prices.

Auberge Gavroche, 90 Avenue Road (tel: 920 0956). The restaurant is in one of the few remaining lovely old houses on this part of the street. The setting is serene and the classic food rarely disappoints. Its menu and that of **l'Entrecôte**, the less expensive upstairs

bistro, can be sampled on the front patio during the summer. Closed on Sundays. Moderate prices.

Le Bistingo, 349 Queen Street West (tel: 598 3490). Exquisite food prepared with a minimum of fuss and accompanied by sauces that show a masterly hand in the kitchen. Top marks for service and a well-deserved reputation. The ambience is thoroughly French, and the walls are dotted with photographs taken by Claude Bouillet, the restaurant's head chef and co-owner. Reservations are advised. Closed on Saturday lunchtime and Sunday. Expensive.

La Bodega, 30 Baldwin Street (tel: 977 1287). The atmosphere is comfortable with lace curtains adding a homey touch, and the restaurant has a regular clientele which has been coming back for years. Splendid entrecôtes, tender lamb and fresh fish as well as a dessert menu with some of the best profiteroles outside France. A short walk from the Art Gallery of Ontario. Closed on Sundays. Moderate prices.

Corner House, 501 Davenport Road (tel: 923 2604). With Casa Loma towering on the rise above, you can set your own scene for a romantic evening. The Victorian house offers five intimate little rooms where you can enjoy food prepared by the chef in the classic manner. Knowledgeable and very personal service. Closed on Sundays. Expensive.

FOOD AND DRINK

La Grenouille, 2837 Yonge Street (tel: 481 3093). A wide selection of regional bistro dishes served by helpful waiters who do not sneer at a less than masterful touch with the French language. Duck and veal and garlicked frogs' legs as well as flavourful tarts and *parfaits*. Closed on Sundays. Inexpensive.

Paramount, 1507 Yonge Street (tel: 923 2300). An uptown Parisienne brasserie with the prerequisite Impressionist prints and fresh flowers. Good fish dishes and excellent steak and *pommes frites*. You will need to get there early for lunch as it is a popular eating place for nearby office workers. Moderate prices.

Le Select Bistro, 328 Queen Street West (tel: 596 6405). It is so tiny they suspend the bread baskets over the tables. It is always crowded and jolly with folk tucking into *moules marinière* or steak and frites. The bistro also has an extensive wine list and serves excellent food that rarely departs from tried and tested French staples. However, the background jazz and classical music may not be to everyone's taste. Moderate prices.

Greek

The Palace, 722 Pape Avenue (tel: 463 3393). Always popular, with its seafood often singled out for special praise, this place somehow manages to leave you feeling relaxed despite its constant rush of people. Moderate prices.

Pappas Grill, 440 Danforth Avenue (tel: 469 9595). Unlike the majority of the many small Greek restaurants in the area Pappas adds pastas, pizzas and burgers to its menu and while they are good, it is probably the lamb and the *dolmades* (stuffed vine leaves) which draw the crowds. Moderate prices.

Penelope, 33 Yonge Street (tel: 947 1159). Handy for the O'Keefe Centre and with all the appropriate mainstays of a Greek menu. It is perhaps a little less relaxed than its Danforth Avenue cousins but is friendly and consistent. Closed on Sundays. Moderate prices.

Italian

Barolo, 193 Carlton Street (tel: 961 4747). Serves northern Italian cuisine concentrating on simple, well-prepared food. Superbly grilled meats and unexpected additions to the gnocchi make for a pleasant meal in lively surroundings. Closed on Sundays. Moderate prices.

La Bruschetta, 1325 St Clair Avenue West (tel: 656 8622). Typical of the many small restaurants in the part of the city known as Little Italy. Spaghetti, minestrone, veal and salad, plus some unusual dishes you may never have tried before. The staff are eager to explain and recommend. Closed Sundays. Moderate prices.

Centro, 2472 Yonge Street (tel: 483 2211). A combination of Northern Italy and California in the food and maybe in the décor, too. Once you get your mind on the menu you will find

*A classic Italian meal –
pasta, red wine and salad*

excellent pastas, shellfish and a wonderful fresh sorbet and fruit platter. A spectacular wine list and one that is priced for good value. Phone ahead because the place draws big crowds. Very expensive.

Il Fornello, 55 Eglinton Avenue East (tel: 486 2130). This highly popular chain of pizzerias has made its name through top quality pizzas, all of which are cooked in wood-burning clay ovens and can be created to order from a choice of over 100 toppings. Other branches can be found at 86 Bloor Street West (tel: 588 5658), 1560 Yonge Street (tel: 920 8291), 214 King Street West (tel: 977 2855) and 486 Bloor Street West (tel: 588 9358). Inexpensive.

Grano, 2035 Yonge Street (tel: 440 1986). This lively and very Italian family-run affair started out as a simple bakery and take-out delicatessan. These days it is a fully-fledged restaurant that has not lost sight of its humble origins. The food is Italian home-style cooking at its best (with plenty of vegetarian options), while wooden tables and simple décor lend a suitably informal air. Closed Sunday. Moderate prices.

Il Monello, 1392 Yonge Street (tel: 968 0030). Elegant Italian with a decidedly French accent. Perhaps Boston bluefish or red snapper grilled with a herbed butter, good *bruschetta* for starters and smoothly sauced fresh pastas. The desserts are highly praised. Moderate prices.

Oggi Bistro, 254 Eglinton Avenue East (tel: 489 3777).

FOOD AND DRINK

Spend a morning in the antique shops of Mount Pleasant and you can lunch in this gracious family-owned-and-run restaurant. Pastas, chicken and seafood are served in a

Take a break in one of the many bars in The Beaches

relaxed atmosphere. Closed Sundays. Moderate prices.
Orso, 106 St John Street (tel: 596 1989). What was once a blacksmith's premises now houses what many reckon to be one of the city's best eateries. Slightly austere décor but the hand-painted service plates and

innovative food bring it all to life. Chic pizzas on the lunch menu and quietly efficient service. Closed on Sundays. Expensive.

Trattoria Giancarlo, 41 Clinton Street (tel: 533 9619). Casual and comfortable with fresh pastas, sauces and well-grilled seafood. And it possesses what every self-respecting neighbourhood trattoria should have – a small front patio for summertime dining. Closed Sundays and Mondays. Moderate prices.

Japanese

Katsura, 900 York Mills Road in the Prince Hotel (tel: 444 2511). This is a showplace for all that is exquisite in Japanese culture and food. *Teppanyaki* chefs do their stuff and the *sushi* and *tempura* counters do brisk trade. Expensive.

Sasaya, 257 Eglinton Avenue West (tel: 487 3508). Good *sushi* and *tempura* bars and a large menu which often needs explanation unless you are an expert. Fortunately help is always on hand from an efficient and friendly staff. Inexpensive.

Seafood

Filet of Sole, 11 Duncan Street (tel: 598 3256). Near the Metro Toronto Convention Centre and the theatre district. Fresh fish and lobster daily along with oysters shucked at Henry's Oyster bar. Very extensive menu which includes steak and chicken. Lots of fun and casual, but not so much so that you don't need reservations. Moderate prices.

Josos, 202 Davenport Road (tel: 925 1903). Exotic nudes adorn the walls of this intimate Mediterranean-style restaurant and between the food and the atmosphere it is hard not to have a good time. Pricey, but with large portions of fresh, grilled fish, deep fried calamari and pastas. Closed on Sundays. Expensive.

The Old Fish Market, 12 Market Street (tel: 363 0334). Popular with St Lawrence Market shoppers and any number of nearby business people, this bustling place, decorated with a nautical theme, is best approached on foot or by taxi. Satisfying, with fresh catches of the day (menus are printed twice daily), an oyster bar and good seafood. Vegetables are sometimes not all they might be. Inexpensive.

Phebe's, 641 Mount Pleasant Road (tel: 484 6428). An oyster bar and friendly neighbourhood restaurant. Service can sometimes be a bit hit-or-miss but even JR Ewing would approve mightily of the Texas barbecued shrimp and luscious pies. Closed on Sundays. Inexpensive.

The Whistling Oyster, 11 Duncan Street (tel: 598 7707). In the basement of Filet of Sole. An informal place with a popular bar thronged with singles. Seafood and lots of pastas. Many dishes are also based on Asian flavours. Inexpensive.

Steakhouse

Barberian's, 7 Elm Street (tel: 597 0225). Arguably the best place for the noble sirloin, T-bones and Barberian's own

FOOD AND DRINK

Delmonico cut, perfectly served by knowing waiters. No-fuss dressing on the Caesar salad and the apple beignets with ice cream are mouthwatering. Open until 01.00hrs Monday to Saturday; Sundays until midnight. Expensive.

Bardi's Steak House, 56 York Street (tel: 366 9211). This smart and intimate place has been in business since 1966, and prides itself on using only top-grade Aberdeen Angus beef that has been properly aged and expertly cut on the premises. Moderate prices.

Carman's Dining Club, 26 Alexander Street (tel: 924 8697). Excellent steaks but be warned: you have to be a lover of garlic because it is laid on with a heavy hand. Within walking distance of Maple Leaf Gardens, venue for such events as National Hockey League games, rock concerts and recitals. Expensive.

Gatsby's, 504 Church Street (tel: 925 4545). You eat in an elegant Victorian-era dining room, all glittering gilt and chandeliers. Steaks are what they do best but there is a whole range of other Continental dishes, too. Near Maple Leaf Gardens. Closed on Sundays. Expensive.

George Bigliardi's, 463 Church Street (tel: 922 9594). A popular restaurant in the Italian manner. Attractive atmosphere with a variety of veal and seafood, too. Dependable steaks and excellent Caesar salads are also served. Open for dinner only, Monday to Saturday 17.00–00.30hrs. Closed Sundays. Expensive.

Swiss

Mövenpick, 165 York Street (tel: 366 5234). Only the Swiss could run a chain this well. The place is large – actually three distinct areas in one – with the formal Rossli being the most expensive. Sit up at the wine bar (offering rare wines by the glass) or in the surrounding Belle Terrasse to enjoy authentic Swiss food. The bread is baked daily and special menus are themed to seasonal produce. Open Monday to Saturday 07.30–01.00hrs; Sunday 07.30hrs–midnight. Inexpensive. There is also a Mövenpick at 129 Yorkville Avenue, Monday to Friday: 07.30–02.00hrs; Saturday and Sunday: 07.30–01.00hrs.

Thai

Thai Magic, 1118 Yonge Street (tel: 968 7366). The ambience here is smarter than in many Asian restaurants, but the sumptous Thai-style décor of tumbling plants, carvings and bamboo screens make it an attractive place to eat if you want to treat yourself. Reservations recommended. Closed Saturday lunchtime and Sunday.

Vanipha Lanna, 471 Eglinton Avenue West (tel: 484 0895). This is a popular and bustling restaurant whose colourful and lively atmosphere matches the superlative Lao-Thai food on offer. Everything is crisp and light, and beautifully presented, and though the food can be slow coming at busy times, and the tables cramped, no-one seems to mind the wait. Reservations recommended. Closed Sunday. Moderate prices.

SHOPPING

Any visitor in the grip of the
'shop till you drop' syndrome
will feel at home in Toronto
where every opportunity is
afforded to spend, spend.
Whatever you are after, it is
here somewhere in the city's
shopping centres, boutiques
and markets, the ubiquitous
surburban malls, or the
individual shops of its
neighbourhoods. However, it is
no duty-free paradise. You pay
the going rate and you get
quality. There are department
stores such as Eaton's,
Simpsons and The Bay for
middle-of-the-roaders. Holt
Renfrew and Creeds cater to the
carriage trade and for big
spenders there is a wealth of

branches of internationally
renowned companies and
imports from all over the world.
There are lots of items made in
Canada but Inuit soapstone
carving makes the most
uniquely Canadian memento or
gift. But be alert. There are
many imitations and inferior
works around so look carefully
before you buy.

High on anyone's list of places to
shop are the more than 300
shops and services of **The
Eaton Centre**, designed along
the lines of Milan's Galleria, all
soaring glass and light, and one
of Toronto's top tourist
attractions.

It is anchored to the north and
south by Eaton's and Simpsons,
and Michael Snow's sculpted
flock of Canada geese hovers
high under the arched glass of
the roof.

(Beautiful as the geese are,

*Eaton's store in the Eaton Centre,
a must for all shoppers*

SHOPPING

Sculpted Canada geese hover over shoppers beneath the arched glass roof of the Eaton Centre

Torontonians seemed to be taking them for granted until a few years ago when the Centre's publicists decided to festoon them with red ribbons at Christmas. Such a howl arose from the artist and public that the geese were returned to their unadorned splendour in short order.)

The Centre is easily reached by subway, bus or streetcar and there is a mind-boggling variety of things to buy and do, as well as some of the best fast food and speciality snacking in the city. **Queen's Quay Terminal** on the water's edge at Harbourfront

Underground City

The Eaton Centre is, of course, just one of many ways to dive into Toronto's **underground city** with its more than 1,000 shops, restaurants, nightclubs, movie theatres and other facilities. At its north end the underground begins at The Atrium on Bay, from which it runs south beneath the Eaton Centre, Simpsons, the Sheraton Centre, First Canadian Place, the Toronto Dominion Centre and the Royal York Hotel, ending, or beginning, as the case may be, at Union Station. On any given day there are masses of people eating, banking, buying clothes or shoes or television sets, seeing their doctors or dentists, stocking up on groceries or just indulging in dinner and a movie.

Apart from all of that, the underground is a marvellous way to escape the snows and winds of winter and the moist heat of midsummer.

(In winter people have been known to drive their heated cars out of their heated garages in the morning, arrive downtown and park in underground garages, take elevators to their offices, dive underground for lunch, then reverse their trips at day's end, never having felt the nip of frost. Or, in summer, the enervating heat of a humid day.)

contains many small boutiques and speciality shops, some of the best novelty items in the city and excellent food. If you want to take a gourmet picnic over to the Toronto Islands (and you should), stock up here.

There is a large number of imports in the shops, together with much that is Canadian. Do not miss the **Tilley Endurables** shop for safari-style clothing for men and women. It is nicely designed and exceptionally well made. So well made, in fact, that the labels on many items carry the succinct washing instructions: 'Give 'em hell'.

This may just be the most glamorous building in Toronto. For years it was known as the terminal warehouse, built (in 1926) like a fortress.

So much like a fortress that when the developers came along, a few years back, they decided it was easier to convert it and stack high-priced luxury condominiums on its roof than demolish it.

A short walk from there and you're at the **Harbourfront Antique Market**, Canada's largest and not to be missed. It is so big that you can spend the better part of a day there if you are really an antiques hound.

Bloor-Yorkville

Bloor Street West, from Yonge Street to Avenue Road, offers a run of shops that carry all the good things in life, so much so that one would need a whole book just to list them. But here are a few, to set the tone:

The ManuLife Centre, 55 Bloor Street West. Home to **Creeds** (where the assistants are so well dressed it is hard to tell them from their customers), plus two levels of shops including **Marks**

and Spencer and **Birks**, a major Canadian jewellery firm.

William Ashley, 50 Bloor Street West, sells premium china, silver and crystal at sharply discounted prices and the selection is incredible. If Ashley's does not carry it, it probably has not been made.

Clothesline, 50 Bloor Street West, second level. Take a breather from European designer labels and look at these well-tailored Canadian examples. Vibrant clothes and accessories from Canadian designer **Marilyn Brooks** are also on this level. Do not miss them if you want something that is up to or way ahead of the times.

Davids, 66 Bloor Street West. Shoes and boots from Jourdan and Maud Frizon, among others. Top prices but watch for frequent sales.

George Jensen, 95A Bloor Street West. Across from the Danish Food Centre. Furniture upstairs and Royal Copenhagen china everywhere, but it is the classic silver jewellery which is always the real Jensen showstopper.

Harry Rosen, 80 Bloor Street West. Huge selections of elegant men's wear at this stylish outfitters (also caters for women).

Holt Renfrew, 50 Bloor Street West. High fashion for women with Canadian exclusives on many of Europe's best designers (for which you will need a 'price is no object' attitude), plus men's and children's wear. The café on the top floor is a prime spot for tired shoppers.

The Irish Shop, 110 Bloor Street West. Some of the best and brightest in Irish design here, along with tableware and books.

Separate entrance to the men's store.

A short walk north on Avenue Road and you are in the midst of Yorkville, an enclave of exclusivity which embraces Yorkville and Hazleton Avenues, Cumberland and Scollard Streets and part of Avenue Road. Back in the days when the flower children held their brief reign this area was full of hippies, folk artists, coffee houses and more than a few illegal substances. It was beguiling, of a summer's evening, to wander around, stop for coffee, and wonder at the kids.

Now the place holds the heartbeat of café society – and is still the best place in town for people-watching, although now the streets are lined with expensive cars and the jeans

Toronto hosts a huge range of stores that are sure to offer something for everyone

have designer labels.

The old townhouses of Yorkville Avenue have been renovated to house chic boutiques and galleries, the restaurants are legion and in the summer months the sidewalk cafés sprout bright umbrellas.

Hazelton Lanes, 55 Avenue Road. An elegant complex full of boutiques around a posh outdoor restaurant (dismantled in winter to make way for a skating rink).

The Compleat Kitchen, 87 Yorkville Avenue. Utensils, gadgets, cookbooks – just about anything that can (or should) be used in a well set-up kitchen can be found here.

Fetoun, 97 Scollard Street, Antique lace, Persian rugs, a chandelier and a statue of Anna Pavlova adorn this opulent four-storey monument to *haute couture*. Fabulous ball gowns and classic suits emanate from the workroom and even most of the off-the-peg is one of a kind.

The General Store, Hazelton Lanes, lower level. Great place for gift-shopping with everything from kitchenware to bathrobes, books and glassware to … well, just about anything you can think of.

Innuit Gallery of Eskimo Art, 9 Prince Arthur Avenue. Perhaps the best place in the city to see beautiful examples and get some idea of what to look for when you are ready to buy.

Irene Dale, 9 Yorkville Avenue. Canadian-designed children's clothing with a beautiful attention to detail, colour and an awareness of a child's activities.

Mirvish Village, Markham Street south of Bloor, a block west of Bathurst Street. The same Mirvish of theatrical and restaurant fame (see **Eating Out**) has made this little block of Victoriana a pleasant place to stroll, shop for antiques, collectables, art and books, or enjoy a meal. At the north end, where the streets intersect, stands the cornerstone of his empire, **Honest Ed's**, the blockbuster of all bargain stores. It's big, it's tacky, it's got the world's largest electric sign on its roof and just getting around in it can be like going the wrong way on an escalator, but if you are feeling really strong, there are definite bargains to be had.

Going West

Queen Street West, west from McCaul Street over to Bathurst Street. This area has the city's most avant-garde flavour and it is where the artists and musicians hang out. The fashions (in the shops and on the street) are outrageous and there is a lot of pink hair, black leather and new wave. But there are bookstores, record stores, vintage clothing shops and many exceedingly good cafés and restaurants. Don't miss it.

Village by the Grange, 49 McCaul Street. Hard by the Art Gallery of Ontario, this complex contains over 60 shops and boutiques and five restaurants. You can buy everything from personalised stationery to exotic birds and it is a good place for unusual gift shops. There is also an international food market with 25 kiosks selling tastes from all over the world. Free parking underground, evenings and weekends.

Markets

Kensington Market. This is a delight which was born in the early part of the century and survives to this day, despite the occasional short-lived plan to knock it down and build something tidier and antiseptic. Bounded by Bathurst Street and Spadina Avenue and Dundas and College Streets, it sprawls over a residential area which in 1815 was a place of wide sweeping lawns. Fifty years later the land had been split up and British immigrants arrived to take up residence. There was no market in their time but after them came Jews from Europe,

for whom markets were essential, and by the 1930s the Kensington was flourishing. Hungarian and Italian immigrants had their innings but by far the biggest influence since the original Jewish impetus was that of the Portuguese, who arrived from the Azores in the 1950s and who now account for at least half the area's population.

Today, with their blessing, Augusta Street throbs with soulful *fado* music, the wares from the tiny shops and stalls spill over what passes for pavements and everywhere there is life and vitality.

The market also attracts the West Indian community, just to the south, and recently the Koreans and Vietnamese have joined the fray.

(It is hard to understand the reasoning but some people are intrepid enough to actually drive through Kensington's cramped and crowded streets. As the no parking signs in New York city say: 'Don't even think about it'. Much better to be an innocent observer as the horns start hooting and the jostling for every inch of every illegal parking space begins.)

St Lawrence Market, 92 Front Street East (corner of Front and Jarvis Streets). The best in produce, fish, poultry and meat is available here, as well as cheese, breads and other foodstuffs. But even if you do not want to shop for groceries, it is well worth wandering around while you enjoy a cup of coffee and one of the hot Canadian-bacon-on-a-bun sandwiches sold by several food stalls. On

Saturdays the market across the street adds another 60 stalls to the mix.

The Neighbourhoods

And then there are Toronto's many neighbourhoods, each as different as the citizens' ethnic backgrounds, but all with one thing in common – interesting shopping and walking areas. It would take up far too much space in this book (and be needlessly repetitive) to list shops within each area.

Shop window in the Beaches, a good area for original shops

Suffice it to say all the neighbourhoods contain them along with restaurants and cafés and each is well worth a visitor's time, not only for the shops themselves, but to gain some knowledge of what holds the city together.

The Beaches. One of the most relaxed areas of the city, with access to the waterfront, its parks, boardwalk and lovely houses are reminders of the past. It retains the allure it once had as Toronto's long-ago summer retreat, despite booming property values. Shopping is eclectic and original.

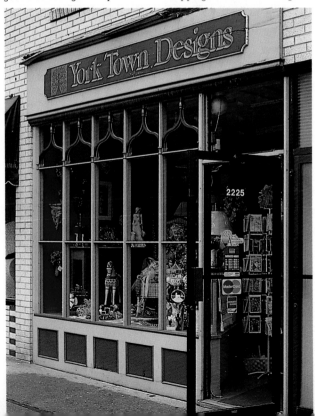

SHOPPING

Make for Queen Street East, between just east of Woodbine Avenue and along to Victoria Park Avenue and you will find folk art, Oriental rugs, junk stores, bookshops and cafés, as well as some good British-type pubs.

By wandering on through some of the area's residential streets, you will come across everything from mock-Tudor on tiny cottages to imposing Victorian beauties.

Chinatown, west of Spadina Avenue to Bay Street, College Street to south of Dundas Street.

Bloor West Village

A real riches-to-rags-to-riches story happened here when the east–west subway line made downtown shopping easily accessible in 1966. What had been a vital part of the community quickly went into decline as people deserted the neighbourhood for the bigger city stores.

Businesses closed down and the street was rapidly sliding into a slum when a few owners decided to fight back by funding a revitalisation scheme with higher business taxes. Today the markets, delicatessens, pastry shops, high fashion and antique stores are not only filled with residents, but they are a magnet for shoppers from all over Toronto. More European than North American with influences from all over that continent, the wide tree-lined street is once again bustling, the cafés and gift shops filled with people. The village, easily reached by subway, is at Jane and Bloor Streets.

The third largest Chinatown in North America (San Francisco and New York are the leaders), this one had its origins in 1878. The shops, stalls and restaurants are always bustling but on Saturdays and Sundays things go into top gear – it seems that every member of this large community is out shopping, eating or just gossiping over a counter.

It is a place of bakeries and herbalists, fish and meat markets, craft stores, clothing – and many restaurants. There was a time when Chinese food in Toronto meant Cantonese food but these days a Chinese meal is just as likely to be Hunan or Szechuan and there are more than a hundred restaurants from which to choose.

The Danforth, between the Don Valley and Woodbine Avenue. If you cannot find a first-class Greek meal on the stretch near Pape Avenue it is possible that you have no taste buds. There are fish markets and fruit markets and the bouzouki music pours out on to the street. The only thing that is not completely reminiscent of Athens is the traffic.

Little Italy or Westclair, St Clair Avenue West and Dufferin Street area. When Italy took home the World Cup in 1982 there were reckoned to be half a million Italians out celebrating in this area. Go there for the pastas in the little family-owned restaurants or the hot sausage sandwiches or settle into one of the many sidewalk cafés on a balmy summer evening and enjoy what may be the world's best ice cream.

ACCOMMODATION

Toronto has well over 24,000 hotel rooms but there are times when it is hard to find one, especially in the summer months when the ranks of vacationers and businessmen are swelled by thousands of conventioneers. The range of hotels runs from luxury in the grand manner to smaller establishments with efficiency (kitchenette) units. It is also possible to find B&B accommodation (see Tight Budget section page 105). Toronto's hotels are scattered across the city, from downtown to the suburbs, and to help make some sense out of it all, the

Choose a downtown hotel to be at the heart of the city

following selective listings are broken into general areas. For a complete listing of all Toronto hotels contact Accommodation Toronto on tel: 629 3800; fax: 629 0035. Hours of operation: 15 May to 1 September: daily 09.00–21.00hrs; 2 September to 14 May: Monday to Friday 09.00–21.00hrs; weekends to18.00hrs. The average cost of a double room in Metro Toronto's hotels runs between $75 and $150 for, say, Holiday Inn-style accommodation and from $175 and up for luxury hotels such as the Harbour Castle Westin. Because prices change constantly the following listings indicate only the general range into which each hotel's room rates fall:

ACCOMMODATION

Downtown
Best Western Chestnut Park Hotel, 108 Chestnut Street West (tel: 977 5000). 522-room hotel by City Hall's Nathan Phillips Square. Complete recreation facilities include indoor pool, health club and gymnasium. One of the world's few hotels to be connected to a museum – the Canadian Museum for Textiles, with ceremonial cloths, carpets, etc from around the world, with emphasis on China. Moderately priced.

Best Western Primrose Hotel, 111 Carlton Street (tel: 977 8000). Close to business centres, shopping and entertainment areas, this 350-room hotel has an outdoor swimming pool. Moderate to expensive.

Clarion Essex Park Hotel, 300 Jarvis Street (tel: 977 4823). A former apartment building converted to a 102-room hotel, 15 of which are efficiency units,

handy if you plan a long-term visit. Inexpensive.

Crowne Plaza Toronto Centre, 225 Front St West (tel: 597 1400). One of two reliable Holiday Inns in downtown. Adjoining the Metro Toronto Convention Centre, its 587 rooms are an obvious draw for visiting conventioneers and crowds are a matter of course. Close to Roy Thomson Hall and the Royal Alexandra Theatre, it has a full-service recreation club which includes two squash courts. Wonderful suites (even if some of them do overlook the railroad tracks). Moderate.

Delta Chelsea Inn, 33 Gerrard Street West (tel: 243 5732). Some kitchenettes in this 997-room hostelry. Special attention to children with a Creative Centre for those aged three to eight and a kids-style menu in the dining room where those under six eat

University Avenue in downtown

The Harbour Castle Westin, 'the downtown resort on the lake'

free. The Chelsea Bun lounge is noted for excellent jazz. Good value. Moderately priced.

Harbour Castle Westin, 1 Harbour Street (tel: 869 1600). A luxurious hotel with 967 rooms, a terraced swimming pool, patio and jogging track and a revolving restaurant, the Lighthouse, perched on its roof offering spectacular views. Very popular hotel and comfortable, despite the fact that it has an entrance that is almost hidden from pedestrians. Expensive.

Hilton International Toronto, 145 Richmond Street West tel: 869 3456). This 601-room hotel is the home of Trader Vic's (well worth a visit if you feel like exotic Polynesian food and drink) and it is popular with travelling business types and legal eagles from the nearby

law court. Expensive.

Holiday Inn Downtown, King Street West (tel: 599 4000). The second decent, downtown Holiday Inn. (There are others in Toronto including two near the airport plus one in York Dale and one in North York. For all Holiday Inn reservations tel: 486 6400.)

Hotel Admiral, 249 Queen's Quay West (tel: 203 3333). This small, recently opened hotel is well placed for the activities of Harbourfront. Great harbour views from its upper outdoor pool area and its 157 rooms are very well appointed. Moderate to expensive.

Hotel Victoria, 56 Yonge Street (tel: 363 1666). Within easy walking distance of the O'Keefe Centre and the St Lawrence Centre, this hotel has been completely renovated and improved. Rooms are small and there are only 42 of them. Good dining room and two cosy, comfortable lounges. Very good value for money. Moderately priced.

The King Edward Hotel, 37 King Street East (tel: 863 9700). A hotel in the grand manner and a landmark since 1900. With all its renovated glories, the 318-room hotel, set in the financial and theatre district, is truly deluxe.

Chiaro's is one of the best hotel dining rooms in the city and Sunday brunch at its Café Victoria is an event (see Food and Drink, page 61). Very expensive.

Your stay in Toronto may include a visit to the SkyDome to see the Blue Jays in action

Novotel Toronto Centre, 45 The Esplanade (tel: 367 8900). With 266 rooms, the hotel is located right behind O'Keefe Centre, a short walk from the St Lawrence Market. Its turn-of-the-century architecture complements many of the surrounding buildings. Moderately priced.

Royal York Hotel, 100 Front Street West (tel: 368 2511). The best known hotel in Toronto, it stands across Front Street from Union Station at the south end of the underground city. It has 1,600 rooms, many restaurants and lounges and the Imperial Room nightclub. (It also has Louis Janetta, the legendary *maître d'* who is said to know everyone worth knowing in Toronto and without whom the hotel would probably fall apart.) Expensive.

The Sheraton Centre, 123 Queen Street West (tel: 361 1000). The underground city also runs through this massive hostelry and it has, as well, over 60 shops and two cinemas on its property. A centre for business meetings and seminars of all kinds, its recreational facilities include an indoor and an outdoor pool. Well located, across from City Hall, its 1,427 rooms and public areas are always busy. Expensive.

Toronto Colony Hotel, 89 Chestnut Street (tel: 977 0707). Behind City Hall and steps from Chinatown. Indoor and outdoor pools and other big city facilities in the usual chain hotel manner. It has 715 rooms and a very popular dining room. Moderately priced.

Midtown

The Bradgate Arms, 54 Foxbar Road, Avenue Road and St Clair area (tel: 968 1331). Close to the shops and restaurants of the Yonge and St Clair neighbourhood, this small (110 rooms) and charming European-style hotel is also handy for the mansions of

ACCOMMODATION

exclusive Forest Hill. Getting down to the Avenue Road/Yorkville/Bloor Street shops and the Royal Ontario Museum is also easy. Comfortable bar and very good dining room. Moderately priced.

Comfort Hotel Downtown, 15 Charles Street East (tel: 924 1222). Another small hotel with 110 rooms, one block south of Bloor Street just off Yonge Street. It is the sort of hotel you can find in Manhattan – if you are a native or have connections – with a good dining room, a piano bar and a patio which operates May to September. This one is a real find. Moderately priced.

Days Inn, 30 Carlton Street (tel: 977 6655). Nothing fancy, this is an economy hotel close to Maple Leaf Gardens and Yonge Street, with 536 rooms, a restaurant and two bars. There is also a special money-saving plan called Seniors Service for those aged 60 and over. (The plan also applies to the Chestnut Park Hotel and the Carlton Place Hotel.) Inexpensive.

Four Seasons Hotel, 21 Avenue Road (tel: 964 0411). Set in the midst of fashionable Yorkville, the luxurious touches that are a byword with Four Seasons are everywhere in this 379-room hotel. First-class dining at Truffles and two always-popular bars. Only one criticism: as happens at the Harbour Castle Westin, guests are unfortunately asked to compete with cars at the main entrance. Very expensive.

Hotel Inter-Continental Toronto, 220 Bloor Street West (tel: 960 5200). The 209 rooms here (plus 11 suites) enjoy 24-hour room service twice-daily housekeeping and a whole host of other small frills and services to ensure a comfortable stay. There is also a fitness centre with sauna, massage room and swimming pool. Special rooms are available for visitors with disabilities. Expensive.

Hotel Plaza II, 90 Bloor Street East (tel: 961 8000). It is actually six floors of a large apartment building and is connected with The Bay department store on Bloor Street, just east of Yonge Street. With 256 rooms and a private health club for its more active guests, it is supremely well situated for midtown attractions. Its Greenery dining room is justifiably popular. Expensive.

Howard Johnson Plaza Downtown, 475 Yonge Street (tel: 924 0611). Handy for Maple Leaf Gardens, it is not a glamorous hotel but its 540 rooms are comfortable and its restaurant, Creighton's, always dependable. Moderately priced.

Park Plaza Hotel, 4 Avenue Road (tel: 924 5471). This stylish old hotel in the heart of the Yorkville district has recently changed owners and multi-million dollar renovations have been under way on its south tower. Meanwhile it is business as usual at the north tower, which fronts Prince Arthur Avenue and where all its restaurants and lounges are located. With 258 rooms and 40 suites (some on non-smoking floors), an award-winning restaurant and a fitness centre, there are plenty of facilities to

Movie star favourite, Sutton Place is sumptuous in both décor and service

attract the visitor. Though, to the despair of many long-time patrons (especially writers), the Roof Garden bar is temporarily closed, too. Expensive.

Sutton Place Grande Hotel Le Meridien Toronto, 955 Bay Street (tel: 924 9221). The financial district and Queen's Park are on the doorstep of this truly luxurious 280-room hotel. Grand European-style service here and it is a favourite haunt of visiting movie stars. The Sanssouci dining room is famed for its décor almost as much as its food. Expensive.

Town Inn, 620 Church Street (tel: 964 3311). Another good

bet for long-term visitors, the Town's well-priced accommodation includes mini-suites with fully equipped kitchenettes. As well, there is a sauna, indoor pool and tennis court. Inexpensive.

Venture Inn Toronto Yorkville, 89 Avenue Road (tel: 964-1220). A 71-room hotel which includes a small continental breakfast in the room rate. Moderate.

North Central

Novotel Hotel-North York, 3 Park Home Avenue, North York (tel: 733 2929). Just west of the northern reaches of Yonge Street and close to Highway 401, it is a well-run, comfortable hotel of 262 rooms, with pool and exercise room, restaurant and bar. Moderately priced.

ACCOMMODATION

Children will enjoy watching the re-enactments of the battle at Fort York

Roehampton Hotel, 808 Mount Pleasant Road (tel: 487 5101). Close to the excellent little shops of Mount Pleasant and the nightlife of nearby Eglinton Avenue, this small residential hotel has an outdoor pool and discounts for senior citizens. Inexpensive.

East
Four Seasons Inn on the Park, 1100 Eglinton Avenue East (tel: 444 2561). The only resort hotel in the city, it sits on 17 acres (6.9 hectares) next to a 500-acre (200-hectare) park. With three year-round tennis courts, five squash and racketball courts and everything from shuffleboard to cross-country skiing (in season), guests are unlikely to be bored. All-day supervised activities for children. Close to the Ontario Science Centre and what should be easy access to downtown via the Don Valley Parkway.
(There are less direct but ultimately faster routes than what is often – because of its susceptibility to traffic jams – termed the Don Valley parking lot.) Good restaurants. Expensive.
Howard Johnson Toronto East Hotel, 40 Progress Court, Scarborough (tel: 439 6200). There's a 24-hour restaurant and mini arcade in this 192-

room hotel, with indoor pool and exercise room plus the usual restaurants and lounges. Moderately priced.

The Prince Hotel, 900 York Mills Road (tel: 444 2511). With 15 acres (6 hectares) of parkland, three tennis courts and a complete health club, this large (406 rooms) hotel also boasts the most beautiful Japanese restaurant in the city (see **Katsura**, Food and Drink section, page 69.) Other good restaurants and lounges, too. Expensive.

Ramada Hotel-Don Valley, 185 Yorkland Boulevard, Willowdale (tel: 493 9000). All the usual Ramada facilities with 285 rooms, an indoor pool, patio barbecue and a rose garden. Moderately priced.

Sheraton Toronto East Hotel & Towers, (formerly known as the Ramada Renaissance), 2035 Kennedy Road, Scarborough (tel: 229 1500). Handy for visiting the Metro Toronto Zoo, this hotel has a tropical feeling with an atrium rising over its swimming pool, a great attraction in the depths of winter. As well, there is squash and racketball, a putting green, a sauna and an exercise room. This is a good choice if you are travelling with children. Several restaurants, of which **Santara** (Japanese) is the prettiest. Moderately priced.

West

Holiday Inn Yorkdale, Central Reservations tel: 486 6400. Moderately priced.

Valhalla Inn, 1 Valhalla Inn Road (tel: 239 2391). Situated midway between Lester B Pearson airport and downtown. Its 250 rooms overlook a garden courtyard and there are three restaurants, three bars and a lounge for dinner dancing. Recreational facilities close by and limousine service to and from the airport. A convenient base if you need to stay in the west end of Metro. Moderately priced.

Airport Environs

Airport and Dixon Roads (known as the Airport strip) are lined with hotels, large and small. Most, if not all, run shuttle buses to and from the airport and in the following selection these are either free or at a minimal cost of from $1 to $2 per person. Accommodation costs can vary but can be easily checked via the courtesy hotel telephones at the Arrivals level of the airport terminals.

The Bristol Place Hotel, 950 Dixon Road (tel: 675 9444).

Days Inn, 6257 Airport Road (tel: 678 1400).

Hilton International-Toronto Airport, 5875 Airport Road (tel: 677 9900).

Holiday Inn-Toronto Airport, 970 Dixon Road (tel: 675 7611 or Central Reservations: 486 6400).

International Plaza Hotel, 655 Dixon Road (tel: 244 1711).

Regal Constellation Hotel, 900 Dixon Road (tel: 675 1500).

Toronto Airport Marriott Hotel, 901 Dixon Road (tel: 674 9400).

For Youth Hostel accommodation see **Directory**, Student and Youth Travel, page 124.

CULTURE, ENTERTAINMENT AND NIGHTLIFE

Whether you go for Swan Lake or tap, Sondheim or Neil Simon, Dixieland or Vivaldi your tastes can find an outlet in Toronto. If sports are what turn you on you can spectate or participate, according to the season, to your heart's content and although it is not a 24-hour place for nightlife, Toronto can certainly keep you going till the wee small hours.

In the lounges, bars and nightclubs of the city you can hear every kind of music from rhythm and blues to reggae. You can dress up to the nines for a glamorous evening of dining and dancing, try a bit of foot stomping, country-style, ogle a belly-dancer or mingle with the trendy crowd at an after-hours club. The possibilities are limitless, depending only upon your tastes, stamina and willingness to spend.

You can dance at Horizons, the world's highest nightclub and bar, atop the CN Tower; put on your best and carry your memories of the big bands to the Imperial Room at the Royal York. Or you can elbow your way through the crush at Albert's Hall in the Brunswick House for rock, country and Dixieland, settle in for the evening with jazz at George's Spaghetti House, or venture uptown for dancing at the informal Chick 'n' Deli.

Then there is the theatre. The range runs from traditional fare, in plush surroundings, to contemporary and experimental theatre where the patrons perch on hard-backed chairs or benches. You can see cabaret or a satirical review, get involved (from the audience) in solving a murder mystery, critique the performance of stand-up comedians in what they hope will be the first step on the road to stardom, or take in opera and ballet at the O'Keefe Centre and a symphony concert at Roy Thomson Hall. On a long visit there is no reason why you should not try them all.

For real night-owls there is a myriad of bars and lounges, after-hours clubs and places to

CULTURE, ENTERTAINMENT AND NIGHTLIFE

Roy Thomson Hall, one of the centres of musical nightlife

dance the night away, some of them sophisticated models of restrained elegance, others crowded, pounding mob scenes that tempt one to invest in hearing aid futures.

The movie houses are as many and as varied as you would expect to find in a major city and, although Toronto's restaurants don't all operate on a late-night basis, it is easy enough to find a snack after the show.

In truth, it is a big city and anything you might want is available somewhere. You can amble around the museums, shop for art in the galleries of Yorkville, indulge a passion for antiques and books, take in football, hockey or baseball or enjoy the theatre. In fact, anything you can afford you can usually find.

Toronto is – perhaps rather surprisingly – the second largest centre for live theatre in North America (New York is tops), and this means the play's the thing (or opera, ballet, concerts, drama, comedy, etc) all over the city.

Where does it all happen? On the next few pages are listed some of Toronto's gathering places:

St Lawrence Centre for the Arts, 27 Front Street East (tel: 366 7723). Toronto's civic cultural centre with concerts, plays, films and public forums.
Massey Hall, 178 Victoria Street (tel: 593 4828). A landmark since 1894 and former home of the Toronto Symphony, this venerable old lady is now hostess to a variety of performers and events.
O'Keefe Centre, 1 Front Street East (tel: 872 2262). Home of the Canadian Opera Company and the National Ballet of Canada and the setting for Broadway shows and star names.
Premiere Dance Theatre, Queen's Quay Terminal (tel: 973 4000). Contemporary and traditional dance in a beautifully intimate theatre. (Free shuttle bus runs every 15 minutes from Union Station to Queen's Quay Terminal.)
Royal Alexandra Theatre, 260

The O'Keefe Centre, Toronto's largest theatre

King Street West (tel: 872 3333). An elegant, turn-of-the-century gem staging some of the city's best plays and musicals.
Roy Thomson Hall, 60 Simcoe Street (tel: 593 4828). Home of the Toronto Symphony and the scene for international performances of jazz, comedy, classical music and the like.

Some Other Notables
Bathurst Street Theatre, 736 Bathurst Street (tel: 588 6800).
Bayview Playhouse, 1605 Bayview Avenue (tel: 481 6191).
Bluma Apel Theatre, St Lawrence Centre, 27 Front Street East (tel: 366 7723).
Centrestage, 27 Front Street East (tel: 366 7723).
Factory Theatre, 125 Bathurst Street (tel: 864 9971).
Leah Posluns Theatre, 4588

Bathurst Street (tel: 630 6752).
Poor Alex Theatre, 296
Brunswick Avenue (tel: 927
8998).
Tarragon Theatre, 30 Bridgman
Avenue (tel: 531 1827).
Theatre Passe Muraille, 16
Ryerson Avenue (tel: 504 7529).
Toronto Free Theatre, 26
Berkeley Street (tel: 368 2856).
Young People's Theatre, 165
Front Street East (tel: 862 2222).

Comedy
Rivoli, 334 Queen Street West
(tel: 596 1908). Revues and
comedians.
Second City, The Old Firehall,
110 Lombard Street (tel: 863
1111). Satire and parody.
Yuk-Yuk's, Downtown: 1280
Bay Street. Stand-up comedians
and a chance to polish your act
at amateur nights. Uptown: 2335
Yonge Street. Mississauga: 300
Dundas Street East. For
information on all three, tel:
967 6425.

The Royal Alexandra Theatre,
for red plush grandeur

Dinner Theatre
La Cage Dinner Theatre, 279
Yonge Street, Second Floor (tel:
364 5200). Top celebrity
impersonators.
Harper's Restaurant, 38
Lombard Street (tel: 863 6223).
Comic cabaret and razzle-
dazzle magic.
His Majesty's Feast, Inn on the
Lake, 1926 Lakeshore
Boulevard West (tel: 769 1165).
Medieval hijinks with Henry VIII
and a lunatic court.
Limelight Dinner Theatre, 2026
Yonge Street (tel: 482 5200).
Scaled-down versions of hit
Broadway shows.
**Stage West Theatre
Restaurant**, 5400 Dixie Road,
Mississauga (tel: 905/238 0042).
High-quality buffet and a variety
of comedy acts and musical
plays.
You can frequently buy half-
price tickets for productions at
the major theatres on the day of
performance from Five Star
Tickets, which shares a booth
outside The Eaton Centre at
Dundas and Yonge Streets with

the Metro Visitors Association. Tickets for Stratford and the Niagara-on-the-Lake Shaw Festival can often be bought there, too, on the day before the performance. *Open*: Monday to Saturday noon–19.30hrs; Sunday 11.00–15.00hrs. (Best bet for theatre, entertainment and nightlife listings and information: the three Toronto newspapers, *The Toronto Star*, the *Globe & Mail* and the *Toronto Sun*, with special emphasis on *The Star's* Friday 'What's On' section; the free tabloid *Now*, a comprehensive entertainment guide found on news-stands and in restaurants all over the city, and the monthly listings in *Toronto Life* magazine.)

A few places to join the night-time glitterati: **Esplanade Bar and Grill** on the Esplanade, is packed at lunchtime and even more so in the evening when the dancing begins. It is one of the most consistently popular spots in the area and it connects with neighbouring Scotland Yard (pub food and more music with a lot of regulars).

Over at the **Hothouse Café** the corner of Wellington and Church Streets, the singles are out in force and at weekends they are lined up outside, champing at the bit to get on to the dance floor.

As the well-heeled shoppers of Yorkville make for home they are replaced with up-and-comers who favour watering holes such as **Hemingway's** and

Remy's (with a patio which accommodates hundreds), and **South Side Charlie's**; serious jazz lovers who hang out at **Meyer's**; and those who want to – really want to – see and be seen at the **Bellair**, where there are two levels of dancing and a bar scene which never stops. Dance, too, at the **Copa**, with its video screens and lasers (it can hold close to 2,000 people!) and then wander over to the '**22**', at 22 St Thomas Street, in the Windsor Arms, for a quiet drink in what can only be termed more gracious surroundings. Move uptown to **Berlin** for rhythm and blues but don't be

The Limelight, one of a number of spots for informal dinner theatre

too casual about it. Berlin likes to advise its customers to dress elegantly and, judging by the crowds, the customers do not mind at all.

Close by are the two most popular bars in the area, **Sweetwater Bar and Grill** and **Friday's**, always packed and queues at weekends. (No jeans or running shoes at the Sweetwater please.) Down on Queen Street West is the **BamBoo**, serving up a mixed bag of musical acts that run the gamut from country blues to rock and reggae. Good Caribbean food and owners who know their stuff.

In the East end there are, among others, the dining/drinking/ dancing spots such as **Panama Joe's** and **Spectrum**, as well as several popular pubs.

At the **Amsterdam** (sister to the **Rotterdam**) you can indulge a passion for beer and watch it being brewed, too. It will have to be a noisy passion, mind you, because the bar area is huge and the outdoor seating area a magnet for summer crowds. Pubs such as the **Madison**, and the **Jack Russell** probably come closest to an authentic British pub, although there are many others scattered through the city and a game of darts can be taken just as seriously here as any place in Britain.

Three places in Toronto consistently recommended by locals should not be missed – the **Chick 'n' Deli** on Mount Pleasant for great jazz; the **Bluenote** on Pears Avenue for what many agree is the best rhythm and blues, and **El Mocambo** on Spadina Avenue for rock.

CULTURE, ENTERTAINMENT AND NIGHTLIFE

A Quick Reference Guide to Night Spots:

Albert's Hall, Brunswick House, 481 Bloor Street West (tel: 964 2242).

Amsterdam, 133 John Street (tel: 595 8201).

BamBoo, 312 Queen Street West (tel: 593 5771).

Barracuda, 21 Scollard Street (tel: 921 4496). Superb disco.

Bellair Café, 100 Cumberland Street (tel: 964 2222).

Berlin, 2335 Yonge Street (tel: 489 7777).

Big Bop, 651 Queen Street West (tel: 366 6699). One of the city's trendiest clubs.

Chick 'n' Deli, 744 Mount Pleasant Road (tel: 489 3363).

Esplanade Bar and Grill, 58 The Esplanade (tel: 364 6671).

George's Spaghetti House, 290 Dundas Street East (tel: 923 9887)

Hemingway's, 142 Cumberland Street (tel: 968 2828).

Horizons, CN Tower, 301 Front Street West (tel: 362 5411).

The Jack Russell, 27 Wellesley Street East (tel: 967 9442).

Hothouse Café, 35 Church Street (tel: 366 7800).

The Madison, 14 Madison Avenue (tel: 927 1722).

Meyer's Deli, 69 Yorkville Avenue (tel: 960 4780).

El Mocambo, 464 Spadina Avenue (tel: 324 9667).

Panama Joe's, 124 Danforth Avenue (tel: 463 0085).

Pimblett's, 263 Gerrard Street East (tel: 929 9525).

Remy's, 115 Yorkville Avenue (tel: 968 9429).

South Side Charlie's, 121 Yorkville Avenue (tel: 929 0316).

Spectrum, 2714 Danforth Avenue (tel: 699 9913).

StiLife, 217 Richmond Street (tel: 593 6116). Smart club for older crowd.

Sweetwater Bar and Grill, 150 Eglinton Avenue East (tel: 487 9281).

Top O' The Senator, 249 Victoria Street (tel: 364 7517). Top jazz club.

Wayne Gretsky's, 41 Peter Street (tel: 979 7825). Sports bar and restaurant.

Bellair Café – the place to be seen

WEATHER AND WHEN TO GO

Toronto has a pleasant climate, all in all, though the average first frost does come on 29 October and the average last frost doesn't melt away until the dawn of 21 April. In between those dates it can get really frigid, but usually not in any sustained way. In fact, the presence of Lake Ontario keeps the Toronto area relatively warm compared with nearby points in Ontario, and the direction of the prevailing wind dumps the bulk of the winter's snow on poor old Buffalo, NY, to the south of the lake.

Not that Toronto gets no snow. Visitors coming between early December and late March should carry clothing – sweaters, overcoats, scarves – that can be worn in layers and will keep them warm in freezing temperatures. The clothing may not be needed every day but a little extra baggage weight is better than turning blue in an Arctic blast.

Have rubber or plastic outer footwear, too, or waterproof boots, because road gangs in Canada throw enough salt to create the Dead Sea at every corner and the saline solution that results is almost as corrosive on leather as it is on ice. And there does not have to be a heavy snowfall to bring out the salt trucks, just frost conditions and water on the roads.

Average temperatures in January and February run just under freezing and in March daytime averages move above that point, but none of that means there will not be a blizzard or a cold snap, which is not all that bad if you are wearing layered clothing and are prepared for it.

To step outside when the air is like chilled wine and the snow crackles under your feet is to feel an aliveness no southern clime can impart. Or so Canadians keep telling themselves.

Summer average temperatures are moderate, too, but averages only reveal the middle range. The reality is that in July or August visitors can expect at least some days that are well above 30°C (90°F) with a humidity near the top of the scale. Book air-conditioned accommodation with or near a swimming pool and rent cars with air conditioning. Then relax and enjoy the heat, as Canadians do, with a retreat conveniently at hand.

Take the lightest summer clothing you own plus a light jacket or top to deal with the

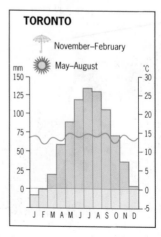

TORONTO

November–February

May–August

chills of air conditioning. And while shorts and brief sundresses are fine for Harbourfront and the Islands, they are rare elsewhere.

Men will need jacket and tie in the better restaurants, winter or summer, and women a dress or dressy trousers.

Unless it is a really gala event there will not be much in the way of formal evening gowns and dinner jackets in Toronto. All in all, big-city wear is much the same now the world over and the city has more than its fair share of designer jeans.

HOW TO BE A LOCAL

In spring, summer and early fall this involves getting caught up in Blue Jay fever, being a fan, talking incessantly about Blue Jays and joining the crowd at the city's superb SkyDome for home games. And, if you really want to fit in, wear one of those long-visored Blue Jay baseball caps that make you look like Admiral Nimitz – or Daffy Duck! But when Toronto empties on Friday evenings in the summer forget the games and join the exodus to cottage country in Muskoka north of the city, to enjoy the pleasure of woodland and lake. Travel Ontario (tel: 203 2500) can give you a list of the resorts.

Less expensive ways of melting into the crowd include relaxing at Harbourfront or Ontario Place in the summer, picnicking on Toronto Islands and canoeing the lagoons, visiting St Lawrence Market on Saturday mornings for coffee any time of the year and skating on the reflecting pool in Nathan Phillips Square in winter.

Caribana: the Caribbean festival starts with a parade

SPECIAL EVENTS

Every year new events crowd the calendar, then disappear, but there are some that stand steady down the years – festivals and celebrations that have caught the hearts or the minds of the public and are welcomed back like old friends when their season rolls around. Such are the following:

Canadian National Exhibition

The oldest and largest annual exhibition in the world, the Ex is held annually in the last two weeks in August and the long Labour Day weekend and is, in effect, a traditional country fair grown gigantic. Just like those small-town autumn celebrations it has hot dogs and booths and the old army game (betting on the spin of a wheel) and prize cows and dog shows and baseball games. But its attractions also include one of the world's great air shows (on the Labour Day weekend), exhibits from other nations and a grandstand show that features Hollywood and Las Vegas entertainment – or such spectacular performers as the massed bands of the Highland regiments. It is strictly Big Time on the entertainment circuit, despite the hoopla, thrill rides and bingo barkers. It makes for a great day in the outdoors – but it attracts hundreds of thousands of people so you have to like crowds.

Caribana

This wild week of Caribbean reggae, food, limbo dancing and mirth begins with a shimmering, strutting parade down University Avenue and a ferry ride to Centre Island for steel band concerts, floating nightclubs and gyrating celebrants. Stage areas on the island throb with loud music and spectacular dancing, impromptu outbursts of exuberance and swirling colour. And while all this goes on the crowds keep coming until the island is crammed with costumed revellers. Labour Day week, September. For information tel: 925 5435.

Festival of Festivals

This celebration of world cinema starts on the first Thursday after Labour Day and runs for 10 days. The films play at downtown cinemas and apart from avid fans the festival attracts a horde of international movie makers, buyers and critics, not to mention some of the stars themselves. During this period the élite meet at all the best places and the entertainment pages of the morning newspapers are crammed with who was seen where, doing what, with whom. In other words, it is a major event, as testified by this comment from a *New York Times* film critic: 'Studios now consider this festival the main testing ground for new films.'
The Festival of Festivals' box office opens in mid-July. Tel: 966 4217 for all information.

Metro International Caravan

A nine-day festival with more than 50 pavilions scattered about the city offering food, drink, crafts and entertainment from countries around the world. Held in the second half of June, it is an ethnic celebration run by the local representatives of each culture, with churches, community halls and clubs serving as temporary pavilions and it is as authentic as a trip back home.

Entertainment is as wide as the world – dance groups, choirs, floor shows, musical theatre, jazz, folk songs, gymnasts – and entrance is by Caravan passport, obtainable at any pavilion. Special buses travel from pavilion to pavilion but you will never make it to more than two or three in an evening without bursting or toppling over from strong drink. For information tel: 977 0466.

The Molson Indy series races take place on the city streets

Molson Indy

The premier open wheel racing series in North America, the CART/PPG Indy Car World Series, comes to Toronto every mid-July with weekend races on the city streets around the Canadian National Exhibition grounds. The world series is a run of 15 events, including the Indy 500 and the Toronto races, which take place in cities all over North America for the National Championship. The powerful cars are not all that different from Formula One cars, though they have retained the turbo engines which have now been banned in Formula One vehicles. For ticket information tel: 260 4639.

Player's International/ Player's Challenge

Canada's top tennis tournament is played at the National Tennis Centre on the campus of York University for the one week in late August directly preceding the US Open. It is actually a two-

Toronto's different ethnic backgrounds join in the annual Metro International Caravan. Above, a Chinese lion dance

kind in the world, attracting competitors and spectators from as far away as Japan to ogle everything from giant Clydesdales to rutabagas (swedes). The best in horses, cattle and farm produce are on exhibit and a highlight is the Royal Horse Show, which draws jumping teams from around the world.

The time is mid-November and the setting is the Coliseum at Exhibition Place. For information tel: 393 6401.

CHILDREN

Toronto offers a whole world of entertainment for children, ranging from museums, hockey, skating and skiing in winter to watery pursuits in the heat of summer, but the following have been chosen with an eye to providing parents with some entertainment, too. For that reason some items duplicate, in part, listings in other sections of this book.

city affair (Toronto and Montréal), with the men's event, the Player's International, and the women's event, the Player's Challenge, alternating cities each year. The hard court tournament attracts many of the world's top-ranked international players. For information tel: 665 9777.

Royal Agricultural Winter Fair

Every autumn Toronto gets back to its roots with this 10-day winter fair, a far more dignified – and top drawer – event than the Canadian National Exhibition. It is the largest of its

BLACK CREEK PIONEER VILLAGE

1000 Murray Ross Parkway (near Jane Street and Steeles Avenue)
Pigs, cows, horses and sheep, wagons and sleighs, farm buildings and 19th-century toys are all spread out for the delight of youngsters who head back to pioneer times at this restored village. In winter there is skating, cross-country and horse-drawn sleigh rides, in summer there is the blacksmith and farm hands to watch, all dressed in the costumes of the day. For information tel: 736 1733 or (a 24-hour tape) tel: 661 6610.

Canada's Wonderland – a theme park paradise for children

CANADA'S WONDERLAND
9580 Jane Street, Maple, Ont
Commercial, noisy, expensive and crowded but tops on any youngster's hit parade with a man-made mountain, 33 rides, fast foods, a Salt Water Circus of sealions and dolphins and fantasy lands where children can be photographed with the Flintstones or the Smurfs or other cartoon characters. A day will go quickly and so will your cash. For information tel: 832 7000.

CASA LOMA
1 Austin Terrace
Here is a castle where they can act out their fantasies, with real turrets, a secret staircase and hidden passages just like the ones in all those horror movies, and battlements from which to withstand the foe. It is the answer to every youngster's dream and if you cannot afford to build or buy one, a day tour here is the least you can do. For information tel: 923 1171.

CENTREVILLE
Centre Island
A pint-sized children's amusement park modelled on a turn-of-the-century village, with 15 inexpensive rides, games, arcades, miniature golf and a small petting zoo. And all with the bonus of a ferry ride over to the island and back.

CHILDREN'S BOOK STORE
604 Markham Street
A treasure trove of books for the younger set, all the classics you remember and the new ones, too. And on Sundays in the spring and autumn there are often readings or concerts. Open seven days a week. For details tel: 535 7011.

HARBOURFRONT
Queen's Quay
Full of activities of all sorts to please young people.
Kaleidoscope, Saturdays and Sundays and some holidays, 11.30–16.00hrs, offers youngsters and their parents a chance to work together at arts and crafts, finger painting, doll making, basket weaving. There is no charge and you can take your work of art home. **Kid's Stage** throughout the summer puts on outdoor performances by mimes, puppeteers, singers and performers of all kinds; **Summer Fun**, daily arts, craft and music demonstrations in which children can get involved; and, in May, a week of appearances by performers from around the world at the **Milk International Children's Festival**. For information on these and other activities tel: 973 3000.

HIGH PARK
Queen Street West
It takes a little bread (literally) for children to have a ball feeding the geese, ducks, swans and other birds on Grenadier Pond. There are other animals in the park, too, and if you take along some extra bread there are plenty of places for that joy of childhood, a picnic.

KORTRIGHT CENTRE
Kleinburg, Ont
The full name of this 400-acre (160-hectare) nature park is the Kortright Centre for Conservation and it offers everything a young naturalist would find fascinating: nature trails, plant and wildlife studies, bat nights, birdhouse building, maple syrup tours, beekeeping, wildflower and autumn colour walks, and more. Winter or summer there is always something going on at the centre, which is just one of 13 valley areas controlled by the Metropolitan Toronto and Region Conservation Authority. So if you do not find what you want at Kortright, which is open 10.00–16.00hrs daily, try one of the others. For information on any of them tel: 661 6600 between 08.30 and 16.30hrs Monday to Friday, and 08.00 to 14.30hrs Saturday and Sunday.

METRO TORONTO ZOO
Meadowvale Road,
Scarborough Highway 401
Any zoo is a fascination for children but this is one of the good ones, with the animals given some space to move about and even, on occasion, privacy. There are camel and pony rides and feeding sessions and young animals to see and, all in all, it could be a long and exhausting day. But they will love it … and remember it.
Open: every day but Christmas; 09.30–16.30hrs in winter, 09.00–19.30hrs in summer. Easiest to reach by car but accessible on public transit with a long bus ride. For information tel: 392 5900.

CHILDREN

ONTARIO PLACE
Exhibition Place
This is a delight on a summer day, with a Children's Village full of innovative play equipment and a play area for the small fry, 12 or under, where water squirts and flows and sprays from everything, even bicycles, and the youngsters scream and love it. The bigger folk, including adults, can opt for the Water Slide, which offers 370 feet

(112m) of slippery slopes and tunnels and a final plunge into a pool. These, along with other attractions such as the Owl Discovery Centre, which presents a 15-minute puppet show telling children about science, put Ontario Place at the top of the wish list for youngsters. For information tel: 314 9900 (recorded message) or 314 9811.

ONTARIO SCIENCE CENTRE
770 Don Mills Road at Eglinton Avenue East
Here is a place where it is hard

Ontario Place, an amusement park with something for everyone

to decide whether children or parents are getting the most enjoyment out of the experiments and props. Act for and run video cameras, get charged with electricity, watch bees at work – there are hundreds of things to do, all designed to amuse and entertain, and teach you as well. It gets top rating. Reachable by public transit on a long ride. For information tel: 429 4100.

THE PUPPET CENTRE
171 Avondale Avenue, North York
This is a museum with 25 exhibits

of puppets down the ages and around the world and puppet shows on Saturdays at 15.00hrs. It has a gift shop as well where you can buy hand, rod or finger puppets or marionettes, from the very cheap to the very expensive. The centre is on the lower level of Glen Avon School and there is an admission charge if you attend a puppet performance. For information tel: 222 9029.

RIVERDALE FARM
Riverdale Park
The site of Toronto's old zoo has been transformed into a real farm where children can visit the 19th century and mingle with farmyard animals, horses, ducks, chickens, cows, goats and such, and pet the little ones. And all right in the heart of the city. There is no fee and the farm is open all year, roughly 09.00–16.00hrs in winter, 09.00–17.00hrs in summer. For information tel: 392 6794.

ROYAL ONTARIO MUSEUM
100 Queen's Park
Not everything at this superb museum will interest children but there are things that cannot fail – the totem poles and dinosaurs, for instance, and the Chinese dragons and the bat cave. And if they are six or older they will love the Discovery Gallery where they can actually handle and experiment with ancient artefacts. You may have to hurry through some galleries where you would like to linger but it will be a day to remember nevertheless. For information tel: 586 8000.

CHILDREN

YOUNG PEOPLE'S THEATRE
165 Front Street East
A professional theatrical company that performs plays for children during a season which runs from September to June. The range of works includes everything from Shakespeare and *Kidnapped* to adaptations of Canadian novels. Performances are usually presented Friday and Saturday evenings, with matinées on Saturdays and Sundays. Audiences range from six to 15 years of age and information can be obtained during the season on tel: 862 2222 (the box office) and throughout the year on tel: 363 5131 (the main office).

Two all-time favourite restaurants for children are **Ginsberg & Wong**, Village by the Grange, 71 McCaul Street and at 390 Steeles Avenue West, and **The Organ Grinder**, 58 The Esplanade.

Note: The tabloid *Kids' Toronto* is an excellent monthly publication which lists a wide range of activities for children of all ages. Available free, at the Ontario Science Centre, Royal Ontario Museum, Art Gallery of Ontario and some shops.

Crowds of young people take to their skates when the pool in Nathan Phillips Square ices over

TIGHT BUDGET

With rates less than $20
**Hostelling International
Toronto** is undoubtedly the least
expensive place to stay in
Toronto. The local representative
of Hostelling International
(formerly the IYHA), it has no age
restrictions and offers 200 beds
in dormitories and semi-private
rooms. Better yet, it runs the
Youth Hostel Travel Agency,
which offers reduced-rate tours
and even discounts on
transportation to the airport and
tickets to local attractions. Both
the hostel and the agency are at
223 Church Street Toronto, Ont
M5B 1Y7, and can be reached by

telephone on 368 0207. The
reception desk is open from
08.30 to 23.00hrs.
The University of Toronto has
750 campus rooms available
between 24 May and 27 August.
There is a small fee for the use of
athletics complex facilities and
parking is available (tel: 978
8735).
There are a number of bed and
breakfast places in Metro. Find
out about them through:

**Downtown Toronto Association
of Bed and Breakfast Guest
Homes**, tel: 690 1724 or 368
1420.
The Association represents 25
single and double occupancy
rooms in centrally located,
restored Victorian-era homes in
some of the city's most
interesting neighbourhoods. The
best time to call the main
number is between 09.30hrs
and noon.

**Metropolitan Bed and Breakfast
Registry of Toronto**, tel:
964 2566 or 928 2833.
Some 50 homes are
represented, many conveniently
located for easy access to
downtown attractions.
The least expensive way to get
around the city, using the
Toronto Transit Commission
trams, buses and subways, is in
most cases the best way. For
detailed information pick up a
free Ride Guide at subway
entrances or tel: 393-INFO from
07.00 to 23.30hrs daily.
Half-price theatre tickets for the
day of performance are available
from the Five Star Ticket kiosk
outside the Eaton Centre at
Yonge and Dundas Streets.

DIRECTORY

Contents

Arriving
Camping
Car Rental
Crime
Customs
  Regulations
Domestic
  Travel
Driving
Electricity
Embassies and
  Consulates

Emergency
  Telephone
  Numbers
Entertainment
  Information
Health
Holidays
Lost Property
Money Matters
Opening Times
Personal Safety
Pharmacies

Places of
  Worship
Police
Post Offices
Senior Citizens
Student and Youth
  Travel
Telephones
Time
Tipping
Toilets
Tourist Offices

Arriving

By Air

Toronto's Pearson
(International) Airport has
three terminals, including the
vast new Terminal Three
(opened in 1991), but like
many major airports around
the world it is crowded, in the
air and on the ground.
Canadian Airlines, British
Airways, American Airlines
and other North American
international airlines use the
relatively uncongested
Terminal Three. Terminal Two,
benefiting from a recent
facelift, is home to Air Canada,
USAir and others, while
Terminal One (built in 1964
and showing its age) serves
Northwest and Delta, among
others.
Customs and immigration
clearances are necessary for
passengers arriving in
Canada from other countries
but though there are queues
they move fairly quickly.
British citizens need
passports, but not normally

visas; US citizens need only proof of citizenship such as a birth certificate, though obviously a passport would prove that too. Citizens of some other countries need visas. Check before setting off.

There are porters available in the baggage claim area (tip about $1 per bag) but there are also free baggage carts, except in privately-run Terminal Three, where you have to pay for them. If there are none available when you arrive, wait a few moments, as trollies are constantly being collected and returned.

Just outside the Arrivals level at each terminal are bus stops for coaches that travel to hotels in downtown Toronto, about 20 miles (32km) away, or connect with the Toronto Transit Commission (TTC) subways. The TTC bus (No 58A) travels from Terminal Two only to the Lawrence West subway

With a daytime service running every five minutes, you'll never have a long wait if you miss the tram!

station. An Airport Express
Aeroport bus (tel: 905/564 6333)
goes to the York Mills and
Yorkdale subway stations, a
second goes to Islington subway
station and the third goes to
downtown hotels.

Airport area hotels have shuttle
buses (you will find hotel ads
and telephone numbers on the
Arrivals level) and there are
taxi ranks and limousines
where, at busy periods,
customers queue for transport.
Fares to the city on both run in
the $25 to $40 range,
depending on distance and
traffic – it is a matter of personal
choice, but if you want a
limousine don't be fobbed off
with a taxi, particularly if you
are not headed for downtown
Toronto, where most cabbies
want to go. For trips into
remote or rural areas
limousines are a far better bet,
so make sure you are joining
the correct queue. (Transport
Canada's centres at the airport,
incidentally, can be reached on
tel: 905/676 3506 for
information on the airport,
flights and tourist attractions.)

By Rail

Toronto is served by VIA Rail,
which handles most passenger
train traffic in the country, with
some services from Amtrak, the
US public rail carrier, and the
Ontario Northland Railway,
which runs trains as far north as
Moosonee on James Bay. All
carry passengers into majestic
old Union Station on Front Street
across from the Royal York
Hotel and within a block of
Yonge Street deep in the heart
of downtown Toronto. Union is

*Double-decker trains wait in the
sidings. Union Station is in the heart
of downtown Toronto*

the hub of the subway's system,
too, and the terminal for the
local GO (Government of
Ontario) commuter rail system
and it has a taxi rank at the front
so there is no problem finding
local transportation.

VIA Rail, which is the agent for
Amtrak and for the Ontario
Northland, can be reached on
366 8411, while Amtrak itself is
toll-free on tel: 1-800/872 7245.
GO Transit can be reached on
tel: 869 3200.

By Bus

Out of town buses arrive and
depart from the Bus Terminal at
610 Bay Street, just north of
Dundas Street. Fares and

schedules for all the bus companies can be obtained by contacting tel: 367 8742.

Camping

There are no campgrounds within Metro Toronto but a number are within easy reach by car. Among the closer ones are:
Indian Line Tourist Campground, 7625 Finch Avenue West, off Hwy 427 (tel: 905/678 1233; off-season tel: 661 6600); open mid-May to mid-October; the closest site to Metro Toronto, located close to the Wild Water Kingdom.
Glen Rouge Campground, 1 Eastville Avenue, Scarborough, Ont M1M 2N5 (tel: 416/392 2541 or 392 8092, May to October only); has showers, beach near by, playground, and is near public transit.

Milton Heights Campground, RR 3, Milton, Ont L9T 2X7 (tel: 1-878 678); has 450 sites, huge pool with solar heating, recreation hall, showers and games room.
Toronto West KOA Kampground, PO Box 198, Campbellville, Ont L0P 1B0 (tel: 1-854 2495); has 100 sites, a playground, recreational room, swimming pool, laundry, groceries, TV room, showers, fire places.
For information on other campgrounds call Ontario Ministry of Tourism on tel: 416/314 0944 or the toll-free number for most of Canada and the US outside the city, tel: 1-800/668 2746. Or write ahead for the booklet called *Camping* to Ontario Ministry of Tourism, 77 Bloor Street West, Toronto, Ont M7A 2R9.

Car Rental

Renting a car in Canada can be quick and easy. You must be 25 years of age, produce identification and a valid national or international driver's licence and be able to pay, whether with cash, travellers' cheques or credit cards.
All the major international car rental companies are represented in Toronto, along with Tilden, a major Canadian company. You will find them listed in the Toronto telephone directory Yellow Pages under Automobile Rental, but meanwhile here are some numbers:
Tilden, tel: 922 2000; Hertz, tel: 620 9620; Budget, tel: 673 3322; Thrifty, tel: 673 9308; Avis, tel: 1-800/879 2847.

DIRECTORY

Chemist
See **Pharmacies**

Crime
Toronto has little crime for its size, at least by North American standards, but it is a big city and growing, so the possibility is always present.

You can walk the downtown streets at night in safety, as residents claim, but as in any big city it is wise to use discretion. Do not take short-cuts through dark alleys or linger on deserted industrial streets. Use common sense and if, despite that, you are robbed or assaulted or injured in any way phone the Metro emergency number, 911, immediately. Any pay phone will accept your call without coins, and following it policemen, ambulance attendants, firemen – whoever you need – will be sent to the scene.

If you want to contact police in a non-emergency situation tel: 324 2222.

Customs Regulations
Canada has no restrictions of currency or on most personal possessions but there are limits on the amount of duty-free liquor (40 fluid ounces/1 litre) and the number of cigarettes (200). Also there are strict controls on agricultural materials, fruits, vegetables, meats and plants and on any product using any part of an animal belonging to an endangered species.

Domestic Travel
Public transport in and around Metro is provided by four basic transportation authorities: The Toronto Transit Commission (TTC) which runs the streetcar,

Getting around: by taxi, on buses – which cover the whole city...

... or by streetcar. The system is efficient, inexpensive and easy to follow

bus and subway systems within the community; Metro Parks Department, which operates the ferries to Toronto Islands; Gray Coach Line, which supplies services to nearby communities and offers tours and coach trips; and GO (Government of Ontario) Transit, which operates commuter trains and buses to communities outside the Metro boundaries. The TTC is by far the largest operation and the one visitors encounter most frequently.

Subway
TTC's best-known operation, the subway describes a huge narrow U through the city with the Bloor/Danforth line forming a cross stroke. One arm of the U starts at Finch Avenue in the north and runs south under Yonge Street before making a slow turn west through Union Station and travelling north again under University Avenue and Spadina Avenue to Wilson Avenue in the northwest.
The Bloor/Danforth line runs from Kipling Avenue in the west to Kennedy Road in the east, with the Scarborough Rapid Transit Line extending the service north and east at ground level to Scarborough City Centre.
The subway system runs from 06.00 to 01.30hrs Monday to Saturday and from 09.00 to 01.30hrs on Sunday.

Streetcars, Trolley Buses and Buses
Busy downtown routes run a five-minute service during the day with slightly greater intervals between vehicles in the evenings

but there can be delays. Surface stops are usually every two blocks and are marked by a red and white sign on utility poles. If you stand by the sign, the bus or tram will stop for you. Drivers will be helpful if you are uncertain about your stop, which you may request by tugging on the wire that circles the interior just above the windows.

Trams and buses connect with subways and a single ticket, with transfers (get them when you board your first tram, bus or subway train, not as you leave), will carry you through the whole system. Tokens (buy them at stations) and tickets are interchangeable and since exact fares are required on streetcars and buses it is a wise idea to buy a few in advance. There are Sunday and holiday passes that allow unlimited travel. For details check the number below.

Tram and bus hours vary, depending on the route, with some providing overnight service, though most do not. For information on any part of the system or to ask for a routing, tel: 393 4636 (07.00–22.00hrs daily).

Ferries

Since there is a small permanent population on Toronto Islands and some other citizens like to walk the chill lake shores in winter, there is a ferry service all year from the city. But hours and frequency change not only with the seasons but with the day of the week, so call the Metro Parks Department on tel: 392 8193 for schedules at the time of your visit. Summer, obviously, is the popular

season, with a frequent service, and it is the best time to visit the Islands. But it is advisable to stay away at weekends when there are queues for the ferries and the parks are packed (well, more populated than they are during the week). Do your island tour Monday to Friday.

Gray Coach

Operating out of the Bus Terminal at 610 Bay Street, just north of Dundas, this provides services to other nearby Ontario communities and also offers some excellent tours to such places as Niagara Falls and Stratford as well as excursions to celebrations, festivals and such special events as the September/October colour show in the hardwood forests to the north. For information tel: 393 7911.

Taxis

These may be telephoned or hailed on the street when the overhead light is on to signify that the cab is vacant (it goes on when the meter is turned back after a fare is paid). Most cabs use standard North American type cars, not special taxi bodies, and have far less room for people, hats or luggage than London cabs (for example) and they have no division between passengers and driver. Nor are drivers as knowledgeable about Toronto streets as, say, London cabbies are about their city. So hesitation and use of street directories is common. A proposed regulation to prohibit smoking totally in taxis has been the cause of some heated debate.

*A ferry service operates
year-round to the Toronto Islands*

The meter starts at $2.20 whenever you hire a cab and jumps up by 20 cents each 200m, $1 each km. The three major cab companies in Metro are **Co-Op**, 364 8161; **Diamond**, 366 6868; **Metro**, 363 5151.

Chauffeur-driven Cars

Toronto's status as a prime movie location may have something to do with the Hollywood-like profusion of posh vehicles available. Want a bar, a VCR, a TV or a cellular phone back there with you? No problem. Everything but a wine cellar is available in the cars parading through the more than 13 pages of listings for luxury chauffeured automobiles in the Yellow Pages, anything from an antique Rolls-Royce to the newest and shiniest of stretched Cadillacs. Just look under Limousine – and be sure to have your credit card ready.

Driving

Metro drivers are fast and not overly courteous, with a tendency to rapid lane changes and tail-gating (coming up close to your rear bumper).

The importance of a car within Metro is dubious. Taxis and public transit will take you everywhere, parking is high-priced and difficult and the stress can be extreme.

Driving is on the right. There are no roundabouts; huge X signs at the roadsides mark crossings where pedestrians have the right of way; you can make a right turn on a red light provided you come to a full stop first and the way is clear.

Accidents

All accidents involving personal injury or property damage over $700 must be reported to the police and you are required to stay at the scene until given permission to leave (in Metro contact police on tel: 324 2222 and in rural areas call the Ontario Provincial Police by dialling 0 and asking the operator for Zenith 50000).

Car Breakdown

Pull over to the side of the road, if possible, and put up the hood (bonnet) of your car as a signal

A car is a doubtful asset. Use public transport or taxis

of distress. Police will stop and help you get to a phone or radio for you, and fellow drivers may well stop to help. Car rental companies will replace vehicles if there is a breakdown and there are a number of firms providing towing and emergency road service, all of them listed in the Yellow Pages under Towing. If you are an AAA, AA, AIT or RAC member the Canadian Automobile Association will provide club services. The number for road emergencies is tel: 1-800/222 4357.

Documentation

The only document necessary is a valid driver's licence, unless you bring your own car, when you will need a valid registration or ownership form and proof of insurance. The minimum liability insurance in Ontario is $200,000.

Parking

The best bets for parking are the publicly owned Toronto Parking Authority lots found throughout the city by following the signs which show an arrow and a white capital P on a green background. For information on lots and rates tel: 393 7275 or (at weekends) 393 7336.

Regulations

Use of seat belts for all occupants of a car is mandatory; infants must be strapped in infant car seats. You must stop behind the rear door of any streetcar discharging or picking up passengers unless there is a safety island at the stop. If you drive out of Toronto and encounter a yellow school bus stopped with all its lights flashing you MUST stop whichever direction you are travelling. All distances and speed limits are in kilometres, not miles; gasoline (petrol) is sold by the litre (4.5 to an imperial gallon, 3.8 to a US gallon).

Road signs

The pedestrian cross-walk X sign is a Metro device, not province-wide. Otherwise road signs are those used generally in North America, with a diagonal stroke indicating a prohibition. Be warned, though, that if you drive through the province of Québec you will find one very important difference: stop signs there do not say 'STOP'. They say 'ARRET'.

Routes

If you plan out-of-town excursions to such places as Niagara Falls and Stratford, then except at rush hours you will find the expressways the fastest avenues out of Toronto. The city itself was laid out in an east–west, north–south grid pattern and the Gardiner Expressway runs east and west across the south, near the lakeshore, connecting to the west with the Queen Elizabeth Way, which will take you to Niagara Falls and the US border. Across the top of the city is another east–west expressway, Highway 401, which will carry you to Montréal in the east or Windsor/Detroit in the west, and squaring off the pattern are two north–south highways, the Don Valley Parkway at the east edge of the downtown area, and Highway 427, toward the western end of Metro.

DIRECTORY

Electricity

Electrical power is 110 volts, 60 amps, alternating current with appliances requiring twin-pronged, flat-tongued polarised plugs.

Embassies and Consulates

Since Toronto is the capital of a province but not a country there are no embassies (they can be reached in Ottawa by dialling 1-613/555 1212 and asking the operator for the number of the embassy you seek). However, Toronto has a number of consulates easily found in the white pages telephone directory under Consulate and in the consumer section of the Yellow Pages under Consulates and Other Foreign Government Representatives.

Emergency Telephone Numbers

Police, fire and ambulances 911. You need not use a coin to dial this number from pay phones.

Poison 813 5900. This number reaches the Poison Information Centre, Hospital for Sick Children.

Child illness 813 5817. The number reaches the Hospital for Sick Children's Medical Information centre, staffed by specially trained nurses 24 hours a day.

Dental service 967 5649 weekdays, 08.30–01.00hrs. Weekends and holidays, 924 8041, 09.00–01.00hrs. The first number reaches the Academy of Dentistry and offers a referral service to dentists, the second number puts you in touch with a dentist.

Medical help For a list of doctors call 'Dial-a-Doctor' on tel: 416/756 6259.

Optical repairs 364 0740 and 863 6221. The first number is Public Optical, 60 Queen Street East, which offers one-hour service on most optical prescriptions and is open until 21.00hrs on weekdays and 18.00hrs on Saturdays. Tel: 638 2998 for Sunday hours. The second number is for United Optical, 27 Queen Street East, which offers same-day service.

Legal help 947 3300. During regular business hours the number reaches the Law Society of Upper Canada at Osgoode Hall, 130 Queen Street West, which offers a free lawyer referral service.

Luggage repairs 598 3469. During regular store hours (which can include evenings) Gold's Luggage Shop will offer repairs while you wait.

Pet problems 465 3501 or 222 5409 for emergency veterinary service. The first number will reach one of several Veterinary Emergency Clinic units, this one at 1180 Danforth Avenue. Telephone numbers of any closer clinic can be obtained there. The clinics deal only with emergencies and are open Monday to Thursday, 19.00–08.00hrs, and from 19.00hrs Friday to 08.00hrs Monday. the second number reaches Willowdale Animal Clinic, 256 Sheppard Avenue West, between Yonge and Bathurst, which is open 24 hours a day and has an animal ambulance. Pets may be brought into Canada provided they have rabies certificates.

Pharmacies open 24 hours a day, tel: 979 2424 or 924 7760/69. The first is for Shopper's Drug Mart, 700 Bay Street at Gerard Street, the second is for Pharma Plus, 68 Wellesley Street at Church Street. Also, some pharmacies are open until midnight. Check the Yellow Pages.

Join the baseball crowds for a taste of Blue Jay fever

Entertainment

The range of entertainment available includes everything from poetry readings at Harbourfront and ballet at the O'Keefe to wrestling at Maple Leaf Gardens and demolition Derby's at the Canadian National Exhibition grandstand. You can troll for huge salmon in the waters of the lake in late summer (*The Star* has a fishing contest that pays thousands to winners) or watch the Blue Jays and the Toronto Argonauts in professional baseball and Canadian Football League action at the city's famous domed stadium; see the fastest game in the world when the Toronto Maple Leafs play hockey at the Gardens, or tee off at Glen Abbey, the course of the Canadian Open in nearby Oakville, or on a score of other courses within easy reach of downtown Toronto.

Sport

For information on Blue Jay American League games or for seats write to the club at 1 Blue Jay Way, Box 3200, Toronto, Ont M5V 1J1, or telephone 416/341 1234 or 341 1111 for ticket information.

For information on Argonaut Football Club action write to the club at SkyDome Gate 9, P O Box 2005, Station 'B', Toronto,

Ont M5T 3N8, or telephone
416/341 5151.

For information on National
League Hockey games write to
the Maple Leafs at 60 Carlton
Street, Toronto, Ont M5B 1L1 or
telephone 416/977 1641.

If you want to do, not watch, and
tennis is your thing then
telephone 495 4215 to find out
about the free use of City courts.
Or, if you are a racing fan, you
will find two forms of the sport in
Toronto – and neither one is
steeplechase. One is the
traditional flat racing with
thoroughbreds and the other is
harness racing, using standard-
bred horses harnessed to light
sulkies. The latter, using sturdy
horses that are less delicate than
thoroughbreds, was a farm
sport that grew into the big time
and now runs at Mohawk
Raceway just west of Metro.
Thoroughbred racing takes
place at Woodbine track on the
city's northwestern edge from
May to October. It is at
Woodbine that the top race in
Canada, the Queen's Plate, is
run early each July. The
province's third track, Fort Erie,
near Niagara Falls, has the same
season as Woodbine.

Note that on Ontario tracks the
horses run counter-clockwise
and bookmaking is illegal. You
can bet, but only at *pari-mutuels*.
For information on flat racing
and harness racing call the
Ontario Jockey Club, 675 7223.

Other Pastimes

The Royal Ontario Museum and
the Ontario Science Centre are
just two of Toronto's sights
where you can while away your
time (see the **What to See**

section of this guidebook for
details). In summer, you can
simply put your feet up and
watch the world go by, picnic at
Tommy Thompson Park (the
Leslie Street Spit) while
birdwatching, or on Toronto
Islands or at Harbourfront, drift
down island lagoons in a canoe
or, if you need some
excitement, try the giant Water
Slide at Ontario Place.

In the evening you can go dining
or dancing, or both, or watch
live theatre or any one of
hundreds of movies, enjoy a
cabaret show with your dinner,
soak up opera or delight in ballet.
For more details of where to find
your heart's desire, pass a
pleasant evening or just gratify a
whim, see under **Culture,
Entertainment and Nightlife**,
pages 88–94. Meanwhile, here
is some useful general
information.

Escape from downtown and watch the world go by from the Islands

Theatre Tickets
You can frequently buy half-price tickets for productions at the major theatres on the day of performance from the Five Star Ticket booth, outside The Eaton Centre at Dundas and Yonge Streets. Open: Monday to Saturday noon–19.30hrs; Sunday 11.00–15.00hrs.

Entertainment Information
Best bet for finding out what entertainment is available during a visit is *The Star's* Friday 'What's On' section which has up-to-the-minute details and reviews covering stage, screen, cabarets, nightclubs, jazz, records, restaurants, galleries, the arts and even community theatre, plus information on other Toronto happenings, everything from a fashion festival at the Metro Toronto Convention Centre to a Harlem Globetrotters basketball game at Maple Leaf Gardens. Other sources include the tabloid *Now*, a very comprehensive entertainment guide found on news-stands and in restaurants all over the city, and the monthly listings in *Toronto Life* magazine.

Drinking
The legal age for drinking in Ontario is 19. Restaurants and clubs serving liquor, beer and wine can be open from 11.00 to 01.00hrs, Monday to Saturday, and from noon to 23.00hrs on Sundays. Bars and other establishments can be open from noon to 01.00hrs Monday to Saturday. They cannot open on Sunday or holidays.
Sale of liquor, beer and wine at ordinary stores is not allowed. Liquor and wine must be purchased at Liquor Control Board of Ontario (LCBO) stores (though some Ontario wineries are allowed to sell their products at a few retail outlets) and beer must be purchased at stores called Brewers' Retail Stores. Hours vary from store to store, though 10.00–18.00hrs are the basic hours, and none are open on holidays. For individual store hours look up the specific outlet under Liquor Control Board of Ontario or Brewers' Retail Stores in the white pages.
Incidentally, there is no such thing as a Happy Hour with reduced price drinks in Ontario. Apparently unhappy with cut-rate competition, some bar owners complained that Happy

Hours were loosing hordes of drunks to wreak havoc on the province's highways. There was not a shred of proof of this, no police or accident statistics that supported the contention, but in its puritanical zeal the province promptly did away with the practice. And politicians and other well-to-do citizens can now feel secure as they sip away at their drinks. The streets outside will be safe when they wend their ways home.

Entry Formalities
See **Arriving**

Health
There are no specific health problems for visitors, nor are any special vaccinations needed, though tetanus shots are recommended, as they are for travel anywhere. Emergency help (ambulance, etc) can be obtained by calling 911 from any phone, or potentially serious medical problems can be taken directly to the emergency ward of the nearest hospital. Hotel staff or taxi drivers can direct you. Unless you are a provincial resident, you are not covered by Ontario's medical insurance plan but you can obtain insurance on arrival from Ontario Blue Cross tel: 429 2661 or Hospital Medical Care tel: 340 0100 (toll-free from elsewhere in Canada 1-800/387 4770) among other agencies.

Holidays
Christmas and Boxing Day, New Year's Day, Good Friday, Victoria Day (always a Monday, 24 May or preceding Monday), Canada Day (1 July), Civic Holiday (first Monday in August), Labour Day (first Monday in

Sculpture on Royal Bank Plaza

September), Thanksgiving Day (second Monday in October).

Lost Property

First check the store, hotel, taxi company or public transit authority where the loss may have occurred. If not successful try the police department since any property found on Toronto streets is taken into divisional police offices, then – if not claimed – to a central lost property office. To find out the location and number of the division involved call the central police tel: 324 2222.

Money Matters

Canadian money is divided into cents and dollars (100 cents) with the notes having different colours to allow instant identification. Two-dollar bills, for example, are orange, and five-dollar bills blue. The old green one-dollar bill is no longer in circulation, having been replaced by a golden-coloured $1 coin called the Loonie after the bird (a loon) depicted on one face.

Banks and Exchange

All banks have foreign currency departments and will exchange bank notes or travellers' cheques, as will many trust companies. Many stores, hotels, restaurants and tourist sites will also take US currency but usually give a less favourable rate than would a bank. Basic banking hours are 10.00–15.00hrs but there are variations on that which vary not only from bank to bank but from branch to branch so it is wise to check by telephone (listings will be found in both white pages and Yellow Pages).

If you want to change currency on a Sunday or holiday you must do it at your hotel or at exchange kiosks at Pearson International Airport or Union Station, which tend to charge a fee over and above the profit made on the actual exchange. For that reason it is sometimes better to exchange money at hotels rather than at exchange kiosks even though the rate at the latter may seem better. For other monetary transactions credit cards will do, of course, and those ubiquitous automatic banking machines are everywhere – malls, shopping centres, street corners .... Some are designed to work with international cards, others are less generous.

Taxes

There is an Ontario room tax of 5 per cent on all accommo-dation and an 8 per cent sales tax on most things you purchase. There is also a federal Goods and Services Tax (GST) of 7 per cent (a Value Added Tax). You will never see the room tax again but non-residents who purchase goods worth over $7 and have them shipped out of Canada within 60 days can claim a GST refund on certain items. A GST refund is also available for accommodation expenses over $100 during a maximum period. Ask about the pamphlet/application form in hotels, shops, airports and any Canadian embassy, and keep your original receipts. Photocopies will not do.

DIRECTORY

Opening Times

The business day is 09.00–17.00hrs for offices and light industries, with many retail stores open 09.00–18.00hrs early in the week, 09.00–21.00hrs Thursday and Friday, 09.00–17.00hrs on Saturday and from noon until 16.00hrs on Sunday. But there is no absolute overall pattern. Some stores close on Monday and stay open every evening, some close every day at 18.00hrs, so if there is something you particularly want, go during regular hours or check the closing time by phone.
Dining lounges and clubs open at 11.00hrs and bars at 12 noon. Both close at 01.00hrs. Attractions tend to open at 09.00, 09.30 or 10.00hrs, with varying closing hours depending on the season and other factors. For exact times check the **What to See** section.

Personal Safety

There are no particular hazards except in the general way of a big city, though visitors from the UK must constantly remember to look left before stepping off kerbs and also that vehicles can make right turns at red lights. A Canadian winter, even in Toronto, is somewhat colder than that experienced by most residents of Europe or parts of the US so they should remember to overdress on really cold days rather than wear too little. Wear layered clothing so that you can add or subtract as needed. Summer, on the other hand, tends to be pretty hot, and should be approached with caution, suntan oil, wide-brimmed hats and light clothing.

Pharmacies

You will find the pharmacist under Pharmacies in the Yellow Pages telephone directory but in normal Canadian speech he is a druggist and his base of operation is a drugstore. They are numerous, easy to find and sell most of the same products sold in pharmacies in Britain and drugstores in the US. For 24-hour operations see **Emergency Telephone Numbers** above.

Places of Worship

Toronto has always been known as a city of churches and that is as true today as it was 100 years ago, but now there is a little more diversity, as a glance under that heading in the Yellow Pages will soon reveal. There are three crowded pages of temple listings, from Roman Catholic through Christadelphian, Byzantine Slovak, Baha'i and African Methodist Episcopal to Buddhist and Muslim. However, for the city's synagogues, look under that heading. Also, most major hotels will have listings of local churches and hours of service.

Police

A Metro-wide police force of 5,000 administers the law within the municipality, aided by a detachment of Royal Canadian Mounted Police working on violations of federal law such as drug smuggling and tax evasion. Highways on the outskirts are patrolled by the Ontario Provincial Police.
All uniformed police wear guns

and are empowered to use them but not one citizen in a thousand has ever seen it happen other than on television. Uniformed police on the street and in cars are invariably polite and ready to help visitors with information and advice.

Post Offices

Canada is not noted for the speed of its mail delivery but that has not kept the cost of mailing letters down. It takes a 45-cent stamp to move an ordinary letter within the country these days, 52 cents to send it across the border to the US and 90 cents to carry it to Europe. Stamps can be bought at hotels and stores and there are small branch post offices in many shopping malls as well. If you need more than a stamp you can find the closest post office by looking in the white pages of the

phone book under Canada Post (it is no longer a government department so stay away from the blue pages at the back of the book).

For postal information from 08.00 to 18.00hrs, Monday to Friday, tel: 979 8822.

Senior Citizens

Senior citizens pay reduced admissions at most attractions in Metro and several hotels offer special room rates. They can also buy half-price tickets on GO trains and reduced fare tickets (60 years or older) on VIA Rail. But they will not get a penny off Toronto Transit Commission fares. There are reduced fares for senior citizens on the TTC but you

Canadian Police are always ready to help visitors

must live within Metro to qualify. And it is not a case of discrimination by the TTC against tourists. They will not sell the seniors' tickets to neighbours who live just over the Metro boundary, either.

Student and Youth Travel

There is only one hostel in Toronto that is tied in directly with Hostelling International or HI (formerly the IYHA) and that is the Hostelling International Toronto at 90 Gerard Street West, Toronto, Ont M5G 1J6, tel: 1-416/971 4440, which also serves as the local representative of HI.

It has 180 beds in dormitory and semi-private rooms, there are no age limits and its rates can scarcely be beaten. It has a kitchen and laundry and a lounge and the reception is open 24 hours a day, seven days a week.

It also runs the Youth Hostel Travel Agency, which offers reduced-rate tours and even discounts on transportation to the airport and tickets to local attractions. It shares the Gerard Street address with the hostel and you can reach it as well as HI and the hostel on tel: 971 4440.

The Association of Student Councils, 234 College Street, tel: 977 3703, is also an excellent source of information on student and youth travel.

Telephones

Pay telephones cost 25 cents for local calls, which have no time limit. You can talk for ten seconds or an hour and the rate is the same. That applies as well

to local calls from telephones in private homes or hotels.

Long-distance (trunk) rates are highest from 08.00 to 18.00hrs, drop 35 per cent during the 18.00–23.00hrs time period and are reduced again (to 40 per cent of the daytime rate) from 23.00 to 08.00hrs, all times being at the point of origin. For calls within Ontario and Québec those 60 per cent discount rates also apply from 23.00hrs Friday right through Saturday and Sunday to Monday at 08.00hrs. On calls to the rest of Canada and the US the 35 per cent discount applies all day Sunday.

Some useful numbers:
Emergency, 911;
Accommodation Toronto, 1-905/629 3800; Canadian Automobile Association (CAA) road emergency service, 1-800/222 4357; Canada Customs information, 973 8022; Canadian immigration, 973 4444; GO Transit, 869 3200; Gray Coach, 367 8747; Hostelling International, 971 4440; Metro Toronto visitors' information, 203 2500; Metro Toronto police information, 324 2222; Taxis, 366 6868, 364 8161 and 363 5151; Toronto Transit Commission (TTC), 393 4636; Travel Ontario, 314 0944.

Time

Toronto is on Eastern Standard Time in the third time zone west in a country which has six time zones and so, like New York City, is five hours behind Greenwich Mean Time. Newfoundland is one and a half hours ahead of Toronto and Halifax is one hour ahead;

Winnipeg is one hour behind, Calgary two hours behind and Vancouver three hours behind. Clocks are moved one hour ahead to Daylight Saving Time the first Sunday morning in April and are moved back on the last Sunday morning in October.

Tipping

Tips of 15 per cent are expected in cafés, restaurants, bars, taxis, etc.

Toilets

There is a long, long trail a-winding between the two main public toilets operated by the City of Toronto. One is at 406 Keele Street and the other at the Cumberland Terrace shopping complex, at 2 Bloor Street West. But take heart, just about every shopping centre, mall and the like has public toilets (known as washrooms) and in desperation you could ask at a bar or restaurant.

Tourist Offices

Tourist information can be obtained from Toronto Convention and Visitors Association, 207 Queen's Quay West, Suite 590, Box 126, Toronto, Ont M5J 1A7 (tel: 1-416/203 2500 or 1-800/363 1990).

LANGUAGE

While Canada is a bilingual country, with English and French as official languages, English is the usual language of business in provinces outside Quebec. The English language in Canada is a product of social, ethnic and historical factors. British settlers in the 19th century naturally brought their language with them and some older English words remain. Early American prospectors and pioneers, along with the continuing influx of immigrants from around the world have also played a role in the development of Canadian English.

Below is a short glossary of some common Canadian words and expressions:

Anglophone English-speaking person

back of, in back of behind (a remnant of 18th-century British English

bar a drinking place; also a ridge of sand or gravel in a stream or river where gold may be panned, as in Boston Bar

Canuck slang for Canadian

CBC the Canadian Broadcasting System

chinook mature spring salmon

chum dog salmon, called qualla (striped) by the Indians

coho Salsih Indian word for silver salmon or fall fish

dim sum Chinese breakfast or lunch

fender wing

Francophone French-speaking Canadian

hockey usually means ice hockey

Inuit Eskimo

logging lumbering

lumber timber

Mountie RCMP officer

province a political division of Canada

RCMP Royal Canadian Mounted Police

slug in city bars slang for a single drink

Stanley Cup a national hockey trophy for the best team of the season

INDEX

Page numbers in
italics refer to
illustrations

ACKNOWLEDGEMENTS

Acknowledgements
The Automobile Association would like to thank the following photographers and libraries for their assistance in the preparation of this book:

J BEAZLEY took all the photographs in this book (© AA Photo Library) except:

AA PHOTO LIBRARY 82/3 Blue Jays baseball (Jean-François Pin)

J ALLAN CASH PHOTOLIBRARY 36 Church, 46/7 Beaver pond trail, 48 Beaver.

MILLER COMSTOCK INC. 6/7 Old City Hall (E. Otto), 34/5 City Hall (E. Otto), 57 Kensington market (W. Griebling), 59 Café (E. Otto), 60/1 Breaded rabbit (M. Saunders), 64 Chinese food (P. Croydon), 67 Pasta (F. Ptazak), 79 At night (E. Otto), 90 O'Keefe Centre (W. Griebling), 104/5 (R. Chambers), 117 Baseball (R. Chambers), 118/9 View (E. Otto).

METROPOLITAN TORONTO CONVENTION & VISITORS ASSOCIATION 19 Black Creek pioneer village, 27 Zoo, 92/3 Limelight Theatre, 96 Caribana, 98 Molson Indy, 98/9 Lion dance, 100 Wonderland, 102/3 Waterfront.

NATURE PHOTOGRAPHERS LTD 50 Chipmunk, 52 Yellow warbler (K. Carlson), 53 Swallowtail (S. C. Bisserot), 55 Long-tailed duck (P. R. Sterry).

PICTURES COLOUR LIBRARY 56 Québec, maple trees, 74/5 Toronto, Yonge Street stores, 94 Yorkville, 106/7 Toronto tram

SPECTRUM COLOUR LIBRARY 8 Skyline, 40/1 Falls at night, 44/5 Canada geese.

ZEFA PICTURES LTD Cover Toronto skyline at dusk, 4 Spinnaker, 37 Niagara Falls, 42 Moose, 88/9 Roy Thompson Hall, 120 Royal Bank Plaza.

Contributors for this revision:
Copy editor: Audrey Horne; Verifier: Tim Jepson